WHAT'S LEFT BEHIND

A JOANNE KILBOURN MYSTERY

GAIL
BOWEN

MCCLELLAND & STEWART

McClelland and Stewart is an imprint of McClelland & Stewart, a division
of Random House of Canada Limited, a Penguin Random House Company

McClelland and Stewart and colophon are registered trademarks of
McClelland & Stewart, a division of Random House of Canada Limited, a
Penguin Random House Company

Library and Archives Canada Cataloguing in Publication

Bowen, Gail, 1942-, author
     What's left behind : a Joanne Kilbourn mystery / Gail Bowen.

ISBN 978-0-7710-2405-4 (paperback)
ISBN 978-0-7710-2404-7 (ebook)

     I. Title.

PS8553.O8995W43 2017   C813'.54   C2015-907736-2

Published simultaneously in the United States of America by
McClelland & Stewart, a division of Random House of Canada Limited,
a Penguin Random House Company

Library of Congress Control Number is available upon request

Cover design: Leah Springate
Cover image: © Justin Gilliland Photography / Getty Images

Printed and bound in USA

McClelland & Stewart,
a division of Random House of Canada Limited,
a Penguin Random House Company

I 2   3   4   5   21 20 19 18 17
www.penguinrandomhouse.ca

WHAT'S LEFT BEHIND

Other Joanne Kilbourn Mysteries
by Gail Bowen

12 Rose Street
The Gifted
Kaleidoscope
The Nesting Dolls
The Brutal Heart
The Endless Knot
The Last Good Day
The Glass Coffin
Burying Ariel
Verdict in Blood
A Killing Spring
A Colder Kind of Death
The Wandering Soul Murders
Murder at the Mendel
Deadly Appearances

For Maggie Siggins and Gerald Sperling,
who have supported artists and
the arts for so many years

with gratitude and love

CHAPTER

1

When I picked up the phone on the morning of my son Peter's wedding and heard Warren Weber's deep, bourbon-cured bass, I smiled. Warren and his wife, Annie, were among my favourite people, but Warren was eighty years old, and he didn't believe in preamble, so my pleasure was short-lived.

"I hope this is an unnecessary phone call, Joanne, but I thought you and Zack should know that my son signed himself out of Valleyview this morning. His doctor doesn't believe Simon is ready to be released, but he entered Valleyview voluntarily so he was free to leave."

My nerves clenched. "Do you think Simon plans to show up here?"

"I don't know, and the doctor didn't say, but Simon's obsession with Lee Crawford drove him to the hospital in the first place. Lee is her sister's maid of honour. We have to consider the possibility that Simon may be headed for the wedding."

"Lee's been worried about that," I said. "Did Simon's doctor have any advice about how to handle the situation if he does show up?"

"Dr. Fidelak suggested that we focus on preventing that from happening," Warren said. "Annie and I are still in the city. One of my oldest friends died this week, and I'm helping his widow with the arrangements. As soon as I'm through, Annie and I will come straight to Lawyers' Bay. If we haven't heard from Simon by then, we'll park outside the gates and wait. If Simon arrives, we'll get him across the lake to our cottage before he does anything we'll all regret."

"Thanks," I said. "I don't know what else we can do. I just hope you don't have to wait around on the road."

Warren chuckled. "Sitting in an air-conditioned limousine with a beautiful twenty-five-year-old who loves me? I'll be fine, Joanne. So will Annie. And so, I hope, will Simon. One way or another we'll see that he gets the treatment he needs."

"I hope so. Zack was still at Falconer Shreve when Simon started with the firm, and he thinks highly of him."

"Good because I may need Zack's help getting my son back to the hospital," Warren said, and then he broke the connection.

Every season has its own rhythm at Lawyers' Bay. In summer, the lake is alive with the squawk of shorebirds, the thrum of motorboats, and children's shrieks of terror and delight as they leap off the high board of the diving tower. In fall, the cheers and groans of touch football and the honking of Canada geese flying south echo across the water. In winter, the screams of tobogganers shrill through air sharp and clear as ice. But on that foggy May morning, the only sounds in our silent world came from Zack's all-terrain wheelchair rolling along the sand and my footfalls. Ahead of us on the beach, our dog, Pantera, chased a squirrel.

The wedding would take place in front of the gazebo at the tip of the bay's west arm. The setting was striking. So was the gazebo, an octagonal structure of wood and glass supported by stones carefully chosen and trucked down from Northern Saskatchewan. Noah Wainberg, the husband of one of Zack's law partners, was a gifted carver, and one of his most eloquent pieces hung from the base of the structure like a figure on a ship's prow. The carving was of a woman: her arms and legs long and graceful, her breasts full – a powerful woman, but her face was etched with an ancient and private grief.

As Zack and I moved towards the point, the mist that had shrouded the familiar markers was lifting. Two summers earlier, our daughter, Taylor, and her friends Isobel Wainberg and Gracie Falconer were captivated by a book that showed how our ancestors created landmarks to guide those who came after them. Inspired, the girls built a series of inuksuit along the shoreline of Lawyers' Bay. As the eerily human, ghostly figures emerged from the haze, I remembered the determination on the girls' young faces as they pushed rock-laden wheelbarrows through the sand to ensure that future travellers could find their way. It was one of my best summer memories.

Being alone with my husband on a beach that was as much a part of us as our handprints was another gift to savour, so I hadn't mentioned Warren's phone call. But when I saw the solitary figure standing inside the gazebo looking out at the water, I lowered my voice instinctively. "That's Simon Weber," I said.

Zack turned his head abruptly. "I thought he was at Valleyview."

"He was," I said. We were well out of earshot but we spoke in whispers. "Warren called when you were in the shower. Simon checked himself out this morning."

"Because he knew Lee would be here for the wedding?"

"That's Warren's guess. Mine too. Let's hope Simon doesn't know Lee's already here. Warren and Annie were planning to come over a couple of hours before the wedding, wait outside the security gates, and spirit Simon away if he showed up."

"But Simon short-circuited their plan," Zack said. "Valleyview's just outside Fort Qu'Appelle – less than half an hour away. He must have come straight to Lawyers' Bay." Zack's gaze was still on Simon. "Did Warren have any idea what shape his son is in?"

"Simon's been in the hospital for a month," I said. "He might have made some progress."

"He had a long way to go," Zack said. As we talked we'd continued to move towards the gazebo; now Zack took my arm and we stopped. "Jo, I never told you, but Lee came to me about Simon last month. She's a strong woman, but Simon had spiralled out of control. He'd never had a problem with alcohol, but he was drinking heavily and showing up at her farm at all hours threatening to kill himself if she didn't come back to him. The night before he checked himself into the hospital, Simon arrived at Lee's farm after midnight, drunk and incoherent. He pounded on her door until she answered it, then tried to push his way into her house. Lee slammed the door on him, but he was too drunk to drive, so she went back outside to try to get his keys. He put up a fight and knocked her down. She's sure it was an accident because when he saw her, flat on her back in the driveway, he started to cry, said he was a worthless human being who didn't deserve to live. He begged her to forgive him. Lee's fall had knocked the wind out of her, and it took her a moment to get her bearings. By the time she was on her feet, Simon was in his car, gunning the motor. In his haste to get on the road, Simon ran over Lee's old tomcat. She called the police, gave them Simon's licence number, and told them he was drunk and driving on Highway 33 about seventy-five kilometres south of the city. Then she wrapped her cat in a towel and took him out behind the barn and buried him."

"Oh God. Poor Lee. I had no idea the situation was that bad."

"Lee didn't want anyone to know. She was trying to protect Simon, but when she came to see me she was desperate. She'd been too keyed up to sleep, and the police had been unable to find Simon. You know how it is around Lee's place – a lot of gravel roads and abandoned farms with outbuildings. Simon probably pulled in somewhere and passed out. Anyway, he was still officially with Falconer Shreve, so we couldn't take on Lee as a client. I arranged with Eddye Kirke to meet with her and have a restraining order issued."

"Zack, Simon is the son of one of your major supporters. I should have known about the restraining order sooner."

"I agree, but Warren wanted as few people as possible to know about it. Not long after Simon was served, Falconer Shreve put him on medical leave and he checked himself into Valleyview."

"Now he's signed himself out," I said.

"Yes. And it's time to see how he's doing." Zack's tone was resigned. "Ready to talk to him?"

"As ready as I'll ever be," I said.

Simon seemed rooted to his spot in the gazebo. I'd only met him twice, and both encounters had been brief, but in retrospect they seemed significant. The first was the previous July at Falconer Shreve's annual Canada Day party at Lawyers' Bay. Simon was with Lee. It was mid-afternoon, and they'd been waterskiing. Lee was tanned, and like her twin sister, Maisie, she had shoulder-length copper curls. She was just a shade under six feet tall, and in her form-fitting one-piece ivory suit she was stunning. Simon was tall and fine-featured with black hair cut short. His body was boyishly slender, and he had the kind of fair skin that sunburns easily. His face, chest, and back had already turned scarlet. He was oblivious. The woman at his side captured his complete attention.

Later that afternoon, I watched Simon choose a beach towel from the stacks we'd piled on a trestle table near the water. He went through the piles twice, rejecting snazzy cabana stripes and cartoon whales to finally settle on a matching pair in denim-blue soft cotton.

"Good choice," I said.

He hugged the towels to his body. "Do you believe in love at first sight?" he asked.

"Maybe not quite first sight," I said. "But sometimes knowing that you've met the right person doesn't take long."

Simon nodded. "Today I found the person who can save me." His smile was heartbreaking. "Now comes the hard part – convincing her."

The next time I saw Simon was at the firm's black-tie Christmas party. Like Simon, our son Angus was an associate at Falconer Shreve. The two men often worked out together in the firm's weight room, and in the five months since I'd last seen him, Simon had developed the physique of a man who looked good in a tux. That night he and Lee were a head-turning couple but not a happy one. Simon was painfully solicitous, and Lee was kind, but her smile was distant. She had moved along. Auden's poignant lines "If equal affection cannot be, let the more loving one be me" flashed through my mind.

In the weeks and months that followed, Simon paid a high price for being "the more loving one." But Lee paid an equally high price for being the one more loved. Until Simon went to Valleyview, he and Lee had been locked in a symbiosis that sucked them both dry. The man staring out at Lawyers' Bay was a man who had seemingly lost everything.

Pantera wandered into the gazebo to check out the stranger. As Simon turned to acknowledge our dog, Zack's intake of breath was audible. Simon's body was skeletal. His clothes hung on him and his face was pale and clawed by sorrow.

"Where's your other dog?" he said. "You have a bouvier like Lee's."

"Willie died in February," I said. "He was twelve."

"I'm sorry," he said softly. "I know how much it hurts to lose a part of your life."

Zack wheeled towards him. "Joanne and I miss Willie every day," he said. "It's good to be with someone who understands that. But, Simon, you know you shouldn't be here today."

Simon's grey eyes were beautiful – large, clear, and long-lashed – but they were filled with despair. "I couldn't stay away," he said. "Lee will be here for the wedding. For the first time in a month, I'll be close to her."

I moved to Simon's side and touched his arm. "Your father talked to your doctor at Valleyview this morning. Leaving the facility is a big step. Dr. Fidelak's not sure you're ready."

Simon laughed jaggedly. "I'll never be ready," he said. "Did my father tell you that Dr. Fidelak, like all the other psychiatrists I've seen, can't come up with a diagnosis of what's wrong with me? Apparently, I exhibit classic signs of borderline personality disorder, a condition – I'm quoting now – 'that produces intense and unstable interpersonal relationships.' Sound familiar? But no one seems able to tell me for sure. It doesn't matter. The words wouldn't change anything. I've read about borderline personality disorders online. The literature is filled with admirably careful wording about treatment and possible outcomes." His voice tightened. "Must have been drafted by lawyers, Zack. Apparently the only magic bullet for people diagnosed with BPD is the one they use on themselves."

Zack gave Simon a comforting pat on the arm. "Whatever the diagnosis, you're not alone," he said, and his voice was strong and convincing. "Joanne and I will do whatever we can to help. But right now you have to get out of here. You have enough to deal with without violating the restraining order. Can I give you a lift?"

"I came in my canoe," Simon said. "It's down there, farther along the beach. My father's cottage is just across the lake, remember?"

"Of course," Zack said. "Are you going to be staying with your dad and Annie for a while?"

The question was meant to be innocuous, but it ignited something in Simon. His face darkened and he leapt away from Zack, chopping the air with his hands. "I don't know where I'm going to be. Don't you get it? If I can't be with Lee, I don't care where I am." Zack and I exchanged a glance. We were both overwhelmed at the quicksilver change in Simon's mood. He had been stoic about the bleakness of his prognosis, but suddenly he was falling apart.

Simon's face crumpled. He looked desperately from Zack to me. "Please, talk to her. Tell her I'll do anything to be in her life again. I won't ask for intimacy. I just want to have a room in her house. I want to see her every day. I want to know she'll never leave me. I need to know that I'll never be alone again." He reached out to me as he pleaded, grabbing hold of my wrists.

His intensity frightened me, but I tried to keep my voice even. "Simon, what if it's impossible for Lee to do what you're asking?" I said.

"You're afraid I'll harm her, aren't you?" he said. When I didn't respond, his eyes narrowed and his hands tightened on my wrists. "You don't understand. I would never hurt her. She's the only one who can lift me from loneliness. She's my last chance."

Zack placed two warning fingers on Simon's right arm. His voice was gentle but firm. "Simon, you're hurting Joanne. Please let go of her."

Simon looked in disbelief at what his hands were doing. "I'm sorry," he said. "I didn't mean to . . . " He was obviously contrite, but he seemed confused, and it was at least a minute before he loosened his grip, released my wrists, and darted from the gazebo. As he started down the beach, his eyes were wild. I went after him, but he was fast. When he came to the yellow canoe, he pushed the boat out into the lake and climbed in. It was a solo canoe, so as soon as Simon took his place, it levelled in the water. Grasping his paddle, he began knifing the waves. I called his name repeatedly, but he didn't answer. Simon was an expert canoeist, and it wasn't long before the yellow canoe disappeared from view and I returned to Zack.

His brow was creased with concern. "Are you all right?"

"I'm fine," I said. "But Simon needs to be back in Valleyview. He's out of control." I rubbed my wrists. "And he's strong."

Zack took out his phone. "I'll call Warren." He entered the number and then shrugged. "Straight to voicemail," he said.

"Warren's helping a friend's widow with funeral arrangements," I said. "Let's wait for him to call."

A peal of laughter greeted us when we came into the cottage. Our sixteen-year-old daughter, Taylor, and Lee Crawford were in the kitchen emptying the dishwasher and enjoying each other's company. Lee looked up when she heard us. "I'm here because I was in need of company," she said. "My sister, the blushing bride, and her bridesmaids are in the other cottage sleeping. They were awake half the night re-enacting lacrosse triumphs."

"How did they manage lacrosse inside a cottage?" I said.

"They'd had a few beers, and they were highly motivated," Lee said dryly. "No property was damaged, and nobody lost a tooth, so no harm done. Anyway, Taylor took pity on me and showed me where the eggs and the frying pan were."

"And now that Lee's eaten, we're going to look at the video I made when we were out at her farm last week," Taylor said. "I can't stop thinking about those heritage birds you raise, Lee. Plus, I got a great shot of you squirting goat's milk into Lena's mouth after she dared you."

"Our granddaughter will remember that goat-milk squirt when she's a hundred years old," Zack said. "Taylor, Joanne and I haven't seen the video. Let's all watch it together."

J. M. Barrie once said that human beings can't retrace happy footsteps, but that morning as the four of us watched the video, we came close. The week before, my daughter, Mieka, and her daughters, Madeleine and Lena, had come to Lee's farm with Zack, Taylor, and me. The weather had been picture-perfect. There were new lambs and baby goats and there were two old mares that had been the Crawford twins' thirteenth-birthday present. In return for carrots, the mares took Madeleine and Lena on a ride to the pond where the heritage geese and ducks swam. Lee and her bouviers, Gabby and Esme, followed along, watchful but unobtrusive.

Taylor's birth mother had been a gifted artist, and Taylor had inherited her talent. Smart collectors were already purchasing Taylor's own work. She had an eye for beauty, and the heritage birds intrigued her. Even their names evoked another time: Blue Andalusians, scarlet-combed Langshans, Swedish Flower Hens, Ridley Bronze turkeys, and pink-billed Aylesbury ducks. Taylor had created a colourful montage of the birds that captured their eccentric charm. The closing shot of Taylor's video was of Lee, flanked by her bouviers, standing on her driveway waving goodbye.

As soon as the video ended, Lee jumped up. "That was great, Taylor. Really great, and Citizens for Planned Growth can put it to good use. The video shows so much of what's at stake." Lee turned to Zack. "Yesterday I discovered that Lancaster Development has purchased another section of the land that borders on my farm. That means they own half the property around me. I've been fighting them off since I inherited this land. They want me out, but I'm not going to let that happen."

"You're not alone," I said.

Since he'd been sworn is as mayor the previous November, Zack had been battling Lancaster, a corporation of strategic planners, developers, realtors, and contractors that had dominated urban development in Regina for over a decade and had been pushing their highly lucrative developments farther into outlying rural areas with each passing year.

The quid pro quo between Regina's previous civic regime and Lancaster was simple and corrupt: in exchange for political donations and support, the mayor and city councillors gave Lancaster carte blanche when it came to development permits. As soon as Lancaster had secured corporate funding to build a new big-box store large enough to anchor a mall, the city handed over the development permits, and Lancaster purchased land in prime locations with proximity to the new mall. After their construction crews had built row upon row of cookie-cutter houses on the newly purchased land, Lancaster's investors sat back and waited for the shopping centre's grand opening when the mayor would trumpet the praises of the mall and of the shining new development that was so conveniently located near all the seductive new stores. And then the cash would really begin to flow.

It had been a sweet deal for Lancaster, but it had ended on election night.

From the day he announced he was running for mayor, Zack had sought out people who understood what made a city work. One of his most trusted advisers was David Christopher, the director of City Planning and Development, who had been fired the day Zack's predecessor as mayor took office.

Zack's first act as mayor was to reinstate Christopher. Their mutual vision for the city was progressive and workable. Christopher believed in limiting urban sprawl, encouraging development that valued diversity, and creating a city that fostered a shared sense of civic identity in Regina's citizens. He also believed that the public should have access to all decisions coming from the City Planning and Development office. Zack and his cohort of progressive councillors quickly announced their plan to create bylaws that put strict regulations on developers so that the city could ultimately ensure that mixed-income, mixed-use developments were given priority.

The new broom was sweeping clean, and when Zack made the announcement, Lancaster struck back with a vengeance. They dug up and publicized some of Zack's morally questionable actions from his days as a trial lawyer. They ran an expensive ad campaign accusing Zack and the new city council of deceiving the people of Regina and hinting at dark connections and secret deals. They rallied their allies in the business community to speak out against what Lancaster claimed would be a hazardous change in the city's future direction, and they bought media spots in which generously paid experts touted the benefits of untrammelled expansion.

The issue had proven to be divisive for the city, and Zack knew it was time to lance the boil. Though his council would very likely have passed the bylaws, he believed Regina's citizens wanted and deserved to have a voice in shaping their city. The Tuesday after Easter he announced that on June 17, there would be a civic referendum on the proposed bylaws. It was a gamble, but Zack had rolled the dice, and he never looked back.

Taylor's video was a powerful tool, and Lee couldn't wait to use it. "We have to keep pushing," she said. "When it comes to power and resources, CPG is David and Lancaster is Goliath."

Zack grinned. "And we all know who won that battle," he said. "We just have to be smart and hang in there. How are you with a slingshot, Lee?"

"Deadly," she said. "I'm a farm girl."

"And you've had a membership surge in Citizens for Planned Growth since the referendum was called," Zack said. "Your organization may just be the stone that brings the giant to its knees."

There was a widespread belief that CPG had sprung up during the last civic election when Zack and the progressive slate highlighted the issue of responsible development. In fact, the group's many factions had been in Regina for years, attempting to draw attention to the dangers of laisscz-faire civic growth. Construction companies, realtors, and suppliers that for over a decade had been elbowcd out of contention by the behemoth Lancaster lobbied for an even playing field. Farmers and environmentalists protested the city's assault on arable land. Activists and other concerned citizens staged rallies and awareness campaigns with the aim of creating a city that served all its people.

During the civic election campaign, these groups had discovered that, despite areas of sharp disagreement, they all believed that the goal of future development should be to build a sustainable, livable city that preserved farmland and respected Saskatchewan's rural heritage. And so Citizens for Planned Growth, a coalition fervent in supporting Zack's proposed bylaws, was born. When Lee had styled CPG's attempts to block Lancaster as a David-and-Goliath battle, she'd been right on the mark. Lancaster's supporters had deep pockets, and CPG was a shoestring operation.

However, the members of CPG struck gold when Lee Crawford became their unwitting spokesperson.

As part of their referendum coverage, NationTV had recently done a long piece on how, after the death of her guardian, Colin Brokenshire, eleven years earlier, Lee had taken over the family farm. Brokenshire had been a well-respected local farmer committed to breeding heritage ducks, geese, turkeys, and chickens, tending an orchard of heirloom apples, and growing large gardens of heirloom vegetables. Viewer response to Lee's tour of her farm and her explanation of Citizens for Planned Growth's goals had been largely positive, but feelings ran deep, and Lee had incited more than a few heated Facebook conversations and collected her share of angry tweets.

At the rehearsal dinner, Lee had taken Zack and me aside and confided that recently she'd been the target of what she termed "pranks." She was curious about whether we'd been on the receiving end of similar tasteless jokes. The incidents she described were far from laughable: a load of manure dumped on a plot of land where she was raising heritage fox cherry tomatoes; Photoshopped pictures of her in obscene positions with her prize Nigerian dwarf goats; a freezer bag filled with bulls' testicles stuffed in her mailbox with an ugly note.

We told Lee that we hadn't been targeted and urged her to call the RCMP. She rejected the suggestion. She said she could handle the situation on her own, believing the best strategy was to ignore the incidents and concentrate on building support for the bylaws.

But on the morning of the wedding, Taylor's vivid montage eclipsed the ugliness and Lee was fizzing with excitement. "There's plenty of time before the ceremony," she said. "Taylor, if you're cool with the idea, I'll upload the video onto YouTube. It's a beautiful piece, and it'll get a ton of hits."

Taylor grinned. "I'm cool with the idea. Let's do it. But afterwards could you help me decide whether to wear my hair up or down?"

"You've come to the right woman," Lee said. "My sister and I spent many hours debating that very question, but commitments first. Let's upload that video."

After they left, Zack turned to me. "Feel better?"

"I do," I said. "Lee's good company. Zack, do you think we should have told her about seeing Simon?"

"Probably, but Lee's been having a helluva time lately. I figured she deserved a few carefree moments."

Warren called just as the van from Gale's Florist arrived with the wedding flowers. Zack took his phone into the living room away from the delivery hubbub. By the time he finished his conversation and came back to the kitchen, I'd checked through the floral boxes to make sure we had everything we'd ordered and the young women from Gale's were at the gazebo putting up garlands.

"So what's the latest?" I said.

"I didn't hold back when I told Warren about our encounter with Simon this morning. I said that you and I had both been shocked at the suddenness and intensity of Simon's mood shift. Warren apologized to me, asked me to convey his apologies to you, and assured me that he'll do everything in his power to get Simon back into Valleyview."

"But the decision to re-enter Valleyview has to be Simon's," I said.

"And there's the rub. Warren talked to Dr. Fidelak. She feels that Simon doesn't pose a physical threat to himself or others, but she believes he requires intensive treatment. Warren and Annie are heading for their cottage. They're hoping Simon will be there and that they can convince him to return to Valleyview. Anyway, now that they know

Simon's at the lake, Warren and Annie are going to stay at their cottage until it's time for the wedding. If Simon arrives when Warren and Annie are here, the housekeeper will call and the Webers will go home."

"So the situation is in hand."

"Not by a long chalk," Zack said. "Apparently there's a history of mental illness in Simon's mother's family. Warren didn't go into details about his first wife's medical history, but he said enough to keep me on high alert. We can talk about it later. Right now, let's keep our focus on the fact that in a few hours our son and a terrific woman are getting married."

CHAPTER

2

The afternoon of Peter and Maisie's wedding day was worthy of a haiku – seventeen syllables praising the lyric beauty of May. The hills around the lake were bright with new grass; the trees were in full leaf; the lake was mirror smooth; and the air was filled with birdsong and the sweetness of spring.

On the stroke of four, the string quartet that had been playing Mozart while the guests took their places hit the first notes of *Lohengrin*'s "Wedding March." Madeleine and Lena, in matching dresses of shell-pink eyelet, petal baskets in hand, hesitation step mastered, started down the aisle that had been created between the rows of guest chairs. Taylor was a junior bridesmaid, and she and the other bridesmaids wore simple, sleeveless cotton dresses in lavender. All five carried bouquets of deep-purple calla lilies.

Lee was maid of honour. As she passed us on her way up the aisle, elegant in an ankle-length crocus-purple dress, she gave us a discreet wink. The past few months had been hard on her, but on that gentle May afternoon, she was enjoying herself and I was glad we hadn't told her about Simon.

Every bride is beautiful, but Maisie was a knockout. As she strode up the aisle in her strapless white gown, she exhibited an athletic purposefulness that I felt boded well for her marriage to Peter. Maisie claimed her thick, springy bronze locks were permanently out of control, but that day her stylist had managed to anchor the curls into a single braid that hung over the flawless skin of her right shoulder. She carried white calla lilies.

When I looked at Peter's face, I knew I had never seen a happier man. Mieka sat beside us in the front row, and when she caught her brother's eye she flashed him the "V for victory" sign. As the dean of our Cathedral began the familiar words of the marriage ceremony, I gave myself over to the joy of watching two people I loved commit themselves to each other.

Zack was the first to notice Simon Weber seated in his yellow canoe about three hundred metres from shore. He whispered Simon's name in my ear. I looked towards the bay and my pulse quickened. When Lee spotted the canoe, she tensed and the lilies in her hands began to tremble. But she mastered her nerves, squared her shoulders, and focused on her sister. Peter and Maisie had eyes only for each other, but Angus, who was Pete's best man, shot us an anxious look. Angus was fond of both Simon and Lee and he knew the situation was fraught. But like us, he realized there was nothing to do but carry on.

When the dean pronounced Peter and Maisie husband and wife, Maisie raised her arms in a gesture of triumph, and Peter followed suit. Zack and I kissed.

The wedding party followed the bride and groom down the aisle, but when the guests began moving towards the reception area, Angus doubled back to talk to Warren and Annie. We joined them.

As always, Warren looked dapper. His snowy hair was freshly barbered and his Tom Selleck moustache was pristine.

Warren's wardrobe reflected his passion for vibrant colours. His wedding outfit was striking: plum tuxedo jacket, white dress shirt, plum bow tie, cream slacks, and black loafers worn without socks. Annie's honey-blond hair was knotted loosely at the nape of her neck. She wore a fuchsia chiffon mini with matching strappy sandals. She had a beautiful mouth, and that day her plush lips glowed with gloss the deep pink of a watermelon heart. Both Webers were smiling. Warren shook Zack's hand and Annie embraced me. "That was an absolutely gorgeous wedding," she said.

"And without incident," Warren added.

"But not without a potential complication," Zack said. As he explained what was happening, the Webers's gaze moved towards the yellow canoe. Warren spoke first. "Zack, I assume there's nothing illegal about what my son is doing."

Zack nodded. "Legally, Simon is in the clear," he said. "He has to stay at least one hundred metres away from Lee, and that canoe is well over one hundred metres from shore."

Angus was clearly worried. He smoothed back the unruly forelock of dark hair that had dogged him since he was a child. "Simon looks so alone out there," he said. "Should I take a boat out and talk to him?"

"Simon's behaviour is unpredictable," Warren said. "Approaching him might exacerbate the problem. Through no fault of her own, Lee's at the centre of this. I think the decision about how we handle the situation should be hers."

I looked across the grass. "Well, she's headed our way."

The glow was gone. Lee's face was drawn and her eyes were troubled. "I recognized the canoe," she said. "I was afraid something like this would happen."

Warren's family business was farm machinery, and he loved the land and those who farmed it. He and Annie were generous supporters of Citizens for Planned Growth and they had come to know and respect Lee. "Angus just offered to go out and talk to Simon," Warren said.

Lee turned to Angus. "Thanks," she said. "But I think we shouldn't do anything until the wedding's over." She scrutinized her fingers. The manicurist had done her best, but Lee's nails were bitten to the quick. "Simon isn't doing any harm out there. Maisie and Peter deserve a perfect day. Simon needs to return to Valleyview, but that can be dealt with after everybody leaves." Lee smoothed her dress. "Right now, I should get back to the others. The party's starting."

Our gift to the newlyweds was the reception. Together, we had decided on an informal catered meal. Chefs stood behind a row of barbecues cooking ribs, planked salmon, rolled prime rib, vegetable kabobs, hot dogs, and hamburgers. There were trestle tables heavy with appetizers, salads, fruit platters, breads, and an impressive variety of cheeses and antipasto. A kids' table tempted the fussiest palates with sliders, crustless peanut butter and jelly sandwiches, macaroni and cheese, and whimsical animal sculptures made of vegetables and fruit. The caterer had stashed a tent in our garage to use in case of wind or rain, but the weather held, so the caterer's servers set up tables outdoors and we provided blankets for those who preferred to sit on the grass.

My position of choice at gatherings of more than twenty people is anywhere on the periphery of the action, but I was the mother of the groom, so that afternoon I mingled. As I wove through the crowd, I saw many familiar faces. Elder Ernest Beauvais and Peggy Kreviazuk, old friends whose advice Zack sought and followed, shared a blanket with Noah Wainberg and his three-year-old grandson, Jacob. The adults were teaching Jacob the names of birds, and when a whir of gold flew past us and Jacob said, "That's a flicker," they all beamed.

Our friend Margot Hunter and her family had also opted for a blanket. Her sixteen-month-old daughter, Lexi, wasn't spending much time on it, but her three-month-old son, Kai, an easy and remarkably handsome baby, seemed content to let his mother sing "Itsy Bitsy Spider" to him – over and over and over again. Margot had been forty-three and widowed when she gave birth to Lexi. Not wanting Lexi to be an only child, Margot approached our friend and colleague Brock Poitras to be her sperm donor. Brock was Aboriginal, and Kai had inherited his biological father's thick black hair and tawny skin and his mother's cornflower blue eyes and elegantly sculpted features. It was a dynamite combo. Home from university for the summer, Margot's eighteen-year-old stepson, Declan, and Brock were taking turns running after Lexi, scooping her up and bringing her back to the blanket. A modern family.

Maisie's bridesmaids had kicked off their pumps and were tossing a Frisbee around with Peter's groomsmen. As the game heated up, some of the more adventurous guests joined the wedding party. I was watching them when Maisie approached me. She pointed out a solidly built man with a sandy brushcut and a ruddy complexion who had ditched his suit coat and was running for the Frisbee with competitive zeal. Maisie called to him and he stopped, waved, and gave her a smile that was as wide as the prairie sky.

"That's our neighbour Bobby Stevens," Maisie said. "When Lee and I were growing up, he was our best friend. He doesn't know it yet, but he's about to win the lottery."

"You're going to have to run that one by me again," I said.

Maisie's eyes danced. "Bobby has loved my sister forever, and five minutes ago she told me that she's finally ready to marry him."

"And you're pleased," I said.

"I'm ecstatic," Maisie said. "Bobby's terrific. He and Lee want the same things from life – kids, farming, life in the community they grew up in. They'll have a good marriage."

"Do you think seeing you and Peter so happy made Lee realize that Bobby was 'the one'?"

Maisie averted her eyes. "Bobby isn't 'the one,' Jo. Lee's been honest with him about that. But Bobby says he's in love enough for both of them. They'll make it work."

For the second time that day Auden's lines about the more loving one flashed through my mind. The images of Simon, alone on the lake consumed by his impossible dream, and of Lee, marrying a man with whom she wasn't in love, filled me with an ineffable sadness.

Maisie picked up on my mood change. "Jo, Lee is fine with this. When she told me about her decision, she said, 'It took a while, but I finally realized that I should cherish what I've been given.'"

"Your sister's a wise woman," I said.

"She is," Maisie said. "And she has a good heart. After everything she's been through with Simon, she's still concerned about how he's going to take the news. Lee thinks that before her engagement becomes general knowledge, Warren should tell his son. There's no way to cushion the blow, but Lee feels that if Simon's doctor was nearby, she might be able to help. Could you and Zack talk to Warren?"

"Of course."

"Good. Lee and Bobby want this kept quiet until Bobby has a chance to tell his mother and Piper Edwards."

I was taken aback. "Piper Edwards, the city councillor from Ward 4?" I said. "Were she and Bobby . . . ?"

"They dated on and off for the past eighteen months," Maisie said, "but they were never a serious romance. On Bobby's side, the relationship was casual, but I gather Piper was doing everything she could, short of hiring a skywriter, to convince Bobby they should make the relationship permanent. Piper's a spitfire, and Lee would be happy if Bobby left well enough alone, but he's a gentleman and he feels he should talk to Piper before the news goes public."

"So the engagement is under wraps until Lee and Bobby make it official."

"Exactly." Maisie's attention had shifted to the area behind me. "And we settled this just in time," she said. "The mother of the groom-to-be is looking our way, and we should go over and say hello." Maisie waved to a handsome, silver-haired woman, and we began walking towards her. "When Lee and I were growing up, Bette Stevens was like a mother to us. She taught us how to clean out a poultry pen, plant a garden, and can Saskatoon berries." Maisie's lips curved towards a smile. "The womanly arts for Saskatchewan rural women."

"Bobby's mother will be getting a daughter-in-law in her own image," I said. "She must be over the moon."

Up close, Bette was impressive, with flawless skin, arctic-blue eyes, and a ready smile. She wore stilettos and a sleeve-less teal dress that showcased her enviably toned upper arms. She did not look like a woman who'd ever cleaned out a poultry pen. When Maisie introduced us, Bette's face lit up. "I've met your son, of course, Joanne. Last week one of our cows was having problems calving, and Peter stepped in. I'm really pleased to meet you."

Bette's voice was deep, and her handshake firm. Maisie smiled at her fondly. "You look lovely, Bette. It's good to see you again. Lee was just saying the other day that it's been too long since the three of us had a real visit."

"These days I keep track of Lee through the media," Bette said. "She's everywhere."

I noticed the edge in Bette's voice. So did my new daughter-in-law. "Protecting rural life is a cause Lee believes in," Maisie said.

"So do I," Bette said. "But many families, including mine, are divided by the issue. The wounds from these political battles run deep. My brother has stopped coming to the farm for Sunday dinner. He and his wife, Quinn, are opposed to CPG, Quinn bitterly so, and if Mansell even says a word against CPG, Bobby's on the attack. It would be so much easier for us all if Lee just kept a lower profile."

Maisie draped her arm around Bette's shoulder. "You know my sister," she said. "She's never walked away from a fight. Now come on, it's my wedding day, let's forget politics and just remember the good times."

Bette's face softened. "There were so many," she said.

"Especially when Colin was alive," Maisie said. Bette stiffened. Maisie reached out to touch her arm. "I'm sorry, Bette. I wasn't thinking."

"What's done is done," Bette said. "No matter how much we wish we could change it. We have to hold on to what we can."

CHAPTER

3

Except for the presence of the yellow canoe at the edge of the bay, the afternoon was perfect. But the canoe never moved; neither did the man sitting in it. The newlyweds had a flight to Winnipeg at seven the next morning, plus another flight and a long drive to get to their honeymoon destination of Jan Lake. They had a big day ahead of them, so before the sun began dipping towards the horizon the caterers whisked away the leftovers and reconfigured the chairs and tables to create a space for dancing. After some urging from Zack, Maisie and Peter had chosen Bill Evans's "Waltz for Debby" as the music for the bride-and-groom dance. Peter was six foot one and his chin grazed Maisie's forehead. As they danced under a cottonwood tree the sun shone through the new green leaves, bathing them in dappled light – lovers from a painting by Monet – but the moment that would stay with me forever came next.

Lee had taken the microphone from the deejay. "This is the time when the bride traditionally dances with her father," she said. "Maisie and I barely remember our parents. We were six years old when the accident happened, and our

parents' best friends, Colin and Fiona Brokenshire, agreed
to raise us. Fiona wasn't into parenting, but Colin stayed
the course. I'd give anything if he could be here today, but
he's not. Now there's just Maisie and me.

"So this is a dance for the ones who are left. It's called 'For
Good' from the musical *Wicked*. It's about two women who
change each other's lives. Some of you will see significance
in the fact that the two women are witches: one is Elphaba,
the Wicked Witch of the West, and the other is Glinda, the
Good Witch of the South. You can decide who's who." Lee
smiled at the laughter and held out her arms to her sister.

The deejay played the Kristin Chenoweth and Idina
Menzel version of "For Good." As I listened to the two soar-
ing female voices sing about how they had changed each
other's lives and watched Maisie and Lee, two confident and
beautiful women, dancing on the soft grass, I had to choke
back the tears. Zack and I had taken Taylor to see *Wicked*
and I knew that "For Good" is Elphaba and Glinda's fare-
well. After that moment, they will never meet again.

Zack moved closer to me. "Are you all right?"

I tried a smile. "Just being the mother of the groom," I
said. But it was more than that. The wedding had been everything Peter and Maisie hoped it would be, and the gazebo
draped in magnolias was beyond beautiful. But like an Alex
Colville painting, the yellow canoe on the bay had the cool
menace of the unknown, and as the guests applauded Maisie
and Lee's star turn, I remained frozen.

Zack wheeled close and broke the spell. "I gave the deejay
twenty bucks to play the Beach Boys' 'God Only Knows,'"
he said. "It's our song. Would you rather dance or smooch?"

"These shoes are killing me," I said. "Let's just smooch
and watch the dancers."

And so we smooched and watched. When Bette Stevens
waltzed by with her brother, Mansell Donnelly, I tensed.

For years Mansell had been a loyal lieutenant of Graham Meighen. The year before the civic election, Mansell resigned from Lancaster and with Graham's blessing set up a consulting firm and ran for city council in a ward that had always been solidly behind Lancaster's handpicked candidates. He won. It was an open secret that Mansell was Lancaster's choice to reclaim the mayor's chain of office, and since being sworn in, he had done everything he could to undercut Zack's administration.

I touched Zack's arm. "If seven months ago, someone had told me that Mansell Donnelly would be dancing at our son's wedding, I would have asked what they were smoking."

Zack grinned. "Maisie apologized to me a dozen times for inviting him, but apparently Mansell was like an uncle to the twins when they were growing up and Maisie couldn't bring herself to leave his name off the list."

"And now you're number one on Mansell's hit list," I said. "The capricious nature of fate."

Zack took my hand. "You know the importance of keeping the door open in politics. Tomorrow we might need Mansell's help or he might need ours."

"What have *you* been smoking?" I said. The song ended. Bobby Stevens approached his mother, and Mansell made a beeline for me. "If he asks me to dance, I'll throw up," I said.

Zack smiled broadly. "Remember *The Godfather*," he said. "No Sicilian can refuse any request on his child's wedding day."

Mansell was still a few metres away, but he was already extending his arms to me. I gritted my teeth. "We're not Sicilians," I said, and then I moved to embrace my dance partner.

Mansell was a big man, tall and fleshy with the same silver hair and arctic-blue eyes as his sister. The cologne he was wearing had a pleasant mossy scent. When he took me in his arms, I didn't shudder. Neither did he. "It's a beautiful wedding," he said. "And you look particularly lovely, Joanne."

"Thank you. You look very handsome yourself. There's something about a man in a summer suit that's very appealing."

"I'm glad I please you." His gaze was piercing. "I had a reason for asking you to dance."

"I assumed you did."

"My wife wanted me to convey her regrets that she wasn't able to attend the wedding. She had another commitment."

"It's a busy time of year," I said.

"That's very gracious. Joanne, Quinn had another message for you." He moved closer and lowered his voice. "She wanted you to know that from now on Slater Doyle will be heading up Lancaster's campaign against the development bylaws Zack's proposing."

"Was Satan unavailable?"

Mansell frowned. "That's a little harsh, isn't it?"

I shrugged. "Maybe to Satan. Mansell, I don't get this. After the hash Slater Doyle made of your candidate's re-election campaign, I thought Lancaster would hang him out to dry." Then the penny dropped. "But Quinn has hung him out to dry, hasn't she? Slater Doyle is desperate. He'll do whatever Quinn tells him to do. He'll take all the risks and if Lancaster's referendum campaign blows up in his face, he'll take the fall. Slater will be finished once and for all, but Quinn will live to fight another day."

Mansell made a moue of annoyance. "You disappoint me, Joanne," he said. "I thought you were an idealist, but it turns out you're a cynic."

"Am I wrong?"

Mansell chuckled. "Time will tell," he said. We finished our dance in silence. When the music stopped, Mansell gave me a courtly bow, thanked me, and walked away.

Zack groaned when I broke the news about Slater Doyle. "So Quinn Donnelly has chosen a reckless, damaged man to lead the campaign of our chief opposition," he said. "This does not bode well for civil discourse."

"No," I said. "The shit is well on its way to hitting the fan. But there's nothing we can do about it. Let's just be grateful Quinn didn't come to the wedding and deliver the news about Slater personally."

"Agreed. Quinn gets under my skin. When she drops in on city council meetings, she sits right in my line of vision so she can stare daggers at me."

"Next time Quinn tries that, go full bore. 'Is this a dagger which I see before me? The handle toward my hand. Come, let me clutch thee. I have thee not, and yet I see thee still.'"

Zack chortled. "I haven't thought of Macbeth since high school."

"St. Bartholomew's did the Scottish play when I was in Grade Thirteen."

"And you played Lady MacBeth?"

"I was the prompter."

Zack took my hand and smiled. "Then and now making sure everything runs smoothly."

It was a nice moment, but it was followed by a vexing one for Zack.

As Taylor and Declan Hunter danced by, bodies close, eyes closed, Zack's smile faded. After years of friendship, our daughter and Margot's stepson were now a romance, and Zack had taken to harrumphing.

"You're going to have to get used to this," I said. "Taylor's sixteen and a half, and Declan's a terrific young man."

Zack was grim. "I'm working on it," he said.

"I know you are," I said. "And you're not the only who's finding it difficult to face facts. Look over there." Zack followed my gaze.

Margot and Brock were standing by the deejay, holding up Lexi and Kai so they could watch the deejay at work. All four were intent. Margot and Brock made a handsome couple, and they were devoted to Lexi and Kai. I knew Margot was in love with Brock, but Brock was gay, and he was still in love with his ex-boyfriend, who, irony of ironies, was married to Slater Doyle. "Falling in love with the wrong person can be heartbreaking."

Zack took my hand. "We were very lucky, Jo."

"I never stop being grateful," I said.

"Neither do I," he said.

Across the lawn, Lee and Bobby were dancing barefoot. Shoeless, they were the same height, and they were laughing, clearly easy in each other's arms.

"It's good to see Lee having fun," I said.

"Her dance partner is certainly happy," Zack said. "He looks as if he's won the lottery."

"Maisie used that same phrase earlier when she told me that Lee has agreed to marry the man she's dancing with. His name is Bobby Stevens. The twins grew up with him, and apparently he's been in love with Lee for years."

Zack frowned. "This is going to be devastating for Simon," he said.

"I know," I said. "So does Lee. She wants us to tell Warren, and she's hoping he can do something to cushion the blow."

"Nothing will be able to cushion that blow," Zack said. "I checked a few minutes ago. Simon's still out on the bay in his canoe. It must be excruciating for him to watch Lee dancing with another man. I don't think he'll get over this, Jo."

The reception continued to follow the well-worn grooves of wedding receptions from time immemorial. Angus's toast to the bride referred too often to Maisie's prowess as a lacrosse player, but it was affectionate and funny. Lee's toast to Peter was light-hearted, but in a poignant moment at the end, she said, "Take good care of my sister. She's all I have." When Bobby Stevens leaned close and whispered in her ear, Lee's face softened with pleasure.

As Maisie positioned herself to throw her bouquet, it was apparent that the bridal calla lilies were intended for Lee. However, Maisie's lacrosse teammates were competitors who instinctively jumped for the prize. When two of the women collided and lost their balance, Taylor reached from behind them and caught the bouquet.

Angus gave her the high-five sign, and Taylor and Declan exchanged a private smile. Luckily, Zack had gone up to the house for a bathroom break so he missed the moment.

Mieka came over to me. "So is Declan the one?"

"He's already like family," I said. "I think for Taylor that's part of the appeal. Professionally, she's starting to cope with art dealers, collectors, and people who want to use her art commercially. Zack's there to guide her through the contracts, but Taylor is determined to learn the business."

"That's a pretty high-powered world for a sixteen-year-old," Mieka said.

"It is," I agreed. "I think that's why Taylor wants to keep her private life safe and uncomplicated."

"And her relationship with Declan is both," Mieka said.

"He and Taylor have known each other for years, and they're good together," I said. "Zack worries that Taylor's too young to be involved, but if she were dating a slew of boys, he'd be worried about that too."

"I am *not* looking forward to my daughters' dating years," Mieka said. "However, since I'm planning not to allow the girls to leave the house with boys till they're thirty-five, I don't have to deal with that today." She scanned the crowd. "But I do have to round up Madeleine and Lena and get

back to the city. We've been invited to a Victoria Day picnic
tomorrow – very elegant: dresses, gloves, and fascinators."

"Wow!" I said. "Madeleine and Lena with fascinators.
Take plenty of pictures."

After Peter and Maisie changed out of their wedding clothes
and rejoined their guests, there was a final round of hugs
and tears. I was standing with Maisie and Lee when Mansell
approached them. The twins both smiled, but Lee looked
reluctant. Mansell kissed the bride and then, after hesitat-
ing for a moment, he kissed her maid of honour.

"Thank you for inviting me," he said. "I've known you
two for twenty-seven years. It meant a great deal to me to
see you walk down the aisle and marry a good man, Maisie."
One of Lee's curls had escaped her chignon. Mansell reached
over and tucked the curl back into place. As he did, the
tension in Lee's expression melted and she and Mansell
grinned at each other. Then, in unison, all three groaned,
"That danged hair!" As the twins and Mansell laughed at
what was clearly an old private joke, I felt the warmth that,
despite their differences, still existed among them.

After Mansell walked away, I turned to Maisie. "I was
dubious about the wisdom of inviting Mansell to the ceremony, but I'm glad you did. You and Lee were obviously
very close to him when you were growing up."

"We were," Lee agreed.

"Politics can be brutal," I said.

"It wasn't just politics," Maisie said quickly. "It was
Quinn. She's a bad influence."

Lee's headshake was barely perceptible, but it was enough
to cut the conversation short. Maisie embraced her sister,
murmured, "Sorry," and then gave me a final hug. A few
minutes later, the newlyweds jumped into Peter's truck,
eager to begin the next stage of their life together. For the

next two weeks their life would be idyllic: shore lunches, fishing, boating, and hiking on their choice of the dozens of tiny islands that dot Jan Lake.

Angus had a trial starting the next week so he went back to the city to prepare. Lee stayed until she'd thanked the last guest for coming, then she went into our cottage and changed into jeans and a polo shirt. She had unpinned the chignon the hair stylist had created and her untamed curly mane fell loose around her shoulders.

"More comfortable?" I said.

"Infinitely. You can take the girl off the farm, but you can't take the farm out of the girl." She breathed deeply. "Before I head out, I want to check the lake."

I could see the concern on Lee's face, and I knew that Simon's presence would always shadow her memories of this day. "I'll go with you," I said.

The sun was just starting to set as Lee and I walked past the gazebo. The yellow canoe hadn't moved. Lee glanced at her watch. "Eight-ten," she said. "He's been there since four o'clock. Four hours and ten minutes. As we looked out at the water, the figure in the yellow canoe lifted his paddle and the boat began to move. "He's going home," she said and then hesitated. "Or he's going somewhere else."

I felt a frisson of apprehension. "Lee, why don't you stay with us tonight?" I said. "It's a holiday weekend. We can have a lazy day tomorrow."

Lee's voice was tentative. "That's a tempting offer, and I *am* tired. Simon showing up in that canoe touched a nerve. I don't even want to think about what he'll do when Warren tells him I'm getting married. Bobby offered to stay at the farm with me tonight, but if Simon arrived and found Bobby there – "

"It would be terrible for everyone," I said quickly. "It's best that you spend the night here."

"That's such a relief. Bobby can tell Bette our news and then drive into town and tell Piper Edwards." Lee shuddered. "I'll be glad when that's behind us."

"Maisie told me that Piper and Bobby had been dating," I said.

"It was never serious," Lee said. "At least not for Bobby. You must know Piper through city council."

"I do but not well," I said. "When Zack announced he was running for mayor, he talked with a number of people. Piper was one of the first to sign on to run as a candidate for the progressive slate. She was a natural. She knew what she had to do to win and she did it. We ran a check on all the candidates running as part of the slate, and some of Piper's real estate colleagues said she had a mean streak, but I never saw any evidence of it during the campaign."

"Let's hope she keeps her cool with Bobby," Lee said. "There's no reason for him to drive all that way to tell Piper something that never existed is over, but Bobby is a good guy. He really is. I don't know why it took me so long to realize that."

Warren called at a little after five the next morning, waking me up. "Simon's car is gone," he said. "He must have come some time in the night and taken off. I called Lee at the farm, but there was no answer."

"Lee stayed with us last night," I said. "We should have let you know. I'm sorry."

"As long as she's all right." The relief in Warren's voice was palpable.

"She's fine," I said.

"I wish I had that certainty about Simon," Warren said.

Bobby Stevens had done Lee's evening chores and volunteered to do her morning chores as well, but mid-May is a busy time on a farm, so Lee planned to drive back to her place after breakfast.

I'd just poured us all a second cup of coffee when the land-line rang. Lawyers' Bay was a gated community, and Milo O'Brien had come to call. I buzzed him in and within seconds the rumble of his Harley shattered the perfect quiet of the morning.

Milo was an expert at shattering perfect quiet. He was thirty-four years old, but he seemed much younger. His wild, kinetic energy; his constant texting and tweet-ing; his machine-gun rat-a-tat-tat conversations; and his continual intake of Crispy Crunch bars drove Zack crazy, but Zack was smart enough to know what he didn't know and he knew that he needed Milo.

Zack won the mayoralty by 241 votes, and I was con-vinced that the ground game Milo had created played a key role in giving him the win. As soon as I saw the final results on election night, I knew that if we were going to get citi-zen support for our programs, we needed to keep the ground game going. Five minutes after Zack gave his acceptance speech, I asked Milo to stay in Regina and work for the new administration.

Part of Milo's job was to monitor all of the available media channels to spot problems so we could deal with them before they got past us. He was our goalie, and as Ken Dryden once explained, the goalie's job is to know what's coming next and insert himself like a stick into the spokes of a bike and stop the action.

Lately, most of Milo's stick-handling had involved the upcoming referendum. The campaign was heated, but Milo thrived on political debate, and as he bopped in, motorcycle helmet in hand, he was in a mellow mood. When he saw Lee, he positively beamed. "Wonder Woman," he said. "That video you posted was wicked. And your message was killer.

'A way of life is at stake. On June 17, vote Yes for the proposed bylaws.'" Milo put his helmet on the kitchen counter, took a Crispy Crunch from his pocket, and offered it to Lee. "Kudos," he said. "You and your weird-ass chickens have gone viral and the Yes side is picking up support."

"And you rode all the way out here to tell us?" I said. "That was very thoughtful."

Milo's long fingers tapped out a riff on the table. "Hey, it was a great day for a ride," he said. "Too great maybe. Just outside Fort Q a cop gave me a Fast Riding Award."

When Lee looked puzzled, Zack translated. "A speeding ticket," he said.

"A small price to pay for nirvana," Milo said sagely. "The wind booms. The bumps in the pavement rise up to meet me; the world streaks by. Riding a bike is a whole-body experience." Milo picked up his helmet. "Speaking of, it's time to get back on the road." It was clearly an exit line, but when Milo's phone rang, he answered and then motioned us to stay put.

After he ended the call, Milo said, "Gather round, children. The CEO of Lancaster Development has words to share."

Zack frowned. "What's this about, Milo? You and Quinn Donnelly aren't exactly confidants."

"Right you are, big man, but Ms. Donnelly's message comes to us indirectly. Last night Lancaster Development celebrated its twenty-fifth anniversary with a party at the Scarth Club. Apparently, the CEO's speech rallying the troops against the bylaws is worthy of note." Milo beckoned us over. "Let's see for ourselves. A guy bussing tables shot this video and sent it to me. He's a buddy of mine, and he works three minimum-wage jobs, so he's not one of the 'contributing' members of society Ms. Donnelly values so highly."

Milo's buddy appeared to have shot the video from the side and slightly behind Quinn Donnelly, but he was close enough to catch her venom. Quinn was not a natural beauty. Her jaw line was weak and her features sharp, but by her mid-forties, she had learned to make the most of what she had. Her closely tailored outfits flattered her whip-thin body; her makeup was skilfully applied, and her platinum hair was attractively tousled to draw attention to her deep-set hazel eyes.

In her public utterances, Quinn Donnelly always appeared cool and focused, but that night she was in a room full of friends and she let loose. As Quinn spoke to the packed dining room, the crowd was hushed. She was not a dynamic speaker. There were no rhetorical flourishes, no dramatic pauses, no ingratiating asides. Her voice was emotionless and her enunciation was clipped, giving each word she spoke heightened significance.

She began with a quick sketch of Lancaster's history, starting with an encomium to its founder and Quinn's mentor, Graham Meighen. As she described how, through brains, guts, and savvy political alliances, Meighen transformed his wife's family's small, marginally profitable construction company into a multimillion-dollar international corporation, Quinn's eyes shone with the incandescence of the true believer.

Her eyes hardened when her focus shifted to us – the people who in Quinn's view had destroyed Meighen's life and now sought to dismantle his legacy. I was first on her enemies list. "Shreve's wife writes most of his speeches and they're mindless pap," she said. "Mrs. Shreve is the one who came up with the Rise and Shine campaign that tells drug dealers and other criminals they're the most valuable resource in their community and that they can build a shining future for everyone. Meanwhile, Shreve wants to pass bylaws that would seriously impact the ability of companies like ours to generate the taxes that are already paying for the law courts where we bring the fine folk of the city's core to justice; for the prisons where we house them when they kill each other, sell drugs to our children, or rob or vandalize our homes; and for the hospitals that save their lives when they're too drunk or stoned to realize they're endangering their lives and the lives of the rest of us.

"The Shreves and the city councillors who support them have to be stopped before they destroy the city that Graham Meighen and the rest of us worked so hard to build." Quinn then segued into disparaging the work of Citizens for Planned Growth and ended with a surprisingly vicious personal attack on Lee Crawford. When Quinn described Lee as "a slut who uses her body to get what she wants," Milo hit Pause. "We've heard enough," he said.

Lee pressed her lips together. "It's all right, Milo. We should know what they're saying."

We listened to the end. Quinn's closer was a call to arms. "We have a vision for this city, and it's a solid vision. Shreve and his councillors and organizations like CPG are going to hamstring us. They have to be stopped. Do whatever it takes to defeat their proposed development bylaws on Referendum Day."

I turned to Lee. "There are a number of people working on the Yes side of this referendum. Do you have any idea why Quinn demonized you?"

Lee's answer was evasive. "We have a shared history," she said. "It's just unfortunate that Quinn ended up being married to Bobby's uncle."

"Whatever your shared history was, don't let her spook you," Milo said. "Be proud, Wonder Woman. You and your Lasso of Truth are going to defeat evil."

Lee's eyes were wide as she watched Milo make his exit. "Milo is a trip," she said.

"He *is* that," Zack said. "Joanne is very fond of him."

"And you're not?" Lee said.

"I admire Milo's skills and I'm grateful he's on our side," Zack said.

I was nettled. "Not exactly a ringing endorsement for a man who works 24/7 tracking and shaping public reaction to your initiatives."

Zack shrugged. "It's the truth," he said. "You and Milo understand politics in a way that I never will. You both instinctively make the right decisions, and you enjoy each other's company. Milo takes a huge burden off your shoulders and that means everything to me because you mean everything to me. Can we leave it at that?"

"I guess we'll have to," I said.

Lee's smile was mischievous. "Is it safe to leave you two alone?"

Zack wheeled over and took my hand. "It *is* safe, isn't it?"

I leaned down and kissed the top of his head. "It's safe," I said.

"In that case, I'm going to move along," Lee said. She picked up her breakfast dishes and carried them to the sink. "I have a job list waiting for me at the farm, and thanks to a good night's sleep and Zack's breakfast, I'm ready to tackle it."

Zack and I went out to Lee's truck with her. She took out her keys and inhaled deeply. "I love the loamy smell of spring," she said. "It's like a promise." When she climbed into the driver's seat, the cobwebs of fear and anxiety that had clung to me since I saw the yellow canoe fell away. Lee was smart and capable. She and Bobby would have a solid marriage. Warren and Annie would find Simon, and we'd all make sure he had the help he needed to deal with the fact that Lee was going to marry Bobby Stevens. The universe was unfolding as it should.

———

Five minutes after Lee left, Warren and Annie Weber arrived. Annie's honey hair was in a ponytail and her scarlet lipstick matched her shorts and the poppies on Warren's Hawaiian shirt. A festive couple, but their faces were grim. When a twenty-five-year-old blonde who manages a biker bar marries an eighty-year-old millionaire, there are certain assumptions. But Annie and Warren were a love match, and that morning as I ushered them into the living room Annie's heart-shaped face was tense because the man she loved was dealing with a problem that was eating him alive.

After we settled into the wicker chairs that looked out onto the lake, Warren began. "I've always been a straight-shooter," he said, "but I withheld information from you because I truly hoped it wasn't relevant. About an hour after Annie and I got back from the wedding, Simon showed up. We called Dr. Fidelak immediately, and she was with us when we told Simon about Lee's engagement. She was a god-send. Simon was devastated. It was terrible to witness some-one I love going through that kind of agony again. Anyway, Dr. Fidelak was able to give Simon medication that calmed him and she stayed with us till he slept. This morning when we discovered that Simon was missing, Dr. Fidelak con-vinced me that Simon's family history is significant, so it's time for full disclosure."

Annie moved closer to her husband and linked her fingers with his. "You're the finest man I know," she said. "You don't deserve this." Her voice was throaty and sensual. For a beat Annie and Warren simply gazed at each other, drawing strength for what lay ahead. It was a moment of such inti-macy that both Zack and I lowered our eyes.

Finally, reluctantly, Warren returned his focus to us. "Simon has had problems throughout his life," Warren said. "But there have been long stretches where he was fine – not just fine but wonderful, brilliant, generous, funny – one of the best people you could ever hope to meet. I want to give my son a chance to find that part of himself again."

"He deserves that chance," Zack said. "That's why Falconer Shreve put him on medical leave. We believe in him too."

"I appreciate that. So does Simon," Warren said. "I've known for years that Simon was afflicted with some variant of the illness that took his mother. But in both cases it was easy to ignore the truth. The image Caroline projected to the world was not that of someone with an illness.

"She was an architect and a successful one. Publicly, she was strikingly confident, the woman who had it all together. Privately, it was a very different matter. She was needy, demanding. She vacillated between terrible depression and self-loathing and fury because she felt I wasn't giving her enough attention and love. Simon was not a planned child. I didn't believe Caroline was stable enough to be a parent. I wanted her to terminate the pregnancy – a fact she repeatedly threw in my face and in Simon's."

"How terrible for all of you," I said.

"Caroline was a very sick woman. Watching her disintegrate was like being pelted with stones," Warren said. "The worst part was that there were always flashes of the woman she was – smart, funny, realistic about her situation. And then the dark Caroline would take over. It was as if there were two people inside her. When the dark one took over, she hated everyone close to her, and she was determined to destroy us all. Finally, I told her I'd give her whatever she wanted or needed, but the marriage was over and I was going to raise Simon."

"How did Caroline react to that?" Zack asked softly.

"She fought me, of course, but there were medical records, and by this time, many people, including our housekeeper, had seen her raging and threatening. Caroline knew there was no way a judge would award her custody. Finally, the darkness swallowed her. She hanged herself in the garage of our house in Regina." Warren's paused. "Simon found her. He was five years old."

Annie rested her head on her husband's shoulder. She was crying and he stroked her arm rhythmically to comfort her.

Zack rolled his chair close to the Webers. "I'm so sorry," he said.

"I am too," Warren said.

"You did everything you could, babe," Annie said. "Nobody could have done more."

After that, the four of us were silent. When my phone shrilled, I took it out on the deck.

Lee's voice was small. "During the night someone came to the farm and killed my heritage birds – the chickens, the geese, the ducks, the turkeys, the pigeons – all of them. Bobby says the birds were fine last night, but this morning they're dead. He's certain they were poisoned." Her voice broke. "Colin spent a lifetime preserving those breeds. Now they're gone."

"I can be at the farm in half an hour," I said.

"Jo, you don't have to come. I'm fine. Really. Bobby called the RCMP. He's on his way over to give me moral support."

"You're sure you don't want me to come?" I said.

"I'm sure."

"Lee, who do you think did this?"

"I don't know," she said, "but I blame Quinn Donnelly. The video of me with my birds was generating a lot of support for our side. We heard Quinn urge people at Lancaster's anniversary party to do whatever it took to defeat the new development bylaws."

"It wouldn't be Quinn or anybody from Lancaster," I said. "Quinn's colleagues are many things, but they're not stupid. Killing your birds was a cruel act that will garner sympathy for you. Lancaster doesn't want to alienate people who may be on the fence about the referendum question."

Lee sighed. "You're right, of course," she said. "At the moment, I'm not thinking clearly." She paused. "Jo, there was another note in my mailbox. It said, 'Now you know how it feels to lose what you love.'"

"Handwritten?" I said.

"No," she said. "A printout."

The defeat in her voice concerned me. "Lee, I'm going to call Angus. It's always wise to have a lawyer when you're dealing with the police, and Angus is familiar with the situation, so you can be open with him."

My mind was racing as I went inside. When Zack saw my face, he began wheeling towards me. "What's wrong?" he said.

"There's been an incident at the Brokenshire farm," I said. As I gave my account of the bird slaughter, Warren and Annie were clearly shaken, but Warren was controlled.

"The note certainly points to Simon," he said. "But Simon would never kill a bird. From the time he was young, he felt a kinship with them. He was always bringing home birds that were in distress. He never gave up on them. If they died, he always gave them a very solemn burial under the elm tree in our backyard."

Warren's description perfectly limned the image I had of Simon as a gentle, loving man, but I had seen the other side of Simon, a man whose escalating rage frightened me and turned him into a stranger. I wanted to be convinced, but the memory of his fingers on my wrist was fresh, and the note was damning.

There was a heaviness in the room, and Zack did his best to dispel it. "Anyone could have written that note," he said. "In the video Lee was clearly a woman who was living a purposeful, joyous life. Someone struggling might have been driven over the edge by the fact that she had found answers."

"The RCMP has jurisdiction out there, so they'll investigate," I said. "I guess we'll know soon enough. I told Lee I'd ask Angus to go out to the farm. She may need the kind of support he can offer."

Warren stood. "Annie and I will go back to our place. I'll have Dr. Fidelak on call in case Simon shows up. I hope to God he does."

"So do we," I said. "Zack, you and I need to get back to the city."

"Agreed," Zack said. "Warren, if there's anything we can do, let us know. Meanwhile, this story will need to be managed. It's only a matter of time before the media gets wind of the incident at the Brokenshire farm."

CHAPTER

4

It was a little after noon when we pulled up in front of our building on Halifax Street. Taylor and her cats were staying with Margot and her family till Monday, so it was just Zack, Pantera, and me.

The poisoning of Lee Crawford's heritage birds had sickened us, but it had also created an opportunity, and Zack was determined to seize it. He'd once told me that criminal law was a prize fight – that in boxing, for every bout that ends with a knockout punch, ninety-nine bouts are decided on feints and small, well-placed blows. Zack saw civic politics as a prize fight too, and he believed that, in the end, feints and small, well-placed blows would win the day. What had happened at the Brokenshire farm was a tragedy, but properly handled it could land some well-placed blows on Lancaster and their agenda. Before we left the lake, Zack had called Milo and Brock Poitras and asked them to meet us at our place at one o'clock.

Brock had a condo in our building, and as soon as we'd settled in, he was at our door. In the past two and half years, Brock had become Zack's go-to guy. Together, they had spearheaded building the Racette-Hunter Training and Recreation Centre, a multi-use facility for the residents of North Central, the area a national magazine had designated as "Canada's Worst Neighbourhood." Since Brock had been elected councillor for our ward at the same time that Zack became mayor, they were together at City Hall. They shared a vision for our city, a passion for sports, and a friendship based on mutual respect and admiration. Zack had campaigned with the promise that he would be a one-term mayor and my unspoken hope was that Brock would succeed him.

When we sat down at the table in our kitchen to wait for Milo, Brock whipped out his tablet and showed us some photos from the wedding. There were some great candid shots of the wedding party and some tender photos of Margot and Brock with Kai and Lexi. They were a handsome group, and the pictures of the four of them sitting on the grass in their wedding finery brought a rush of recent memories.

I held the device out to Zack. "I can't believe that was less than twenty-four hours ago," I said.

Zack exhaled slowly. "Neither can I."

We were all relieved when Milo buzzed from downstairs and we were able to stop contemplating the ephemeral nature of happiness and deal with the business at hand.

After she and I had spoken that morning, Lee had written and posted on Facebook a graceful elegy she'd written about the death of her birds, and according to Milo, the issue was catching fire online. Speculation was growing that the slaughter of Lee's heritage birds was a warning from Lancaster and their allies that they would do whatever it took to force their agenda. Slater Doyle tweeted that Lancaster could not be held responsible for the act of a disturbed person and deeply regretted the killings.

Milo unwrapped what must have been his tenth Crispy Crunch of the afternoon. "Is it just me or does Slater Doyle's statement sound as if Lancaster knows who killed the birds but they're not ready to throw the guilty party under the bus?" he said.

"It sounds that way to me too," I said. "But there's another possibility, and this one has me worried. Lee Crawford has a very disturbed ex-suitor, Warren Weber's son, Simon. She has a restraining order against him."

Milo frowned. "Jo, I should have known about this. Warren Weber's a major supporter of our campaign. I need to be aware of anything that might be used against us."

"I agree," I said, and the words hung in the air.

Zack turned his chair towards Milo. "For the record, Jo and I discussed this, but Simon's a lawyer at Falconer Shreve and Warren's a friend, so I wanted to do what I could to limit the number of people who knew about the restraining order. It was a mistake and I won't repeat it."

Milo gave Zack a long and assessing look. "Fair enough," he said finally. "So do you think this dude decided to get Lee's attention by killing her birds?"

"Simon was in Valleyview for the past month, but he signed himself out yesterday," I said. "Whether or not he was involved, he would be a convenient scapegoat. By focusing attention on Simon and his psychiatric problems, Lancaster would be able to divert suspicion away from them."

"Got it," Milo said. "So what do we do about the dead bird sitch?"

"Looks like the sitch is in hand," Brock said. "Zack just needs to let the public know that the RCMP is handling the investigation and that those responsible for the slaughter will be brought to justice."

Zack pulled out his phone and began tapping. "Done," he said.

"And I'm out of here," Milo said.

"I'll walk you to the elevator," I said.

Zack glanced at me questioningly, but I ignored the look.

When we got to the elevator, neither Milo nor I pushed the button. "I'm sorry I didn't tell you about Simon Weber," I said. "I just learned yesterday myself. But you should have had that information as soon as I did."

Milo's smile was wry. "I gather you tried to make that point with the big man."

"I did," I said.

Milo moved closer. "Jo, the restraining order thing is minor, but it reveals a problem that could become major. The big man is accustomed to running his own show. I get that. He has a city to run, and I'm cool with that too. But politics is our territory, and he has to trust us to do our jobs."

"I'll talk to him," I said. "Milo, I don't want to lose you over this."

Milo stepped nearer. "Don't worry about it," he said.

We were still standing close when Zack wheeled out of our condo and came down the hall towards us. "You both should come back," he said. "There's something you need to see."

Brock was waiting at the door. As soon as we were inside, Zack handed his phone to Milo. New tweets kept popping up on the screen. Milo narrowed his eyes, perusing the list. Finally, he said, "There's the link."

We gathered around Zack's phone so we could all watch as the video came up. A voice-over from Lee accompanied disturbing footage of the dead birds. "Until yesterday, these were living beings – a significant connection to our history – the birds that our ancestors raised. Colin Brokenshire saw himself as a steward charged with keeping the past alive. When Colin died, I continued his work. Now, because somebody decided these emissaries from another time should be pawns in the fight against a better way for our city, they're lifeless. Today I'll bury them and our world will be a little poorer.

"My name is Lee Crawford. What happened to these birds will happen to a way of life if you vote for big-block stores and tract housing. On June 17, please support Regina's mayor and the overwhelming majority of our city councillors. Vote Yes for their new progressive regulations." The footage Taylor shot of the birds running around the yard – odd, beautiful, and alive – filled the screen. Then Lee's voice-over came in again. "This is one example of what we're fighting for."

We all stood, stunned, until Milo broke the silence. "Head for the hills," he said. "Lee just lobbed a grenade into the enemy camp." He opened the door to the hall and then turned to face us. "Tell Lee I'm sorry about her birds," he said. "They really were dope."

After Milo left, Zack wheeled towards the refrigerator. "Why don't I get everybody a beer?" He opened three bottles of Stella and I brought out a bag of Fritos and a tin of bean dip.

"So where do we go from here?" Zack said.

"I think we have to anticipate the worst," I said. "Even if Lancaster isn't behind this, with Slater Doyle in the mix, all bets are off. We may be in for a replay of the horror show that went on during the campaign."

"Joanne's not the only one anticipating the worst," Brock said. "I ran into Michael at Racette-Hunter this morning. He's very uneasy about Slater's involvement with Lancaster again."

Michael Goetz and Brock had been a couple before Michael married Slater Doyle. In my opinion, Brock was well rid of Michael. After months of investigating the roles Slater and Michael had played in covering up the rape and death of a minor, the Crown decided it lacked sufficient evidence to win a case against either of them, so the charges were dropped. Clever lawyers had managed to keep both men out of jail, but Michael was a psychiatrist and the ethical standards of the College of Physicians and Surgeons were high. After studying his murky role in the death of a patient and his failure to assist a dying child, the College revoked Goetz's licence to practise psychiatry. He was a man who had lost his reputation and his profession. All he had left was Slater Doyle.

"If anyone would know what's going on, Michael would," Zack said. "So what's his take?"

"Michael's afraid," Brock said. "He thinks you've gone too far too fast with the changes you're trying to make, Zack. If we win the referendum, Lancaster stands to lose a lot of money not just now but in the future."

"And that's why they're pulling out all the stops to defeat us," Zack said.

Brock was sombre. "We might have ruled out the possibility that Lancaster was involved in the poisoning of the heritage birds too quickly," he said. "The slaughter may have been their warning shot across the bow."

"To convince us to raise the white flag?" Zack said. "It's not going to happen."

"But Slater Doyle's job is to make it happen," Brock said. "Michael's worried Slater will do something irrevocable."

"Then Michael will have to stop him," Zack said. "It's that simple. Slater and Michael are married. If Michael feels his husband would do something dangerous, he has to intervene."

"Michael has made so many mistakes. I know it's difficult for you to believe, but at heart he's a decent human being. He'll listen to me."

I walked Brock to the door. "You still love him," I said.

Brock smiled wistfully. "Yes. Seeing each other again today made us both realize what we'd lost."

When I came back into the living room, Zack wheeled towards me. "We need to talk about Milo," he said.

"We do," I said. "Zack, starting now, Milo has to be privy to all the information he needs to do his job. I can't afford to lose him, especially not when we've got Lancaster breathing fire at us."

"Did Milo threaten to leave?"

"No."

"He's staying because of you, Jo."

I could feel the anger rise. "Does that really matter?" I said. "Zack, you have a city to run. Why don't you focus on that and let me deal with Milo?"

Zack looked at me sharply and then gave me the smile that won my heart. "That sounds reasonable," he said. "Look, I haven't made dinner in a while. I could make that pasta thing you like – the one the hookers in Naples invented."

"Spaghetti alla puttanesca," I said. "Good call. I'll make the salad."

The pasta and a shared half-litre of Italian red thawed the chill that had developed between Zack and me when we discussed Milo. We were just marvelling over the photos Mieka had sent us of Madeleine and Lena wearing their fascinators at the Victorian picnic when Angus called. It was a little past six-thirty. "Everything okay?" I said.

"As okay as it can be, I guess," Angus said. "Bobby, Lee, and I just finished doing chores. The goats, the sheep, and the horses are still really spooked by what happened yesterday. We managed to calm down the animals in the barn, but Lee thinks the bouviers must have witnessed the killing. Gabby and Esme are usually so quiet, but all day they've been pacing and whimpering.

"It's really awful, Mum. Bobby and Lee are strong, but we've had to leave the area in front of the poultry house and the pond as is until the RCMP get everything they need.

It looks like a slaughterhouse. Dead birds everywhere. Lee wants a decent burial for them. Bobby dug a pit with his backhoe in that field behind the orchard so that when we bury the birds, the coyotes won't get them. The three of us should be able to get everything cleaned up tomorrow, but until then, it's gross."

"Does the RCMP have any idea yet who did this?"

"If they do, they're not sharing," Angus said. "I'm going to stay over, and Bobby's going to go home and come back in the morning. I'll check in with you guys then."

"Do that," I said. "Give Lee and Bobby our love and try to get some sleep."

Milo called on the landline just as Zack and I were getting ready for bed. "Grab your phone and check out hashtag yellowcanoeman," he said. "We've got to move on this, Jo."

I picked up my phone. #yellowcanoeman showed a torrent of tweets. The messages varied, but they all had attached the same photograph. It was of Simon in the canoe on Lawyers' Bay the day of the wedding. I scanned the messages. "Lee's ex-lover driven mad bc dumped?" "Simon a stalker?" "Restraining order couldn't stop him." "Yellowcanoeman = killer?"

Collectively, the fragments created a narrative that was as ugly as it was persuasive. I showed my phone to Zack. He put on his reading glasses, glanced at the screen, and uttered his favourite expletive.

I stared at my cellphone screen. Milo was still on the landline. "So what do you think?" he said.

"Mansell must have taken that photo," I said. "I'm sure he or Quinn supplied it to whoever first posted it. Bette Stevens would have known about Lee's troubled relationship with Simon. Given Bette and Mansell's closeness to the twins when they were growing up, it would have been natural for Bette to mention Lee's problem to her brother."

"And so Lancaster gets its scapegoat," Milo said. "I'll bet the Donnellys are creaming their jeans about sticking it to Warren Weber's son. They travel in the same circles, and they've always seen Warren's support of Zack as a betrayal. Time for the big man to convince Mansell to put Slater back in his cage before he strikes again."

"I'll pass along the message."

After Milo hung up, I turned to Zack and told him what Milo had said.

He nodded, picked up his phone, and made the call. Zack had just begun his conversation when my cellphone rang. I stepped into the hall and answered. Warren Weber was on the line, and he was livid. "Simon's here at the lake," he said. "He stopped by the house long enough to show us the yellowcanoeman tweets. He's devastated. Simon's well beyond caring what anybody says about him. But he doesn't want Lee to think he killed her birds."

Suddenly exhaustion took hold. The fact that, with his whole world shattered, Simon's only concern was that Lee would think ill of him brought tears to my eyes. "Warren, I'm really sorry Simon's photo has gone viral. I was certain that Lancaster's people were too smart to risk backlash from killing Lee's birds. Now I'm not so sure. Mansell had a camera at the wedding, and his sister might have told him about the restraining order. Simon was the perfect scapegoat."

"So it's a three-cushion shot," Warren said. "The Donnellys put an end to speculation that someone from their camp killed Lee's birds; they throw suspicion on my son; and they lift a middle finger to me."

"Slater Doyle's heading up their campaign against the new bylaws," I said. "This attack on Simon has Slater's fingerprints all over it."

"I'll call Mansell and pressure him to get Doyle fired," Warren said.

"At the moment, Zack's on the phone with Mansell attempting to do that very thing," I said. "But from what he said at the wedding, I think Mansell's policy on Slater Doyle is 'hands off.'"

"A policy guaranteed to please his wife." Warren's voice dripped with disgust. "Quinn's the one with the balls in that family," he said. "I apologize, Joanne. There's no need for me to be crude, but Graham Meighen taught Quinn everything she knows, and she learned her lessons well. She runs Lancaster the way he did: she never forgets a perceived betrayal, and she's vindictive. And of course, there's bad blood between her and Lee Crawford."

Remembering the relish with which Quinn tore apart Lee's reputation in the video of Lancaster's anniversary party, I felt a chill. "Warren, where did you hear about the hostility between Quinn and Lee?"

"From Quinn herself. When she heard that I'd donated to Citizens for Planned Growth, she called to ream me out. She started saying ugly things about Lee. I told her to stop and when she didn't, I hung up. She hasn't spoken to me since."

"So you think yellowcanoeman is payback."

"I know it is."

"I'll have Zack call you. Warren, where's Simon now?"

"He's staying in the flat over the boathouse. We've used it for guests when the house was full. It's comfortable. Simon will have his privacy, and Annie and I will be able to keep close tabs on him." Warren paused. "Joanne, I lost Simon's mother. I'm not going to lose our son."

When he was angry, Zack never raised his voice; he lowered it. He was still on the phone when I came back to our bedroom, and his voice was barely audible. Clearly, he was furious.

"Just to make certain I have this straight, Mansell: you're offering to publicly denounce the yellowcanoeman operation if I get Lee Crawford to take down the video of the dead birds. That's not acceptable. Nothing links Simon Weber to the slaughter of Lee's birds." Zack cast a glance at me and shrugged. We both knew the note left for Lee could incriminate Simon, but Zack soldiered on. "The yellowcanoeman campaign is vicious, baseless innuendo and it's libellous. Slater Doyle may have been disbarred, but he must still have a vague recollection of the fact that libel is actionable.

"Lee Crawford posted a video of something that actually happened. She raised heritage birds and someone slaughtered them. Lee has every right to leave that video up. Now here's a piece of friendly advice, Mansell. Rein in your wife, and suggest that she lock Slater Doyle up somewhere and throw away the key. You and Quinn have plans for this city. They're not my plans; they're not the current city council's plans; but we all know that gutter politics comes at a price. You and I can debate the bylaws rationally and nobody else will get hurt."

When Zack's call was over, I went to him and rubbed his shoulders. "There's smoke coming out of your ears," I said. "I take it that did not go well."

"Nope. Mansell's decided to flex his muscles. His parting words were curious. He said that if we don't get Lee to take down the video, someone else will."

"I don't like the sound of that," I said.

Zack transferred his body from his chair to the bed. "Neither do I," he said. "Neither do I."

CHAPTER

5

When we talked the next morning, Angus sounded more in control. The RCMP had given permission to remove the birds' bodies, and Lee had stood dry-eyed and alone in a field of wildflowers as Bobby and Angus buried them. As soon as she came back to the house, Lee began drawing up lists of what she needed to restart her heritage bird breeding program.

Her fortitude impressed Angus. "Lee is really something else, Mum."

"I agree," I said. "Are you staying at the farm for the day?"

"Bobby will be here all morning. He has a late-afternoon meeting in Saskatoon so I'm going in to work, but I'm cutting out early to come back here to make supper."

"I'm really glad you're pitching in."

"It's no big deal. Bobby and Lee are good people, and they're jumping right back into the fray. Lee's having an emergency CPG meeting here this morning to strategize about how to respond to what happened to the birds."

"She'll have to tread lightly," I said. "There's a lot of anger out there. The slaughter of those birds was an atrocity, but no one should respond in kind. Retaliation will just up the ante."

"That's what Lee feels too," Angus said. "Mum, could you possibly stop by the farm? Bobby will be here, but Lee could use more support."

"She's got it," I said. "What time is the meeting?"

"Ten this morning, and bring a lawn chair."

When the groups that came together to form Citizens for Planned Growth met for the first time, they made one key decision. Since CPG was an ad hoc coalition formed for the purpose of making certain the Yes side won the referendum, the individual member groups would retain their autonomy. Each group would decide the time and place of its meetings, maintain social media contacts with current members, and seek out new members from its natural constituency. Realizing that matters such as advertising and public statements for CPG had to be unified, each group would designate a liaison for more formal meetings of the larger coalition to reach decisions.

My guess was that many of the twenty or so people sitting on lawn chairs in a ragged circle in front of the Brokenshire house were activists who had been allies in earlier political battles. As soon as she spotted me, Lee and her bouviers came over. After I'd fussed over the dogs, Lee held out her hand to show me her engagement ring. It was delicate and lovely: two identical diamonds in a simple silver setting. "It belonged to Bobby's maternal grandmother," Lee said. "She told Bobby's grandfather she wanted a ring that showed their marriage would be the union of two equal partners."

"A woman ahead of her time," I said.

Lee laughed. "Bobby said she was a lot like me. And her initials were the same as mine, LKC."

"Sometimes all the pieces just slide into the place where they belong," I said.

"It feels that way, doesn't it?" Lee's eyes, so like her sister's, met mine. "This will be a good marriage. Bobby deserves the best." She took my arm and we joined the others. "Joanne's going to sit in for a while at our meeting," she said. "Jo, I think you know everybody."

I looked around. Bobby was there, flanked by Bette and Piper Edwards. Apparently, ring or no ring, Piper wasn't giving up. Somehow I wasn't surprised.

A smart, savvy petite redhead with a snub nose, a small but determined mouth, and big brown eyes, Piper had just turned thirty when the Writ was dropped, but she already owned Wascana Realty, a company that had mushroomed during our city's housing boom and continued to flourish.

That morning when I extended my hand to her, I anticipated that Piper would welcome me as a sister progressive. However, her handshake was perfunctory, and after a desultory exchange about the weather, she strolled away.

Bemused, I greeted Bette and Bobby, and then I picked up my lawn chair and joined Elder Ernest Beauvais and my old friend Peggy Kreviazuk. Peggy had tinted her dandelion-fluff hair a pale mauve for Peter and Maisie's wedding, and her complexion glowed with the tan of a passionate gardener. She was wearing a T-shirt with the message TOGETHER WE ARE BETTER. "Great shirt," I said. "Can we buy those by the gross?"

Peggy smiled. "I'll look into it. Lee has asked Ernest to say a prayer before the meeting," she said.

"That's a wise beginning," I said.

Since Zack and I had committed ourselves to bringing the Racette-Hunter Centre into being, Ernest Beauvais had been a part of our lives. The opposition to building a community centre in our city's poorest neighbourhood had been fierce, but those who believed that Racette-Hunter could be the lifeline to our marginalized citizens were determined. Ernest was part of the R-H working team, and later when Zack ran for mayor, Ernest put in long hours organizing voters in North Central. Those were tumultuous times, but Ernest always offered a still point in the storm.

He was a retired ironworker, the grandson of one of the Mohawks from Kahnawake who helped frame New York City's skyscrapers and bridges. His grandfather had married a Cree woman, and Ernest, like his own father, had married a Cree. Although, as Ernest said, his own children were more Cree than Mohawk, all six of them, including the women, were ironworkers who took pride in "walking iron." A big man in every way, Ernest always created an atmosphere of shared strength and hope when he began our meetings with a prayer, first in Cree and then in English.

That morning when Ernest stood, we all followed suit. His prayer was heartfelt.

Nohtawenan saweyiminan oma Ka Kesikak
Our father, bless us this day
Ayis Kiyehewini pimatisiwin
For your breath is life
Sayweyiminan mena ota mamawai Kayayahk
and Bless us here together
Meyinan, muskawisewin mena ayinesewin
Give us – strength and wisdom
Ta natohtamahk menata nahehtamahk
To listen and to hear
Namoya ayiwakeyimowin ta pimitsahamahk
Not to follow enviousness
Meyinan asumena ta wapahatamahk
Give us again to see
Sakastewini mena ka nanskomitinan
Sunrise and sunset
Hiy hiy ki anaskomitinan
Thank you, we are all most thankful
Pitane ekosi teyihki
Hoping that will happen

It was customary to spend a few moments reflecting on an elder's prayer, but Piper Edwards was clearly not in a contemplative mood. Ernest had barely finished when she stepped forward. Piper was known for her eye-catching clothing choices. That day she wore a very short grey cotton shift with a split neckline, diamond-patterned tights in black and grey, and pink suede ankle boots with four-inch heels.

As her eyes swept the circle, they were hard with anger. "It's all well and good to ask for blessings and sunsets," she said. "But let's face facts. We're all sorry about Lee Crawford's birds, but whoever killed them did us a favour. For weeks, Lancaster has been blanketing the media with ads. We don't have the funds to match that kind of blitz, but thanks to the bird slaughter, social media can't get enough of Lee Crawford. Keeping her and the tragic loss of her heritage birds front and centre is top priority."

Piper was a skilled public speaker, and I watched with interest as she turned slowly so she could make eye contact with people in the circle as she spoke.

"Very smooth," I whispered to Peggy.

"Very," Peggy said. "Did you notice that Piper didn't look at Lee?"

"I did, and I know why," I said. "Piper and Bobby Stevens have been seeing each other on and off for a while. As my grandmother would say, Piper 'set her cap' for Bobby, but Bobby has always loved Lee. After the ceremony on Saturday, he proposed to Lee and she accepted. Lee showed me her engagement ring when I arrived."

"So Piper is wounded," Peggy said. "I understand, but we can't afford to be divided." She touched the motto on her shirt. "The only way we'll win the referendum is through solidarity."

"Agreed," I said. But as soon as Lee Crawford spoke, it was clear that this group was going to need more than T-shirts to remain united.

After she'd thanked Ernest Beauvais, Lee turned to the others. "Elder Beauvais prayed for the right things. We all need the strength and the wisdom to listen and to hear. Yesterday when I posted the video of my birds on YouTube, I made it harder for all of us to do just that. This issue has already caused too much anger. I don't want to fan the flames. I'm taking my video down."

Piper stood so abruptly she knocked her chair over. A young man wearing a U OF R Cougars sweatshirt righted the chair, but she ignored him. Piper's hands were balled into fists and her face was a thundercloud. "Lee, you can't do that. For once in your life, you have to think about somebody other than yourself."

When Lee rose again to speak, she was pale. Bobby moved to stand behind her. "I am thinking of someone other than myself, Piper," Lee said softly. "I'm putting CPG first. We're a collective, a group of people with a shared belief. Our strength is in each other. People have come to see me as CPG's leader, but that changes what we are, and it makes us vulnerable."

Piper's voice was cool. "You owe the people here today an explanation, Lee. Tell us why you being the leader would make CPG vulnerable. Your public image is that of a person of honour who fights for what she believes in. How can that image make CPG vulnerable?"

"Because I'm not an image. I'm a person, and I've made my share of mistakes. I don't want to give our opponents a chance to shift the focus from the issues about development to *my* feet of clay."

Lee's tone had been conciliatory, but her words ignited Piper. Her gaze moved furiously around the circle. "A collective uses the strength of each member," she said. "I support Citizens for Planned Growth because I'm the councillor for Ward 4 and the majority of my constituents believe that our city's future development should be rooted in thoughtful planning and respect for our environment. My strength comes from the people who live and vote in Ward 4.

"Lee Crawford's strength as a member of this collective derives solely from the fact that she is a media magnet. No one has ever voted for her. She went on NationTV. She made herself a public personality online. Now it's time for her to get past *her* ego and push forward *our* agenda."

There was no mistaking the rancour in Piper's voice. Peggy nudged me. "We have a problem," she said.

"I'd heard Piper could be mean," I said.

When George Sawchuk pushed himself out of his lawn chair, I relaxed. George and his father, Kostya, had been heroes of mine for years. One of the first farmers to recognize the dangers of pesticides and go organic, Kostya Sawchuk had fought the multinationals to keep them from spraying their crops because the spray drifts. Time and time again, he took the multinationals to court. No matter how many times the multinationals' teams of high-priced lawyers beat him, Kostya kept the faith. When he died, George picked up the torch and carried on.

George bore a striking resemblance to his late father. Compact and powerfully built, both men were sharp-featured with wavy iron-grey hair, high foreheads, and deeply set blue eyes. The resemblance was not simply physical. Like Kostya, George believed that some day, somehow, human beings would get it right, and as he began to speak I knew that, once again, he would appeal to our best selves.

"I'm not a religious man," he said, "but my father was. Every night after supper, he'd read the Bible to us. There are some great stories in there, and there's some solid advice.

Over the years, I've been a part of many groups devoted to important causes who let pride or pigheadedness tear them apart." He gestured towards me. "Joanne here calls it 'the granolier than thou syndrome.' Anyway, whatever you call it, the loser is always the cause the group believes in. There's a passage from Isaiah that we need to remember today. 'Come now and let us reason together.'"

A scruffy young man with a ponytail and attitude had been standing throughout the meeting. He took a few steps towards George. "You're out of touch, buddy," he said. "We're not living in Bible times any more. This is the twenty-first century and it's all about social media. Your generation fucked up everything. Why don't you sit back down and let my generation clean up the mess you left us."

George stood his ground. "It's clear we have differences about how to proceed," he said mildly. "Fine. That means it's time to talk. We have a goal. On June 17, we're going to win the referendum. We can't allow anything to get in our way. As soon as we publicly acknowledge one person as leader, we expose that person to brutal scrutiny by our opponents. We all have feet of clay. Through no fault of her own, Lee has achieved a certain notoriety. The reason why she doesn't welcome that notoriety is her business. As our friend and our colleague, she has the right to take down the video."

Beside me, Peggy breathed, "Amen."

Her body taut with rage, Piper took to her feet again, but Bette Stevens intervened. She touched Piper's arm. "Time for us all to take a deep breath," she said. Bette cast a piercing look back at Lee and then led Piper from the circle, the younger woman following wordlessly.

"Bette's right," Lee said. "Let's take a break. There are glasses on the kitchen table and lemonade in the fridge. My one and only bathroom is on the second floor. Please make yourselves at home."

I went to Lee. "Zack and I have a busy afternoon scheduled, and there's something I should take care of before then. If you need me, I'll stay . . . "

Lee shook her head. "I'll be all right, but let me walk with you. I need to get away for a minute."

"Do you think cooler heads will prevail?" I said.

"I don't know," Lee said. "At the moment, I'm just clinging to the last line of Ernest's prayer."

"'Hoping that will happen'?" I said.

"Yes," she said. "I really do hope Piper and I will be able to work together." Her smile was rueful. "Is that too much to ask?"

"You know the story of Pandora's box," I said. "Sometimes when all the evils of the world have been let loose, hope is all we have."

Lee put her arms around me. "I'm glad you're on my side."

"It's the right side to be on," I said.

Bobby Stevens came through the gate and held out his hand to Lee. "I'm on your side too," he said. "Always have been, always will be."

Lee took his hand. "Thank God for that," she said. "Bobby, I'm glad we're getting married."

Bobby kissed Lee's ring finger. "I've been waiting to do this since I was eleven years old," he said.

Piper had followed Bobby to the gate. When she saw the intimacy between Bobby and Lee, her face contorted with rage. A confrontation seemed inevitable, but at that moment Bette Stevens appeared. In seconds, Bette assessed the scene and whisked Piper away. Once again, Lee's mother-in-law-to-be had saved the day.

———

After Bobby and Lee headed back to the house, I texted Zack to tell him I was on my way. I still felt shaken by Piper's anger as I walked towards my car, scrolling through my messages.

When I heard a car pull into the driveway, I looked up. The grey Lexus was moving slowly, but it was headed straight for me and the driver wasn't changing course. I stepped out of range and after the car stopped, I began walking towards the driver's side.

The window had been rolled down. Behind the wheel sat Slater Doyle with a smirk on his face. The evils of the world were on the march.

Because Slater suffered from photophobia, he always wore wraparound Ray-Bans. In addition to protecting his eyes, the glasses acted as a barrier, shielding Slater against people who might be curious about what they'd find if they peered through the windows to his soul.

That day, instead of squinting into the depths of Slater Doyle, I had to content myself with leaning into the open window of his Lexus. "You're getting sloppy, Slater," I said. "You've always been the surgical strike-and-withdraw type. Threatening to run me down is thug stuff."

"Made you blink," he said.

"What are you doing here?"

"I came upon some interesting information about St. Lee of Assisi. It seems that the beasts of the field and the air aren't the only creatures she's gathered to her breast."

"Don't you ever get tired of being an asshole?" I said.

"You're not going to win this one, Joanne."

"The game's barely begun, Slater."

His smile was chilling. "Oh but it has." He cocked his head. "You really don't know, do you?" he said. He glanced at the cars in the driveway. "Probably best if I delay my tête-à-tête with Lee till she's alone. Besides, anticipation's half the fun." And with that, he floored it and made a U-turn that sent the pebbles of the driveway flying.

I watched the Lexus peel down the road and disappear over the hill, then, nerves prickling with apprehension,

I slid into the front seat of my station wagon. I'd had enough. I called Warren and asked whether he had Quinn Donnelly's cell number. He did. Surprisingly, I got right through to her. When she heard I was her caller, Quinn was all business. "What do you want, Joanne?"

"Five minutes of your time," I said. "Your goon Slater Doyle just drove his Lexus at me. Falconer Shreve are looking into the legal implications of the yellowcanoeman campaign. When they expose you and Mansell as the not-so-merry pranksters behind it, you won't be the golden power couple any more – you'll just be a couple of high school mean kids – the ones everybody hates. You and I have to talk, Quinn. Warren Weber tells me that you have a problem with Lee personally. If she *is* the problem, give me a chance to bring you two together to talk it out. We're all going to have to live with the voters' decision about these bylaws. We can't afford to let personality conflicts derail the discussion. All I'm asking for is five minutes of your time."

Quinn didn't respond. As the silence on her end continued, my spirits sank. But just as I was about to break the connection, she said, "All right. I'm at the office. I'll be here all day."

"Thanks," I said. "This is a good first step, Quinn. I'll be there in thirty minutes."

Lancaster's offices were in a glass tower twin to the building that housed Falconer Shreve's offices. I parked on the street and cut across the spaces reserved for executive parking. It was Victoria Day Monday, a holiday, and there was only one car in the lot, a dark-blue Porsche with a vanity plate DONN-1. As I watched, the Porsche roared out of the parking space onto 11th Avenue. Someone other than Quinn could have been the driver, but instinct told me she was behind the wheel.

Checking was a simple matter. Lancaster's executive offices were on the twenty-fifth floor. I could take the elevator up and see for myself. I didn't even get into the lobby. When I tried the doors, I discovered that the glass tower was locked up tight. I tried Quinn's private number again, but my call went straight to voicemail so I left a message telling her I'd keep calling until she responded and then, frustrated and hungry, I walked to my car.

When I got home, Zack and Brock were at the kitchen table eating thick deli corned beef sandwiches off the paper in which they'd been wrapped. A tub of potato salad and one of coleslaw sat on the table between them.

Zack grinned at me. "Perfect timing." He gestured towards a grease-stained bag on the table. "That's yours, and it should still be hot."

I unwrapped my sandwich and bit in. "Still hot and very tasty," I said. "I guess my run-in with Slater Doyle didn't kill my appetite."

Brock's eyes narrowed. "Where did you see Slater?"

"At Lee's farm. Her group was having a meeting this morning. I went, but I arrived late, so I had to park halfway down the driveway. Slater Doyle must have driven in when I was walking towards my car to leave. I was checking my phone and when I looked up, Slater's Lexus was coming at me."

Zack tensed. "What the hell?"

I waved my hand dismissively. "He was moving slowly. That was just Slater being Slater, but he did say something that disturbed me. He said that the beasts of the field and the air weren't the only creatures St. Lee of Assisi had gathered to her breast."

Zack scowled. "Slimey sexual innuendo – vintage Slater."

Brock shook his head. "There may be more to it than that," he said.

I spooned potato salad onto my plate. "I agree," I said. "Slater seemed genuinely surprised that I didn't realize that he had some presumably damaging information about Lee."

Brock was clearly troubled. "This morning Michael overheard Slater on the phone saying that Lee Crawford and her group had fucked up big-time by putting her front and centre."

"That's just bullshit," Zack said. He saw my face and stopped. "That is just bullshit, isn't it?"

"I don't know," I said. "At the meeting today, Lee suggested that CPG would make itself vulnerable by allowing her to be its public face. She said she'd made a mistake by putting up the video of her with the dead birds and she was taking the video down. I hope for all our sakes she has."

"So do I," Brock said.

"And something else – Warren says there's bad blood between Quinn Donnelly and Lee. Neither side can afford that, so about an hour ago, I called Quinn to try to broker some kind of peace between her and Lee. She told me she'd be in her office all afternoon and agreed to see me, but when I got to Lancaster, Quinn's Porsche was zooming out of the executive parking space, and the building was locked up for the holiday. I called Quinn and left a voicemail saying that I'd keep phoning her until she responded." I glanced at my watch. "No time to call now," I said. "Zack, you and I have to move along. We have an event, and we're already late."

Regina is a city of neighbourhoods, each with its own history, identity, and needs. During the election, Milo had created a series of neighbourhood profiles that identified the average income, level of education, predominant family structure, and issues of concern for the area's voters. As part of our campaign we'd planned wiener roasts in each of our city's ten wards, and they'd been hugely successful.

The importance of community organization had not been lost on us, and that Victoria Day Monday we were having planting parties at newly dug community gardens in five different areas of the city. The price of admission was some bedding plants or a pack of seeds, though we had extras on hand for anyone who wanted to join in. Parks and Recreation were in charge of preparing the soil, supervising face painting and games for the kids, and helping interested adults and kids with the planting. Merchants donated an assortment of veggie chips, freshly squeezed fruit and vegetable juices, and fibre-laden cookies. We'd hired local bands to keep the day swinging.

Obeying the old recreation dictum that it's better to kill an activity than have it die on you, each party lasted two hours, and Zack and I were staying at each party for half an hour. We staggered start times so that any child who cared to could get his or her picture taken with the mayor and a teenager in a Bugs Bunny suit. The number of takers surprised us, and it was a little after three-thirty when Zack and I arrived at the last stop, the Racette-Hunter planting party.

Over the course of the afternoon, I'd called Quinn Donnelly three times, but she never picked up, and as I took my place at the face-painting table, I was tired and irritable. My spirits rose when Margot and Brock arrived with Lexi and Kai, both wearing floppy hats and sunglasses. As Margot settled the babies on Zack's lap to get pictures, he groaned but, always a party guy, he was clearly enjoying himself. Margot, Brock, and I visited as I painted the kids' faces, and chatting with them made the time pass quickly. After they'd taken Kai, Lexi, and a flat of tomato plants to the community garden area, I checked my watch. It was almost four o'clock. The end was in sight.

I glanced over at Zack. Only one more child remained in line to get his picture taken with the mayor and Bugs Bunny.

I was attempting to paint a pink butterfly on the cheek of a three-year-old girl who had a firm idea about exactly where a pink butterfly belonged on her cheek when my cell rang,

The voice on the other end of the line was wafer-thin. "Mum, it's Angus."

"You don't sound like you," I said. "What's wrong?"

"Everything," he said, and his voice quivered.

The three-year-old picked up the hand mirror from the makeup table, gave her face a final critical glance, then, satisfied, she skipped off.

"Angus, what's happened?"

"It's Lee, Mum," he said. "She's dead."

CHAPTER

6

We left as soon as the photographer had taken the last photo of Zack and I had the chance to fill him in. The drive from our end of the city to the Brokenshire farm took half an hour. By the time we pulled into the driveway, I still hadn't been able to reach Peter and Maisie. The cabin where they were staying was too remote for cellular service. I had a number for the cabin's landline, but they weren't answering and it didn't have voicemail. It was imperative that I reach them, but I was grateful they were being given a few extra minutes of happiness.

Regina police don't have jurisdiction in rural Saskatchewan, but the RCMP officers were already on the scene. Angus stood with three officers on the west side of the driveway. Lee's bouvier, Esme, was leashed and next to him. Close to the barn and directly across from them, officers spoke to Simon Weber.

One of the men talking to Angus spotted us, broke away from the group, and approached. When he stopped at our car, Zack held out his ID. "I'm Angus Kilbourn's stepfather, and this is his mother, Joanne. Our daughter-in-law, Maisie, is

Lee's only relative. We've been trying to reach her, but so far no luck. I'd like to talk to my stepson."

"He's being questioned, Mr. Mayor," the officer said.

Zack was sanguine. "Then he'll need a lawyer," he said. "And I also happen to be just that."

Inspector Carl Lovitz was fortyish with a thinning tonsure of greying hair; a narrow, suspicious mouth; and the trim appearance, erect bearing, and precise enunciation of a man who was accustomed to being obeyed. He took his time deciding on how we would proceed. Finally he said. "You may see Mr. Kilbourn. But I'll bring him here. Don't move your car. Extraneous tire marks and footprints will hinder the investigation."

"Fine," Zack said, and he opened his door, reached into the back seat, pulled out his wheelchair, snapped it together, and transferred his weight from the driver's seat onto the chair.

Angus looked terrible, very young, and, I feared, on the verge of shock. When I embraced him, he held tight.

"Lee was shot, Mum. She was a mess. One of the officers said she was shot twice – once in the shoulder and once in the chest. Gabby's dead too. He must have tried to attack the person who killed her." Angus's voice was flat, toneless.

"Angus, you didn't touch anything, did you?"

"I covered Lee with my jacket," he said.

"Don't worry about it," I said.

Two more squad cars pulled up and parked on the side of the road. Each car carried four officers, who unloaded with practised ease the paraphernalia necessary to investigate death by violence and carried the equipment to the barn.

Inspector Lovitz addressed Zack first. "We've finger-printed Mr. Kilbourn; we've done the GSR test to see if he fired a gun recently. Mr. Kilbourn voluntarily supplied us with a DNA sample, and we'll have an officer bag the clothes he was wearing when he found the victim. You can never tell what might be useful."

"That's certainly true." Zack motioned Angus to stand beside him. Angus's colour was returning, and he seemed to be more in command of himself.

Inspector Lovitz took a paper notebook and a fountain pen from his breast pocket. His hands were small and dainty. "Tell me exactly what happened here," he said. "Take your time. And try not to leave anything out, no matter how insignificant."

Lee's dog strained at the leash. Bouviers grow frantic if they're separated from their owners. I took the leash from Angus and bent to reassure Esme. Hearing a woman's voice seemed to calm her.

My son gave me a faint smile, and then he took a deep breath and began. "Yesterday morning when I heard about Lee's birds being killed, I came straight to the farm. I stayed overnight. This morning Lee's fiancé, Bobby Stevens, and I buried the birds. When we'd finished and cleaned up, I went back to Regina. It was eight-thirty. I'm a lawyer, and I have a big case coming up. I offered to work on it here, but Lee said she would be fine on her own."

Inspector Lovitz looked from his notepad to Angus. "And your relationship with Ms. Crawford is . . . ?"

"My brother, Peter, is married to Lee's sister, Maisie."

"Anything more than that?"

"Friendship. We enjoyed each other's company," Angus said. "Bobby is at a meeting in Saskatoon this afternoon. He thought he might be late getting back to the farm, so I told Lee I'd come back and make supper and we could watch a movie together and wait for Bobby. I worked through lunch and left the office at two-thirty to go grocery shopping."

"Where did you shop?"

"At the Co-op in the east end."

"Did you see anybody who might remember you were there?"

"This is Regina," Angus said. "You always see somebody you know. I saw Camilo Rostoker, a guy who was on my Ultimate Frisbee team. He was picking up a cake for his son's birthday party."

"Approximately when did you see him?"

"Probably between two-thirty and three."

"We'll need to talk to him. Can you supply us with contact information?"

After Angus supplied the information, Inspector Lovitz pressed on. "Did you see anybody else, Mr. Kilbourn?"

"I stopped at the liquor store to buy a bottle of wine for dinner," Angus said. "Lee's a vegetarian, and I was planning to make moussaka. I asked one of the men who works at the liquor store if he could recommend something suitable."

"And he did."

"He suggested a Cabernet Sauvignon. It's in the kitchen. When I got to the farm, I called for Lee. She didn't answer so I put the groceries away and went outside to look for her. Her truck was here, so I knew she hadn't gone far."

Inspector Lovitz gave Angus a sharp look. "You weren't concerned?"

"No. Not at first." Angus pointed to the black car parked beside Lee's truck. "I'd noticed the BMW in the driveway, of course, but I assumed that Lee and whoever drove it were in the barn or checking out the orchard. Then I realized I hadn't seen the bouviers since I got back from town. Lee has . . . " Angus took a breath and corrected himself. "Lee had two bouviers. They never left her side. So I called them. Only one of them – Esme, the one with my mother – came out of the barn but she ran back in again. She started howling. I'd never heard either of the dogs make that sound before. That's when I knew there was something wrong.

"I followed Esme into the barn. Simon Weber was just inside the door. He was stripped to the waist and he was washing himself with water from the trough. The water was bloody. I think I asked him what had happened. He didn't answer me. He just kept washing his body with that bloody water. I went to the back of the barn. Lee was lying on some straw on the barn floor. Her dog Gabby was lying beside her. He was dead." Angus swallowed hard. "The front of Lee's shirt was covered in blood. Her jeans and her underwear were pulled down around her ankles. I took her pulse, but there was nothing. I put my jacket over her and called 911 and then I called my mother. My brother and his wife are somewhere up north on their honeymoon, and I thought my mum would know how to get in touch with them."

"We know about Ms. Crawford's restraining order against Simon Weber. Was she afraid of him?"

"No. He'd checked himself into Valleyview – it's a private facility for people with emotional problems."

"Valleyview is not far from where your brother's wedding took place," Inspector Lovitz said. "Tell me what you know about Simon Weber's activities after he left Valleyview Saturday morning."

"The wedding took place at four o'clock. Lee was maid of honour and Simon spent more than four hours in a canoe on the lake watching the ceremony. When the wedding was over, he left. Lee stayed the night with my parents."

After Angus finished, Inspector Lovitz flipped the page in his paper notebook. "Do you know of other enemies Lee Crawford might have had?"

"Yesterday Lee showed me printouts of some antagonistic emails she'd received about the referendum," Angus said. "And she kept a log of hostile phone calls. I didn't pay much attention to the email addresses, and most of the callers were anonymous. You can see the emails for yourself,

Inspector Lovitz. Lee kept meticulous records of everything she dealt with."

"Was she afraid of the people who attacked her?"

Angus narrowed his eyes in concentration. "She seemed more perplexed than afraid. Lee was an idealist. She believed people are good, and that, if we had the will, we could work out our differences."

"Is there anything you'd like to add?"

Angus shook his head. "No, not at the moment."

"Inspector, there is something else," I said. "At the rehearsal dinner the night before the wedding, Lee asked Zack and me if we'd been the object of what she called 'pranks.' She'd been on the receiving end of some very unpleasant practical jokes, and she wondered if they'd been politically motivated."

"Did she suspect anyone in particular?"

"She didn't mention a name," Zack said. "As soon as Joanne and I told Lee that we hadn't been targeted, she said, 'I guess it was just somebody with a warped sense of humour.' I urged her to report the incidents to the police. Lee said she'd think about it. At that point the wedding planner corralled the members of the wedding party to practise something and the subject was dropped. I should have pursued it. Lee had given Joanne and me enough specifics about the 'pranks' to alarm us both."

"Fill me in," Inspector Lovitz said.

As Zack described the incidents, the inspector's pen flew. His face was stony, but Angus was clearly disturbed.

"Inspector, Lee never told me about the pranks," he said. "I know she sloughed off their significance with Mum and Zack, but in retrospect, they could well have been warnings. I think whoever pulled those stunts was working up to killing Lee's birds. After the birds were buried, Lee said that the person who killed them was capable of anything."

"Do you believe that if we find the person behind the 'pranks,' we'll find Lee Crawford's killer?" the inspector asked.

"I think you'll be close," Angus said.

Lovitz peered at Angus intently. "Do you believe Simon Weber could have pulled the pranks and killed Lee's birds?"

Angus paused and looked towards Simon, who appeared as wasted and still as a man could be. Then, meeting the inspector's eyes, my son said, "No. Simon may be sick, but he's not cruel, and he's not a killer."

The inspector closed his notebook without comment. "That's all for now. You know the drill, Mr. Kilbourn. Keep us informed of your whereabouts. As we learn more, we'll have other questions."

When he turned to leave, I stopped him. "Inspector, there's something else. I was at a CPG meeting at Lee's this morning around ten-thirty."

Inspector Lovitz opened his notebook again. "Go on," he said.

"There was friction at the meeting, and it centred on Lee. She was uncomfortable with the public perception that she was the leader of the group."

Inspector Lovitz raised an eyebrow. "She was no longer in support of your husband's bylaws?"

I shook my head. "It wasn't that. Lee's commitment to the cause was firm. She didn't want the fact that she had become a public face to make the group vulnerable. A YouTube video Lee posted of her dead birds has been getting a lot of attention. Lee said that she was going to take it down."

"And others in the group opposed her decision?"

"Yes."

"Can you identify them?"

"I was only there for about half an hour," I said. "I don't know what went on after I left. Every meeting has tensions; most of the time, they're resolved by the time the meeting ends."

"But during the time you were at the meeting, there were people who opposed Lee Crawford's decision to take down the video?"

"Yes. Piper Edwards, the city councillor for Ward 4, was adamant about keeping the video on YouTube, but by the end of the meeting she might have changed her mind."

"Who else was at the meeting?"

When Inspector Lovitz had written down the names I gave him and the role each had played in the meeting, he started to close his notebook again.

"There's someone else you should talk to," I said. "When I left the meeting, Slater Doyle drove in. Slater's handling Lancaster Development's campaign against the bylaws. He made a disparaging remark about Lee. He said that the beasts of the field and the air aren't the only creatures St. Lee of Assisi has gathered to her breast."

The beginning of a smile curled Inspector Lovitz's lips but he suppressed it. "So Mr. Doyle implied that he had information about Lee Crawford's sex life that would damage your campaign?" he said.

"Yes," I said. "But when he realized Lee had company, Slater said he'd delay his tête-à-tête with her till she was alone."

The inspector offered me a wintry smile. "You've been very helpful, Ms. Shreve."

"I want Lee's murderer caught," I said. "Inspector, Maisie and Peter won't be able to make it back here until tomorrow night at the earliest. The animals will have to be taken care of until then. Lee's fiancé, Bobby Stevens, has helped Lee with chores in the past . . . " The realization that Bobby didn't know about Lee hit my husband, my son, and me simultaneously. Mute, the three of us stared at one another. Finally, Angus reached into the breast pocket of his jacket and took out his phone. "I have Bobby's cell number," he said. When Angus stepped away to make his call, I took out my phone. "I'll call George Sawchuk," I said. "He'll know someone who can handle chores."

The inspector scowled. "We can't have people tromping all over the place. This is a crime scene, Ms. Shreve."

"The animals don't know that," I said.

George had known Lee since she was a child and he was heartbroken at the news of her death, but he said he'd do chores tonight and work with the neighbours to take care of the farm until Maisie and Peter returned.

Angus had been on the phone for at least five minutes, but when he rejoined us, he said that he hadn't been able to get through so he was going to stay at the farm till he connected with Bobby. During Inspector Lovitz's questioning, Esme had been whining and straining at the leash. It was clear she was desperate to be with Lee. I turned to Zack. "You and I should get back to the city. I know neither of us has the stomach for dealing with the fallout from this, but we'll have to make some decisions. Inspector, we'll take Lee's dog with us. Esme will be miserable, and she'll be a distraction for your officers."

Zack raised his eyebrows, but he didn't object. He got into the driver's seat and started taking apart his chair. Angus and I coaxed Esme into the station wagon and closed the tailgate. I hugged Angus goodbye. "How are you doing?"

"I'm okay." He kneaded his temples. "I still can't believe this. And every time I think about Bobby . . . "

"I know . . . ," I said. "Call if there's anything we can do."

Zack finished stowing his chair in the back seat. "Does Simon have a lawyer?" he said.

Angus swore softly. "I must have had my head up my ass. I should have called somebody."

"You were dealing with a lot," Zack said gently. "I'll get Asia Libke. She has no connection to Falconer Shreve. She's smart and perceptive. She'll know how to protect Simon."

———

I managed to get in touch with Peter just as we came to the city limits. It was the most painful call I'd ever made, and I knew the grief had just begun.

Angus phoned not long after I had talked to his brother. "Asia just arrived. Apparently, she and Simon knew each other in law school so she's confident he'll trust her. Bette Stevens is here too. As soon as she heard the news about Lee, she came over. She's hoping she can get a call through to Bobby and break the news to him before he shows up here."

"That makes sense," I said.

"It does. Ms. Stevens is pretty shaken up herself, but she says the best place for her son right now is at their farm. I'm going to check with Asia and if there's nothing I can do here, I'm coming to your place. I don't want to be alone right now."

Zack and I were making dinner when Angus arrived at the condo. "We're having bacon and eggs," I said. "Interested?"

"Thanks," Angus said, "but what I'd like is one of Zack's martinis."

"I didn't know you drank martinis," I said.

"I've never had one," Angus said. "But today seems as good a time as any to start."

"There's a pitcher in the fridge," Zack said. "I'll get the glasses. Your mother and I will join you." Zack poured the martinis and we settled in the living room.

"So what do we know that we didn't know earlier?" Zack said.

Angus took a gulp of his first martini and grimaced. "That's a body slam," he said, putting down his glass. "Well, there is news. Bette Stevens talked to Bobby. She didn't tell him what's happened, just that there'd been a family emergency, and she needed him to come home as soon as possible." He swirled the drink in his glass. "I know I'm a coward, but I'm grateful Bobby's mother is taking charge."

"Bette's been running her farm since her husband died," I said. "She's strong, but Lee's death must be excruciating for her too," I said.

"I asked Bette to call if there's anything I can do." Angus's tone was derisive. "As if there's anything anybody can do now."

Zack wheeled closer to Angus. "How's Asia handling Simon's situation?"

"Carefully," Angus said. "Asia suggested to the RCMP that her client spend the night in the psych ward, and they wisely agreed. My guess is they have him on suicide watch."

"Is he talking yet?" Zack asked.

"Yes," Angus said. "And he specifically asked me to tell Lee's family what happened. Asia cautioned him, but Simon was adamant. He swears that he did not kill Lee."

"So what's his story?" Zack asked.

"According to Simon, sometime after three this afternoon, he got a text from Lee saying, 'I'm hurt. I'm in the barn. Help me.'"

"Was he sure the text was from Lee?"

"It was from her phone," Angus said.

"Whoever killed Lee could have used her phone to send the text," I said.

"Yeah, I guess. Simon says he drove out to the farm, and when he got there, Lee and Gabby were both on the barn floor, motionless and bleeding. He says he tried to resuscitate Lee and that he put his head on Gabby's chest to listen for a heartbeat. That's why he was covered in blood. When he realized they were both gone, Simon snapped. He remembers seeing me walk into the barn, but he says he wasn't aware until then that he was washing the blood off himself in the trough."

"And you believe him?" Zack said.

"I do," Angus said. "And if you'd seen Simon, you would have believed him. When he was talking about what happened, he was reliving the moments. I hope to God I never see anybody in that much agony again."

Zack and I exchanged a look. Remembering the suddenness with which the anger and darkness swallowed Simon the morning of the wedding, I rubbed my wrist. There was still a faint bruise on one of the places where his thumb had pressed my flesh.

Like all of us, Taylor was devastated by Lee's death, but she had apparently decided it was up to her to shepherd us through the terrible evening ahead. She helped with dinner, insisted on clearing the table herself, and suggested that we watch *Blazing Saddles* together.

The choice was significant. Taylor and Angus had watched *Blazing Saddles* together a dozen times. During dinner Angus had been unreachable, but Taylor knew that if anything would, the film's new-sheriff scene would draw him out. Taylor sat beside Angus on the couch, and as Cleavon Little rode into town, she reached over and squeezed her brother's arm. He smiled, and I knew he'd taken the first step on the road back.

When the credits rolled, Zack clicked off the movie. "It's time for this day to be done," he said. He wheeled over to Angus. "How are you doing?"

"I'm dented," Angus said, "but I'm okay. If it's all right with you guys, I'll stay here tonight. I'm beat and I don't want to go back to my apartment."

"This is a night to be together," Zack said. He held out his arms and Angus leaned down to be embraced.

———

At sixteen, our daughter still liked us to say goodnight to her in her room. That night she had left the door open, and she was perched on the bed surrounded by pictures of the heritage birds she'd taken the day we visited the Brokenshire farm. She held out a closeup of a Blue Andalusian. "I'd never seen that shade of blue before," she said. "Look at the way he holds himself. He's an aristocrat, and he knows it. I'm going to paint Lee's birds." Taylor's voice was steely. "That way everything won't be lost."

We kissed her and then Zack pointed his chair towards the stairlift. As always, I waited at the foot of the stairs with Pantera until Zack had made it safely to the top. But that night, Esme waited with us, and as I started upstairs, she stayed at my side.

When Zack and I settled into bed, Pantera sprawled on the floor beside Zack and Esme flattened out on the floor beside me.

Zack wrapped me in a hug. "I take it Esme's not just here for a sleepover."

"No. She belongs with us."

For a few moments Zack and I were silent, absorbed in our private thoughts. "I'm glad when Lee walked into that barn she knew Angus was coming back to the farm to make moussaka for supper," I said. "And I'm glad she and Angus were planning to watch a movie together till Bobby came home."

"The miracles of everyday life," Zack said, drawing me closer. "We're never grateful enough, are we?"

"No," I said. "We never are."

CHAPTER

7

Tuesday morning the wind shuddering against the windows awakened the dogs and me. The view from the bedroom window was not encouraging. A sky dark with clouds threatened rain, and wind whipped the graceful forsythias on the lawn behind our condo. Esme had whimpered most of the night, but when I began donning the clothes I wore for running in wet weather, and Pantera lumbered to the bedroom door, Esme got the picture. I opened the door, and both dogs hit the stairs. Angus emerged from the guest room, yawning and scratching his head. "I guess I'm in for the run," he said.

"It'll do you good," I said. "Clear your head."

Before we left, I checked on Taylor. She was sleeping, the photos of the heritage birds still scattered on her bed. When we got off the elevator we found Brock in the lobby stretching. He winced when I told him about Lee's death. He had not known her well, but Lee's fervent desire to protect the land had impressed him, and as he took Pantera's leash, I could feel his grief. Angus felt it too, and he tried to lighten the mood. He reached for Esme's leash. "Mum,

I can't remember you ever running without a dog," he said. "Are you up for the challenge?"

"Always," I said, opening the door to the street. Brock and I stepped outside, but when Angus tried to follow, Esme wouldn't budge. He coaxed her and I handed him a treat, but she was stubborn.

Finally, I held out my hand. "She can come with me," I said. As soon as I took the leash, Esme trotted off like a show dog. For most of the run, she and I led the pack, while Pantera followed along behind with the men. The rain started after we'd run ten blocks, but we carried on, mud-splashed, wet, but invigorated.

Zack had the coffee on and the towels ready when we got back. Brock joined us to help with cleaning up and feeding the dogs. The humans were all relieved to be distracted.

Peter had called when we were running. He and Maisie had managed to book a flight that would get them back to Regina by four in the afternoon. The day loomed, and it was going to be a doozy. Zack had already talked to Milo. He was on his way over. We agreed that after Angus, Brock, and I had showered and changed, Angus would head for Falconer Shreve and Brock would come back to our place for a break-fast meeting with Milo, Zack, and me. There was only one item on the agenda: come up with a way of dealing with a death that was on the cusp of being transformed from a per-sonal tragedy into a headline news story.

It was 6:45 a.m.

Among Milo's many strengths was the fact that nothing fazed him. When he came through the door and a one-hundred-and-ten-pound bouvier, whom he'd never clapped eyes on before, checked him out, he let Esme sniff, then bopped into the kitchen.

"We're in for a rough ride," he said. "Lee Crawford's murder has become national news. Over one hundred thousand people have watched her YouTube piece on the dead birds."

"Lee was planning to take that video down," I said. "I guess she changed her mind."

"Either that or somebody made sure she ran out of time," Milo said tightly. "But that's a job for the cops, and we have our own situation. There's some scary stuff going on in tweetsville. People are calling Lee a martyr, a woman who was prepared to die to protect a way of life. Some are blaming Lancaster for her death. And Lancaster is fighting back. They're suggesting that there was a side to Lee that was very different from her public image and that her own actions might have brought about her death."

"Which is tantamount to accusing Simon," I said.

"He's not in an enviable position," Milo agreed. "First, the yellowcanoeman operation and now he's at the scene of the crime." He unwrapped one of his chocolate bars and turned to Zack. "Time to step up to the plate, big man. You can't win if you don't show up."

Zack pulled out his BlackBerry and tapped away. When he was finished, he read out loud the tweet he'd just written. "Lee Crawford's death is heartbreaking, but the RCMP will learn the truth and justice will come. Remain calm."

"Good," I said. "I'll ask Norine to arrange a press briefing for your statement about Lee's death. Does nine this morning work for you?"

Zack nodded. "Yep. At nine-thirty I'm meeting with city council."

"So Piper Edwards will be there?" I said.

"I imagine so," Zack said. "Why do you ask?"

"She may *be* the problem," I said. "At the meeting yesterday, Piper led the attack on Lee. She was adamant about Lee's obligation to keep her video online."

Milo's fingertips tapped out a riff on the butcher-block table. "And she got her wish," he said.

"She did," I said. "Zack, I don't trust her. Keep an eye on her at the meeting. See how she's reacting to Lee's murder."

"Will do," Zack said.

I looked at my watch. "We have time for a swim," I said. Zack nodded and Milo beamed. He loved to swim and he was graceful in the water. The moment he dived in, all his ticks and jitters disappeared. Water was Milo's element and he knifed through it with barely a ripple. "I'm in," he said and jumped off his stool and tapped his way down the hall. "Angus, I've been wearing an old suit of yours – the one with Spider-Man on it. Okay if I wear it today?"

Angus smiled. "No problem," he said.

My suggestion that we go for a swim was not whimsical. Zack and I were as close as two people could be. We talked about everything except the one subject that kept me awake at three in the morning: Zack's health. Before we were married, Zack was determined that I understood exactly what I was signing on for. He arranged an appointment for both of us with his friend and physician, Henry Chan.

Henry had been forthright. Paraplegia compromises everything, including the workings of internal organs, the blood's ability to flow without clotting, and the skin's ability to heal. As a paraplegic, Zack was vulnerable to respiratory ailments, renal failure, pulmonary embolisms, and septicemia. The list had been daunting, but I was deeply in love, and I said that we were all going to die of something and I wanted to die married to Zack.

When I picked up my coat to leave, Henry asked me to stay and talk to him alone for a few minutes. He was a plainspoken man and as soon as Zack left the room, he went straight to the point. "Everyone who loves Zack is glad you came along, Joanne. He's been living like an eighteen-year-old with a death wish for far too long. Booze, fast cars, too many women, too much pressure, no exercise, not enough sleep, eating only when he remembered to eat. It's taken its toll, but I know Zack's making an effort to change the way he lives. He wants to grow old with you."

"That's what I want too," I said.

"And you're doing all the right things," Henry said. "But you have to accept the fact that you can't change the man Zack is. I've known him for over twenty-five years and there's no half-measure with him. He is fully alive only when he's working. If you ask him to cut back on the number of cases he handles, he'll do it because he loves you, but his frustration will shorten his life."

"How long do we have, Henry?"

He shrugged. "None of us knows the answer to that, but I would say with luck, you and Zack will have ten years together."

My heart sank. I had counted on at least fifteen. "That's not enough," I said.

"Make the most of what you're given," Henry said. Words to live by, and I did my best.

Zack's long-time executive assistant, Norine MacDonald, had agonized over whether to follow Zack to City Hall. She had been with Falconer Shreve from the beginning – twenty-eight years. Recently, the firm had been expanding rapidly, and the partners agreed that they needed Norine's knowledge of their history and culture and her management skills to preserve what was best about Falconer Shreve while the firm adjusted the expectations of young lawyers who were reluctant to put in twelve-hour days until the loyalty kicked in and they could work to the point of collapse at their desks.

The firm's managing partners had been persuasive, but in the end, Norine's loyalty to Zack won out. From the day he was sworn in, Norine was in the office adjoining his and I was reassured. Zack's schedule as mayor was punishing, but I did what I could to carve out periods of time for him to rest and exercise. Every Sunday night Norine sent me a copy of Zack's schedule for the week ahead. I would go through it, circling events Brock or I could handle, and send it back. Because of the holiday weekend, scheduling for this week had been particularly heavy, and as Zack was towelling off and getting dressed for the briefing, I called Norine to see what could be done to lighten the load. As always, she was way ahead of me. She'd drafted a note to many of those with whom Zack was scheduled to meet, explaining that for the next few days family obligations would take precedence and apologizing and rescheduling.

After three years of marriage, my loins still twitched when Zack came into the room dressed for the day. That morning his suit was lightweight mochaccino, and he was wearing a matching shirt and a patterned mochaccino-and-turquoise silk tie. "You are such a good-looking guy," I said. "Now I wish I'd put our swimming time to better use."

Zack gave me a satyr's smile. "I offer rain checks. Are we taking both cars to City Hall?"

"Yes," I said. "I need to keep busy. After you deliver your statement to the press, I'm going to UpSlideDown. During all the pre-wedding festivities, Lee always found time for Madeleine and Lena and they were very fond of her. It'll be difficult for them to accept the fact that she's gone."

"Difficult for all of us," Zack said.

"Yes. Anyway, I'm going to see Mieka and find out how the girls are doing, and then I'll meet you at the downtown library. Your reading with the preschoolers is scheduled for ten-thirty."

———

The mayor's office was a large, utilitarian space, more than adequate for the number of journalists who normally showed up for a briefing. When I arrived, Norine was standing outside Zack's office checking the press credentials of a journalist I didn't recognize. Norine had always been a Max Mara woman, but lately she'd been adding outfits created by a local First Nations designer. The clothing was conservatively stylish with subtle but striking Aboriginal details: a pattern of eagle feathers on an ivory scarf; a beadwork flower on a lapel; a swirl of powwow bright colours on the collar of a black silk blouse. That day she was wearing beige slacks, a creamy turtleneck, and a pair of exquisite turquoise and silver drop earrings.

As soon as the journalist went inside, I joined Norine. It seemed important to keep the mood normal. "I love those earrings," I said.

Norine was wry. "If we'd been living in my great-grandmother's time, that compliment would mean I had to give you the earrings."

I raised an eyebrow. "So . . . "

She laughed softly. "Not a chance," she said. "But I'll make sure Zack gets the number of the woman who makes them." Her face became grave. "The hysteria has already started," she said. "I've made it clear that Zack's only making a five-minute statement – no questions. But I had to have extra chairs brought in."

"How's Zack doing?"

Norine's brow furrowed. "Zack rolls with the punches, but I think the magnitude of the response to Lee Crawford's death has surprised him." She gestured to the open door. "We might as well join the circus."

TV cameras and reporters from the three networks that had affiliates in Regina crowded the office, but other than the TV reporters and print journalists that covered City Hall,

I didn't recognize anybody. When Zack saw me, he gave me a fleeting smile and wheeled his chair from behind his desk so he was closer to the press.

"Let's get started," he said. Camera people positioned themselves. TV lights glared. Flashbulbs went off, and the event was underway.

Years in the courtroom had taught Zack how to dominate a room. Pushing his weight in a wheelchair eighteen hours a day had made his upper body powerful, and as he leaned forward it was impossible not to feel his strength. He had an actor's voice, full-timbred, rich, and strong, which brought genuine feeling to whatever he was saying. When all else failed, Zack had what Milo referred to as Zack's "fucking amazing schtick" – his wheelchair.

Zack had been careful about the wording of his statement, but he spoke without notes, and with true emotion.

"Yesterday, Lee Crawford died. She was thirty-three years old. A lifetime of potential and possibilities died with her. She was bright, devoted to preserving the land, the heritage birds, and the heirloom orchards and gardens her guardian, Colin Brokenshire, left her. After her birds were killed, Lee said, 'The world is a little poorer because they're gone.' My family and others who were part of Lee's life know that today the world is a little poorer because she's gone.

"We don't know who killed Lee Crawford. The RCMP is investigating. If, as citizens, we have information that might help in the investigation, we should go to the RCMP. Other than that, we must leave them to their work. They will find the person or persons who did this, and at that point, the law will take over and justice will be done.

"Like everyone who takes a public stance, Lee had opponents. She was on the receiving end of ugly pranks, vicious emails, and anonymous phone calls. Yesterday, one of the

RCMP officers asked our son Angus if Lee was afraid of the people who berated her.

"Lee was more perplexed than afraid. She was an idealist who believed that people are good, and that if we could lower our voices and really listen to one another, we could work things out." Zack moved his wheelchair closer to the media people. "It's time to lower our voices and listen," he said.

Norine and I didn't stay as we both knew that Zack wouldn't be answering questions. As we stepped into the hall, Norine looked worried. "What do you think?"

"He said all the right things, but the day Lancaster hired Slater Doyle to manage their referendum campaign, the evil genie got out of the bottle."

"Zack has always found a way to put evil genies in their place," Norine said.

"Let's hope he hasn't lost his touch," I said.

It was raining hard when I got to UpSlideDown. Parking on 13th was always a problem, so I nosed the Volvo into the employee-parking space behind the building. When I came through the back door, Mieka's face pinched with concern. "Mum, you're soaked, and you look like you're freezing."

"I'm fine," I said. "I'm not staying long. I just dropped by to see how Madeleine and Lena are doing."

Mieka sighed. "They seem okay, but they're not."

"Just like the rest of us," I said.

"This morning Lena asked me when we'd be happy again."

"What did you say?"

"I said I didn't know." Mieka's laugh was short and angry. "Not much of an answer, was it?"

"It's the truth," I said. "Mieka, we're all just hanging on."

My daughter's green eyes were miserable. "Lee's death is just so wrong," she said. "Mum, if I get you a towel and some dry clothes, could you hang on with me for a few minutes?"

"Of course," I said. Luckily, Mieka and I were the same size. After I changed my clothes, she poured me a mug of coffee.

"We can sit in the café," she said. "But you might want to stay here. Slater Doyle's husband, Michael Goetz, is out there."

"By himself?" I said.

"No, with Slater's daughter, Bridie. They've become regulars. They're always here on the weekend and Michael often brings Bridie in for lunch. I know you don't like him, Mum, but he's devoted to Bridie and she really is a sweetheart."

"I met Bridie here with Slater one day during the election campaign. She's very sweet. It would be impossible not to like her." I sipped my coffee. "Did you hear Zack's statement this morning?"

"I did." Mieka's smile was impish. "Your turn to listen, Mum. Go for it."

Michael was sitting at a table for four by the quiet-activity area. Because of the rain, there were plenty of kids around, but Bridie played alone, carefully moving plastic royalty through the rooms of a pink castle. She was a fairy child – delicately boned, with wavy white-blond hair and porcelain skin. Michael sat watching her, totally absorbed in her play.

Mieka touched his arm. "Michael, I think you know my mother, Joanne."

He was taken aback but gracious. He stood and smiled. "Of course," he said.

"Mind if we join you?" I said.

"It would be nice to have company," he said. "As Mieka can tell you, I'm not an expert on castles and princesses, and Bridie often has questions."

I had never liked Michael Goetz. The first time I met him he burned with self-righteous anger and lashed out with ugly accusations. As details of his medical malfeasance emerged and he was stripped of his licence to practise psychiatry, my assessment was harsh. But humiliation and loss had changed him. That morning the suffering in Michael Goetz's eyes moved me.

Hearing our voices, Bridie came over. She cocked her head and examined my face carefully. "I remember you," she said. "You were here one time when I came with my daddy. Then we stopped coming. Did you wonder where I was?"

"Yes," I said. "I did."

"Well, now you don't have to wonder because I'm back," she said and then returned to arranging the complex lives of plastic royalty.

The look on Michael's face as he watched Bridie would have melted a harder heart than mine. "Bridie's a beautiful child," I said.

"She is," he agreed. "And now that I no longer have a practise, I have plenty of time to spend with her. Bridie is my silver lining."

A tussle over a rocking horse threatened the peace in the quiet-activity area, and Mieka went to calm the combatants. Michael watched her as she walked across the room, then he turned to me. "Thank you for coming to sit with me, Joanne. Given our history, I know it wasn't easy."

"We have to start somewhere," I said.

"I heard Zack's statement this morning when I was driving here and I've been following his tweets," Michael said. "He's right. Lee Crawford's death should force us all to examine what we're doing."

"Does Slater share your feelings about that?" I said.

Michael fingered his gold wedding band. "Slater and I don't share much of anything any more."

"If you explain to Slater that we all have to take a step back, will he listen to you?"

His mouth hardened. "Slater only listens to me when he's desperate."

"And he's not desperate now," I said.

Michael ran his hand through his close-cropped hair. "Joanne, I'd really rather not talk about Slater."

It was an awkward moment, and I was grateful when Mieka returned. "I should take off," I said. "Zack's reading to a group of preschoolers at the library downtown, and I promised I'd catch his act."

Michael stood. "It was good talking to you," he said.

"Let's keep talking," I said. "For all our sakes."

I said goodbye to Bridie at the pink palace, then Mieka walked me through the kitchen to the back door. "I never thought I'd feel sorry for Michael Goetz," I said, "but I do."

"He's miserable," Mieka agreed. "What I can't understand is how a man like Michael would marry a snake like Slater Doyle."

"Michael and Slater were lovers for years before Slater came out," I said. "They've been through a lot together."

"And now Michael's stuck in a loveless marriage," Mieka said.

"But he has Bridie," I said.

The shoe rack outside the children's library was a sea of crayon-bright rubber boots. Zack was already chatting with the kids when I arrived. He waited until I'd found a place to sit before he began. The audience was comprised of preschoolers, but Madeleine and Lena were not long out of preschool when Zack and I married, so he knew how to wow the junior set. First, he read *The Pigeon Finds a Hot Dog*, one of our granddaughters' summer favourites. When he read the pigeon's description of a hot dog as being "a celebration in a bun," the kids smiled with satisfaction. And as Zack pretended to stumble over the words of *The Very*

Hungry Caterpillar, the children chimed in. By the time he got to *Where the Wild Things Are* and *Goodnight Moon*, the performance had become a collaboration, with the children's reedy voices supporting Zack's bass.

Then it was question time. There were questions about caterpillars, about what Zack liked to put on his hot dog, and about whether it was fun to be mayor. Then a boy wearing Harry Potter glasses, who was perhaps four, tossed Zack a high hard one. "Why did somebody kill that lady and her birds?"

Zack moved his chair closer to the boy. "I don't know," he said. "All I know is that the police will find that person. Until then, we have to tell people that hurting others is never the answer."

"I could tell people that," the Harry Potter boy said. "But I'd have to ask my parents."

"Understood," Zack said. "I'd be happy to talk to your parents whenever they'd like to talk." He wheeled back so he could focus on the whole audience. "I'd be happy to talk to any of you about this or anything else," he said. "I'll leave business cards with my contact information at the circulation desk. Please take a card and keep it handy. We're all in this together."

When we got outside I turned to Zack. "That went well," I said. "The little guy with the Harry Potter glasses was a challenge, but his question was fair, and you treated him with the respect he deserved."

The creases that bracketed Zack's mouth like parentheses had deepened. These were not easy days for him. But the rain had stopped, the unmistakable scent of a street vendor's tube steaks was in the air, and Victoria Park was close.

I reached down and massaged Zack's neck. "I'm in the mood for a celebration in a bun. Are you up for that?"

Zack's shoulders relaxed. "Tube steaks and you are my two unslakeable lusts."

Victoria Park was in full summer mode. Lovers embraced on benches. Drunks weaved along the paths. Pigeons paid their respects to the statue of Sir John A. Macdonald. Daycare kids clambered over the guaranteed child-friendly, eco-friendly play structures while their minders checked their messages. Zack and I had just loaded up our hot dogs and found a bench in the sun when my cell rang. It was Peter calling from La Ronge.

He was on edge. "Mum, Maisie is determined to spend the night at the farm. I'm afraid it'll be a circus."

"You're right to be concerned," I said. "When we were out there yesterday, it was chaotic, but Bobby Stevens is in seclusion at the Stevens's farm, George Sawchuk has organized the neighbours to handle the chores, and we brought Esme back with us."

Peter laughed softly. "You and dogs," he said. "Is everybody getting along?"

"We're doing fine," I said. "Pantera's only interest is Zack, and Esme seems to have taken a shine to me. But see for yourselves. Why don't you and Maisie spend the night with us? She shouldn't have to deal with seeing the home she grew up in turned into a crime scene."

"Let me ask her."

It took a while, but when Peter came back the decision had been made. He and Maisie would spend the night with us and we'd all deal with what had to be dealt with tomorrow morning.

By the time I hung up, my appetite for a street vendor tube steak with all the condiments was robust. Zack and I turned our attention to munching and watching the world go by. We had twenty minutes of glorious mindlessness before our idyll was cut short.

Zack's phone rang just as we were wiping the mustard off our faces and fingers. It was the RCMP. After he hung up,

Zack passed along the news. Lee's body would not be released until next Tuesday, but despite the nakedness from the waist down, there was no evidence of sexual assault.

"Do you think someone was trying to implicate Simon?" I said.

"Could be. Could be someone's sick idea of a joke."

"I don't get it," I said.

Zack's voice was harsh with contempt. "In that video of her call to arms, Quinn Donnelly said that Lee used her body to get what she wanted," he said. "Maybe someone wanted the whore image to stick."

That afternoon, when Peter and Maisie came through the doors into the arrivals lounge, it was impossible to believe they were the same glowing couple who had driven off in Pete's truck to begin their new life together. The first time I met Maisie, she'd come straight from lacrosse; she strode across the room, curls damp from the shower, hand extended, lip split but still smiling. She always radiated confidence and optimism, but that night in the harsh light of the arrivals room, she looked grey and hollowed out by grief. Peter had his arm around her shoulders and she was leaning into him as if she found standing difficult.

Zack and I spoke in low tones. "My God, what do we do?" he asked.

"Just be there, I guess."

He took my hand. "We can do that," he said.

Margot said Maisie was tough, and she was. During the next few days there were many spirit-crushing moments, but, with one exception, Maisie remained dry-eyed and resolute. She faltered only when she walked into our condo and saw Esme. The sight of Lee's dog hit Maisie like a physical blow. She crumpled and wept. Esme went to her and Maisie clung to her sister's dog until the tears stopped. "I'm sorry," she said. "It's just that I've never seen Esme without Lee." Peter handed his wife a tissue, and she mopped her eyes and blew her nose. "I guess there's a lot I'm going to have to get used to," she said. Then she sat down at the butcher-block table, took a deep breath, and said, "Tell me everything."

It was an excruciating evening. Angus's account of the scene that met him when he walked into the barn was factual and he managed to keep his voice emotionless, but there was no way to blunt the horror of what had happened. When Angus said the police believed that the first shot would have killed Lee instantly and that she would not have suffered, Maisie was bleak. "There's no way the police could know that. Lee would have seen the person holding the gun. Even if her awareness only lasted a split second, she would have died with the image of her murderer in her eyes." Maisie steeled herself. "So whose image was it? Do the police have a theory?"

"They've questioned Simon Weber," I said.

"Asia Libke is representing him," Zack said. "At Asia's request, the police put Simon in the psych ward overnight Monday."

"Where is he now?" Maisie asked.

"I don't know," Zack said.

"Asia's sharp," Maisie said. "At this moment, her client is undoubtedly walking among us. But I guess he did what he wanted to do."

"I don't believe Simon killed Lee," I said.

Maisie's eyes widened. "On what evidence?"

"None that would stand up in court," Angus said. "But if you had seen Simon's face when the police were questioning him, you'd believe he was innocent too."

"Instinct isn't enough," Maisie said tightly.

"Simon's version of what happened is plausible," Angus said. "He says Lee texted him around three asking him to come out to the farm because she was in the barn and she was hurt."

Maisie's tone was withering. "So she texted the man against whom she had a restraining order, asking him for help."

"I know what he said doesn't make sense," Angus said. "But if he did get a text from Lee's phone, he wouldn't think for a moment that it was a trick. When it came to Lee, Simon wasn't rational. All he wanted was to get Lee back. His obsession with Lee was no secret. And Simon swears he's innocent. He says that when he got to the barn Lee and her dog were already dead. The RCMP say Lee wasn't sexually assaulted – that might point to someone else."

"Who?" Maisie asked.

"We don't know," I said. "The police are following every lead, but there's so much craziness out there. First the birds and then . . . "

Maisie's hand flew to her throat. "What about the birds?"

"Oh God. Nobody told you," Angus said. "After the wedding Lee stayed overnight at Lawyers' Bay. When she went home the next morning, someone had killed all the heritage birds."

Peter took his wife's arm. "How were the birds killed?"

"They were poisoned," Angus said.

Maisie closed her eyes against the image. "And Lee was alone when she had to face that," Maisie said

"She wasn't alone," Angus said. "Bobby and I came to the farm as soon as we heard what had happened. I stayed overnight. Bobby wanted to, but we all agreed that if Simon showed up, Bobby would be a raised red flag, and I'd be someone Simon could talk to. I had to go into the office the next morning, but I promised Lee I'd cut out early and come back and make dinner."

"And when you came back, Lee was dead." Maisie leaned into Peter. "I've had enough for one day," she said.

"We all have," Peter said. And then hand in hand they walked down the hall to the guest bedroom.

CHAPTER

8

Maisie had trouble sleeping. Peter said she finally dropped off around three, and it was close to ten when she came into the kitchen for breakfast. She'd showered, anchored her still-wet curls into a ponytail, and dressed for the day in blue jeans, a crisp white shirt, and the white and lime-green Cloudracer running shoes Zack and I had given her for her birthday last year.

Forewarned is forearmed, and I was grateful that Peter and I had time to deal with reminders of the outside world before Maisie had to face it. For the second day running, the front page of our local paper featured pictures of Lee. Today's had one of her kneeling to feed her birds, and another of her body being loaded into an ambulance. Peter tossed the newspaper in the recycle bin within seconds of its delivery. Other problems were not so easily solved.

Zack called twenty minutes after he got to City Hall, and he was clearly nettled. "It's bizarro mondo out there," he said. "I had to wheel through a gauntlet of very angry people to get into the building."

"What was their message?"

"Take your pick," Zack said. "There were signs calling our opponents land rapists, blood suckers, and murderers. There were signs calling Lee a martyr. And there were pictures of Lee that had the word *whore* written in dripping red paint across her face."

"That line has Slater's fingerprints all over it, and it makes my stomach heave," I said. "Did you talk to the protestors?"

"Yeah, I gave them my standard message about lowering our voices and listening, but they were screaming so loud they didn't hear me."

"Not the sunniest way to start the day."

"No, and when I got to my office Stefani Laustig from communications greeted me with tapes from the local morning news shows. Apparently there was a vigil at the Brokenshire farm last night. The media were there, and the organizers went the whole nine yards: candles, flowers, teddy bears, guitars, and letters to Lee telling her they loved her and they'd carry on her work."

"That sounds innocent enough," I said.

"Some of the mourners were carrying signs saying 'An Eye for an Eye.'"

"Not so innocent," I said. "So that's what Maisie, Pete, and I are going to be walking into."

"No. According to Stefani, when the vigil was over, two men came out of Lee's house and sent everyone packing."

"Probably George with a neighbour," I said.

"Whoever they are, they're still there this morning and other neighbours are coming to help, so it's likely safe to go out to the farm."

"Zack, how are you going to handle this?"

"Play it as it lays, I guess. The situation is explosive. Stef says media from outside the city smell a red-meat story and they're on their way. Of course, their presence will be catnip for the crazies. But we'll jump off that bridge when we come to it. Gotta go. I love you."

"I love you too," I said. "I'll call you from the farm."

Maisie ate a healthy breakfast. The night before, she'd managed only a cup of weak tea, crackers, and a few spoonsful of chicken soup, but Thursday morning she cleaned her plate and when she carried it to the sink to rinse, her colour was good. Peter had already packed up their overnight things, so when Angus arrived with Pete's truck, we were ready. Angus was headed for work. Maisie and Peter were going to the farm in the truck. Esme was still glued to me, so she and I were driving out in our station wagon.

I was apprehensive but hopeful. The sun was shining and the air was fresh with the promise of early summer. As I drove past trees turning from blossom to fruit, and fields pale green with sprouting crop, I felt a stirring of optimism. Perhaps we would find a way through this after all.

As soon as I approached the Brokenshire farm, I knew Zack had been overly positive about the situation there. The entrance to the driveway had been blocked off with pylons and police tape, but there were several cars parked on the shoulder of the highway, and I spotted three media vans. I angled around towards Esme. "What fresh hell is this?" I said. She rewarded the Dorothy Parker line with a neck nuzzle.

Peter's truck was ahead of me. As soon as he pulled his vehicle up to the driveway, George ran over to the window on the driver's side. He talked to Peter and Maisie for a few minutes, then he cleared a path through the pylons and police tape and waved our vehicles through. As soon as we cleared the entrance, George replaced the pylons and the tape and resumed his watch.

I parked and joined my son and daughter-in-law. "So what's going on?" I said.

"George told us that when he came over last night to do chores, the vigil people and the media were here," Peter said. "The police had sealed off the barn, but sightseers were taking pictures of the inside of the house through the windows and tromping through the garden and the orchards. Apparently it was quite a show.

"George set up a schedule with the neighbours so there'll be people patrolling the driveway until the sightseers find another diversion," Maisie said. "It's good to be part of this community. If Pete and I had to deal with this on our own, I would spontaneously combust."

Peter squeezed her shoulder. "Let's go inside."

Maisie squared her shoulders. "Not yet," she said. "I need to go the barn – I might as well get that over with."

I was unsure about how Esme would react to being back on the farm, so before we got out of the car I had clipped on her leash. When Maisie and Peter turned towards the barn, Esme whined and strained to go with them. "No," I said. "You're staying with me." As I turned towards the house, Esme pulled hard and began to keen. I squatted beside her. "It's over," I said. "We're going to be okay. We just have to hang in there for a while."

The day Taylor had shot her video at the farm we'd eaten in the farmhouse kitchen. It had a wood stove, but Lee used it only in the winter, so on that spring day just a couple of weeks ago, she had served lemonade cooled in a venerable round-shouldered fridge, wild rice bread, and Lunenburg beans baked in the oven of an Admiral stove that had seen decades of service.

The lives of the sisters who had grown up on the Brokenshire farm had been ripped asunder, but the house Esme and I walked into that Wednesday morning was still the house where the Crawford twins had practised piano, shelled peas, played hide-and-seek, worked on homework, and dreamed dreams.

There was a vase of red and yellow tulips on the chrome kitchen table where Lee had served us lunch. The realization that, in all likelihood, Lee had picked the tulips for the dinner she and Angus were planning was a fresh blow.

I put the kettle on and called Zack to fill him in on the situation at the farm.

He had news too. "It's insane here," he said. "There are a dozen issues that need attention, but the protestors outside City Hall are still making noise and we're getting dozens of calls and emails asking us for further comment on Lee's death. Milo, Stefani, Norine, and I are huddled in my office trying to get a sense of where the story is going and the effect it's going to have on the referendum."

"Any conclusions?"

"The networks are picking up the story about the vigil for Lee. The footage is dramatic. All those innocent, candlelit faces, but the anger isn't far beneath the surface. Someone's put together a montage of photos of Lee at the farm and uploaded the video on YouTube. They used that old Louis Armstrong song 'What a Wonderful World' as background music. People are sharing and retweeting the link. Milo says Lancaster is already striking back."

"Against who?"

"Against Lee," Zack said. "The rumour that Lee was a slut who used her body to get she wanted is making the rounds. And you know where that particular piece of garbage started."

"With Quinn Donnelly," I said. "Zack, I know she hated Lee, but Lee's dead. Why would Quinn feel the need to continue to sling mud at a dead woman?"

"Because she wants to contradict the image of Lee as a martyred saint. And I'm sure Slater Doyle is right beside

Quinn digging away to make certain she doesn't run out of mud." Zack paused. "Jo, Milo's been checking out Lee's personal life. Simon wasn't the only man who fell hard for Lee. She wasn't a nun."

"She never claimed to be," I said. "She was an attractive, intelligent, unattached thirty-three-year-old woman, and men were drawn to her. Zack, there's something more to this than just sex. It's the twenty-first century. People are no longer shocked to learn that a woman has a robust romantic life."

"But you think there *is* something damaging in Lee's past."

"I do," I said. "At the CPG meeting, Lee was adamant about not being the public face of the organization. She said she didn't want her lapses to make CPG vulnerable in the referendum."

"And Lee didn't elaborate on the nature of her lapses," Zack said. "If Lancaster has dug up something that will stick, it will be useful to know what they've got, and when they might use it." For a beat Zack was silent, and then he said, "Jo, Maisie would know about Lee's past."

"She probably would," I said. "But right now Maisie's in the barn where the sister who was part of her life since before she was born was murdered. I'm not going to ask her."

"It doesn't matter," Zack said. "We'll know soon enough."

Esme had been sitting quietly at my feet while Zack and I talked. Suddenly, she tensed and started barking. A shiny red truck had pulled up in the farm's driveway. "We have company," I said. "I'll call you later."

"Be careful," Zack said.

"Whoever's here made it past George," I said. "This is rural Saskatchewan, and there's been a death in the family. My guess is that our visitor will be a family friend bringing food."

I was right on the money. Bette Stevens was behind the wheel of the red truck, and when she rolled down her window, I saw that there was a casserole, a salad, and a Tupperware container of cookies in the picnic basket on the passenger seat.

"Maisie and Peter are in the barn," I said. "I'll get them. I was just about to make tea."

"Another time," Bette said. At the wedding, I'd been struck by Bette's vigorous health. Lee told me that she had been widowed young and she'd run the farm herself for many years. She had been a striking figure that afternoon. Her complexion glowed with the vitality of a woman accustomed to outdoor physical labour, and her bright blue eyes were clear. Today, she hid her eyes behind sunglasses and she picked up the basket slowly. I could feel the heaviness of her grief.

"Lee told me how close you've always been to her and Maisie," I said. "I know this is devastating for you."

"Devastating for us all," Bette said. "Bobby's like a zombie. She was finally going to marry him. He's always been quiet, but after he put the engagement ring on her finger, he couldn't stop talking about the life they were going to have together." She shook her head as if to clear it. "Anyway, none of it's going to happen now."

"Bette, there are no words to tell Bobby how sorry I am, but please let him know we're thinking of him."

"I will," she said. "And thank you. Bobby will be all right. He's like me – the farm will save him. Right now, he's in the barn working on an old seeder. We haven't used it for years, but Bobby will take it apart, clean the pieces, put it back together, and the seeder will be like new."

For a few moments we were silent, lost in our own thoughts. Then Bette opened the door of her vehicle and handed me the picnic basket. "I didn't know whether Maisie and Peter were planning to spend the night here or in the city, but I figured wherever they were, they'd have to eat, so I've brought a shepherd's pie over. It's Maisie's favourite."

I took the basket. "Maisie and Peter will be glad they don't have to worry about dinner," I said.

"Any time," she said. Bette paused. Clearly there was something else on her mind. "Joanne, do you have any idea what Maisie and Peter's plans are? I'm not prying. I'm sure that among the neighbours we can handle the chores for as long as necessary, but if Maisie is going to need someone long-term, we should talk about how to find the right person. It's been years since she lived out here, but I know the community."

"I'll pass that along," I said.

"Could you also tell Maisie that the neighbourhood ladies will make the lunch after the funeral. I don't know where she's planning to have the service, but Colin played the organ at the United Church every Sunday for thirty years, and after . . . after he was gone, Lee took over."

"I'll let you know as soon as they make a decision," I said.

Esme's bark was growing hoarse, but she didn't quit. "Lee's dog is really suffering," I said.

Bette was matter-of-fact. "Purebreds don't make good farm dogs," she said. "They're too high-strung."

"Esme misses Lee," I said. "But we're doing the best we can."

"That's all any of us can do," Bette said. She reached forward to turn the key in the ignition and winced. "Sciatica," she said.

"I understand that's very painful."

"There's worse pain," she said tightly.

As Bette turned her truck and headed for the road, Esme was still howling. Before going back inside, I bent and rubbed her head. "We're going to have to work on that barking," I said.

After I put the casserole and salad in the refrigerator, I took
the kettle off the stove, warmed the pot, and made tea, and
then Esme and I wandered through the house. The living room
had the air of a place unchanged for generations. The furniture was all solidly built – sturdy but plain; the hardwood
floors gleamed and the deep red geraniums on the window-
sills were flourishing. Two pianos faced each other across the
room. When she had taken us on a tour of the house, Lee sat
down and played a few minutes of one of the Brandenburgs.

Zack, who played by ear, was dazzled. "I wish I could do
that," he said.

Lee's smile was impish. "Take lessons from the time
you're six, and practise every day with Colin Brokenshire
sitting across the room from you, and you'll nail it."

"Did you rebel?" I said.

"No. I loved the piano. I've always loved everything about
this place, but Maisie wanted more. If you push her, she
will admit that the discipline of all that practising helped
her in law school and sports. But the piano was never her
thing – just as this farm was never her thing."

"So you both ended up where you belonged," I'd said.

"We did," Lee agreed.

Lee's office at the front of the house was a hybrid of present
and past. The computer, printer, scanner, and shredder were
new, but Lee's desk, her chair, the filing cabinets, and the
bookcases were made of oak that glowed with the patina of
wood that for generations has been lovingly polished. Two
shelves of the bookcase nearest the desk were devoted to
leather daybooks. On the desk, there were two silver-framed
photographs: one of Colin Brokenshire flanked by Lee and
Maisie. The twins appeared to be in their late teens; Colin
was greying and his complexion was weathered, but his
eyes were alive with intelligence, and his smile was a young

man's smile, open and full of hope. The second photo was of three adolescent boys: Colin, Mansell Donnelly, and George Sawchuk. They were clowning for the camera and clearly having the time of their lives.

When Esme started barking again, I went back to the kitchen. Peter and Maisie were walking in from the barn. I arranged the tea things and some of Bette's cookies on a tray.

"My grandmother would say you must have smelled the tea," I said.

"Thanks for staying around, Jo," Maisie said. "It would have been hard coming into an empty house."

"I'm glad I was here. Bette Stevens came by with a shepherd's pie and salad for your dinner. I put everything in the fridge."

"Shepherd's pie," Maisie said, pulling out one of the chrome chairs. "It's great to have neighbours."

"It is," I agreed. When the tea had steeped, I poured. Maisie held out the plate of gingersnaps to Peter and me, and then took one herself. "So did Bette say anything about Bobby?"

"Not much, but she's optimistic. She says the farm will save him."

Maisie eyes were thoughtful. "She could be right. This farm saved Lee after Colin died." She took a breath. "Jo, Pete and I have been talking pretty well non-stop about what we'll do with the farm. We've decided to move out here permanently."

Peter reached across the table and laced his fingers through his wife's. "We want to carry on Lee's work," he said. "It's the right time of year to put in a garden and get the orchards in shape and we're going to re-establish the heritage poultry-breeding program. There's a lot to be done. The farmhouse will need renovating. The house isn't accessible and we want to open it up, so there's more room and more light."

"That's a major change, of course, for both of you," I said. "Are you sure this is the right decision?"

"It's the only decision," Maisie said. "Jo, I can't lose this farm – it would be like losing Lee all over again. As long as I can sleep in this house, and walk on this land, Lee will be with me. If we sell the farm, the buildings will be torn down, the orchards will be ripped out, and the fields will be ploughed under. Everything Colin and Lee cherished will be lost."

"We're not going to allow that to happen, Mum," Peter said. When I heard the resolve in his voice, I knew the discussion was over.

"Then let's do what needs to be done," I said. "Where do we start?"

Peter gave Maisie a searching look, and when she smiled and nodded, he cleared his throat. "How about with some good news?" he said. "Maisie and I are expecting twin boys at the end of September."

My eyes welled. "Twins at the end of September – that's only four months! And you're hardly showing. That's amazing. And you're feeling well?"

"Very well. Everything was perfect until . . . "

"I know," I said. "But, Maisie, you're not alone. Everyone in our family is ready to help."

Maisie gave me a small smile. "Are you ready to help now because I'm having difficulty staying focused on the idea of a service for Lee. All I've come up with is a book called *The Tibetan Book of Living and Dying.* Have you heard of it?"

"I read it a few years ago," I said. "I was impressed."

"Lee certainly was. Wait till you see her copy." Maisie disappeared down the hall and returned with a dog-eared, water-swollen book. "Lee backpacked across Tibet with this," she said. "After Colin died, she and I read parts of it together. One sentence keeps coming back to me." Maisie opened the book and read, "'Death is a mirror in which the entire meaning of life is reflected.'" Her gaze was steady. "Lee lived a meaningful life. Her death doesn't reflect that. But her funeral can. Jo, I want people to understand the entire meaning of Lee's life. I want them to leave the church committed to making her vision a reality."

"We'll start planning tomorrow morning," I said. "In the meantime, try to eat some of Bette's shepherd's pie and get some sleep."

"I am tired," Maisie said.

"Curl up on the couch," Peter said. "I'll walk Mum to her car, then I'll come back and get lunch started."

When Esme followed me, Peter shot me a curious glance. "It's weird how Esme has latched on to you."

"She probably smells Pantera on me," I said.

"She probably smells those dried liver treats you always carry in your pocket," Peter said.

"Those treats have kept Zack panting after me for three years," I said. When Peter laughed, I put my arm around his waist. "Esme seems to have decided that she belongs with us and that's fine with me. I miss Willie, and you and Maisie don't need to deal with a heartsick dog. You've had four major life changes in the past few days."

"Three," Peter said. "The babies were started well before the wedding."

I hugged him. "Something is lost and something is gained. That seems to be the pattern."

Peter lowered his eyes. "That doesn't make the losing any easier," he said.

At five o'clock, Zack called to say he had three interviews with media scheduled, a shitload of messages to return, and he was ready to snap hubcaps with his bare teeth.

"Sounds like you're at the end of your tether," I said. "Declan and Taylor have plans for the evening, and I don't feel like cooking. Why don't I meet you at the Sahara Club for a full-bodied red, a sizzling porterhouse, and some cool jazz?"

"You're on," he said. "I'll be there at seven."

The Sahara Club is on Dewdney Avenue, six blocks from our condo in a strip called "nightclub row." Most of the clubs lost their glitter decades ago, but in summer they keep their doors open, and while the bands inside blare, kids too young or too broke to be inside a club dance on the sidewalk, pleasantly buzzed on weed, music, and the joy of life in the Warehouse District. The area was sketchy, but if the weather was pretty, Zack and I often wandered over there in the evening. I'd always savoured nightclub row's rakish charm, but since the previous September when a former client of Zack's died and left us, among other holdings, the building that housed the Sahara Club, I'd viewed the area from a new perspective. Once Milo agreed to stay in town after the election, I suggested he move into the spacious, comfortable apartment available over the Sahara Club, and he'd been living on Dewdney ever since. As I walked past the lot reserved for restaurant guests and the building's single tenant, I checked to see if his motorcycle was parked there. It wasn't.

The Sahara Club is an anomaly. For one thing, it is not a club. It's a steakhouse and piano bar, and in a down-at-the-heels neighbourhood, it is as lovingly maintained as the overripe beauty of an aging showgirl. The steps are always swept or shovelled. The window boxes are always seasonally celebratory: tulips in spring; geraniums and ivy in summer; chrysanthemums in fall; and fragrant evergreen boughs in winter. The black paint on the club's front door is always glossy, and, whatever the season, the legs of the neon camels marching on the sign over the entrance move with the precision of the Rockettes. The website description of the Sahara's dining experience nailed it: "The best steaks, big wines, all the while you are surrounded by a surplus of polished oak and red velour booths."

All in all, the Sahara Club was the perfect place to recuperate from a tension-filled day. Zack grinned and began wheeling towards me as soon as he came through the door. "Life just got better," he said and he moved in close.

When the server came to take our drink order, I turned to Zack. "I walked over, so I'm the designated driver tonight. Go crazy."

"In that case I'll have a very dry double martini," he said. "And thank you."

"Water's fine for me," I said. "I'll have a glass of wine with dinner."

After the server left, Zack took my hand. "Tell me something good."

"How's this for good," I said. "Peter and Maisie are expecting twin boys at the end of September."

Zack smiled widely. "That is the best news." His brows knit, and he leaned across the table. "I'm no expert, but if Maisie's five months pregnant with twins, shouldn't she be showing?"

"Women carry differently," I said. "Maisie's tall, and she's in fantastic shape, but those little boys will make their presence known soon enough. What matters is that everybody's fine. And, Zack, we have to do everything we can to make sure it stays that way. There are going to be many changes in Peter and Maisie's lives. They've decided to move to the farm permanently and carry on Lee's work."

Zack raised an eyebrow. "That's a big decision."

"It is, but they're convinced it's the right one."

"I can't imagine Maisie giving up law," he said. "She loves the courtroom."

"My guess is that Maisie will stay at Falconer Shreve. Renovations aren't cheap, and she and Pete will need a source of income."

"We're in a position to help them."

"We are," I said. "But Peter and Maisie are well-educated, independent people and they're proud. We can help, but we'll have to take our cue from them."

"I can drive a tractor," Zack said.

"You're kidding."

"Nope, I had a client who was a farmer and a paraplegic. After his trial was over, we went out to his farm and he showed me how to drive his tractor. The tricky part was transferring my body from the chair to the tractor cab, but once I was behind the wheel, I was king of the world. The tractor had hand controls, so I could control the clutch and gas. I drove around for about an hour. Fresh air. Sunshine. Freedom." Zack stretched his arms widely, embracing his agrarian future. "Give me the simple life," he said.

"Maybe we should cancel that double very dry martini," I said. "You're already euphoric."

Zack craned his neck so he could see the bar. "Too late," he said. "It's already on its way."

It didn't take us long to decide on our order. As always I steered Zack away from the thirty-two-ounce Kobe Tomahawk he longs for and we chose the Chateaubriand for two.

Despite the maelstrom that surrounded our lives, Zack and I managed to stick to our rule about keeping dinner conversation light. Zack genuinely loved children, and the prospect of being the grandfather of two baby boys thrilled him. He was also pleased that Peter and Maisie's renovations included making the main floor of the house wholly accessible. And experienced tractor driver that he was, the idea of playing a role in a working farm intrigued him. We took time with our meal, and we both ordered dessert.

It was close to nine o'clock when we decided to leave the restaurant.

The sun had set, and I felt the frisson of anxiety I always felt when Zack and I were in our neighbourhood after dark. But the parking space was brightly lit, so after a quick check of the area around our car, I slid into the driver's seat.

"Don't put on your seatbelt yet," Zack said. "I'm in the mood for love."

"We'll be home in five minutes."

"Just one kiss," Zack said. "But we'll make it a good one." As soon as he was in the car, Zack drew me to him. "We need more evenings like this," he said. "No tensions. No complications."

"The simple life," I said. "You on your tractor, and me waiting at the door with your martini at the end of the day."

Zack shrugged. "Sounds good to me," he said, and then he zeroed in for another kiss.

CHAPTER

9

Thursday is liver lovers' day at the City Hall cafeteria. Since he'd become mayor, Zack and I had made Thursday lunches at the cafeteria part of our weekly routine. Filling our plates, then sitting down at a big table and waiting to see who joined us was always an adventure. Shoptalk was encouraged, and we were both learning a great deal about what worked and what could be improved in the various city departments. The impromptu lunches should have failed for a dozen reasons, but despite the odds, they succeeded. People were eager to talk about their jobs; colleagues had a way of making certain no one monopolized the conversation and that the table talk didn't turn into a grievance session. Zack and I enjoyed the company and we both loved liver.

When Zack called as soon as he got to the office to say he was swamped and lunch was out, I phoned Peggy Kreviazuk and asked her to join me at City Hall at noon. She was quick to accept. "I'm available and I'm gardening all morning, so I'll be hungry." She paused. "Joanne, could I invite George Sawchuk to join us? He called me this morning and he's down in the dumps about Lee."

"Of course," I said. "Colin Brokenshire, Mansell Donnelly, and George were close when they were boys. Lee had a picture of the three of them on her desk. George must have known her from the time she was little. It may help him to be with people who cared about her."

As soon as I said goodbye to Peggy, Peter called to ask if I could come out to the farm to talk about Lee's service. I was free until lunchtime, so three-quarters of an hour later, I was sitting in the farmhouse kitchen with Maisie, Peter, and Chesney Langen, the minister from Wesley United Church, drinking lemonade and talking about the funeral.

Chesney was a diminutive, middle-aged woman with hair the colour of dark honey and the keen intelligence and clear, carrying voice of a person to be reckoned with. Maisie had told me that when Chesney was chosen as circuit minister for Wesley United and three other rural congregations, she and Lee became friends. Like Lee, Chesney was fascinated by the nature of faith, and she and Lee spent hours mulling over the similarities and differences in the world's religions.

When it came to making decisions about the spiritual aspects of the service, Chesney was firm. Maisie wanted a service that reflected the meaning of Lee's life, and in Chesney's view it was essential that both the music and the readings should indicate that at the time of her death Lee was still searching.

Her insistence surprised me. "I assumed that since Lee played the organ for church services, she'd found her answers," I said.

Maisie laughed. "Colin played organ there for thirty years and he was a confirmed Darwinist. You know those metal fish signs some people have on their cars to show that they're Christians? Colin had a fish sign on his old Buick, except his fish had legs to show that it was evolving. He was a regular at Wesley United because he liked playing the organ and he believed in community. It was the same for Lee."

Chesney snapped her laptop shut. "So Joanne and I will look into the music and readings. The ladies in the community are taking care of the lunch after the service, and Bobby Stevens called to let me know that a group of his friends are arranging for extra chairs and loudspeakers so people who can't find a place in the church can at least hear what's going on inside."

"How's Bobby doing?" I said.

"He didn't say, and I've learned not to ask."

"Very wise," I said.

Maisie picked up her napkin and began pleating it. "I called Bette Stevens to let her know that we were putting together some preliminary plans for the service. She reminded me that around here families make a memory board with photos of the person they've lost so people can reminisce during the reception. Bette says she has albums full of pictures of Lee and me, and she invited me to come over and choose the photos I wanted to include." Maisie's eyes found mine. "Jo, I had an appointment with my OB/GYN earlier this morning."

I felt a sting of anxiety. "Is everything all right?"

"Everything's fine. The babies are doing well and so am I, but Dr. Vollett says I should do what I can to minimize the level of stress in my life. I'm not ready to look at pictures of Lee yet."

"You won't have to," I said. "I'll call Bette as soon as I get home."

"Thank you." Maisie used her pleated napkin to wipe off a drop of lemonade on the Formica table. "Jo, yesterday was Bette's birthday. Lee and I have always taken her out for lunch. This time I didn't even call. Please tell her how sorry I am. There's just been so much."

Bette had been cordial when I called to ask if I could look through the photos for the memory book with her. She'd suggested I come for afternoon tea, so my day was taking shape.

Peggy, George Sawchuk, and Ernest Beauvais were waiting at the cafeteria door when I arrived at City Hall. George offered his hand, and I took it. "I'm so glad you were free for lunch today," I said.

"Peggy felt I needed to be with other people."

"Was she right?"

George smiled. "Isn't she always?"

I turned to Ernest. "You're a welcome surprise."

"I'm a big fan of organ meat," Ernest said. And with that, we picked up trays and joined the line of liver lovers.

The half-portion of the liver and onions lunch cost $6.75 and the portions were generous — three slices of liver, four slices of bacon, a scoop of fried onions, a scoop of mashed potatoes, a scoop of coleslaw, and a scoop of homemade gravy.

After we found a table and unloaded our trays, George's eyes scanned the room. "This was a good idea," he said. It seemed he was relaxing, but the next second he froze. I followed the direction of his gaze. Mansell Donnelly and Piper Edwards had arrived at an empty table near us. Piper had just taken her plate from her tray when Mansell spotted us and whispered something to Piper. She put her plate back on her tray and they went off in search of another table.

"I guess Mansell was afraid sitting close to me would put them off their lunch," I said.

It had been an idle comment, but it seemed to strike a nerve with George. He sighed heavily and picked up his fork. "I wish I understood what's going on with Mansell."

I stirred the gravy into my potatoes. "Don't worry about it," I said. "I'm sure Mansell was just following orders.

Quinn Donnelly sees politics as a blood sport and I'm on the wrong side."

George lowered his voice. "It isn't you," he said. "It's me."

I looked at him closely. "But you were friends. Yesterday I saw a photograph of Colin, Mansell, and you when you were teenagers. You looked like you were having a lot of fun."

"We did have a lot of fun. For years we were inseparable, but that was before Colin died. Since then, Mansell's been avoiding me."

"Why?"

Pain knifed George's features. "Joanne, it's very hard for me to talk about that time, especially now that Lee's gone too." He stared at his plate. "At least they're together now."

I leaned across the table. "I spent the morning with Maisie, planning Lee's service. Maisie wants people to leave the church understanding why they have to fight for what Lee and Colin Brokenshire believed in. We're all heartsick about Lee's death, but we have to carry on."

Ernest covered George's hand with his own. "My people believe that after four days, we can't cry for the one we lost. In order to help the spirit undo its ties with us, we have to stop crying and start living. Old friend, it's time to let Lee go so she can be at peace."

"I know you're right. It's just that I can't stop remembering how happy they were." George stared at his plate for a long time. Finally, he picked up his fork and began to eat. It was a silent meal. There was nothing more to say.

Peggy and I stood together on the lawn in front of City Hall watching our lunch companions walk down Victoria Avenue to their cars. "Not the liveliest lunch we've ever had," Peggy said.

"No, but at least George wasn't alone," I said. "Peggy, do you have a few minutes? I have to be at Bette Stevens's at three, but it's only one-thirty, and there are some things I'd like to talk about."

"Of course, but let's go to my place and sit in the rose garden. We'll be more comfortable there, and roses have a way of putting problems into perspective."

"I could use a dose of perspective right about now," I said.

The sun was peeking out by the time I arrived at Peggy's pretty bungalow. She was sitting on an old-fashioned porch swing and when she saw me she leapt up and I followed her down the path that led to her backyard. Peggy gardened seriously, and from the first crocus of spring to the last October marigold, her garden celebrated colour and scent. June was the month for roses in our part of the world, and even before we came into the yard, the strong, rich, complex aroma of damasks filled the air. Peggy had an English rose garden, a riot of pinks and reds where something was always budding or blooming.

"It's so tranquil here," I said. "And so beautiful."

"Make yourself at home," she said. "Can I get you anything?"

"After that lunch?" I said. "No, thanks. Let's just talk."

"Fine with me," Peggy said. "What's on your mind?"

"For starters, you can tell me what happened at the CPG meeting after I left."

Peggy shook her head. "I've been through it with the police, and over it in my mind a dozen times. That was such a terrible morning – all those strange currents and jagged edges. The fact that Lee was murdered just hours later puts everything into an even more sinister light. I keep thinking that I must have missed something or that there was something I could have done . . . "

My pulse raced. "Do you think someone at the meeting killed her?"

Peggy was clearly distressed. "I don't know. People behaved badly. Things were said." She fell silent.

"When I was there, Piper Edwards seemed to be leading an attack," I said. "She was merciless."

"And that continued," Peggy said. "Piper kept hammering away at Lee about how taking down her video before it had 'maximum impact' would be a betrayal of everyone in CPG. Lee tried to explain that she wanted to protect CPG from the potential fallout of personal attacks on her, but she didn't get far before Piper cut her off. Piper's assault was personal: it was ugly, and it was very effective. I'd say that at the beginning, the majority of people at the meeting supported Lee, but when Piper talked about the individual's need to sacrifice for future generations, I could feel the wind shifting. So could Lee."

"She knew she was beaten?" I said.

"She did," Peggy said. "George tried to pour oil on the troubled waters. He said there were many struggles ahead and if we were going to prevail we had to respect one another and work side by side."

I smiled. "He's a wise man."

"Not everyone shares your opinion. That young man with the ponytail who attacked George when you were still at the meeting waded in again. He said he wasn't about to take advice from someone whose father spent all his time losing lawsuits." George tried to respond, but the young man shouted him down.

"The situation was out of hand. Piper moved towards Lee, and she was furious. Bobby stopped her, and then he announced that the meeting was over and asked Ernest to say a prayer. After Ernest finished, everyone went his or her separate ways. I didn't want Lee to feel that she was without allies, so I stayed behind. Bobby was with her. I congratulated them on their engagement, admired Lee's ring, said that political conflicts blow over but love endures, and then I left.

"My perennials needed some tending, so I took care of

them and started supper. That's when you called to tell me that Lee had been killed."

"Peggy, do you think it's possible Piper murdered Lee?"

"I don't number myself among those who believe that in a desperate moment, we're all capable of murder," Peggy said.

"Neither do I," I said. "But Piper is known to have a problem with controlling her temper, and she was already fuming when she arrived at the meeting. She'd just found out that Lee was marrying the man she wanted, and she believed Lee was on the verge of sinking the referendum campaign."

"I hope you're wrong," Peggy said.

"So do I. Piper has so much to offer." I checked my watch. "Peggy, I have another question. Do you know what's going on between Mansell Donnelly and George Sawchuk? I'm sure you noticed that Mansell wouldn't sit near us today. I assumed it was because Quinn had warned him that I was persona non grata, but George told me Mansell's been avoiding him since Colin Brokenshire died."

Peggy frowned. "That's sad. Those three were such good friends. I would have thought the tragedy would have drawn Mansell and George closer, but the workings of the human heart are a mystery. I guess Mansell still feels guilty . . . " The sentence drifted off, incomplete.

"Why would Mansell feel guilty?" I said.

Peggy looked baffled. "I assumed one of the twins would have told you by now," she said. "Mansell was driving the truck that killed Colin. I'm not sure of the details. All I know is that it was a late harvest, and Mansell and Bette were helping Colin get his crop off before the weather changed. The truck Mansell was driving was one of those heavy-duty farm vehicles. It was after dark, and everyone was tired. The police investigated, of course, but it was clearly just one of those terrible agricultural accidents. Kostya told me once that Mansell was never the same after that night. I guess seeing George brings back painful memories for Mansell."

"It's been eleven years," I said.

Peggy's eyes met mine. "You know what they say, Joanne. 'Time heals the wound, but no amount of time can erase the scar.'"

CHAPTER

10

Until the last decades of the twentieth century in Saskatchewan, it was not uncommon to see millions of dollars' worth of equipment in a grain farmer's yard and the farmer's family living in a house that had been built fifty years earlier but unimproved, except for an occasional lick of paint. The feminist movement changed many things. Farm wives became recognized as farmers in their own right, and their contribution to the success of working farms was reflected in the handsome new farm homes that sprang up across the prairie, like mushrooms after a three-day rain.

Bette Stevens was a striking example of the new breed of female farmers. She met me at the front door of her home wearing smartly fitted jeans, a classic white chambray shirt, and a pair of western boots with a pattern of hearts and scrolls tooled into their buttery leather.

"I'm so glad we could arrange this," she said. "Maisie's fortunate to have you."

"It's a terrible time for everybody," I said. "How's Bobby?"

Bette's lips tightened. "He's tough. He'll make it."

"And he has you," I said.

She looked at me questioningly, as if weighing my words. "That's true," she said finally. "Bobby has me. Now come inside and let me show you around." As she led me into the kitchen, I noticed Bette was still moving carefully. I didn't mention her sciatica. She'd made it clear that the Stevens family handled its pain privately.

The kitchen was a comfortable room with an open fireplace, a well-used maple table and chairs, state-of-the-art appliances, and a generous working space. It was a kitchen designed for a dedicated cook who liked people to gather while she worked. I could easily imagine Bette there teaching the Crawford twins the intricacies of making Saskatoon berry jelly.

The family room, too, was a welcoming space, filled with overstuffed and comfortable furniture and a very large big-screen TV. "Colin wasn't a huge fan of TV," Bette said, "but he and the girls used to come over and watch Riders games and the Stanley Cup."

"Sounds like you and your families had a lot of fun together," I said.

"We did," she said. "But that's over now."

Her bleak words underscored the magnitude of the losses the two families suffered. Bette looked at me searchingly. "You're suffering too," she said. "Let me take you to the place where I've found solace during these last terrible days."

The room she led me to was adjacent to the family room. As soon as I stepped through the French doors, I felt the bloom of peace. Everything in the simply furnished room was white, but the effect was soothing rather than sterile. A wall of floor-to-ceiling windows looked out on a manicured emerald lawn and a pond in which six swans glided serenely.

The scene was, quite literally, breathtaking. "That's incredible," I said. "How do you keep swans in southern Saskatchewan?"

Bette winked. "Sorcery," she said.

"Well, it's benevolent sorcery," I said. "I could look at those swans forever."

"I could too," Bette said. "I built this house the year after my husband died. Rob and I had been happy in the old place, but it was full of memories and I wanted to start afresh. I had a farm to run and a son to raise. I needed a place where I could find peace and remember that there was beauty in the world." Bette's laugh was low and warm. "As you can imagine, those swans were the talk of the neighbourhood. Everyone except Colin thought I'd lost my mind."

"From what I've heard, Colin would have been supportive."

Bette's face softened. "He was a rock. Joanne, I know you and I have a difficult task to tackle, but I suspect you haven't had many peaceful interludes lately. I've made us strawberry shortcake. Let's just enjoy the shortcake and the swans for a while before we look through the albums."

"I'd like that," I said.

When Bette stood, my eyes were drawn again to her boots. "Bette, I know this sounds strange, but would you mind telling me where you got your boots? Maisie has a birthday coming up. Her first birthday without Lee is going to be very difficult. It just occurred to me that since she's moving back to the farm, a pair of western boots might be a thoughtful gift."

Bette's face flushed with pleasure. "Boots would be a perfect gift," she said. "And these are beautiful, aren't they? But I'm afraid the only information I have about them is that they were specially made. They were a gift from a friend – a very dear friend." For a moment she seemed lost in memory, then she shook her head impatiently. "The tea isn't going to pour itself," she said. "I won't be long. Have a look around. There are some photographs in the family room you might find interesting now that you're getting to know us."

The mantel above the fireplace in the family room was crowded with birthday cards. Most were either greeting-card sentimental or greeting-card humorous, but Mansell's card for his sister was a photograph of her swans and the message inside was handwritten and affectionate. Interestingly, Quinn Donnelly hadn't signed her sister-in-law's card. I did a quick check, and Quinn hadn't sent a separate card. Clearly the sisters-in-law were not bosom buddies.

A solid oak credenza held a number of framed family photos, and I took my time looking at the photographs. The largest was a portrait of Bette and her now-deceased husband, Rob Stevens, exiting the church on their wedding day. A handsome couple, they glowed with vitality and hope. Five years later, Rob suffered an embolism while he was combining. Lee told me that Bette found Rob when she drove out to see why he was late for dinner. There were other photos: of Bette with Bobby as he received sports awards and graduated from high school and university.

However, the photo that drew my eye was of Bette and her son with Colin Brokenshire and the Crawford twins. The children looked to be about ten, not thrilled at having their picture taken, but obviously easy in one another's company. The photo had been taken during harvest, and Bette, Colin, and the children, surrounded by hay bales and pumpkins, were bathed in the warm glow of a September sun. I was holding the photograph when Bette came back into the family room carrying the tray with the shortcake and a pitcher of iced tea. She looked over my shoulder at the photo. "I love that one," she said. Her voice broke.

"Lee said you were like family."

"We were," Bette said, and her voice was dead. "We were like family." She breathed deeply. "Now, let's go into my little hideaway, enjoy our refreshments, and watch the swans."

After we'd had our tea and cake, we cleared away the dishes and Bette brought out a manila envelope of photos. "I'm sparing you from going through all the albums," she said. "I chose some pictures that showed Lee at different ages. Maisie can do what she likes with them, but I've had a copy made of one I hope she'll use."

Bette removed an eight-by-ten photograph from the envelope and held it out to me. "Lee was seven when she asked me to take this. She'd been outside, and she came running up to the house, out of breath, with her hair every which way. The words just seemed to tumble out of her. She said, 'I was lying in that field of grass by the canola watching the sky. All of a sudden the wind came up. When it blew through the field, it sounded like the grass was singing.'"

As she lay on the ground Lee's copper curls were indeed going every which way. With a smudge of dirt on her nose and her smile showing two gaps where her baby teeth were missing, it was impossible to imagine a child more blissful or more triumphantly alive. "I'll make sure this one is included," I said.

Bette's eyes were filled with tears. "Lee was easy to love," she said. "Somehow I'd forgotten that."

Annie and Warren Weber were on the terrace with Zack when I got home. Annie had painted her generous lips the cotton-candy pink of Warren's Bermuda shorts and her golf skirt.

Warren rose when I joined them, and as always, he moved directly to the matter at hand. "We just got back from a meeting with Simon's lawyer," he said. "According to Asia, the situation is not good. The police investigation is closing in around Simon. None of the other leads are panning out. Piper Edwards seemed like a real possibility. The police have questioned the people present at the CPG meeting that morning and everyone remembers Ms. Edwards's animosity

towards Lee, but Ms. Edwards's alibi is holding up – at least
so far. Simon doesn't have an alibi and the circumstantial
evidence against him is damning. When Angus discovered
him at the scene of the murder, Simon didn't know where
he was. He didn't know how he had got to the barn, and he
didn't know how long he'd been there. The police haven't
found the murder weapon. Simon says he doesn't remember
what happened to his phone. Lee wasn't wearing her engagement ring when her body was found, so the police have been
hunting for that. Until this morning, it appeared that the
engagement ring, like every other piece of hard evidence,
had vanished into thin air, but this morning when George
Sawchuk was doing chores, he stuck his pitchfork into a
bale of hay, and there it was."

"And the police hadn't found it before now?" I said.

"No, and they say they had been rigorous, but that old
adage about the needle in the haystack held true until this
morning. Their theory is that the murderer tossed the
engagement ring away after he ripped it off Lee's finger. And
that's more bad news for Simon. It's not general knowledge,
but Lee's finger was bruised and broken by her attacker. Asia
says mutilating the finger is common when a lover kills his
once-beloved. She thinks the Crown will argue that Simon
was enraged that Lee was marrying another man and the
damage to Lee's finger came when Simon pulled off the
engagement ring."

"How's Asia planning to handle this?" Zack said.

"As of now, she doesn't have many options," Warren said.
"She's talked to Simon's psychiatrist and she's talked to
Angus. Dr. Fidelak believes that when Angus saw Simon,
Simon was in a dissociative fugue state caused by the fact
that he either witnessed or committed a traumatic event.
Both Asia and Angus believe the trauma began when
Simon walked into the barn and saw Lee and her dog dead.

They believe that he really did try to revive Lee and that he put his head against Gabby's bloody chest to see if the dog's heart was beating. And they both believe that Simon arrived shortly before Angus did – certainly after the murder had been committed."

Zack sighed. "Unfortunately, Asia and Angus's faith in Simon won't count in a court of law."

Warren was stoic. "It won't. Asia has said all along that the Crown will argue that because of his own mental illness Simon is knowledgeable about psychiatry and that as a lawyer he would be aware of the advantages of feigning a dissociative fugue state to muddy the waters about exactly what happened in the barn. She believes the Crown will argue that Simon's action in washing the blood off himself was premeditated. He knew that by removing any gunshot residue, a GSR test to see if he'd recently fired a gun would be rendered meaningless."

Annie sat next to Warren on a wicker loveseat. She leaned forward so she could look directly at me. "We have to do something, Joanne. If we could prove Simon received a text from Lee's phone, that would help establish the time that he arrived at the barn. But Lee's phone is also missing."

"Unless one of the phones miraculously shows up, there's no proof at all that the text was sent and received," Warren said.

"How is Simon dealing with all this?" I said.

"Not well," Warren said.

"Everyone is under so much stress," Annie said.

"Annie is trying to fit Simon's behaviour into some sort of normal pattern," Warren said. "But his behaviour is becoming increasingly irrational. He spends almost all his time out on the lake in his canoe. He's still staying in the apartment over the boathouse, but he doesn't have his meals with us any more. Three times a day, Annie takes a tray to the boathouse. Simon eats whatever he's given, washes his dishes, and leaves them outside the door. When Annie and I try to talk to him, he answers in monosyllables.

"Dr. Fidelak comes over every day for an hour. She and Simon sit together, but according to her he often doesn't say a word. She believes hypnosis might help him remember the missing details about what happened from the moment he received Lee's text until the moment when he saw Angus. Simon refuses. He says now that Lee's dead, he doesn't care what happens to him."

"Meanwhile, Lee's killer walks around free," Zack said.

"We've tried to make that point," Annie said. "It doesn't seem to matter to Simon."

"Is there a friend who could talk to him?" Zack said.

"Simon never had many friends," Warren said. "And the few he did have have fallen away since he checked himself into the hospital." He turned to me. "Perhaps Angus?"

"Angus would do it," I said. "But he's just started his first major trial and he's still so torn up about Lee's death that he's finding it difficult to focus."

"Then Angus is out," Annie said flatly. "He deserves his chance. Lee was your daughter-in-law's sister. Maisie must be as desperate as we are to know what happened that afternoon. Joanne, maybe you could convince Simon to undergo hypnosis."

Remembering the wildness in Simon's eyes as he told Zack and me he'd do anything to be with Lee, I felt a chill. "The truth might not help Simon," I said.

"Not knowing the truth is killing him," Warren said emphatically. "Joanne, Simon can't go on like this. None of us can. For all our sakes, please talk to Simon."

The image of Simon choosing the perfect matching beach towels at the firm's Canada Day party flashed through my mind. That afternoon he told me he had met the woman who could save him. I wasn't Lee, but if I could save Simon from the hell of not knowing, I knew I didn't have a choice.

"All right," I said. "I'll do my best."

As I set out the next morning, my mood was as sombre as the weather. Lowering skies, light rain, and heavy mist made the familiar landscapes seem alien and unknowable. I was having grave doubts about the wisdom of agreeing to speak to Simon, but it was too late to turn back.

Annie and Warren greeted me at the gate, and then Annie ran into the cottage and returned with two travel mugs of coffee for me to take to the boathouse.

There was a slope between the cottage and the lake. A third of the way down Simon startled me by appearing out of the mist. I handed him one of the mugs, and we walked to the beach together. The rain had stopped. Simon gestured towards two red Muskoka chairs facing the lake. "I've dried these off," he said.

He wore jeans and a white T-shirt. He looked well; his dark hair was long and he was thin, but he was tanned and his eyes were clear.

For a few minutes we sat in silence. The day was cool and the coffee, strong and hot, was welcome. Most often when we visited the Webers on rainy days, we could look directly across at Lawyers' Bay and see rectangles of light from the windows of the cottages that dotted the horseshoe of land around the bay. That day there was nothing – just a thick blanket of impenetrable fog. When I couldn't see our cottage I felt a stab of existential panic. Simon sensed my unease.

"It's terrifying when something that's always been there disappears," he said.

"It is," I said. "But the cottages *are* there," I said. "And when the fog lifts, we'll be able to see them again."

"We don't know that for certain," Simon said, and his despair made my heart ache.

Out of nowhere, a memory came. "When I was young, my grandmother took me to see a revival of the musical *Brigadoon*," I said. "The town of Brigadoon emerges from the Highland mists only once in a hundred years and then only for a single day. In the play a young woman of Brigadoon and a man from 'outside' fall in love. If the young woman leaves Brigadoon, the town will disappear forever. In the end, the young man agrees to join her in Brigadoon so they can be together."

As I told the old story, Simon was rapt. "Even though he'll have to leave his own world behind, being with her will be enough," Simon said, and his voice was a whisper.

"I guess the message of the play is that love transcends everything," I said.

"Even death?" Simon's tone was urgent. "Do you believe love transcends death?"

"I do," I said. "And I believe that love makes it possible to go on living."

Simon gestured towards the lake. "Even when all you can see ahead is grey space and emptiness."

"Even then," I said. "Because although we can't see it, there is something there. Simon, you can't give up. Dr. Fidelak believes hypnosis will provide some answers. Zack always says the only thing worse than knowing is not knowing. We all need to know the truth. Everyone around you will do what they can to help, but you have to take the first step."

"I'll think about it," he said.

"That's a start," I said.

We finished our coffee and Simon walked with me till we were halfway up the incline.

Then, without explanation, he turned and started back towards the lake. I watched until he disappeared into the mist.

———

Late Sunday afternoon, Peter called to confirm that the RCMP
was releasing Lee Crawford's body the following Tuesday, so
the funeral would be held on Saturday, May 30.

"It will be a relief to get at least this part over," Peter said.
"Maybe now Maisie and I can focus on remembering the
person Lee was and continuing her work."

For the first time since Lee's death, it seemed that Peter and
Maisie were finding their footing, and I felt a flutter of hope.

My optimism was short-lived. Not long after I spoke to
Pete, Warren and Annie arrived at our condo. Annie was
carrying a gorgeous double-pink hydrangea. "This is for
your terrace," she said. "Last time we were here you said
you'd lost your last double-pink to frost and you missed it."

I took the plant from her. "You're a good friend to think of
me with everything else that's going on in your life," I said.
"Let me take this outside, and then we can visit." I was back
in seconds. "I found just the right place for the hydrangea,"
I said. "It makes me smile just to look at it. Now, can I get
you tea or a cold drink?"

"Nothing, thank you," Warren said. He leaned forward.
The ordeal had aged him. "Joanne, I want to thank you for
talking to Simon. Dr. Fidelak thinks he may be ready to turn
a corner. She's had Simon on a medication that's intended to
calm him so he can think coherently. It seems to be finally
kicking in. Thanks to you, he's agreed to try hypnosis. He
had one session today, and he was able to supply details that
he hadn't remembered earlier. Dr. Fidelak believes that, at
some point, Simon will be able to put together the pieces of
what happened that afternoon."

"That's good news," Zack said.

"It should be," Warren said. "But as always seems to be the
case with Simon, there's a problem. He's refusing to continue
with the hypnosis. All along, he's believed he was innocent.

Suddenly, he's not sure, and he's petrified. We've tried to talk to him, but he won't listen. Meanwhile, Asia believes it won't be long before the police arrest Simon."

"Asia's a scrapper," Zack said. "She won't be sitting there with her client waiting for the police to come knocking. What's the plan?"

Warren leaned forward. "We've decided to take matters into our hands and look more closely into Lee Crawford's life to see if there's someone else who had a motive to kill her." Warren paused. "We've heard the rumours about her sexual relationships."

I felt a prickle of anxiety. "Warren, I don't like where this is going," I said.

"I knew you wouldn't," Warren said. "But please hear me out. Joanne, someone *did* kill Lee Crawford, and for Simon's sake, for *all* our sakes, we have to find the murderer. I've hired a private detective agency here in the city. I've used Harries-Crosby before, and they're discreet and thorough. Much of what they dig up will undoubtedly be unpleasant. There may be revelations that your family, especially Lee's sister, won't welcome, but we have no alternative."

I tried to tamp down my anger. "Warren, on Thursday I sat down with my son, our daughter-in-law, and the minister of Wesley United Church to plan Lee's funeral. It was excruciating. Lee was thirty-three years old and she was deeply loved by many. Later that day, I went through photographs for the memory board at Lee's funeral with Bette Stevens. When the twins were growing up, Bette was like a mother to them. If Lee had lived, Bette would have been her mother-in-law. I understand your need to protect Simon, but what you're proposing will inflict pain on people who are already broken."

Warren stood heavily. "I'm sorry, Joanne. I'm truly sorry."

"That's not good enough," I said. "My daughter-in-law is pregnant. She has already suffered a devastating loss. Think for a moment what excavating her sister's past could do to her."

Annie stepped forward. "We knew this was going to be difficult for you," she said. "But it's the only way."

"Really? Let me show you something." I took the photo of Lee out of my bag and handed it to Annie. "This is the girl whose memory you'll be desecrating. Lee was seven when this was taken," I said. "She'd been lying in a field at Bette Stevens's farm watching the clouds when the wind came up and rustled the grass. She ran into the house and asked Bette to take a picture so she'd always remember how it felt to hear the grass sing."

Annie's eyes were filled with tears, but Warren was resolute. He took the photograph from Annie and handed it back to me. "I have to save my son, Joanne. I hope you can accept that."

CHAPTER

11

Margot's forty-fifth birthday was on May 29. The invitations to a lollapalooza of a bash on our building's roof garden had been sent out a month earlier, but as Robert Burns wryly noted, "the best laid schemes o' mice an' men gang aft agley." With the funeral set for Saturday, May 30, a big celebration was out of the question. Margot was in favour of scuttling the party altogether, but Maisie was adamant. She suggested a casual barbecue for family and friends. Margot came from a very large family, so she decided to limit the Friday celebration to her law partners and their families and celebrate with her relatives in her hometown on Sunday.

At five-thirty the evening before the funeral, Declan, Angus, Pete, and Zack fired up the barbecues and we waited for the others to arrive. There would be about twenty of us. Together, we had known good times and not so good times. It was a warm night, fragrant with the sweet notes of late spring, but the tragedy of Lee's death hung over us like a pall. No one, including Margot, knew quite how to behave. The birthday wishes offered by family and friends were heartfelt but muted, and as she acknowledged them, the awareness that for Lee Crawford there would be no more birthdays shadowed Margot's face.

For the first twenty minutes, I was convinced the party had been a mistake, but the rising smoke of the barbecues, the exuberance with which Taylor, Gracie Falconer, and Isobel Wainberg chatted about their lives and the kids at their school, the fluty voices of the younger children, and the presence of two very large dogs worked their magic. By blood or by affection, we were family, and it was comforting to be together.

Mieka and Taylor were just bringing out the salads when my cell rang. On the other end of the line, Brock's voice was strained. "Jo, I'm going to have to bail on Margot's party. Michael just brought Bridie by the condo. He wants me to take care of her for a couple of hours."

"Bring her to the party," I said. "Bridie knows Madeleine and Lena from UpSlideDown and she'll have fun with the babies."

"I'll ask her," Brock said. "She's been pretty quiet since Michael dropped her off."

"Tell Bridie that Margot's going to need help blowing out forty-five candles and one to grow on," I said.

Brock's laugh was forced. "I'll pass that along. Thanks, Jo."

Bridie hadn't needed much convincing. Five minutes after Brock and I talked, he and Bridie arrived at the roof garden. She was carrying a gift-wrapped box. There was a table for presents, and Bridie walked to it, placed her gift carefully beside the others, came back, and looked up at me. "What do I do now?" she asked. Her eyes were extraordinary – large, deep blue, and, at the moment, anxious. She was a child who couldn't risk a mistake.

"If you'd like, I can take you over to Madeleine and Lena and you can help them feed the koi," I said.

"I'd like that," Bridie said. "I have a book about fish, but I've never seen one up close." She slid her hand into mine. "Could you come with me? Sometimes I'm shy."

I took her hand. "Me too," I said.

She knit her brow. "But you're not shy right now," she said.

"No," I said. "I know all the people who are here."

"I know five of the people," she said. "Madeleine, Lena, Mieka, Brock, and you. Is that enough?"

"Five is enough," I said.

After introducing Bridie to the koi, I went back to talk to Brock. He was at the beer cooler and he snapped the cap off a Great Western lager and held the bottle out to me. "Ready for this?" he said.

"I am." I gestured towards the three girls kneeling by the fishpond. "Mission accomplished."

I took the lager from him, and he got another out of the cooler for himself.

"So what's the story?" I said.

"I wish I knew. Half an hour ago, Michael called and asked if he could drop Bridie by the condo. Bridie's nanny, Zenaya, had just quit."

"Did the nanny explain why?"

"Michael hadn't talked to her. Slater delivered the news and Michael is baffled. He says Zenaya's salary was more than generous, and her only obligation was to care for Bridie. Michael has a guest house on his property and that's where Zenaya lived. According to Michael, until lately, Zenaya seemed satisfied."

"But that changed."

"Apparently. Michael is convinced he's not getting the whole story and he wants to get to the bottom of what went wrong."

"So you're taking care of Bridie so that Slater and Michael can iron out the problem."

Brock averted his gaze. "From what Michael says, the situation with Zenaya is just the tip of the iceberg."

"He and Slater have other problems?"

Brock nodded. "Serious problems. I know Michael would have left Slater long ago if it weren't for Bridie."

"Does Michael have any legal claim on her?"

"Michael is punctilious." Brock said. "He started adoption proceedings the day he and Slater were married. Legally, Bridie is as much Michael's as Slater's, but custody is not the issue."

"I saw Michael with Bridie at UpSlideDown a week or so ago. He seemed devoted to her."

"He is," Brock said. "That child has already been through so much. Not long before Slater's wife, Kelly, died, she discovered that he was gay and that he'd been having sex with men throughout their marriage. Understandably, it was devastating for her. She was a devout Catholic, so divorce was out of the question."

I glanced over at the girls. Madeleine and Lena were teaching Bridie how to do a cartwheel. Bridie's small body was tense with fear and determination, but when her cartwheel turned out well, her face lit up. "She's a sensitive child," I said. "She would have picked up on the conflict between her parents."

"She did, and then Kelly died." Brock sipped his beer. "And you know the rest. Slater started drinking heavily, engaging in 'risky behaviours,' and fiddling with clients' trust funds. He got disbarred. He was punishing himself, but of course Bridie suffered."

"And Michael doesn't want her to suffer again," I said. "Slater is among my least favourite people on the planet, but for Bridie's sake, I hope that he and Michael can keep her from being hurt."

Brock was silent. During his campaign for city council, Brock had been on the receiving end of vicious racial and

homophobic slurs and remained impassive, but that afternoon, the prospect that Bridie would again be wounded by
the adults in her life was sickening him.

I reached out and touched Brock's hand. "You and Michael
were hoping you could find a way to be together," I said.

"We were," he said softly. "I don't think that's in the
cards any more."

We'd shoved three picnic tables together so our dinner on
the roof would feel more like a party. When it was time to
eat, Madeleine, Lena, and Bridie spread a blanket close to the
big table and Lexi plopped down next to them. While they
waited for their burgers, our granddaughters taught Bridie
and Lexi a clapping game that involved complex rhythms,
split-second timing, and endless giggling. It wasn't long
before Noah and Delia Wainberg's grandson, Jacob, and Kai
began squirming to join the game. Accepting the inevitable,
Noah and Brock, who both weighed in at well over two hundred and fifty pounds, spread a blanket beside the girls and
led Jacob and Kai in a clapalong.

The barbecue was a success. Peter, Angus, Declan, and Zack
handled the grilling. Maisie spent most of the party holding
Kai and chatting quietly about pregnancy and parenthood
with Mieka and Margot. The three women clearly took pleasure in one another's company, and as the late-afternoon sun
glinted off Margot's honey-blond bob, Maisie's tangle of copper
curls and Mieka's ash-blond ponytail, I felt a bloom of peace.

After Margot had opened her gifts, Taylor and Declan
brought out the cake and we sang "Happy Birthday." Brock
proposed the toast to Margot. He held Kai while Margot
held Lexi. Brock's expression was tender, and his words were
graceful. When he took his place beside her, Margot touched
his cheek and murmured, "That was perfect." Zack and I
shared a look. "It's not going to happen," I said.

"I know," Zack said. "But that doesn't stop me from wishing it could."

Lee's funeral was taking place at Wesley United Church at eleven o'clock on a sunny, cloudless, and unseasonably hot morning. At the last minute I had replaced the spring suit and pumps I had planned to wear with a sleeveless summer dress and sandals. Zack and Taylor, too, had dressed for comfort rather than ceremony.

Wesley United was a small church, but Lee's funeral was a big event. The church would be packed with family, friends, and the curious, and the building did not have air-conditioning. Bobby's friends had tested to see how many electric fans they could plug in without blowing a fuse and then purchased a dozen battery-operated fans as backup. I'd bought every paper fan I could find in Regina's Chinatown. We had done our best, but it was 37° Celsius. As Zack drove out of the city, I saw the heat shimmering off the pavement and I knew that our best would not be good enough.

The service Maisie and Peter decided upon was simple and personal. The Christmas before, Bobby had hand-carved a pine box for Lee's collection of Victorian bridal buttons, and Maisie found comfort in the idea that Lee's ashes were in something that had meaning for her. On the altar was the old school desk that Lee used for homework when she was growing up. The pine box was on the desk; beside it, in a frame Bobby had finished just the night before, was the picture of Lee at seven Bette had taken.

All the musical selections came from recordings of Glenn Gould performing Bach. The crystalline beauty of Gould's playing soothed our ragged emotions. Chesney Langen's eulogy celebrated a woman of complexity and commitment. "Lee wasn't a saint," she said. "She was a human being, a fine human being but human nonetheless. She made mistakes, but she always learned from them and she tried to do better. Lee's life was not long, but the real measure of a life is not its length but its depth." Chesney gazed slowly around the church, seeming to take in every face. "Lee lived fully, loved deeply, and made the world a better place. No one could have done more with the number of years she was given."

There were three readings: Bobby Stevens read the Twenty-Third Psalm. Maisie read the Buddhist story "The Mustard Seed," in which a mother grieving for her dead son goes to the Buddha and begs him to restore her son to her. The Buddha says he can cure the woman's son if she brings him a handful of mustard seed, but the mustard seed must be taken from a house where no one has lost a child or a parent. The mother wanders the streets carrying her dead son, but every home has suffered a death. Finally, weary and hopeless, she realizes that death is common to all. She puts aside her selfish grief, buries her son, and returns to the Buddha and the comfort of his teachings.

The final reading was Dylan Thomas's "Fern Hill." It was Lee's favourite. Zack had practised it many times at home so that his voice wouldn't break when he read the poem's final lines: "Oh as I was young and easy in the mercy of his means/Time held me green and dying/Though I sang in my chains like the sea." Zack recited Thomas's poignant words with such fervour that my throat closed. When he wheeled back to the place beside me, I reached out and took his hand.

Mansell and Quinn Donnelly had arrived early. They sat across the aisle from us with the Stevens family. Both Donnellys had on black suits, and both clearly suffered from the heat in the crowded, airless church. Mansell was sweating profusely, and perspiration had started to make inroads on Quinn's careful makeup. Though Mansell showed no emotion, throughout the funeral a small smile played across

Quinn's thin lips. Beside her, Bobby remained calm. Piper Edwards was beside him, watching his face anxiously, but Bobby saw only the carved pine box on the altar. Bette was fighting for control.

Throughout the service, the emotion inside the church had been building incrementally. Just as it seemed the grief was about to crest, Chesney stepped forward to offer a final prayer. I offered a prayer too. I'd asked Milo to stand at the back of the church in case Simon showed up. I had repeatedly glanced towards the door, but Milo was always alone. Simon never appeared. It seemed we'd been spared that sorrow.

Relieved that there wouldn't be an ugly scene, and calmed by Chesney's words and the recording of Glenn Gould playing the Brandenburg Concerto No. 5, I moved down the aisle. Milo was waiting just inside the door. When Zack wheeled out, Milo took my arm and drew me aside. "Look up there," he said, gesturing towards the altar. Mansell Donnelly had picked up the picture of Lec that had been placed on her old school desk and was staring at it. Twice, his wife tugged his arm and whispered something, but he ignored her. Finally, Quinn took the picture from him, returned it to the school desk, and marched him down the aisle. Mansell's face was devoid of expression, his eyes unseeing – the face of a sleepwalker. The Donnellys seemed not to notice us as they walked by.

"What do you make of that?" Milo said.

"I don't know," I said. "None of this seems real."

Milo took both my hands in his. "Are you all right?"

"Yes, just dreading the next few hours."

"Do what you have to do. I've got this. Twenty minutes ago I checked the churchyard. It was a zoo. I called that private security firm Zack uses. They should be here any minute. It won't take them long to get the crowd under control." Milo's hands were cool. For a moment we faced each other without speaking. Finally, I withdrew my hands. "What would I do without you?"

"You'd be fine," Milo said.

The parking area beside Wesley United had long since been filled to overflowing. Media vans, trucks, and cars were parked on the church lawn, in the driveway, on the highway shoulder, and even on the grass in the old cemetery. People with handheld cameras were taping people with microphones talking to people holding signs. Some of the signs had pictures of Lee with the dates of her birth and death; some bore only the cruel and dismissive epithet SLUT. An impromptu memorial of teddy bears and flowers in plastic sheaths had sprung up at the edge of the cemetery. It seemed everyone with a phone was taking selfies. When she saw the circus, Maisie recoiled and buried her face in her hands.

She and Peter were walking ahead of Zack, Taylor, and me. A woman carrying a SLUT sign spotted Maisie and yelled, "There's her sister," and the sea of selfie-takers switched targets and aimed their cameras at Maisie and Peter. Maisie froze. Peter took her arm and led her through the crowd to the cottonwood tree where the ladies of the United Church had set up tables of cold drinks and dainties. Brock, Angus, and Bobby had removed their jackets and ties, rolled up their shirtsleeves, and were now setting out chairs for older people and carrying food and drink from the kitchen of the church hall.

Bette Stevens supervised from a chair by the door to the church hall. She was wan but in command. As people filed by to offer their condolences, our family stood with Maisie in a kind of informal reception line. Some of the faces were familiar to me. When a woman whom I recognized from her organic fruit and vegetable stand at the farmers' market approached, I tensed. Arranging her golden beets and baby eggplants, the woman had struck me initially as gentle and otherworldly, but her messianic zeal for protecting the environment was offputting. Her opening gambit with each customer was the same. "We humans are just travellers on this earth. We come and go, but the land is forever."

I'd dismissed the woman as a flake, slightly askew but harmless, and I'd continued to buy her golden beets and baby eggplants. However, that afternoon as she stood in front of me, her face twisted with rage, I was uneasy. "We have to make sure they pay for what they've done," she said.

"Lee wouldn't want us to be vengeful," I said.

"An eye for an eye," she said, and then, silver hair streaming, she floated off.

Most of the people in the condolence line offered a few words. More than a few were overcome when they saw Maisie and simply embraced her.

I was concerned about Maisie. The heat had grown oppressive, and she was pale. The line seemed neverending, and when she swayed and leaned into Peter for support, I slipped into the church hall to get her a glass of water. When I came out, I saw Quinn and Mansell Donnelly heading away from the church towards the parking area. If there was ever a time to talk about putting an end to the insanity, this was it. After I'd given the water to Maisie, I sprinted towards the Donnellys.

"We need to talk," I said.

Mansell didn't respond. He still had the thousand-yard stare of a man on the edge of shock, but my appearance ignited Quinn.

"Not now," she snapped. The long bangs of her cropped platinum hair were damp with perspiration and there were sweat stains in the armpits of her black silk suit. "Mansell and I have to go back to the office. It's important."

"Look at your husband's face," I said. "He's devastated. We all are. What could be more important than trying to find a way to salvage what we can from the terrible waste of Lee's life? I don't know why you hated her, but Lee's dead now. We need to have the talk we should have had the day she died."

Bette Stevens was walking towards us. She was in ear-shot, but I was too angry to care, and I continued my harangue. "Quinn, you agreed to see me in the early after-noon the day Lee was murdered. I was five minutes early for our meeting, but when I arrived at Lancaster your Porsche shot out of the parking lot. If we'd talked, this tragedy might have been averted."

Quinn's eyes were fiery. "Are you accusing me of killing Lee?"

My intention was simply to remind Quinn that we'd already agreed to talk and it was past time to honour that agreement, but I'd hit a nerve so I kept the pressure on. "I'm not accusing you of anything," I said. "But given what's happened since, I think I deserve an explanation. Why *did* you run off that day?"

When Bette Stevens joined us, she was pale and breath-less. "Quinn drove out to the farm because I needed help," she said. She slid her arm through her brother's and looked into his face, seemingly seeking support. When Mansell continued to stare into space, Bette's confusion was obvious, but she carried on with her narrative. "The pain from my sciatica had become debilitating. I needed to see my neurol-ogist, but I didn't trust myself to drive to Regina. Bobby was in Saskatoon, and I couldn't find Mansell, so I called Quinn. By the time she got out to the farm, the pain was manage-able. Quinn stayed with me until she was sure I was able to cope, then she went back to the city."

"Okay," I said. I turned to Quinn. "We still have to talk," I said. "If you don't want to deal with me directly, choose somebody from your side to talk to somebody from our side. By this time tomorrow, we have to agree on criteria that will ensure fair play for the rest of the campaign. If Lancaster isn't willing to do that, I'll tell the media I made the offer and you refused to cooperate."

When I linked up with our family again, Zack wheeled over to talk to me. "What was that about?"

My husband listened without interruption to the précis of my conversation with Bette and the Donnellys. When I finished, he said, "That should move matters along."

"Fingers crossed," I said. "How are things here?"

"Peter took Maisie back to the farm. The sun and the emotion were too much for her. I told him we could handle the condolences."

And we did. As the line inched forward, we stood in the heat and listened as people reminisced about Lee's childhood and lamented her death. We thanked them for coming and promised to let them know if there was anything they could do to help. When George Sawchuk reached me, my heart lurched. He was holding on but barely.

"I see the wisdom of Ernest's advice about letting go. But I just can't do it," he said. "Even when she was a child, Lee was special. She always stayed at the table to listen when Colin, Dad, and I talked about the kind of farming we were committed to. Young as she was, she never wandered off or interrupted. If she didn't understand a word she'd ask, but apart from that she just sat there taking it all in."

The burden of sadness crushed me, and I turned to watch a water sprinkler on the lawn spinning in the sunlight, filling the air with coolness and rainbow mist.

We went straight from the reception in the churchyard to Lawyers' Bay. May 30 was early for a swim in a prairie lake, but after the funeral we were all hot and miserable and the water was inviting. Zack and I had brought Madeleine and Lena with us. Mieka had two birthday parties to handle at UpSlideDown and the girls loved the lake. Milo was a loner, but there are times when even loners shouldn't be alone, and I asked him to join us for a swim and dinner. Margot and her family were there, as were Brock and Angus. It took four adults to get Lexi and Kai water-ready, but finally we all headed for the dock.

Bouviers like to swim. Esme was already halfway to the raft when we got to the beach. English mastiffs are not fond of water, so Pantera had taken up his customary position at the end of the dock where he could watch Zack slide into the water with his pull buoy and position the figure-eight-shaped piece of foam between his thighs to support his body. With his pull buoy in place, he and I were able to do laps together. As we finally headed for the shore, I could see that the tension had left Zack's body and I could feel the headache that had been moving from the back of my neck to my temples receding.

We were sitting in the sun, Zack in his wheelchair and Madeleine, Lena, and I on beach towels, when Milo arrived. It was almost four-thirty. He'd already changed into his bathing trunks, and he sped past us with a quick wave, ran along the dock, dived in, swam straight to the diving tower, climbed to the highboard, and did a perfect front dive with somersault. The girls, eyes wide, mouths forming Os, watched as Milo swam back to the ladder, climbed to the high board again, and executed a flawless front dive. Before he swam to shore, Milo completed six dives of varying degrees of complexity. When he pulled himself onto the dock, Lena and Madeleine ran to him. "Teach us how to do that," Lena said, and I could almost hear her lower lip quiver. "Please."

"Okay," Milo said. "But we start on the raft."

For the next half-hour, Milo taught Madeleine and Lena the rudiments of the forward dive. Until that day, despite my best efforts, the girls' dives had been haphazard – a grudging step-up from the belly flop, but they were attentive to Milo, aligning their bodies carefully as he spoke.

The water was chilly, and the girls were blue-lipped and shivering when they came back to the dock. Like every child before them, they insisted that they weren't cold, but I sent them up to the cottage to change anyway.

I handed Milo a towel. "That was really great. Where did you learn to dive like that?"

"Here and there," he said airily. "Now, I'd better change and get back to town."

"We're going to build a bonfire on the beach and have a wiener roast," I said. "Why don't you stay? We're making s'mores."

Milo wrapped his towel around his waist in a sarong. He and I had always been straight with each other. He narrowed his eyes. "You guys don't really do that," he said.

"Yeah," I said. "We really do."

"So it's 1956 on Lawyers' Bay," Milo said.

"1956 has a lot to recommend it," Zack said. "In 1956, Don Larsen pitched the first and only World Series perfect game."

Milo's tone was somewhere between adulation and pity. "Big man, you are mind-blowing!" He gave me a private smile. "Thanks for the respite from reality, Jo."

"Any time," I said.

After Milo loped up the hill to the cottage, Zack turned to me. "Milo's pretty mind-blowing himself," he said. "What do we really know about him?"

"Not much," I said. "Since he works for us and not the city, I have his CV, and that's the source for pretty much all my information. He's from Ottawa. He has a BA from

Carleton and an MA in strategic public relations from
George Washington University. He graduated summa
cum laude from George Washington, and since he graduated he's worked steadily on political campaigns in the
States and here in Canada. He's drawn to situations where
the odds are against the candidate, and since he's a strategist not an ideologue, every campaign in trouble wants
him. He's a gun for hire, and in my books, he's perfect.
He's absolutely loyal, and I've never once had to give him
instructions. He loves politics; he knows what needs to be
done, and he does it."

Zack cocked his head. "But you don't know anything
about his private life."

"When he started working for us, I asked him a couple
of 'getting to know you' questions. He shut me down, so I
stopped asking. I think the only thing that matters to Milo
is his work. When he moved into that flat we own above
the Sahara Club I told him to make whatever changes he
wanted and send us the bills. I never heard another word
about it. My guess is that if I told Milo to shut his eyes and
describe his living room, he wouldn't have a clue."

"But he could give you a detailed demographic breakdown
of every district in the city," Zack said.

"Yes, and after eight months here, he has the contact
information of everyone who matters in our small world."

Zack peered over his glasses at me. "Jo, when Milo gave
you *his* contact information, who did he list as next of kin?"

"Me," I said.

"I guess that tells us something," Zack said, and he wasn't
smiling.

That night Brock, Angus, and Declan built a bonfire on the
beach. As promised, we had a weenie roast, made s'mores,
and watched the sun go down. It was the perfect ending to

a day that had been anything but perfect, and as we tucked the girls in, Zack and I looked at each other gratefully.

I was about to turn out the light on my nightstand when my cell rang. It was Milo. "I just had a phone call from Mansell Donnelly," he said. I groaned. "Hold that groan," he said. "This merits perusal. Mansell Donnelly wants the big man to consider joining him for a media statement tomorrow morning. Mansell thinks it's time for a truce – no more craziness, no more personal attacks. Civil discourse only."

"Was Mansell acting on behalf of Quinn and Lancaster?"

"He didn't say. My guess is he was calling on his own hook."

"So Mansell had a 'Saul on the road to Damascus' moment?" I said.

There was a pause. Finally Milo said, "Joanne, sometimes your wig bubbles float right past me."

"Sorry. What I meant was did Mansell suggest how he arrived at this decision? I had an encounter with the Donnellys after the funeral. More accurately, I had an encounter with Quinn. Mansell was physically present, but his mind was elsewhere."

"So, it was just you and Quinn. How did it go?"

"We'll find out," I said. "I gave them twenty-four hours to meet with us and come up with a plan committing both sides to behave rationally until the day of the vote. I told Quinn if they weren't in touch, I'd go to the media and say their side refused to cooperate."

"Hardball. But obviously it worked."

"I wonder," I said. "I don't trust them, Milo."

"It's possible Mansell realizes the situation is out of hand."

"I guess anything's possible," I said. "When he looked at that picture of Lee after the funeral, he seemed shattered."

"So the old bad Mansell fell away and out came a good Mansell?" Milo's tone was ironic. "Jo, we don't even know if there *is* a good Mansell."

"Oh there is," I said. "I got a glimpse of him at the wedding reception. He and the twins shared a moment that made it clear Mansell is a man who feels and cares. The three of them even laughed together at a private joke."

"You think Mansell regrets Lancaster's attacks on Lee."

"I'm sure he does," I said. "But regret is one thing; breaking ties with Lancaster is another."

"Agreed. So let's consider the other options. The obvious one is that the media blitz at Lee's funeral made Lancaster realize that stepping up the attacks on Lee would be dumb as shit, so it was time to chill, and Quinn had Mansell make the call. The Machiavellian one is that Lancaster wants Mansell to be mayor, and that means putting some distance between him and their looney-tunes Meighen loyalists."

"Including Quinn Donnelly? That's pretty hard to swallow."

"It is, but Quinn's smart enough to read the writing on the wall. We're gaining support for our bylaws every day. Sustainability is an idea whose time has come. Barring disaster, we're going to win, and Quinn and her cohorts want Mansell to be on the winning side. By joining Zack and calling for a fair and rational campaign, Mansell moves one step away from the marginalized and one step closer to the mainstream."

"And broadens his base when he runs for mayor," I said. "So we're being used."

Milo was nonchalant. "We're using Mansell too. The optics of the big man and him shaking hands will legitimize our position on the bylaws with a lot of Mansell's on-the-fence voters."

"And it will legitimize Mansell with a lot of our on-the-fence voters, and torpedo Brock's chances of being mayor," I said. "Brock's a good human being who's educated, experienced, and committed. His election would send a signal about the kind of city we are."

"A city where it's possible that a gay Aboriginal man with a boyfriend who's a married psychiatrist who lost his medical licence for malpractice can be elected mayor?"

"You make it sound impossible," I said.

"It's not. You and I can get Brock elected, Jo. It won't be easy, but if we begin early enough we can do it."

"I thought we'd start raising Brock's profile in September. Racette-Hunter will be celebrating its first anniversary on Labour Day weekend, and Brock's the director. There'll be plenty of positive coverage."

"My thought too," Milo said. "That's going to be one mother of a campaign, but we can do it. However, that's in the future. Right now the ball is in the big man's court."

"I'll see what I can do," I said.

Zack had been watching me carefully as I talked to Milo. When I broke the connection, I turned to him. "Want me to fill you in on Milo's side of the conversation?"

"Please," Zack said. "But give me a minute to get vertical." Zack piled his pillows against the headboard and pulled himself to a sitting position. "Okay, I'm ready," he said. "What's going on?"

I explained the situation. "We'll have to make a decision tonight," I said.

"What's your opinion?"

"I think we should say no."

Zack shot me a lawyerly gaze. "But you were the one who issued the ultimatum."

"Zack, what I asked for was a private meeting between the opposing sides, not a media event. We all know that Mansell's positioning himself to run for mayor after your term's up. Milo says that by standing in front of the cameras with you and calling for a reasoned discussion of the issues, Mansell will move from the marginalized to the mainstream."

"And it will encourage the business community to take a second look at what we're proposing and we'll win the referendum."

"What about Brock?"

"Jo, I know you've hoped that Brock would succeed me as mayor, but be realistic. Brock's one of my closest friends. You know how much I respect and admire him, but he has too much baggage to be elected."

"You've never mentioned Brock's baggage before."

"The issue wasn't relevant before. Now that you've thrown down the gauntlet, the issue has become relevant. You gave Lancaster twenty-four hours to make their move, and they did." Zack's voice was even.

"I overplayed it," I said. "I was planning to start positioning Brock to run for mayor in September. Mansell's people will use the footage of you and Mansell presenting a united front to undercut Brock's candidacy before it gets off the ground. I'll call Mansell and tell him we want a private meeting."

"Before you do that, let's call Brock and tell him what's happening."

"No," I said. "I don't want Brock to feel that you turned down Mansell's offer to make a joint statement because of him."

Zack was moving to get out of bed. I watched as he transferred his body onto his wheelchair and picked up his robe. "I'm not turning down Mansell's offer, Joanne. I'm going to call Brock and explain my decision. He'll understand. We were elected to serve *all* the people. Making the joint statement is the best thing for the city. I'll call from the living room so I don't disturb your sleep."

Zack was back in fifteen minutes. "Brock's fine with me making the statement," he said. "And I've called Mansell.

We're meeting in front of City Hall at nine-thirty tomorrow morning. Do you want to talk about it?"

"No point," I said. "It sounds like a done deed."

"Are you angry?"

"Very, and I'm disappointed. I've seen you in court, Zack. I know the lengths you'll go to get the outcome that's favourable to you. But until this moment, I never realized you'd sacrifice a friend to win."

CHAPTER

12

Zack was still sleeping, or pretending to sleep, when I got up. After I let the dogs out, I made two phone calls. Brock was sanguine about the possible ramifications of the joint statement on his own political career. "We were elected to serve all the people," he said. "Winning the referendum is the best thing for the city."

"So you're swallowing Zack's argument hook, line, and sinker," I said. "What about your political future?"

"I spent the night thinking about that. And after I got past my injured pride, I realized that as councillor for Ward 6 and director of Racette-Hunter, I'm exactly where I should be. Racette-Hunter's just starting to realize its potential. I want to do everything I can to make sure the centre succeeds. If I ran for mayor, I couldn't do that."

"But as mayor you could do so much more," I said.

"I could, but Margot and our children would be forced to pay a price they shouldn't have to pay. Jo, Margot and I need to have a private life that's private. The family we have is not traditional, but it works, and it will continue to work if we can simply be the people we are. That means

Margot and I will both be free to have relationships with
other people. Our kids will grow up knowing that there are
other people in their mother's life and in mine, but the central truth will always be that Margot and I love each other
and we love them."

"I understand," I said. "I really do. Brock, I'm sorry if I
pushed too hard."

"You didn't," he said. "To be honest, it was flattering to
be pushed. But we can talk about this later. Margot and I
are taking the kids to Lawyers' Bay for the day, so we'll see
you there."

"Good. I'll feel better when I can see you and know you're
really all right with this."

When I filled Milo in on my talk with Brock he, too, was
sanguine. "Brock's a sensible guy, and given his situation it's
a good decision." His laugh was rueful. "But, wowsers, that
would have been an epic campaign to run."

"There'll be other epic campaigns."

"True, and there are always diversions," Milo said. "For
starters, I just learned that last night Mansell Donnelly
either left or was thrown out of the family homestead."

"You're kidding. So I guess he and Quinn aren't joined at
the hip after all."

"Not any more. Apparently when Mansell called me
about the joint statement with Zack, he was acting on his
own. Quinn was not pleased. They had words, and they did
not share a bed last night."

"Milo, how do you know these things?"

"I'm a good listener," he said airily. "Anyway, hang on to
your toga because there's bigger news. At the media meet
today, Mansell is not only going to join Zack in calling for
civility, but he's also going to announce that he's supporting
the Yes vote in the referendum."

"You're sure of your source."

"Yep, and I'll be standing right beside you outside City Hall when Mansell has his big moment."

"Milo, why don't you ride out to the lake this afternoon? We have a lot to talk about. You can swim, and I'll teach you how to make s'mores."

"An offer I can't refuse. I'll be there."

I could smell the coffee as soon as the dogs and I came up from our run on the beach. The table was set, the dogs' water dishes were filled, bacon sizzled on the grill, and there was a bowl of fresh strawberries at my place. Zack brought me a cup of coffee. His eyes were deeply shadowed. He had not slept well.

"Truce?" he said.

"Truce," I said, and I kissed the top of his head.

By the time we left for the city, Madeleine and Lena were having breakfast in the sunroom with Taylor, Gracie Falconer, and Isobel Wainberg. The drive into town was pleasant. The heat had broken and so had the tension between Zack and me. While the dogs and I were on our run, Mansell had called Zack to tell him he was going to announce his support for the referendum, so the subject of our conversation was how to handle what came next.

A cool breeze snapped the flags in the Queen Elizabeth Courtyard in front of City Hall. Pride Week was on the horizon. Soon the rainbow flag would fly alongside the flags of Canada, Saskatchewan, the Union Jack, Regina, Treaty4, and the Métis nation.

It was Sunday morning, and there'd been no attempt to alert the public to the fact that Mansell and Zack would be appearing jointly to make statements. But TV vans were parked along Victoria Avenue, cameras and microphones were already set up in the Queen Elizabeth Courtyard, and the media were waiting.

Mansell arrived just as we did. In a small cosmic joke it happened that Mansell and Zack had dressed alike: dove-grey suits, pale-blue shirts, and dark-blue paisley ties. They gave each other an appraising glance and smiled. It was an auspicious beginning. When they'd talked earlier, Mansell and Zack had decided that after statements stressing the need for conciliation, cooperation, and civility from the opposing camps, Mansell would announce that he was now supporting Zack's bylaws and would encourage citizens to vote Yes in the referendum. Zack would say that there would be no questions and thank the media for coming out.

Milo was already there in his invariable uniform of black T-shirt, chinos, lace-up black Keds, and ballcap. Mansell and Zack didn't waste time glad-handing. They approached the microphones and delivered their appeal for calm and reason. When Mansell announced his change of position on the new bylaws, a moment of stunned silence was followed by a barrage of questions. The two men shook hands, and then, camera people and print journalists in tow, Mansell headed towards his car. His surprise statement had turned a staged-for-media event into front-page news.

Milo walked us to our car. Zack got into the driver's seat and began taking his wheelchair apart. Milo and I stepped aside to give him room.

"Do you give rain checks on the s'mores lessons?" Milo said.

"Of course. Did something come up?"

"Just some stuff I'd like to check out."

"While you're checking, see if you can find out where Slater Doyle was this morning," I said.

"Slater was up shit creek," Milo said. "That's where he's been since Lee's death. Quinn might have started the rumour, but Slater orchestrated the smear campaign against Lee. Word has it that Lee's funeral got to Mansell and he insisted Quinn deep-six Slater."

"And Quinn refused?" I said.

"So far, she's hanging tough. But my guess is that unless Slater comes up with something fast, even Quinn will be ready to turn her bad boy's ass to grass."

"And you got this information where?" Zack asked.

"Here and there," Milo said.

Brock and the granddaughters were working on an old *Charlotte's Web* puzzle when we got back. "Taylor and Declan took the dogs for a walk," Brock said. "So I'm getting acquainted with Fern and Wilbur."

Zack rolled over to investigate. He was terrible at puzzles, but he never stopped trying. When the girls saw him pick up a puzzle piece, they tensed. "It's okay, Granddad. We're just about through," Lena said.

Zack tried jamming a piece that was clearly part of Wilbur's snout into a cloud and then into a space at the base of some foliage. "But you've still got half the puzzle to go," he said.

"Lena just meant we're done for the day," Madeleine said. She smiled at Zack. "So, Granddad, you can go off and do whatever you want to do."

Brock stood. "Zack, we both have office work we should catch up on."

"And the girls and I have a project of our own," I said.

"Your vegetable garden," Zack said.

"Right. Tomorrow's June 1, I think it's safe to get seeds in the soil."

When Madeleine, Lena, and I decided to plant a garden at the lake, we went online and consulted *The Old Farmers' Almanac*. We were following the almanac's advice to the letter. We had chosen a place behind the cottage that got plenty of sun, over eight hours a day, and offered good drainage. As the almanac advised, we kept our plot small – five metres by three. Noah Wainberg dug the garden, and the girls and I added compost to the soil.

Since the first week in May, we had been gardening on paper. We had ruled eleven rows running north to south to take full advantage of the sun. Each row would be three metres long. Lena had drawn vegetable pictures to indicate what we would plant where; Madeleine had written the names of the vegetables on Popsicle sticks with an indelible felt-tip pen. Finally, we had shopped for seeds. That Sunday armed with the map of the garden, the Popsicle sticks, and the seeds, we set to work. As we planted, we talked about Lee – her life, her death, and what it all meant. The girls had many questions, and I had few satisfactory answers, but it was good to talk while the sun beat down on our backs and our hands were buried in the loamy earth.

None of us wanted our time at the lake to end, so we decided to stay over and go back to the city early the next morning. That night after we got the kids to bed, the adults sat out on the deck with a cooler of Coronas and soft drinks, a basket of tortilla chips, and a bowl of Zack's charred tomatillo guacamole, a dish that was almost as good as he believed it to be. A nearly full moon hung in the dark sky, and the night was quiet except for the slap of the waves against the shoreline.

Zack took a sip of his beer and sighed contentedly. He turned to me. "We need more nights like this, Joanne. When I'm through with the mayor thing, let's make every weekend a long weekend at the lake."

"Fine with me," I said. "But it'll be two and half years before you're through with the mayor thing."

Margot took a handful of chips and scooped some

guacamole onto her plate. "What are you planning to do when you leave City Hall?" she asked.

"Go back to being a lawyer," Zack said. "I miss the rush."

"So do I," Margot said. "In two and half years, Kai and Lexi will be old enough for me to split my time between home and work."

"And with Falconer Shreve now officially a family-friendly firm you'll actually be able to work part-time," Zack said.

I turned to my husband. "Can you get in on that part-time lawyer thing?"

"Zack will be able to write his own ticket," Margot said. "The firm needs him. We have some promising associates, including Maisie and Angus, but Falconer Shreve needs the old bull to share his wisdom about how to survive in the ring."

"I'm not crazy about the bull analogy," Zack said. "Any bull that outsmarts a matador is executed."

"Retribution?" I said.

"No," Zack said. "The theory is that the bull will have learned enough moves to kill his next opponents."

Margot grinned. "You've always known how to gore the next matador, Zack."

"A lot will have changed in two and half years," I said. "The old bull and I will be empty-nesters. Taylor will be in university."

Taylor and Declan were sitting side by side on the porch swing. "In Toronto," Taylor said. "I've decided to go to OCAD."

I felt a pang. "The old College of Art," I said.

Taylor smiled. "Is that what they called it when you were at U OF T? Now they teach drawing and painting, material art and design, photography, printmaking, sculpture, installation, critical studies, and so many other things I'll either need to know or want to know. I've checked online and OCAD is the right place for me. I need to be somewhere where I can see a lot of art and the school is right next to the Art Gallery of Ontario. And I want to be with other people who are making art. Most of all I just want to paint."

"Toronto really does have a great art scene," Declan said, "and it's an hour from New York and Chicago. By the time Taylor graduates from high school, I'll be in my final year at U OF T. We can share a place."

Zack narrowed his eyes. "But just as roommates," he said.

Taylor was gentle. "Who knows? As Jo said, a lot can change in two and a half years." When Zack sputtered, Taylor held out her hand to him. "Dad, would you mind passing the guacamole?"

That night when Zack and I went in to say goodnight to Taylor, I felt the weight of Zack's eyes on me, and after he left, I stayed behind. Taylor's smile was impish. "I'll bet you a loonie I know what you want to talk about."

"I never make a bet I know I'm going to lose. May I sit down?"

Taylor patted the bed. "Of course."

"You know how fond your dad and I are of Declan," I said.

"Then there's no problem," Taylor said. She hugged her knees. With her face scrubbed clean and her breath minty with toothpaste, she seemed like the little girl I'd always known. "I thought you and Dad would be relieved that I wasn't going off somewhere by myself," she said.

"We are," I said. "It's just hard for us to let go. I read once that the love between a parent and a child is the only love that must grow towards separation."

Taylor had her birth mother's expressive mouth. I could always read her mood by looking at her lips. At that moment her mouth showed sadness but also resolve. "I guess that's true," Taylor said. "I love you. You're my family, and you'll always be my family. But after I finish high school, I'll have to find my own way."

"And your own way is with Declan," I said.

She nodded. "We're good together."

"Taylor, didn't you ever think you might want to date other people?"

"No," she said. "I listen to how the other girls at school talk about boys. There's so much drama. One minute a girl is crazy happy and the next she's suicidal. Declan and I know we're right for each other, so why complicate things?"

"I just think that maybe you should both be meeting other people, having other experiences."

"We don't want that. We want what we have. Jo, when did you know Dad was the right man for you?"

"About a week after I met him," I said.

"And you've never wanted to be with anybody else since then."

I hesitated.

Taylor's face pinched with concern. "Are you and Dad having problems?"

"What makes you say that?"

"I heard you last night."

My heart sank. "It was just a political disagreement."

Taylor's voice was small. "Did Milo have something to do with it?"

"Why would you think your dad and I would be having a problem about Milo?"

"Because of the way he looks at you."

"Taylor, Milo doesn't let many people get close to him. He's let me get close, and Milo and I are both grateful for that, but we're friends – that's all. I'm old enough to be Milo's mother, and I love your father."

"I love him too," Taylor said. "And I love you. And I like Milo a lot. He and I have had some really good talks. I was just worried."

"There's nothing to worry about," I said. "I promise."

The next morning, after I dropped Taylor off at school and Zack at City Hall, I went up to the roof garden and stretched out on a lazy lounge with an old copy of *The New Yorker* and tried not to think about the troubling conversation with our daughter the night before. My cell rang just as I finished a vignette in "Talk of the Town" about Neil Patrick Harris's makeup regime for his role as the transgender protagonist in *Hedwig and the Angry Inch*.

It was Margot. "Good. I caught you before you got started on your day," she said. "Where are you?"

"Up on the roof reading about Neil Patrick Harris."

"I *love* him," Margot said. "Got time to come down here for a visit? There are a couple of things I'd like to run by you."

"I'll be there in two minutes," I said.

Margot met me at her condo door with Kai in her arms and Lexi at her heels. "Take a child, any child," she said. "But if you break it, it's yours."

I picked up Lexi. She had an orange mouth and a sodden Cheezie in her hand. She offered the Cheezie to me.

I had eaten many Cheezies of dubious provenance, but this one had toilet paper stuck to it.

"Thank you," I said. "But I'm still full from breakfast."

"Good call," Margot said. "That Cheezie has been around since I was an object of unbridled lust." She stepped aside. "Come inside. Tread carefully. Those Fisher-Price Little People are sneaky."

"I remember," I said. I gazed around Margot's condo. Like ours, it was an open-concept plan with a vaulted ceiling and skylights. Two storeys of light, hardwood, granite, and glass. Margot's original decorating choices had been cool and elegant – soft creamy leather couches, ivory worsted-wool Wilton carpets, a round mahogany dining room table with chairs upholstered in the palest yellow silk. A perfect setting for the sleek, flaxen-haired, immaculate trial lawyer whose dagger nails were always painted the signature red that suggested danger.

As the single parent of two children under the age of two, Margot had made some changes. The Wilton carpet and the mahogany table were bearing up, but the creamy leather of the couches was now protected by bright, washable throws; the silk-upholstered dining room chairs were in a storeroom in the basement, replaced by two high chairs and sturdy, wide, deep adult chairs that a child could not tip over. The dagger nails were now short and unpolished; the flaxen hair had returned to its natural honey blond, and these days Margot's wardrobe was pretty much wash and wear. That morning she was in sneakers, blue jean cutoffs, and a T-shirt that read "Childbirth: A Labour of Love."

She blew a strand of hair back off her forehead. "Can I get you anything?"

"No, I really am still full from breakfast."

"In that case, I'm going to take advantage of having another adult present and feed my hungry boy." We trouped into the living room, where Margot and Kai settled into the birchwood rocking chair that Margot favoured for nursing. A basket filled with bright blocks was on the floor beside her. I squatted, picked up the basket, and held it towards Lexi. "Do you want to play blocks with me?" I said.

"No," she said, and then she came over, plopped down, emptied the basket, and began piling blocks. I joined in. Kai had latched on to Margot's breast and was tugging enthusiastically.

Margot beamed. "Sometimes I just have all the moves," she said. "Before I forget, I called Maisie and asked if she wanted my maternity clothes. She does, and they're all packed up and ready to go."

Lexi was choosing only red blocks to pile atop one another. When I picked up a blue block and set it on the pile, she scowled. "Okay," I said, removing the offending block. "I'll keep blue over here with me." Lexi immediately began handing me blue blocks.

"Smart girl," I said. "I'll take the clothes out to Maisie this afternoon. I always welcome an excuse to drive out there. I don't want to hover, but Maisie has so much to deal with."

"Maisie and I had a good talk when I called about the clothes," Margot said. "It's so hard to know what to say, so I followed her lead. She asked me to tell her how I managed to get through my pregnancy after Leland died."

"What did you say?"

"I told her I kept reminding myself that I was carrying a new life and I had to keep putting one foot in front of the other. When that didn't work any more, I crawled into bed and cried."

"That's about it," I said.

"I also told Maisie to lean on other people when she needed to. I honestly don't know how I would have made it through if I hadn't known you and Zack were just across the hall."

"That goes both ways, you know."

"That's good to hear," she said. Kai was fussing, and Margot adjusted his position. When he snuggled right in, Margot turned her attention back to me. "I saw Zack and Mansell's announcement on the news," she said. "I've been pondering Mansell's one-eighty on the referendum."

"So has everyone else," I said. "It was a shocker, and even more shocking, Mansell's walked away from Quinn and Lancaster over it."

Margot was thoughtful. "Leland said once that Mansell hadn't drawn a breath without Quinn's permission since the day they were married. He knew them both better than I did, of course. Quinn was a competitor, and Leland had some dealings with Mansell back when Mansell was still farming. Apparently, he was a different man then. He loved the land, loved his life, was filled with plans and dreams, and then, about ten years ago, he walked away from it all and ended up as a puppet for Lancaster. That always puzzled Leland. He said it was as if Mansell simply gave up on life."

"Maybe Mansell's decision to break with Quinn and Lancaster is a sign that he's back in the game," I said.

Margot was wistful. "That would make Leland happy."

"That would make me happy too," I said. "The day of the wedding, I got a glimpse of the old Mansell, and I liked him."

"We live in hope," Margot said. "Anyway, I wanted to talk to you about something else. Incredible as it may seem, Peyben's just about ready to start selling houses and condos. I've seen our ad campaign for North Village, and it's going to be a real boon to the Yes side. The ads show concrete proof that there's a right way to reclaim the inner city. Our neighbourhood is a case in point. It was the worst, but Peyben took the time and spent the money on good materials and solid workmanship and we've created a real community."

"You've done a terrific job."

Margot waved her hand dismissively. "The concept was Leland's. He'd already made all the decisions before he died. I just made sure Peyben followed through. I told the ad agency I wanted people to know what can be accomplished when a company commits to developing a mixed-use neighbourhood that will last for generations. They suggested a time lapse ad showing what this area looked like when Leland started and the process that led to what we have today."

"Very smart," I said, "to show that unlike throwing up tract housing, real urban renewal takes time. I have to admit, I was dubious that first year. The neighbourhood looked as if it had been bombed."

"I remember," Margot said. "Leland had to remind me more than once that there could be no phoenix without ashes. But two and a half years after that upheaval and destruction, we have North Village, and it really is what we promised: a place in the city where people of all ages and levels of income can live good lives."

When his mother shifted Kai to the other breast, he attacked hungrily but quickly settled into making glugging sounds.

"No complaints about the grub from that boy," I said.

Margot smoothed Kai's thick black hair and kissed his head. "He's going to be a big guy, like his dad," she said. "Speaking of Brock. He's seen the North Village ad, and he says it dovetails perfectly with what you'll be doing in the past two weeks before the referendum. He loved the footage we included of the countryside just five minutes away from the village."

"A proximity that will be preserved if the new bylaws go through," I said.

"Right. And we hammer away at the fact that the infrastructure and services necessary for North Village – roads, sewers, water, power, public transportation, mail delivery – are already in place so our tax base won't be sucked dry by skyrocketing infrastructure payments, and we didn't spoil prime land outside the city with tract housing. The slogan we're using is 'Building upon what we have.' What do you think?"

"I love it," I said. "It's exactly right. Factual. Evocative and powerful. When do the ads start running?"

Margot smiled mischievously. "Tonight." She looked down at her son. "Okay, bud. Time to close the diner."

As Margot pulled her shirt back over her breast, Kai clouded up. "Don't look so worried," she said. "We open again in two hours." She handed Kai to me. "Can you hold him while I get the clothes?" She knelt beside her daughter and examined the block towers Lexi had erected. "Impressive," she said. "Now why don't you take a break and help me get dolly?" Lexi beamed and ran down the hall. Within seconds, she and Margot came back wheeling an industrial dolly that held three large cartons.

"You're always so organized," I said.

"I didn't want you lugging those boxes downstairs. After you've loaded the clothes into your car, put dolly on the elevator and send her back up. I use that thing all the time." Lexi gave me an orange smile. "Dolly," she said.

"Right," Margot said. "Dolly – Mummy's best friend after you and your brothers."

I was in luck. When I pulled up to the delivery door at the back of our condo, a FedEx truck was behind me and the driver helped me load the clothing into my car. He even took the dolly back and sent it up on the elevator. Margot wasn't the only one with all the moves.

I called Maisie before I left the delivery entrance. She laughed when she heard my voice. "Pete says his family communicates telepathically. I was just about to call you. I'm going through Lee's things, and I could use some company."

"I'll be there in thirty minutes," I said. "And I come bearing gifts."

When she heard my car pull into the driveway, Maisie came out from behind the house. She was holding a carpenter's metal tape measure. "I've been 'doin' some figgerin','' as our hired man used to say. As far as I'm concerned, the sooner we get started on the renovations, the better."

"So fill me in on your plans for the house."

"Follow me and I'll show you." Maisie led me around back and handed me her tablet. "Here's a preliminary sketch of what we want to do. As you know only too well, the kitchen is ancient and really small. Pete and I want to open it up and make a place where we can eat and visit with family and friends, and our kids can visit with their kids. And we want to add a family room down here. There's no bathroom on the main floor so we're putting in an accessible bathroom too."

"Zack will be glad to hear that," I said.

"And he'll be glad to hear we're planning to move one of the pianos into the family room so our kids can press the pedals under the piano while their grandfather plays."

"Zack will love that," I said. "He's crazy about Madeleine and Lena, and we're both really excited about having more grandkids."

"We're being selfish," Maisie said. "Peter and I are counting on you and Zack to babysit when we need a wild and wacky weekend alone together."

"Anytime," I said. "How are you feeling?"

"Surprisingly well," Maisie said. "I'm at twenty weeks. The babies are very active." She touched the curve of her belly. "At times, it feels as if there's a roller derby going on in there."

"It's an amazing time," I said.

"It is," Maisie said. "And I'd love to talk about our plans and the babies all day. But there's a task we have to deal with and the sooner I get it over with, the better."

Few exercises are more painful than disposing of the clothing of a loved one, and I could feel Maisie steeling herself as we walked down the hall towards the stairs that led to Lee's bedroom. When we came to the office on the main floor, Maisie stopped. "Lee kept meticulous files, and so did Colin." She went over to a bookcase on the far wall.

The shelves of the case were lined with leather daybooks. Maisie's fingers ran lightly over them. "The black note-books were Colin's. Thirty-three of them – one a year from the time he started farming until the day he died. The dark-green ones are Lee's. She began keeping them when she was fourteen, so there are nineteen of them. Pete says having all that information is going to make starting the breeding program over a lot easier."

She bit her lip. "I decided I'd read the notebooks chrono-logically, but it's hard. They're filled with information, but they're newsy too – about the weather and who came to visit. Colin's have notes about how Lee and I were doing at school and piano, and he kept track of things the three of us did together – berry-picking, fishing, hunting gophers, trying to catch fireflies, horseback riding, tobogganing, skating. Colin always made a rink for us out back. Lee has these very orderly accounts of her farm 'projects,' but every so often she veers off to complain about how I wrecked a sweater of hers I'd borrowed and how my snoring keeps her awake."

Maisie turned away from the bookcase. "We had the best lives. I don't know how I'm going to go on without Lee. I feel as if I've been ripped in two."

I held her tight. "I'm around. That's all I can offer you, but whenever you need me, I'll be here."

"Hugging helps," she said. "Does being your daughter-in-law give me unlimited crying-on-your-shoulder privileges?"

"Any time, day or night," I said.

Maisie's voice was small. "You may be sorry you offered," she said.

The boxes were already lined up in Lee's bedroom, neatly labelled with a Sharpie. There were three categories: Value Village, Recycle, Garbage. We worked well together. I held up an item of clothing, and Maisie told me which box to put it in. She never hesitated, and we were making good time

when we heard someone pull into the driveway. Maisie
went to the bedroom window.

"It's Bobby," she said. "He's been amazing, but we're both
hanging on by a thread." She gestured to the clothing on
the bed. "I want to finish this before I fall apart. Would you
mind telling him I'll call him later?"

"Of course not," I said.

Bobby had taken a cooler out of the back seat of his truck
when I opened the door to the porch. "More food," he said.
"There's a casserole of scalloped potatoes in there and a
couple of pies. I'm sure by now Maisie and Peter's freezer is
full, but living in the country means that no neighbour
is ever allowed to go hungry."

"I like that philosophy," I said. I took the cooler from him.
"Bobby, how are you doing?"

He shrugged. "Not great, but making myself useful
helps." He spotted the boxes in the back of my station
wagon. "Can I give you a hand with those?"

"You can," I said. "They're maternity clothes a friend sent
out for Maisie."

"One less problem for her to deal with," Bobby said.

The concern in his voice disturbed me. "Bobby, you don't
have to answer this, but do you get a sense that Pete and
Maisie are in over their heads? Pete's closing his walk-in
clinic, but it's going to take time to wrap that up, and he
wants to get the breeding program started. Maisie is going
back to work this week. I worry that it's going to be too
much. Is there somebody in the area we could hire to help
them get through the next few months?"

Bobby ran his hand over his brushcut. "Me," he said. "I've
already signed on to take care of the day-to-day business of
the farm, help Pete set up the breeding operations, and give
Maisie a crash course on farm living. It's been fifteen years
since she lived out here."

"That's very generous of you," I said.

Bobby lowered his eyes. "Just self-preservation," he said. "Our hired man has a teenaged son keen to pick up some spending money this summer, and of course, there's my mum. With four of us, there's no problem handling the farm, but there are a lot of hours in the day, and I need to fill them."

By the time I rejoined Maisie, she'd already finished with the clothing from the closet and cleaned out all but the two bottom drawers of the bureau. I pulled the drawers out and placed them on the bed. Winter scarves and mitts filled one, and the other held mementos – loose photographs, birthday cards, letters.

Maisie swallowed hard when she saw the contents of the drawer. She picked up a plastic storage box and handed it to me. "Jo, would you mind just putting everything from that drawer in here? Someday I'll go through it all, but I'm not ready yet."

"I understand," I said, and I began packing the mementos away. At the bottom of the drawer there was a framed portrait of Lee in the convocation robes of a Ph.D.

I took it out. "I didn't know Lee had her doctorate," I said.

"She didn't talk about it," Maisie said, and she began to sort through the mitts and scarves. Clearly, the subject was closed. I placed the picture face down in the storage box. We moved on, but Maisie's eyes kept returning to the box. Finally, she reached over, took the portrait out, and gazed at it. "Lee was so proud that day. She had offers of tenure-track positions at three universities, but Colin had died two years earlier, so she accepted the offer from University of Saskatchewan. She felt she could work out a schedule that would allow her to teach on campus and still be actively involved in the farm."

"What happened?"

Maisie's sigh was deep. "A mess. Lee was twenty-seven when she defended her dissertation. She worked very closely with her adviser. He'd been a friend of Colin's, so he took her under his wing. Unfortunately, he also took her into his bed. Along the way, he gave her an interesting piece of research that he told her he'd done on prairie restoration. It was rudimentary but promising. Lee followed through on it, and it became the heart of her dissertation. It turned out the research was the work of a master's student the good professor was also supervising. The other student only found out about what had happened after Lee had been awarded her doctorate, and her dissertation was published."

"So what happened?"

"The adviser convinced the other student to back off. She was realistic. She realized what she was up against: a tenured faculty member with a decade of glowing departmental performance reviews, an immensely promising home-grown doctoral candidate, and a dissertation that had taken a master's student's preliminary research and used it to formulate sophisticated strategies to conserve and restore high-quality prairie."

"So the master's student went away quietly."

"Not quite. She went to Lee and showed her that the research she used in her dissertation was plagiarized. When Lee knew the truth, she confronted her lover. He said he'd lose his job if Lee reported what had happened, and he pointed out that Lee *had* done the bulk of the research herself."

"So Lee didn't report him," I said.

"No. She ended the relationship, but she felt her doctorate was a sham, so she turned down the tenured position at U of S and came home."

"What happened to the adviser?"

"Nothing. He had tenure."

"Did you ever find out what happened to the master's student?"

"She reinvented herself. She started working out, became a blond, got a great haircut and slick new wardrobe, switched her thesis topic to municipal planning, and after she got her degree she went to work for Graham Meighen at Lancaster. When he died, she took over as CEO."

I was incredulous. "The other student was Quinn Donnelly?" I said. "Warren said there was bad blood between Quinn and Lee. That would certainly explain it."

"Lee tried to apologize to Quinn when it happened. Lee told her she believed the research had come from her adviser and that she'd acknowledged his contribution in her dissertation. Over the years, Lee held out the olive branch several times, especially after Quinn and Mansell were married, but Quinn was never in a forgiving mood."

Remembering the smile that had played on Quinn's lips during the funeral, I felt a chill. I shook it off, picked up the drawers, and slid them back in place in the bureau. "We're through here," I said. "Pete can carry down the boxes."

Maisie smoothed the white chenille bedspread on Lee's bed and straightened a photograph of Colin Brokenshire on the nightstand. Her fingers lingered for a few seconds on the photograph's silver frame. "Is it too soon for me to ask for a little more time on your shoulder," she said.

"No," I said. "It's not too soon." I held Maisie in my arms until she stepped away, "I'm okay now," she said.

"Good," I said. "Let's go downstairs so we can look at what you'll be wearing for the next four months."

Throughout her pregnancies Margot had continued to be involved in decision-making at Peyben Development.

Her maternity wardrobe was extensive: casual clothes and some very smart business attire and eveningwear.

Maisie held up a gorgeous peacock-blue, full-length silk gown. "Check the neckline on this," she said. "I've never worn anything cut that low in my life."

"I guess the idea is to showcase your burgeoning assets," I said.

She cocked her head at her mirrored self. "Actually, just this morning Pete complimented me on my burgeoning assets." She smiled, and for the first time since Lee's death, her smile was not shadowed by sorrow. She hung up the dress and looked thoughtfully at a blouse the colour of a cut peach. "Did Bobby tell you that he's going to help us at the farm till we find our feet?"

"He did," I said. "And I think it's a terrific plan."

"It's a godsend," Maisie said. "Bobby is familiar with every millimetre of this farm." She turned from the mirror to face me. "And right now he needs us as much as we need him." Maisie folded the peach blouse and replaced it in the packing box. For a few moments we were silent, lost in our private thoughts.

Maisie picked up a silky summer nightgown, held it against her cheek, and smiled. "Pete is going to love this nightie," she said.

"And you're going to love seeing Pete loving you in that nightie," I said. "Maisie, you two have so many good times ahead."

Her eyes met mine. "I know," she said. She closed her eyes and when she opened them, I knew that the idyllic moment she had been holding in her mind had been replaced by other pictures – pictures that would never exist.

"Lee should have had a chance to experience this kind of happiness."

"But she never did?"

"Just once, and she cherished it. She was on the brink of having everything she'd ever wanted and then, in the blink of an eye, it was gone. You read about people dying of a broken heart. For months after she lost the man she loved, I was afraid my sister would die of a broken heart."

"But she didn't," I said.

"No. She came back, but she was changed. She enjoyed the company of men and she liked sex, but she always kept the men with whom she was involved at a distance. I'm sure it was because she couldn't risk the pain of loving anyone deeply again. So, it was always no strings."

"And the men Lee was with accepted this?"

"Lee thought so, but since she died I've spent many nights wondering if she was wrong about one of them. When she was in a relationship Lee was always monogamous and the affairs often lasted months, so I came to know the men in her life. They all seemed like fine people, even Simon before he got sick. None of them seemed capable of violence. Of course, some were initially bitter about the breakup, but in time they all ended up being friends with Lee." Maisie's gold-flecked eyes were troubled. "But who knows? Sometimes, I wonder whether any of us can ever truly know another human being.

"Court dockets are filled with cases where seemingly normal people have committed unspeakable crimes because they believed a lover betrayed them. I've handled a few of those cases myself – spousal murder cases are the worst – the 'wronged' partner often feels the need to mutilate the spouse's wedding ring finger.

"When I went to the morgue to see Lee's body, the first place I looked at was at her ring finger. The skin was torn and the finger itself appeared to be broken. Lee's killer mangled her finger, ripping the engagement ring off. Who did that?

Was it Simon? Was it one of the men whom Lee believed was reconciled to the breakup but who carried a smouldering hatred that finally burst into flames? What's driving me craziest about Lee's murder is not knowing *why* it happened. What set of circumstances made the killer come into the barn with a gun that afternoon? Who decided that May 17 was the day Lee Crawford would die?"

CHAPTER

13

Tuesday morning, I'd just finished showering when Warren Weber called me. "You and I have some fences to mend," he said, "and there's no time like the present. Are you free for lunch today?"

"I am, and, Warren, I really am looking forward to seeing you."

I could hear the relief in his voice. "Zack has suggested once or twice that you might enjoy my club. Would that be acceptable?"

"More than acceptable," I said.

"I'll send my driver to pick you up at half past noon. The club is famous for its Old Fashioneds, and I'd like you to enjoy one without worrying about the drive home."

"That's very thoughtful," I said.

When I came into our bedroom, Zack was laying out his clothes for the day. "You look pleased," he said.

"I am pleased. That was Warren Weber. He wants to have lunch with me so we can mend fences. My guess is Warren also wants to personally deliver his private investigators' findings about Lee's life."

"And you're not still angry about that?"

"Not as angry as I was. Yesterday when I was out at the farm, I could see that not knowing who killed Lee is tearing Maisie apart. She can't take much more uncertainty. As painful as it might be, our daughter-in-law needs to know the truth. I'm hoping there's something in the report that brings us closer to knowing what really happened that afternoon."

Zack wheeled towards me. "We all need to know the truth," he said. "But at the moment, I'm just relieved you and Warren are getting together. I understood why you were angry about what he was doing, but Warren's been a good friend to us."

"Agreed," I said. "He's even sending his driver to pick me up and take me to the Scarth Club for lunch."

Zack chuckled. "And I'll bet Warren suggested that you would enjoy one of the Scarth Club's Old Fashioneds. They really are something else – the bar has been using the same recipe for a hundred and twenty-five years and it's dynamite."

"They knew how to mix drinks back then when men were men and women weren't allowed in the club," I said.

"Point taken," Zack said. "And maybe if women had been allowed in the club back in the day, the food wouldn't still be so lousy."

"Is the food bad?"

"The worst," Zack said. "The chef gets a great cut of beef and cooks it till it's grey. The vegetables taste like they've spent hours on the steam table, which they have, and you can stand a spoon up in the gravy."

"And no one complains?"

Zack shrugged. "It's part of the charm, like the pictures of all the old farts who served as club presidents, and that great motto carved in the mantel over the fireplace in the Portrait Gallery: 'They builded better than they knew.'"

Warren's driver arrived at twelve-thirty on the nose. Warren, tanned and seemingly relaxed, jumped out to greet me. He was well turned out in a vibrant cobalt blazer, white shirt and trousers, and cobalt loafers. As we drove to the club we exchanged pleasantries. Warren was courtly, and after his driver had helped me out of the car, Warren took my arm and escorted me up the front steps and into the bar. We ordered Old Fashioneds, and when they were in hand, Warren asked if he could show me around.

He didn't have to ask twice. After we'd explored the Portrait Gallery and cruised the dining room with its steam table of vegetables, Warren led me across the hall to a room with closed double doors. "This used to be a private dining room," he said, "very charming in my father's time, but it was showing its age, and people had stopped using it." He opened the doors with a theatrical flourish. "They're using it now," he said.

We stepped inside. The room had high ceilings and large windows. The floors were gleaming pine planks, and the dark oak hutch, sideboards, mismatched dining tables, and chairs were in mint condition. "This is absolutely stunning," I said.

"All the furniture came from farm estate auctions," Warren said. "We've had the pieces refinished, of course, but they are old beauties, aren't they?"

I nodded. "Your decorator did a great job."

Warren beamed. "Annie was the decorator. She had help, but she made the decisions."

"Annie has a good eye," I said. The paint on the walls was the colour of clotted cream, and the long feature wall was filled with framed black-and-white photographs.

"All the photographs are of rooms in abandoned Saskatchewan farmhouses," Warren said. "Some of them were taken in the Dirty Thirties." He pointed at a silvery photograph of a kitchen. The oilcloth-covered table was set for a meal. There was a kettle on the woodstove and a Crisco can by the sink. "That Crisco can brings back memories," Warren said. "My mother always kept a Crisco can in the kitchen so she could reuse grease." He laughed. "My father was a millionaire, but my mother lived through the Dust Bowl years, and she knew families who lived in houses like these – hard-working people so beaten down that they just walked away, leaving tables set, laundry drying, and family Bibles open at the Twenty-Third Psalm."

I put on my reading glasses to examine the photos more closely. "These are heartbreaking," I said. "Where did you get them?"

Warren's face lit with pleasure. "Simon," he said. "Photography's his hobby. He scoured the province, unearthed these, and restored them. I don't know what process he used."

"Whatever he did worked," I said. "These photographs look as if they were taken yesterday."

"And restoration isn't my son's only talent," Warren said. "He's an excellent photographer in his own right. Come have a look."

I followed Warren to an alcove off the dining room. More photographs of abandoned farmhouses lined the walls. They, too, were stunning. "These make me think of Walker Evans's work," I said.

Warren sipped his Old Fashioned. "I'll pass that along to Simon. We're having a collector's edition of Simon's photographs hand-bound for the official opening of the private dining room on Saskatchewan Day. Annie and I are hoping that some public acknowledgement of his gifts will rekindle Simon's passion for photography. At any rate, when the collector's edition is ready, I'll make sure you and Zack get a copy."

"We'd appreciate that," I said. "We need to be reminded of our history."

"We do," Warren said. "And Simon came up with a title we all like. We're calling the collection *What's Left Behind*. My son chose the epigraph too. It's from Ansel Adams. 'Not everybody trusts paintings but people believe photographs.'"

"That packs a punch," I said. "Warren, it's so good to learn about this side of Simon," I said. "How is he doing?"

"Not well. The police haven't made a move, but we're all on edge. Simon still doesn't remember anything, and despite our entreaties, he won't go further with the hypnosis. He's taken to driving around aimlessly all day. He has his camera with him, but when Annie or I ask if he's taking pictures, he doesn't answer. Sometimes I wonder if I ever knew my son at all." Warren tried a smile. "But I guess we're all icebergs to one another," he said.

"Maisie and I were talking about that very topic yesterday."

Warren's expression was concerned. "How's she doing?"

"She's coping, but it's not easy."

"Let me know if there's ever anything I can do."

"I will," I said.

"I never make an offer of help I don't mean, Joanne."

"I know that. I promise I'll call on you if the need arises, and, Warren, I want you to know that you can always call on me."

"Thank you," he said. "Now, you must be hungry. Let's go in to lunch."

I had spent thirteen years in a boarding school. Overdone beef, overcooked vegetables, and wallpaper-paste gravy held no terrors for me. I spooned gravy over everything and cleaned my plate. The choices on the dessert menu were straight out of 1970: baked Alaska, a Harvey Wallbanger cake, cherries jubilee, and a chocolate malted milkshake. It was a tough choice, but it had been decades since I'd thought about Harvey. When I tasted the cake's Galliano-vodka-orange glaze, it was 1974 all over again.

Our lunch together had reminded us that we were genuinely fond of each other. When we sat down in the Portrait Gallery to enjoy our coffee, I told Warren that Maisie was paying a high price for her uncertainty about why her sister died and that if he was ready to talk about his investigators' report, I was ready to listen.

Warren's relief was obvious. He touched my hand. "You've taken a load off my mind, Joanne. I'll send you a copy of the investigators' findings and I strongly suggest you hand it along to Maisie. I should tell you at the outset that the report does not provide any dramatic revelations. The best we can hope for is that the details might jog Maisie's memory and point the police in a new and useful direction."

Clearly Warren had read the report thoroughly and frequently. He spoke without notes or hesitation. "From the time she was twenty-two until the time she died at the age of thirty-three, Lee had a number of romantic relationships. The investigators determined that when Lee was in a relationship, she was always monogamous, so we can conclude that over that eleven-year period, she had relationships with ten men. The names of the men and dates indicating the span of their respective affairs with Lee are in the report."

I was taken aback at what seemed to be an unusual omission. "Warren, I find it very difficult to believe that Lee didn't have a sexual relationship until she was twenty-two."

"I questioned that as well," Warren said. "Harries-Crosby are the best in the business, but I was sure they'd missed something, so I asked them to go through Lee's activities during her undergraduate years again. In her program at the College of Agriculture and Bioresources there were four students Lee had known since high school. Apparently, the group studied together, partied together, and even shared a house. They all still live in Saskatchewan, and they were very cooperative with the people from Harries-Crosby. They were devoted to Lee, and they want the person who killed her brought to justice. They all said the same thing: Lee had plenty of friends, but she didn't date. She went home to the farm every Friday as soon as classes were over and drove back to Saskatoon early Monday morning."

"Maybe there was someone back home," I said.

"Not according to her friends," Warren said. "They claim that the five of them discussed everything. Lee was always open about what she'd done on the weekend, and she never mentioned dating anybody. Her university friends are certain there was no man in her life."

"That seems odd for an outgoing young woman like Lee, doesn't it?" I said.

"Yes," Warren agreed. "It does. Perhaps if you show Maisie the report, she'll have something to add."

"I'll talk to Peter, but I'm sure he'll agree that Maisie should see what your investigators came up with."

"Thank you." Warren pulled his chair closer to the table and lowered his voice. "There's something else. Mansell Donnelly came to see me this morning."

"He's had some big changes in his life."

"He has, and I'm glad of it. As you can imagine, Mansell has a great deal on his mind. He needs to talk, but he doesn't know whom to trust. I seem to fit the bill. His late father, Aidan, and I were friends, and I knew Mansell and Bette when they were children."

"They seem very close. Were they always that way?"

"Tight as ticks," Warren said. "Bette used to lead Mansell by the nose."

"And now Quinn leads him by the nose – or did."

Warren nodded. "You're correct in using the past tense, Joanne. That marriage is definitely over."

"I never liked Quinn," I said. "But it is sad when a marriage ends. This referendum is taking a terrible toll."

"It is," Warren agreed. "And that brings me to my final point. This may be nothing, but Mansell told me that Quinn called very early this morning to goad him. She said that Slater Doyle is about to deliver a game-changer that will make Mansell regret he jumped ship."

"I don't suppose Quinn elaborated."

"No, but I think her taunt merits serious attention." Warren sipped his coffee, grimaced, and pushed away his cup. "The coffee here is almost as bad as the food," he said.

"The Old Fashioneds make up for everything," I said and stood. "Thanks for lunch. I had a fine time, but the party's over. It's time to see what Slater Doyle is up to."

As we were waiting for Warren's driver, I called Milo and asked him to meet me at the condo. When we pulled up in front of our place on Halifax Street, Milo's Harley was parked near the building's entrance and Milo himself was sitting on the stoop waiting. It was a pretty day, so I sat beside him and told him about Quinn Donnelly's call to Mansell.

Milo's response was surprisingly explosive. "Well, shit fuck. In my spare time lately, I've been stalking Slater – nothing serious, just playing with his head. Every time he catches me, he mutters about unleashing a master plan. I've ignored him because most of the time he's so stoned he forgets to pee downwind."

"Slater's into pharmaceuticals?" I said.

"Pharmas, street drugs, booze, and questionable dates," Milo said. "Slater has become one wild and crazy guy, but I should have taken him seriously. Even a blind pig finds an acorn once in a while." Milo turned to look at me. His eyes were so dark they were almost black. "Jo, do you have any idea what this could be about?"

I shook my head. "What I have is so nebulous, I don't know if it's even a starting point."

Milo had cut back on the Crispy Crunch bars, but these were desperate times, and he whipped one out and unwrapped it without hesitation. By the time I delivered my précis of the Harries-Crosby report, the bar was gone and Milo had begun drumming on his motorcycle helmet with his long fingers. "You think Quinn and Slater found something incriminating Lee did during those four years?"

"I don't know," I said. "It could be something all together different. Slater has played the slut card ad nauseam, and we continue to pull ahead in the votes."

"So we dismiss Lee as a late bloomer when it came to romance and focus on the political angle."

"Let's split it up," I said. "I have a gut feeling that the motive for Lee's murder was personal. This so-called game-changer is political. Why don't I follow the Lee angle and you keep spooking Slater?"

"Fair enough," Milo said. He stood and started to put on his helmet.

"It's getting hot," I said. "Let's go for a swim before we explore the possibilities."

Milo and I had never swum together alone, and after we completed a few laps, we discovered we swam alike: smooth, straight-armed, deep catch strokes; rhythmical rotations of the core with each stroke; and bilateral breathing – inhales on the right for one length of the pool and on the left for the next length. We swam in perfect cadence, and there was an intimacy in the unison of our movements.

When finally Milo and I pulled ourselves out of the pool and started for the elevator, we were silent. Neither of us wanted to break the invisible bond between us. I showered and changed in my bathroom and Milo used the guest bathroom. As he walked down the hall towards me, dressed again for the outside world, Milo was beaming. "That swim was transcendent," he said.

"It was transcendent for me too." I said. We took our suits to the terrace and hung them on an old wooden drying rack I'd bought at a garage sale; then, still warmed by memory, we picked up our phones and started making calls. My first call was to George Sawchuk, asking him if he had time for a conversation with me about Lee. He did, and Milo and I were on our way out the door when Zack came in, jacket slung over the back of his chair and tie loosened. He looked hot, exhausted, and miserable.

I kissed him hello. "This is a pleasant surprise," I said.

"The air-conditioning in the office quit, I was averaging about thirty calls an hour, and I'd dealt with everything that needed immediate attention. I still have a city council meeting at five-thirty, so I thought you and I might have a swim and I'd make us a gin and tonic."

"I'm sorry," I said. "I wish you'd called. There've been some developments and Milo and I were just going our separate ways to deal with them."

Zack sighed. "My loss," he said. "So what's up?"

I filled him in on the report from Harries-Crosby, underscoring Lee's apparently man-less undergraduate years, and told him that I was meeting George Sawchuk at four-thirty to talk about Lee's life during that time.

Milo said that was he was going to hit the gay bars to see if any pals of Slater's had started the cocktail hour early and were in the mood for a chat. Milo and I were making our second attempt to get out the door when Taylor came home from school.

From the moment they met, Milo and Taylor had clicked,

and that afternoon when she greeted him with a hug as she always had, I was relieved that she had taken me at my word when I said that Milo and I were simply friends.

As it turned out, Milo had news for our daughter. "T, when I was in Calgary last week I saw copies of two of your paintings in Corydon."

Taylor's eyes widened. "How was the placement?"

"Primo," Milo said. "The store has this wicked open winding staircase in the middle of the main floor, and *Blue Boy 21* and *Endangered* are at the head of the stairs. I started to snap some pictures for you, but Corydon's staff are protective of their clientele's privacy."

"Thanks for trying. And thanks for telling me about the great placement. I get a lot of tweets from people ragging at me for selling out because I'm letting my work be used commercially."

Milo put his hands on Taylor's shoulders and looked into her eyes. "Remember what Bob Marley said. 'Flee from hate, mischief, and jealousy.' Taylor, I would never have seen *Blue Boy 21* and *Endangered* if they hadn't been in that store. You're bringing something beautiful into the lives of people like me. Be proud."

As quickly as it came, the moment ended. Milo tossed Taylor a Crispy Crunch and told her it was a token from a patron of the arts. When he left, she offered to walk him to the elevator.

After the door closed behind them, I turned to Zack. "Another side to Milo," I said.

"Corydon is a very cool store," Zack said. "It's also very gay. I wonder what Milo was doing there."

"Buying gotch," I said. "Brock, Milo, and I were hanging around waiting for you last week and Milo asked if either of us knew of a place in Regina that sold Andrew Christian boxer briefs. I didn't, but Brock told Milo that Corydon in Calgary carries Andrew Christan. I guess Milo dropped by."

"A lot goes on around here that I don't know about," Zack said.

I kissed him on the top of his head. "We try to shelter you," I said. "Now I'd better get a move on."

As soon as I parked in the driveway of the Sawchuk farm, George came out, accompanied by two black German shepherds. "You're okay with dogs, aren't you?" George said.

"More than okay," I said. "I've been a dog lover my entire life, and I've never seen a shepherd with an all-black coat. These two are gorgeous."

"They're my boys – Conrad and Cyrus," George said. "Let them get a sniff and they'll wander off."

I held out my palm. As George predicted, after a quick sniff, the boys loped off in search of fresh adventures.

"Come inside where it's cool," George said.

To get to the kitchen we had to pass through the front porch, where a ginger cat was nursing a litter of ginger kittens. I stopped to watch.

"Are you a cat lover as well as a dog lover?" George asked.

"Our daughter, Taylor, is the cat person in our house. She has a tortoiseshell and a combo. She'd love a ginger."

"When these little guys are ready to leave their mother, Taylor can take her pick," George said.

"I'll pass that along," I said.

The Sawchuk kitchen was much like the kitchen in the home where the Crawford twins had grown up: the same 1950s chrome dinette set, the same round-shouldered refrigerator, the same wood stove. A calendar from Weber Farm Machinery, Warren's family's company, hung on a nail beside the old, wall-mounted telephone.

George poured two glasses of lemonade, put six Peek Freans Digestive Biscuits on a plate that had been placed between us on the table, ripped off two paper towels for napkins, and then disappeared down the hall. He returned with a framed eight-by-ten photograph of himself with Colin Brokenshire and Mansell Donnelly that he laid on the table in front of me. The photo in Lee's office had captured the exuberance of three adolescent boys eager to grab everything the shining world had to offer. In this photo, the men were middle-aged, hair greying or thinning, flesh sagging slightly, eyes wary with the knowledge that everything the world offers comes with a price tag, but their smiles were unforced.

George pulled his chair close so we could look at the photograph together. For a few moments he was silent. Finally, he shook his head as if to bring himself back to the present. When I'd called George earlier, I told him how important it was to discover if Lee had any men in her life when she was doing her first university degree, but from the beginning George's conversation veered off in a direction that seemed only tangentially relevant.

"Colin, Mansell, and I met in kindergarten," he began. "And we were best friends until the day Colin died. After that – well, you saw in the cafeteria how things are between Mansell and me."

"Do you have any idea why he turned against you?"

"At first I thought he felt guilty about the accident, but I never blamed him – how could I? In a way, Colin's death was the end of Mansell's life – at least the end of the life he wanted. Farming was in his blood, but after Colin died, Mansell handed over responsibility for the farm to Bette, moved to Regina, and got involved with commercial and rural real estate. He hated that work. I could see it in his face. And he broke off with the woman he'd been with for years – a really fine woman, a teacher who wanted the same things from life he did. I knew he was punishing himself.

"And we were all suffering. My marriage broke up. I started having panic attacks when I was around other people. My ex-wife told me it was survivor guilt, but whatever the cause, the attacks were debilitating. It was months before I could leave the farm."

"But you're doing all right now?"

"Some days are better than others," he said simply.

I looked again at the picture. "So much pain for all of you," I said.

George stared at the photograph. "At least Colin died happy. I'll always be grateful for that."

"It must have made him happy to know the twins' lives were on the right path," I said. "They'd both finished their undergraduate degrees. Maisie was starting at the College of Law and from what Peter tells me she never had a shortage of suitors. Lee had obviously found her passion in agriculture. Had she found the right man to share her passion with?"

I waited, but George didn't reply. Instead he picked up my glass. "Refill?" he asked.

When I shook my head, he took the empty glasses to the sink. "So now you know our history," he said.

"Not all of it," I said. "Was there a man in Lee's life?"

George turned and his eyes met mine. "Joanne, let Lee take some parts of her history with her," he said. "Let her rest in peace."

I headed home burdened with shards of information I couldn't fit together and questions I couldn't answer. Why did George avoid talking about Lee's past? Why had Mansell shut George out and broken his heart and his health? Why had Mansell punished himself for eleven years for an accident? As I waited for the condo parking gate to lift, I remembered an exchange between Alice and the White Rabbit in *Alice in Wonderland.* Alice asks the White Rabbit, "How long is forever?" He replies, "Sometimes, just one second."

On a hot September night, Mansell Donnelly had momentarily lost his focus and the lives of everyone close to him had been changed forever. I drove into the darkness of the parkade wondering if Mansell had ever read *Alice in Wonderland*, and, if he had, whether the White Rabbit's response to Alice's question had haunted him as I knew it would haunt me.

CHAPTER

14

The next morning I was watering the flowers on our terrace when Milo called. "Nothing to report from the gay bar scene. I had to hang around for a few hours till the crowds picked up, but I met some nice guys. Everybody knows Slater, and the ones who know him best are worried. Apparently he's indulging in the drugs, booze, and risky sex to stave off his desperation. When he's high, he's euphoric, king of the world, babbling on about his secret plan to decimate our vote – no specifics, of course. When he comes down, he's so depressed some of his acquaintances fear he's suicidal. A few of the men I talked to said Michael Goetz is the only one who might be able to get through to Slater, but Michael's not part of the bar scene and nobody I spoke to knows him well enough to approach him."

"Brock and Michael are still close," I said. "Maybe Brock can encourage Michael to make an intervention. We've already taken the dogs for their run, but I might be able to catch Brock before he goes to work."

"Text me."

"I will," I said.

The suits Milo and I swam in were still on the wood drying rack. I took them off and was smoothing them just as Zack came through the terrace door. "Everything okay?" he said.

"As okay as it ever is these days," I said. "I'm going downstairs to see if I can catch Brock before he goes to Racette-Hunter."

Zack eyed the bathing suits. "Looks like you got your swim in yesterday after all," he said.

"Milo and I did some laps before you came home yesterday afternoon. If I'd known you were coming, I'd have waited."

The corners of Zack's mouth tightened. "Would you?" he said, and then he turned his chair and rolled inside.

Zack was on the phone when I went back in. I leaned over, whispered, "I'll be right back," and headed for Brock's. When the elevator doors opened at his floor, he was waiting. We both laughed. "Just in the nick of time," he said. "What's up?"

"Milo hit the gay bars yesterday and a lot of men are concerned about Slater's determination to crash and burn. Brock, I don't care what Slater does to himself, but Bridie's part of the equation. No one wants to see her hurt."

"Of course not."

"Any chance you could talk to Michael this morning?"

"He's in Saskatoon."

"When's he coming back?"

"I'm not sure, but it won't be long. He wouldn't have gone at all, but he has a meeting with the College of Physicians and Surgeons."

"He's trying to get back his licence to practise psychiatry?"

"Yes, so it's important. But Michael asked me to drop by his house after work. He's anxious about leaving Bridie alone with Slater."

"Surely, Bridie is safe with her own father. I saw them together during the campaign. He seemed devoted to her."

"That's my feeling too, but Michael's closer to the situation than we are. He was concerned enough to call Bridie's former nanny to see if she'd reconsider her resignation. It turns out Zenaya didn't resign. Slater fired her."

"Why would Slater lie about that?"

Brock shrugged. "Who knows? Anyway, it's a moot point. Zenaya refused to come back. She said that although she's very fond of Bridie, she's afraid of Slater and she's uncomfortable being around him."

"Milo says Slater's using," I said.

"Milo's right," Brock said. "Slater is using everything and everybody. He's self-medicating, and he's using Bridie to keep Michael in the marriage because he's terrified of being alone and he knows Michael won't leave their daughter. It's a lousy situation."

"One more thing to worry about," I said.

"Why don't you let me worry about this one?" Brock said. "You've been carrying too many burdens for too long. Give yourself a day off."

"Sold," I said. "Let me know if you're able to get in touch with Michael."

Busying myself with the tasks of daily life has always been my antidote for fretting. My to-do list was always robust and that morning I didn't have to look beyond the first item. Mieka was bringing Madeleine and Lena by after school for a swim. Over the winter the girls had both grown like the fabled weeds, and they needed new bathing suits. So did Mieka, who seldom bought anything for herself but was gracious about accepting a gift.

I hate shopping, but I found exactly what I wanted at reasonable prices within an hour, and I celebrated by coming home and making Madeleine and Lena's favourite – snicker-doodles. Milo had texted only to say he would come by later to report the latest numbers. He arrived at three-thirty, and the news was good. Our base was holding and we were picking up support from people who self-identified as likely to vote on Referendum Day. I knew Zack could use a shot of optimism and I was anxious to repair the rift between us. When Milo agreed to stick around and give the girls a diving lesson, I texted Zack to come home and join us so he could get an account of the numbers and see that Milo was simply part of a larger picture that included us all.

The weather had continued glorious. It was Goldilocks weather – not too cold, not too hot – just right. Mieka and the girls were enthusiastic about their new suits, and as Mieka, Zack, and I watched Milo show the girls how make a clean, graceful entry into the water, we were relaxed and happy. Seemingly summer was once again working her languorous magic. When I spotted Brock walking across the grass towards us, I called out. "Just in time for the lesson," I said. "Pull up a lazy lounge."

Brock didn't respond. When he came closer, I saw that he had the five-mile stare of a man in shock. "I just had a call from Michael," he said. "Bridie's missing."

My mind raced. "Missing," I said. "Is Michael sure? She could be at a friend's."

"Bridie doesn't have any friends," Brock said.

Mieka's eyes were wide with fear. "How long has Bridie been gone?"

"I don't know," Brock said. "Slater had a party last night, and he was hung over today. Bridie was playing in the backyard, and Slater went back to bed to sleep it off. When Slater checked the yard again, Bridie was gone. Slater searched the neighbourhood and then called Michael in Saskatoon. As soon as Michael heard about Bridie, he drove back to Regina."

Zack's voice was acid. "But Slater *had* called the police," he said.

Brock hesitated. "No. Michael called them when he got back to the house."

"What the hell?" Zack said. "It takes two and a half hours to drive from Saskatoon to Regina. Counting the time Slater was supposedly searching the neighbourhood, by the time the cops were called, Bridie would have been missing for at the very least three hours."

Mieka was pale. "Let me take the girls upstairs to change. They're through their lesson, and you need to be able to talk to Milo."

My daughter and I took towels to the swimmers, and after Mieka shepherded Madeleine and Lena inside, I told Milo about the abduction.

He dried off his hair, wrapped the towel around his waist, and levelled his gaze at me. "So Slater was so deep into street drugs and street boys, he forgot he had a daughter," he said. His black eyes were piercing. "How could anyone with a heart do that, Joanne?"

"I don't know," I said. As Milo and I walked across the lawn, the memory of Bridie's delicately boned hand in mine the night of Margot's party overwhelmed me and I stumbled. Milo took my arm. "I'm here," he said. And for the time being that was enough.

When we joined them, Zack and Brock were still trying to sort through the facts as we knew them. I could feel Zack's frustration. "None of this makes sense," he said. "Why didn't Slater call the police as soon as he realized that Bridie was missing?"

"Michael said Slater thought he needed to clean up the house before the police came," Brock said.

Zack's voice was coldly furious. "I'm not grasping the sequence here," he said. "Slater's a bottom-feeder, but he's not an idiot. He knows that if a child is abducted every minute counts."

"Slater said the party got out of hand," Brock said. "There were a lot of empty bottles and there was drug paraphernalia."

I had seldom seen Zack so angry. "Jesus Christ. Slater used to be a lawyer," he said. "He must have known that he was destroying evidence that might help the authorities find his daughter." He wheeled closer to Brock. "I'm assuming that by now Michael has told the cops everything."

Brock shook his head. "Slater's pleading with Michael not to tell them about the partying. He says that they're married and that Michael owes him loyalty."

Zack snorted with disgust. "A child's life is at stake," he said. "Michael owes Slater fuck all."

"Zack's right," Milo said. "The men I talked to at the bars said that these days Slater's reduced to bringing home dregs. Michael's a wealthy man. Someone at Slater's party last night might have decided that they could get a lot of money for Bridie."

Feeling helpless and impotent, the four of us went up to our condo to wait for news. It wasn't long in coming. We'd just settled in when Michael texted Brock to tell him the police had arrived to interview Slater, and that Michael was going to make certain Slater told the truth. Twenty minutes later Michael texted again to say that Slater had given the police the full story.

Zack's mouth curled in disgust. "I'll bet the cops had Doyle twisting in the wind. I wish I'd been there."

Michael was climbing the walls, and Brock had agreed to meet him for a drink. After Brock left, I went into the kitchen to start dinner. There was a note from Taylor on the butcher-block table. "At my studio. Put something from freezer in oven for dinner. Couldn't tell what it was. Might be chicken."

Zack and I exchanged smiles. "Life's a crapshoot," he said. "Let's have a drink to celebrate the fact that we might be having chicken for dinner."

I invited Milo to stay but, as always, he had places to go and people to see. Milo's inner life was, in Churchill's famous phrase, a riddle wrapped in a mystery inside an enigma, so I never pressed. I set the table and Zack and I took our martinis out on the terrace. We'd taken one sip when Zack's cell rang. He listened, said, "See you in a few minutes," and broke the connection. "That was Debbie Haczkewicz," he said, opening his tablet. "She called to let me know the police have received information about Bridie Doyle."

Zack's expression was grim, and he handed his tablet to me without further comment. A photo of Bridie filled the screen. She was sitting on an old and rough-hewn child's rocking horse. The wallpaper behind her had a pattern of pink cabbage roses. It was faded and, in one place, torn. Bridie was wearing purple jeans and a T-shirt in bubblegum pink, the favoured shade of very young girls. She was clean, and her wavy white-blond hair had been brushed and fastened neatly by pink butterfly barrettes, but her small face was pinched with terror. The photograph was labelled "An Eye for an Eye."

Panic washed over me. "So kidnapping Bridie is retribution," I said. "But by whom and for what?"

"I don't know," Zack said. "Some of the mourners at the vigil for Lee carried signs with that slogan. And we saw some real whack jobs outside the church after Lee's funeral."

"The night Bridie came up to the roof garden for Margot's birthday party, she told me she was shy," I said. "I told her she'd be fine because she had friends at the party. She added up the number of people she knew on the roof: Madeleine, Lena, Mieka, Brock, and me. She asked if five was enough to keep her from being scared. I said five would be enough." My voice broke. "Zack, wherever she is now, Bridie doesn't know anybody. She's absolutely alone except for the person who abducted her."

Zack set down his drink and held out his arms to me. "Debbie's on her way over. We're going to pull out all the stops to find Bridie, and we *will* find her, Jo. Count on it."

I finished my drink, went into the bathroom, washed my face, and freshened my lipstick. Then I checked the casserole. It did indeed appear to be chicken.

Police Chief Debbie Haczkewicz and Zack went way back. Like lions and buffalo, cops and trial lawyers are natural adversaries, but Debbie and Zack had a bond. When Debbie's son, Leo, was in his late teens he was in a motorcycle accident that left him paralyzed from the waist down. Leo isolated himself in his misery and was bitter and abusive to anyone who offered help. Fearful that her son would take his own life, Debbie called Zack. After a month of battles that often ended in physical blows, Leo realized that Zack wasn't going anywhere, and he began to listen. At Zack's urging, Leo went back to school, earned a degree in teaching English as a Second Language, and moved to Japan, where he met Miyoshi, the woman who became his wife and the mother of his son. Debbie credited Zack for the happy outcome.

For years, Debbie had been head of Major Crimes. Zack had seen her in action, and he liked and respected her. Shortly after Zack was sworn in as mayor, the position of chief of police came open. The city hired a consulting firm to recruit nationally for candidates, and Debbie applied. She was experienced; she understood the community; she had been active in the police union; and she was dogged.

As mayor, Zack chaired the board of police commissioners; when the board chose Debbie, Zack was publicly pleased and privately jubilant. He knew he and Debbie could work well together.

As I took Debbie's jacket, I could feel her tension. Zack and Debbie needed to take control of the situation immediately, Bridie Doyle's photograph with the chilling message "An Eye for an Eye" was likely to create a groundswell of hysteria in our city. The stakes were high, and after Debbie joined us on the terrace, she and Zack got right to business.

When I started to leave, they both beckoned me to stay. I didn't hesitate. Bridie needed all the help she could get. Zack deferred to Debbie. "So where does the investigation stand?"

"We have dozens of officers combing the city and surrounding areas. Our public information officer issued a statement to the media telling them what we know and showing the picture of Bridie on the rocking horse. The officer encouraged anyone with information to contact the Regina police or Crime Stoppers." Debbie's voice was wearily resigned. "We're nowhere. Slater Doyle is the key. I sat in on the interview with him. He loves his daughter and he's terrified for her. During the interview his whole body was shaking. That kind of physical reaction can't be faked. Doyle said he would do anything to get his daughter back."

I picked up on the note of doubt in her voice. "But you didn't believe him," I said.

Debbie nodded. "He's holding something back. I've been racking my brain trying to pinpoint the moment when I sensed Doyle had omitted a key piece of information. He gave every appearance of a man who was being absolutely open. He answered every question without hesitation, and he revealed details without being pressed. But I've been a cop for over thirty years, and I know there's something Doyle isn't telling us."

"Do you think he's protecting somebody?" Zack said.

Debbie shrugged. "Why would he sacrifice his daughter, the person he loves most in this world, to save someone else?"

"It's possible that Bridie isn't the person Slater loves most in this world," I said. "He could be covering for someone who was at the party."

"Doyle claims the relationships he had with the men at the party were casual," Debbie said. "There were eight of them. We were able to track them all down and they back up Doyle's story that for them Doyle was just a rich guy with a big house who promised them booze, cocaine, and a place to connect."

"That fits in with the assessment of Slater's behaviour made by the men Milo spoke to in the bars," I said. "They say he's desperate and his use of alcohol and drugs has been reckless."

Zack made no effort to hide his disdain. "And Doyle was so set on destroying himself that he brought strangers into the house where his daughter was sleeping," he said. "It's possible somebody at the party learned that Bridie lived there and realized that, somewhere down the line, she could be useful."

"I don't think so," Debbie said. "They're not poster boys for healthy living, but they all have solid alibis for their whereabouts this morning."

"So we're back to the scenario where a stranger just happened to stroll by the backyard while Slater just happened to be passed out, and the stranger abducted Bridie," Zack said. He turned to Debbie. "I'm assuming the yard is fenced?"

"Yes," Debbie said. "Two-metre-high redwood fence around the perimeter of the yard. Two lattice-top redwood gates: one opens onto the back alley and the other opens onto the lawn leading to the street. The house is on a corner lot. Both gates have keyless combination locks. The gate to the alley was locked. The gate to the street was wide open."

"Doesn't add up, does it?" Zack said. "I guess one of the guests could have left the gate open when he left."

"They all swear they came in through the front door, stayed in the house till the party was over, and left through the front door."

"So that leaves Slater," I said. "I've seen him with Bridie. Slater's a rat, but he loves that child. He'd never purposely leave that gate unlocked."

"He would if he knew she wouldn't be harmed," Debbie said.

Her words, heavy with unthinkable possibilities, hung in the air between us.

Finally, I broke the silence. "Debbie, do you really think this is a sham."

"It's possible," Debbie said. "I know that Slater works for Lancaster. They have a nasty track record, and their referendum agenda has been suffering since Lee Crawford's murder."

"So Lancaster might be behind this?" Zack said. "Their support has been hemorrhaging since the funeral. If they can spin Bridie's kidnapping to make it seem as if the kidnapper abducted Bridie as retribution for Lee's murder, it will stanch the flow."

"An eye for an eye," I said. "My God, what kind of people are we turning into?"

Zack was grim. "Desperate people, and I don't get it. There are valid arguments on both sides of the new bylaws issue. Whoever wins, there'll be a compromise. The world will not come to an end."

"Reasonable people have probably figured that out," Debbie said dryly. "But there are extremists on both sides of the debate, and despite my theory about Doyle, we have to look hard at all of them. Can either of you identify one of your supporters who might have done this?"

"That's my bailiwick," I said. "Zack made his position on the bylaws clear, but he hasn't been involved in the day-to-day strategies for the referendum. I've been working on tactics with Zack's executive assistant, Norine MacDonald, and our political strategist, Milo O'Brien. I'll call them and see if they can meet us here after dinner and come up with some names."

"I'd appreciate that," Debbie said. "In the meantime, Zack, you and I have to figure out how to keep a lid on this situation. Any possibility we could get together after Jo's meeting?"

"Why don't you stay for supper?" I said. "We're having a casserole of something that might or might not be chicken, but I'm going to put some panko and grated cheese on top, so it should be okay."

Debbie smiled. "Best invitation I've had all week," she said. "I've been living on takeout."

After supper we cleared away the dishes, Taylor went to her room to do homework; Zack and Debbie went to the study; and Milo, Norine, and I went into the living room to deal with the depressing possibility that one of our supporters was holding a five-year-old child captive.

The task would have been daunting if it hadn't been for Milo. The alliance of groups in favour of the legislation was a loose one and our numbers had been steadily growing. During the university term, we'd had a number of student supporters: some were idealistic and committed; some were just troublemakers. From the outset Milo had insisted we keep a close eye on our allies. Political movements attract all kinds of people, including those Milo referred to as the bat-shit crazies. To win the referendum we had to control

the message and that meant keeping an eye out for supporters who might have slipped a gear.

Norine, Milo, and I had shared many light-hearted
moments, but that night we were sombre. As we assessed
our most ardent allies, I felt like Judas Iscariot, but the
image of Bridie spurred us on. We all clung to the hope that
Bridie's kidnapper was an extremist whom none of us knew.
Nonetheless, by the end of our meeting we'd red-flagged ten
people who, while perhaps not directly involved themselves,
might be able to identify the person who was.

Piper Edwards was vivacious and persuasive. It was easy
to imagine her convincing a five-year-old to get in the car
with her so they could go on a great adventure. There was
no logical reason for Piper to be involved in Bridie's kidnapping, but I remembered how vicious she had been at the CPG
meeting so I left her name on the list.

When I described the hothead student who'd attacked
George Sawchuk at the CPG meeting at Lee's the day she
was killed, Milo had no trouble identifying him. His name
was Brendan Beverage, and in my career as an academic in
our university's political science department, I had met and
failed many students like him – so certain that they were
right that they refused to listen to counter-arguments, so
busy with protests that they failed to come to class or hand
in assignments. Already on the list, his name moved up a
number of notches. I didn't know the name of the woman
at the farmers' market who believed humans are just travellers on this earth; however, the knife edge in her voice as
she quoted the five-word principle of Babylonian law after
Lee's funeral suggested she was well worth tracking down.
Her waist-length silvery hair and flowing skirts made her
seem charming, and I could imagine Bridie taking her hand
and being led to a place where the woman could mete out
a punishment commensurate with Lee Crawford's murder.

Coming up with a list of people capable of abducting a five-year-old child had been depressing work, but it kept my mind from the horror of imagining what was happening to Bridie. The idea of hands touching her, violating her, made my stomach turn. And as we readied ourselves for bed, Zack watched me with concern.

When I slid into bed beside him and we kissed goodnight, Zack felt the stress in my body. "Do you want me to call Henry Chan," he said. "There's a drugstore on Broad that delivers. Henry could prescribe something that will help you sleep."

"I'm not sure I want to sleep," I said. "I'm afraid of what I might dream."

"Why don't we go for a swim?"

"You're kidding," I said. "We're already in bed."

"But you're not going to sleep, and that means I'm not going to sleep. Swimming always relaxes you. Let's give it a shot."

We swam for half an hour. As I moved through the water I could feel my muscles unknot. When my kids were little they called the loose-limbed fatigue they felt after a day of sports being "good tired." That night when I climbed out of the pool, I was "good tired," and Zack and I both slept deeply and well.

The next morning at seven, Debbie and Zack had a press briefing in the mayor's office. Taylor was still sleeping, so just Brock and I watched from the kitchen table as we ate breakfast after our run. Zack began the briefing by greeting everybody and introducing Debbie, and then the cameras zoomed in on the photograph of Bridie on the rocking horse. The image of the little girl with the white-blond, wavy hair and the terrified blue eyes had burned itself into my consciousness, but Debbie was pointing to the possible significance of details in the room where Bridie was being kept. The fact that the floral wallpaper was faded and ripped in places suggested that the room was in a house no longer in use. Debbie asked for citizen cooperation. Anyone who lived close to or knew of an abandoned house or building was asked to check it out thoroughly for evidence of occupancy.

The task would not be easy. The lower third of Saskatchewan was once almost wholly agricultural. As mega-agricultural conglomerates swallowed up family farms, people moved to town. Simon Weber's haunting photographs had revealed his intimate knowledge of the abandoned farmhouses and outbuildings near our city. He was still the prime suspect in Lee's murder. The night before, feeling like a traitor, I'd told Debbie about Simon's photographs and watched as she drew a line around his name, already at the top of her interview list.

Debbie showed photos of Bridie in happier situations. Even when she was preparing to blow out the candles on her birthday cake, there was a sadness about the little girl that wrenched my heart. Debbie asked people to study the pictures and remember if they'd seen a child who resembled Bridie within the last twenty-four hours. The police were going through security tapes of convenience stores and gas stations, but they were relying heavily on citizens reporting anything that seemed suspicious. The contact information for Crime Stoppers flashed on screen and Debbie urged people to use it.

Zack's statement was short and to the point. He told people not to give in to hysteria or fear but to be vigilant in keeping an eye on their own children and in searching for signs of Bridie Doyle. He finished by saying that the Regina Police Service was doing everything in its power to bring Bridie Doyle's abductor to justice, and he was confident that it was only a matter of time before the guilty parties would be in custody.

When the briefing was over, Brock turned to me. "Did you notice that Zack didn't promise Bridie would be returned to her home safely?" he said.

"I noticed," I said. "Every time I think about what that child is going through, I want to weep."

"So do I," Brock said.

"Has Michael mentioned how the 'father of the year' is doing?" I said.

Brock snorted derisively. "No, and I haven't asked." Brock flexed his hands. "I'm glad we have a justice system, Joanne. Because if we didn't, right now I'd be hunting down Slater Doyle, and when I found him I'd tear him limb from limb."

I spent the rest of the morning doing errands that had fallen by the wayside in the past week: talking to liaisons from the member groups of CPG about their strategies for getting out the vote; grocery shopping; picking up dry cleaning and food for the dogs and Taylor's cats; and choosing bedding plants for the remaining empty pots on our terrace. I'd finished putting everything where it belonged when Zack called.

"I just wanted to hear your voice," he said.

"Is it that bad?" I said.

"Worse," he said. "The city's going nuts – the traffic on Crime Stoppers is unbelievable."

"Anything useful?"

"Nah – just further proof, if we needed it, that there are a lot of very disturbed people out there."

"You sound like a boxer on the ropes," I said. "Let's go to bed early tonight. We'll have two fingers of Old Pulteney, and you can paint my toenails."

"Finally, something to look forward to," Zack said. "Do you still have some of that sexy Petal to the Metal polish?"

"I keep three bottles stashed away in case of an emergency," I said.

Zack chuckled. "This qualifies," he said. "I'll be home as soon as I can sneak out the door."

I had arranged with Mieka to pick the girls up from school that afternoon. As I sat in my Volvo in the parking lot of École St. Pius X, the firestorm that had started with the announcement of the referendum and engulfed so many lives seemed remote. The day was sunny and breezy – shorts and T-shirt weather – and the playground was filled with pretty stay-at-home mums with their preschoolers, toddlers, or babes in arms. Some of the braver kids were trying out the playground equipment. Next year many of them would be in kindergarten. Pius X was a good school, and with luck, the new kindergarteners would be students there for the next nine years.

When the school bell rang, the doors shot open and the kids streamed out. As always, Madeleine came out with friends from her grade, and they stood talking as they waited for siblings. Also as always, Lena was among the last children to come out of the school. Mieka had called to tell the girls' teachers that I was picking them up, so they came straight to the Volvo.

As we drove down Albert Street, our granddaughters were uncharacteristically restrained. They were eighteen months apart, and Mieka always called them her Irish twins. I assumed the peace in the car was just a sign that the Irish twins were growing up. When we got to the condo, Lena grated pepper-jack cheese so that the three of us could have our favourite snack, Triscuit nachos. As soon as the nachos were ready, I poured us all iced tea and we sat down at the kitchen table. When the silence continued, I knew there was a problem.

"Did something happen at school today?" I said.

Madeleine nodded. "Just before we got out of school there was a special assembly in the gym," she said.

"Monsieur St. Amand told everyone about Bridie being kid-napped. He told us we had to be especially careful and that if we saw or heard anything that might help the police find Bridie we should tell an adult."

"That's good advice," I said.

The girls exchanged glances. "Maddy and I know some-thing that might help the police," Lena said. "But we aren't supposed to tell."

I waited. Finally Madeleine said, "Bridie told us that her mother was going to send someone to bring Bridie to her for a visit."

"That's not possible," I said. "Bridie's mother is dead."

Madeleine's face was grave. "We knew that, but Bridie was so excited about seeing her mother again we didn't say anything."

"Bridie's very young," I said. "Her story may just be about something she wished would happen."

Lena's headshake was vehement. "Bridie didn't make up the story. Her father told her that someone was going to come and take her for a visit with her mother. He told her it wouldn't be anybody she knew, but the person was a friend of her mother's, and Bridie would be safe."

I felt a chill. "Did Bridie say if the person coming to get her was a man or a woman?"

The gravity of the situation had struck Madeleine. Her answer was halting. "No," she said. "Just that she was sup-posed to go with whoever came for her."

The girls had a jigsaw puzzle set up in the family room. I sent them in to work on it and called Mieka. Then I called Debbie Haczkewicz. Mieka and Debbie came up in the same elevator. I met them at the door, told them Bridie's story, and then we went into the family room. Debbie talked to the girls separately and together. When she was finished,

I walked her to the elevator. She was angry but controlled. "I knew Slater Doyle was holding something back," she said. "Jo, do you have any idea why he would do this?"

"Because Slater Doyle is out of control and desperate," I said. "Lancaster Development is giving him one last chance. If he doesn't win the referendum for them, Lancaster will throw Slater Doyle to the wolves."

"So Doyle throws his daughter to the wolves to save his job." Debbie spit out the words. "There has to be a special place in hell for a father who would do that. He'll pay for this, Joanne. He'll pay for terrifying his child, and he'll pay for lying to the police."

Our family and Margot's family have small tables for deliveries outside our front doors. When I came back from walking Debbie to the elevator, I noticed a package on our table. It was from the photographer who'd taken the formal pictures at Peter and Maisie's wedding and it was addressed to them in care of us. On the day of the wedding, I'd been intrigued by the skill with which the photographer captured private moments. Now the wedding pictures had arrived, and I couldn't bring myself to look at them. I took the package inside, left it unopened on the sideboard, and went into the family room to check on Mieka and the girls. The puzzle of Aslan talking to Lucy was coming along well. We left the girls perusing the remaining pieces, and Mieka and I went into the living room.

My daughter looked terrible, exhausted, and edgy. "Ever since I heard about Bridie I've been beside myself," she said. "Whenever I think about her . . . " Mieka's sentence trailed off.

"I know," I said. "She's such a vulnerable child."

"They're all vulnerable," Mieka said fiercely. "That's what's driving me crazy. I opened the UpSlideDown play centres because I love kids. I wanted a place where they could be safe and happy and explore new things. I can't stop thinking about the children I know – not just Madeleine and Lena – but all the kids who come through the doors at UpSlideDown and UpSlideDown2." She chewed her lip, always a sign that she was anxious. "No matter what we do, we can't keep them safe, Mum."

I put my arms around her. "Why don't I take the girls to the lake tomorrow after school. We can stay till Monday morning. Give us all a chance to catch our breath."

"The girls need that," Mieka said. "They were whispering half the night, and this morning when I went to awaken them, Lena had crawled into bed with Maddy. She hasn't done that in years. As soon as I close UpSlideDown on Saturday, I'll join you at the lake."

I gave her a final squeeze. "To quote Zack, 'Finally, something to look forward to.'"

That night after we'd eaten, Zack and I took our tea out to the terrace. The evening was muggy and overcast. This was the time when we exchanged news of the day. Often our talk would be punctuated with laughter or mock groans at the weirdness of the world, but that night we were content just to sit in the gloaming and drink our Earl Grey. When Zack's phone rang, I said, "Don't answer it. We need time to lick our wounds, and I've already got the bottle of Petal to the Metal on my bedside table."

Zack gave me a quick grin and checked the caller ID. "It's Debbie," he said. After he'd spoken to her, he shook his head. "Slater denies everything. He says Bridie's five years old, and she often has trouble distinguishing between reality and her fantasies about what she wishes would happen."

"So Bridie's hell continues," I said.

"Yeah," Zack said. "But so does Slater's. Debbie said Slater seemed genuinely stunned when the cop in charge of the investigation confronted him with Bridie's story about the friendly stranger who was going to take her to her mother. Apparently, Slater's sweating bullets, and the cops have no intention of letting up on him. They don't buy his story, and they're going to keep hammering at Doyle till they break him."

"Good," I said. "But meanwhile Bridie's somewhere frightened and alone. Zack, I can't stop thinking about how her hand felt in mine."

Zack wheeled closer and rubbed my leg. "I noticed the unopened package of wedding photos on the sideboard when I came in. The pummelling never quits, does it?"

"No," I said. "But we can't let ourselves be overwhelmed. There's too much at stake. We have to believe that Bridie will be found, and she'll be found safe. I'm certain Slater is complicit in this, but he wouldn't let anything happen to his daughter. The problem at the moment seems to be that Slater has painted himself into a corner. He needs an exit strategy."

"Let's hope he finds one. In the meantime, let's have a long, hot shower together, and I'll give you that pedicure."

CHAPTER

15

The next morning as I dressed for my run, Zack was in the shower singing the old Johnny Cash song "I Walk the Line," clearly steeling himself for whatever came next. I was determined to be ready too. After we'd exchanged rings on our wedding day, Zack drew me to him and whispered, "This is forever. A deal's a deal." As far as I was concerned, the crisis with Slater Doyle was part of the deal, and I was determined to get us through.

The dogs and I met Brock on the stoop of our condo. The day was overcast but breezy – a good day for a run. Brock and I seldom talked when we ran, but that morning after Brock made a fuss of the dogs and took Pantera's leash, he didn't start running. "Michael called a few minutes ago," he said. "Slater Doyle's interrogation by the police did not go well. Michael is certain that Slater is lying when he denies telling Bridie someone was coming to take her to her mother."

"What's Michael going to do?"

"You've seen him with Bridie. He loves her. Michael is through with Slater, but he's convinced that staying with Slater is his best chance of finding out where Bridie is.

Quinn Donnelly is keeping a close eye on how Slater fares with the police. Michael is hoping that Slater will fall apart in the next interrogation, and Lancaster will cut him loose."

"And then Slater will turn to Michael," I said.

"Yes and then, if the stars are aligned, Michael will be able to lead us to Bridie."

As we began our run, the bands that had tightened around my chest when Brock told us that Bridie had been abducted began to loosen. Suddenly it seemed possible that Bridie would come home safely. Without realizing what I was doing, I repeated the last line of Ernest's prayer out loud. "'Hoping that will happen,'" I said.

Brock smiled. "Ptane ekosi teyihki," he said. "Might as well say it in Cree too, Joanne. Just in case the Creator doesn't speak English."

When I came in, Zack had the dogs' water dishes filled and a glass of water on the counter for me. I took a deep sip. "So what's going on around here?" I asked.

Zack handed me his tablet. "The police received a new picture of Bridie this morning and Debbie sent it to me. Check it out – same caption, different setting." Bridie was in an old farm kitchen that had faded gingham curtains hanging on the window and a coal-oil lamp at the centre of a table. A wooden highchair was drawn up to the table. She was clean. Her hair was neatly combed; her barettes were in place, but there was a large bandage on her arm and her eyes were puffy from crying.

"I think the Creator heard us," I said.

Zack shot me a questioning glance.

"I think this picture might be an answered prayer. Who else has seen it?"

"Debbie just sent it a few minutes ago. I imagine she's sitting on it till she figures out what to do."

I looked at the picture again. "Zack, have the police looked at Simon Weber's photographs? Because they should. The houses in both photographs of Bridie are very much like the ones in the photos Simon took that are in the new private dining room at the Scarth Club. I don't know if this is one of them. And I don't know enough about photography to explain why I'm making the connection. I just think the police should look at Simon's photos."

Zack leaned forward. "Jo, you don't believe Simon abducted Bridie, do you?"

"No, not for a single moment. But if he can identify the building where Bridie's being held, the police might have a chance to rescue her."

"I'll call Debbie."

"Good, but when you do, could you ask her to give me an hour before she makes the photo public? I'm going to take this to Slater Doyle."

"You're kidding."

"No, I'm not. Look at that child's face. Enough is enough."

Zack turned his chair towards the door. "I'm coming with you."

"If you come, Slater will start bleating about how you're using the power of the mayor's office to coerce him."

Zack shook his head. "I don't think you should go alone."

"This is no big deal," I said. "I'm just showing a father a picture of his daughter and asking him to do the right thing."

I called Brock, told him my plan, and asked him to find out where Slater was. He got back to me almost immediately. Slater was still at home, and he was still in bed.

"I'll get there before he brushes his teeth. Put him at a disadvantage."

Brock seemed taken aback. "You're really loaded for bear, aren't you?"

"When you see that picture of Bridie, you'll understand," I said. "I have to shower and change. Could you call Michael and tell him I'll be leaving here in fifteen minutes tops? He should probably just let me in, then make himself scarce."

Michael's home was a large split-level in an older, carefully landscaped neighbourhood near the university.

Michael met me at the door with a question. "I'm not sure about this," he said. "Slater is unstable. Who knows what might happen if you confront him."

My heart was pounding, but my voice was assured. "You'll be standing right here with your phone. Slater will be half asleep and hung over. We have to do this." I showed Michael the photo of his daughter. He closed his eyes against the image and stood aside to let me in.

"Where's Slater?"

"Still in bed."

I followed Michael down the hall. He opened a door and I stepped inside. The drapes were drawn and the room was shadowy. Michael called out, "You have a visitor."

Slater's voice was heavy with sleep. "Too early," he said.

"It's after nine," I said.

As soon as he heard my voice, Slater sat bolt upright. "What the hell's going on?" he said.

"An ambush," I said. "Slater, no more games. Find your glasses. The police received a new picture of Bridie this morning."

Slater wasn't wearing a pyjama top. My guess was he wasn't wearing anything at all. Modest as a maiden, he gathered the sheet around him and fumbled on the nightstand for his glasses. I went over to the bed and handed him my tablet. He picked it up, glanced at the photograph, and made a sound somewhere between a sigh and a sob.

"Look at your daughter," I said. "Her arm is hurt. Her eyes are almost swollen shut from crying, and she's petrified. You used her, Slater. You used your own child as a pawn in a fight over *bylaws*." When I spit out the word *bylaws*, Slater cowered. "I'm not through," I said. "You were prepared to sacrifice Bridie so Lancaster could win the referendum and you'd save your job, but it's not too late. You know who has Bridie, and you know where she is. Bring her home. The police will crucify you, and you'll lose your job, but you will have done the right thing and you'll have your daughter back."

I didn't give Slater a chance to reply. I picked up my device and left. Michael was in the living room. "Well?" he said.

I shrugged. "I don't know," I said. "There's not a doubt in my mind that Slater knows where Bridie is. Keep at him."

I was still shaking when I got back to our condo. I was running on empty, and I knew that Zack was too. When I called him at City Hall to tell him about my encounter with Slater, he reassured me. "You did the right thing," he said. "It's in Slater's hands now."

Our family had been counting the hours to the weekend, and it turned out to be worth the wait. Everything clicked. The weather was great. Zack's law partners were all there with their families and we walked, swam, canoed, kayaked, waterskiied, and caught up on one another's news. UpSlideDown closed on Saturdays at three-thirty, so Mieka was at the lake in time for our traditional Saturday-night dinner at Magoos, a diner across the lake that offered succulent burgers, greasy shoestring fries, straw-clogging milkshakes, and a Wurlitzer that played nothing that had been written after 1970. The girls and I checked the garden three times a day to see if anything had sprouted. Nothing had yet, but we live in next-year country, so we were hopeful.

It was an idyllic weekend, but by definition idylls don't last forever. All weekend I had kept an ear open for a call from Michael telling Brock that Slater had brought Bridie home. The call hadn't come, but when Brock's cell rang as we were loading up to go back to the city Sunday night, my nerves twanged. I watched Brock's face for a sign of relief, but he looked increasingly troubled. After he hung up, Brock turned to me. "That was Michael," he said. "Slater's missing."

"Missing," I said. "How long has he been gone?"

"Michael doesn't know. After you left on Friday morning, Slater and Michael quarrelled. Slater accused Michael of betraying him. Slater said he didn't need to involve the police. He was going to handle the situation himself, and then he took off. He didn't come home Friday night or last night. Michael assumed Slater was afraid to face him, and he wasn't concerned until Quinn Donnelly called an hour ago, said she'd been trying to track Slater down for two days, but Slater's phone was going straight to voicemail and he wasn't responding to texts."

"Slater hasn't been a paragon of reliability lately," I said.

"True, but according to Michael, Slater will do anything to keep Quinn from firing him so it's really strange that he wouldn't answer her calls."

"Out of sight, out of mind," I said. "Maybe Slater thinks that if he doesn't answer her calls, Quinn can't give him the axe."

"Maybe," Brock said, but he sounded doubtful.

Slater's whereabouts did not particularly concern Zack or me. I'd written him off long ago, and his apparent refusal to rescue Bridie confirmed my assessment that Slater was not worth talking about. Taylor had driven back to the city with Declan, so Zack and I were on our own. On the drive home, we organized the week ahead. Slater's name was not mentioned once. Had it been, I would have said something unkind. In retrospect, I was glad the subject hadn't come up.

Five minutes after we got back to the condo, Debbie buzzed from downstairs. "I have to talk to you," she said. I let her in, called Zack, and we both met her at the door. "Slater Doyle's dead," she said. "Joanne, we followed up on your suggestion and got Simon Weber to go through proofs of the photos he took for his book on abandoned farmhouses. I'm sure there were well over a thousand photos, but Simon stuck with it. He recognized the house in the first picture of Bridie, he was able to lead the officers to it."

Debbie's laugh was short and sardonic. "God works in mysterious ways, but having the prime suspect in one murder case help our officers find the site where a kidnapped child was held and where, unbeknownst to us, the child's father was murdered is really stretching it. At any rate, both the front and back door of the farmhouse were locked from the outside. The locks were industrial, and apparently our officers had a hell of a time getting them off.

"When they did, they found Slater in the room with the rocking horse. He'd been shot three times in the chest – point-blank. He never had a chance."

"The shooter was someone he knew."

"Apparently."

"And Bridie wasn't in the farmhouse," Zack said.

"No, she's been moved – there was a used bandage on the floor. Forensics will check the blood type, but Bridie had a bandage on her arm in the second picture, so I'm guessing that was a clean one and the one we have in the evidence bag was discarded and the blood type will match hers."

"The officers on the scene couldn't be specific about how long Slater had been dead, but their guess is that it had been a while – at least forty-eight hours."

"So at the end, Slater was trying to do the right thing," I said.

"Let's hope that's how it went down," Debbie said. "From the moment we heard your granddaughters' story, I was certain Slater knew where his daughter was. My guess is that he told whoever was holding her that he was coming to get Bridie, and they moved her. When Slater showed up, they shot him."

I felt light-headed and grabbed Zack's wheelchair to steady myself. "They'll kill Bridie," I said. "While Slater was alive, Bridie was safe because Slater knew who they were. Now that he's dead, they're free to get rid of her."

"That's not necessarily true," Debbie said, but her voice lacked conviction. "I should get back to the office now, but I wanted you to be aware of the situation. It's only a matter of time before the media gets wind of this, and then . . . "

"All hell will break lose," Zack said. "We need to control the narrative, as they say. Are you and the RCMP planning to make a statement tonight?"

"We're waiting for tomorrow morning at eight, so we catch the local morning shows."

"So the situation's in hand," Zack said.

Debbie raised an eyebrow. "Nope, this investigation suffers from scope creep," she said. "We're putting serious money and personnel into it. So is the RCMP, and since Slater's body was found in their jurisdiction they'll be involved in this case as well Lee's. And we're all tired. It seems that for every answer we get, there are four new questions. This kind of investigation is like a house renovation that goes amok – no matter how much you spend or how hard you work, new cracks keep appearing in the foundation."

We escorted Debbie to the elevator. After the doors closed, Zack said, "While we're here, we might as well go down and break the news to Brock."

"He may already know," I said. "Michael is Slater's next of kin. The RCMP has probably notified him."

"You're right. For all we know, Michael might already be at Brock's. Probably best to leave this one alone." Zack frowned. "I know Slater Doyle was a miserable excuse for a human being, but it's sad to know that there'll be nobody to mourn him."

"Bridie will," I said. "If she's still alive to mourn."

Zack and I swam for half an hour before we went to bed, and I smoothed my body with lavender oil before I put on my pyjamas. Two sure-fire relaxation aids, but I slept fitfully and woke early the next morning, feeling apprehensive.

There were dark circles under Brock's eyes too. We did our stretches in silence. Before we started off, I said, "How are you doing?"

"I'm okay. Michael's devastated. Despite the torture they put each other through, it seems Michael was still in love with Slater."

"How can that be?" I said.

"We don't choose the ones we love," Brock said.

That morning, Brock, the dogs, and I ran hard, but when we got back to the condo, I was still on edge. Zack was already at City Hall. He, Debbie, and Inspector Carl Lovitz had decided to make a joint statement about Slater Doyle's death. I filled the dogs' water bowls, poured myself a glass of water, and at eight I turned on the TV.

Zack's statement was going to be short. He would express sorrow at Slater Doyle's violent and untimely death. He would reassure the public that the RCMP and the Regina Police Service were bringing every resource to their investigations. He would ask for calm but alert involvement from the community, and he would refuse to answer questions on the grounds that the investigation into Slater Doyle's murder was ongoing.

Debbie's and Inspector Carl Lovitz's statements would be in lock-step with Zack's. Debbie had just begun to speak when my cell rang. It was Mieka. "I'm watching the news conference," I said. "Can I call you back?"

"No," Mieka said. "I'm at UpSlideDown. Mum, Bridie Doyle's with me. She was standing at the back door when I pulled into our parking space."

My heart was pounding. "Is she all right?"

"She seems to be okay physically, but she's terrified. The minute she saw me she threw herself into my arms and she's still clinging to me."

"I'll be there in ten minutes," I said.

I knew Zack would have his phone turned off, so I called Milo. He listened, said, "I'll tell the big man," and hung up.

I called Michael Goetz, but there was no answer. I didn't leave a message. After that, I watched the action unfold on the TV screen. Milo darted into the picture, leaned down, and whispered something to Zack. Zack waited until Debbie was finished, then he wheeled over and spoke to her and Inspector Carl Lovitz. Debbie went to the microphones and announced that Bridie had been found, and she appeared to be unharmed physically. At that point, as Zack had predicted, all hell broke loose. I turned off the TV, picked up my car keys, and set out for UpSlideDown.

By the time I had parked behind the building, I'd cobbled together a plan that wasn't perfect but was the best I could come up with, then I called Zack.

He was clearly harried. "Jesus, finally," he said. "I've got about fifty people here with their tongues hanging out waiting for this call. What's going on?"

"I'm just about to see Bridie. She was on the backsteps of UpSlideDown when Mieka got to work this morning. Zack, we need time to get Bridie someplace where the media can't get at her. I think Mieka should take her to our condo.

Bridie had a happy time on the roof garden and she likes the dogs.

"I know Debbie and Inspector Lovitz will want to talk to her and I know the RCMP and the city police will want to get doctors and psychologists to examine her, but this child has been through hell. And she's facing a terrible blow when she learns that her father's dead. Can you get Debbie and Inspector Lovitz to hold off for a few hours, so Bridie can at least get her bearings?"

"I'll give it my best shot. Jo, I am so relieved that Bridie is all right. When Slater was killed, I pretty much gave up hope."

"So did I," I said. "It appears our killer has a conscience after all."

The kitchen space at UpSlide Down was large, and Mieka had put a homework table and chairs and a couch in the back corner for the girls. She and Bridie were on the couch. Bridie was curled up on Mieka's lap and her arms were around Mieka's neck. On the floor beside them was a small Dora the Explorer suitcase.

I kept my voice low. "Hi, Bridie. Remember me? I'm Joanne. I was at the birthday party where you fed the koi."

Her blue eyes seemed huge in her small face. She seemed to recognize me, but she didn't speak.

I pulled a chair up close to the couch. "You're safe now, Bridie. No one's going to hurt you, but you need to be in a place where you can be quiet." She clung even more desperately to Mieka. "Would you like Mieka to take you to the roof garden at my house? You had a lot of fun there when you came to the birthday party, and the koi haven't been fed yet. You and Mieka could feed them."

Bridie's only response was to burrow in closer to Mieka.

Mieka stroked Bridie's flaxen hair. "I'd really like to see those koi," she said. "Let's go to the roof garden. It's a beautiful day to be outside, and if you're sleepy we can curl up on a lazy lounge. Just the two of us."

Mieka stood and Bridie took her hand. Mieka turned to me and said, "Mum, can you phone Angela and ask her to take care of things here for a few hours?"

"Of course," I said. I walked Mieka and Bridie to the back door. After Mieka pulled out of the parking space, I called Michael Goetz again. He'd seen the announcement that Bridie had been returned safe, but no one he talked to knew where she was. I told him Bridie was with Mieka and me and asked him to meet us at our condo on Halifax Street. I gave him the security number and told him to make tracks before the media surrounded him. Then I called Angela to tell her that a situation had come up and Mieka needed her to take care of things at UpSlideDown. Angela said she'd be there in twenty minutes. As soon as I hung up, Zack called. Debbie and Inspector Lovitz had agreed to give us till noon before they had Bridie examined, and they assured Zack they would be very careful in their questioning. I started the coffee and muffins, so by the time Angela arrived, the morning routine was underway.

In a perfect world, the new Racette-Hunter Centre would have radically changed the lives of hundreds of North Central's citizens, but ours is not a perfect world. The centre had been open nine months. Brock was proving to be a dedicated and effective director, and some of the programs were unqualified successes. The cooperative daycare was running smoothly; the life skills classes were filled; there were waiting lists for the martial arts classes for women; and the recreation programs were popular.

But the dropout rates from the trade and academic programs were high. The centre had been too quick in establishing a mentoring program. A successful mentoring program requires rigid screening and training of both students and mentors. R-H had jumped right in, hoping for the best, and the best hadn't happened. The centre had a zero tolerance policy for drugs, alcohol, and weapons and it was strictly enforced. Some of the potentially best and brightest students quit because they were unable to stay clean.

There were many setbacks and disappointments, but Angela Greyeyes was not among them. Angela had been off the street for seven months and off drugs for eight, and the change in her physically and mentally was nothing short of miraculous. She had just turned twenty. She was the mother of three and she'd been a sex-trade worker since she was fourteen, but that morning, dressed in bright yellow overalls and a dazzlingly white T-shirt, her face innocent of makeup and her thick, glossy black hair in braids, she looked like a teenager. Her eyes were anxious and her voice, always husky, was low and urgent. "Joanne, I need to know that everything's okay with Mieka and her kids."

"Everything's fine," I said. "Something just came up that only Mieka could handle. I've got the coffee started and the muffin batter is ready. Audrey and Cassie will be in at ten. Do you want me to wait till then?"

Angela smiled. "Nope, I'm good to go. Tell Mieka whatever the problem is, I hope it works out."

"I'll tell her." I started for the door and then turned. "Angela, I'm glad Mieka has you to count on."

A shadow crossed her face. I was puzzled. "Did I say something wrong?"

Angela covered her mouth to hide a self-conscious giggle. "No. Just no one's ever counted on me before," she said. "It's gonna take some getting used to."

I was walking across the back lawn to our building when Michael Goetz called. He was outside the condo, and he was concerned that if he parked there, his rather conspicuous

2015 Range Rover might alert the media to his whereabouts. I met him at the front door and together we drove into the condo's underground parkade.

Mieka and Bridie were already on the roof garden feeding the koi when Michael and I arrived. We were counting on the combination of sunshine, fresh air, familiar faces, and feeding the koi to combat Bridie's terror, but her small face was still strained; her body was coiled-wire tense; she wouldn't let Mieka out of her sight; and she still hadn't said a word.

When she saw Michael, she ran to him, and he picked her up and held her close. With Bridie still in his arms, Michael came over and sat down with Mieka and me. "I don't know how to thank you," he said.

"We all love Bridie," Mieka said. She leaned towards the little girl. "And we're all so glad you're here with us again."

Michael had arrived with a rag doll that he handed to Bridie. "Raggedy Ann is especially glad you're home," he said. "And guess what? I called Zenaya and she's going to come back to take care of us."

Bridie nodded solemnly but she didn't speak. Michael's eyes were questioning.

"Bridie doesn't feel like talking yet," I said.

Michael smiled at his daughter. "Take your time," he said. "Talk when you're ready, munchkin. Right now, Joanne and I need to discuss a few things. It won't take long. We'll be over there by the pink flowers where you can see us."

Michael had been calm and assured with Bridie, but the facade disappeared when he and I were alone. He was a broken man. His eyes were red-rimmed, and he was still fighting tears. "I don't know where to start," he said. "So much has happened, and there's so much pain ahead for her."

"She has you, and, in the end, that will make all the difference," I said. "But there's something that has to be decided now. The RCMP and the Regina police know Bridie's here with us. They agreed to wait until noon to examine her. It's your call. You may want to take her to your place, but I think it would be easier if they talk to her here."

Michael's eyes widened. "Bridie shouldn't be anywhere near our house – not the way it is now. The police are still there, and they're in the middle of an investigation. Being confronted with that chaos would be another blow for Bridie and it would raise questions in her mind about Slater. Jo, how can I explain to a five-year-old child why the father she loved put her in danger, and then died trying to set right the wrong he had done? Right now, this is the closest thing to a safe place Bridie has. She shouldn't be moved."

"If she's staying here, Bridie needs to be fed. We have no idea when she ate last." I stood. "I'll go downstairs and make some sandwiches. Does she have a favourite?"

Michael smiled. "PB&J. We're both partial to those."

"In that case, I'll make a plateful," I said.

I called Zack from downstairs to tell him that the interviews with Bridie were going to take place on the roof garden. Zack had news too. The authorities had decided to talk with Bridie in pairs. The MD from the Regina police and the RCMP psychologist would visit first, and Debbie and Inspector Lovitz would follow up. The media were on the hunt, but they had no idea where Bridie was, and according to Zack, the RCMP and the Regina police agreed that, for the time being, Bridie's location should be kept secret.

Michael asked Mieka to stay with Bridie and him while the doctors examined her. It was a wise decision. Bridie was terrified of being touched by a stranger, and she put up a fight. Finally Mieka calmed Bridie enough to allow the doctors to examine her. Except for the scratch on her arm, she was unharmed, and there were no signs of sexual abuse. Still, she refused to speak, and when the psychologist attempted to get her to choose plastic figures of children and adults and have them play in a dollhouse, Bridie became hysterical. The investigating officers fared no better. No matter how gentle or how leading the question, Bridie refused to answer.

When Debbie and Inspector Lovitz came down from the roof garden, I could feel their fatigue and discouragement. They turned down my offer of coffee but stayed to talk.

"I have some idea about what that child has been through," Inspector Lovitz said. "There were locks on both doors, and I'm sure Bridie was kept a prisoner inside. She was provided for. She had a sleeping bag and a potty. There was a cooler in the kitchen. It was well stocked: juice, milk, fruit, a bag of cut-up vegetables, cold cuts, bread, cookies. That little girl must have been starving but she'd barely touched anything." He compressed his lips. "I've never had children, but I imagine that it's difficult for a child to swallow when she's scared to death."

"Bridie had a Dora the Explorer suitcase with her," Debbie said. "It was filled with her own clothes and some colouring books and markers." Her lips curled with contempt. "I imagine Slater Doyle gave himself points for being such a thoughtful father."

"So what's next?" I said.

"Dr. Goetz asked us if he could take Bridie somewhere for a few days so he can help her reach a point where she's able to talk about what happened," Debbie said. "I know he's lost his medical licence, but he is an experienced psychiatrist and a medical doctor, and he is Bridie's next of kin. Carl and I think it may be our only option. We're not going to get anything from Bridie the way she is now."

Debbie and Inspector Lovitz traded a look. "We're both afraid of what might happen if the media pounces on that child," the inspector said.

"I agree," I said. "Debbie, you know that Zack and I have a place at Lawyers' Bay. To this point, the media have been responsible partners. They made Bridie's face recognizable, and that was exactly what was necessary. But right now Bridie needs privacy. Our cottage at Lawyers' Bay will give her that. It's a gated community, so Bridie will be safe. And it's close to Regina if Michael feels Bridie is ready to talk to you."

Debbie and Carl Lovitz weighed the proposition. "Tell Dr. Goetz he can take his daughter there," the inspector said. "Just give us the contact information."

When I told Michael what Debbie and Inspector Lovitz and I had arranged, he slumped with relief. "Thank you."

"This time of year we go up every weekend, so you'll find everything you need," I said. "Help yourself." I gave Michael the security key and directions to the cottage and he, Mieka, and Bridie left. Then I poured myself a glass of milk, picked up the lone PB&J left on the plate, and called Zack to tell him he could start breathing again.

CHAPTER

16

Zack and I had just finished breakfast the next morning when Milo appeared. He was carrying the morning paper and he used it to beat out a rhythm on the furniture as he bopped in; then, opening the paper, he held it up so the front page faced us.

The headline read "DAD SLAIN. DAUGHTER SAFE." There were pictures of Slater and of Bridie, and there were stories – many, many stories about the back-to-back tragedy of the murdered father and the poignant return of his child.

"The first reference to the referendum is on page eight and it's a paragraph long," Milo said. "Who cares about bylaws that affect development? Since May 18, there've been two homicides and a kidnapping in our little corner of the world. If the Twittersphere is any indication, all people care about is ending the shitstorm."

"We can't wait for the public to regain their interest in the referendum," I said. "Whether they're interested or not, the Yes side has to win."

Milo ripped open a Crispy Crunch, balled the wrapper, and tossed it towards a wastebasket across the room. When the wrapper went in, Milo breathed, "Booyah."

"Three points," Zack said. "Milo, you and I should shoot hoops together sometime."

"Whenever you're feeling up to a challenge, big man," Milo said.

Zack raised an eyebrow. "I'll reserve some time at Racette-Hunter this week. Right now, I have to hit the road." He wheeled over, held out his arms to me, and we had a nice, if brief, moment. "Let me know how the meeting with the volunteers goes," he said, and he sailed off, a man whose most pressing immediate concern was scoring court time at R-H.

The informal quarters for the Yes forces was our former campaign office, the Noodle House. Counting on a larger turnout than the Noodle House could comfortably handle, I had booked the hall at our church for a "get out the vote" meeting at nine-thirty that morning. The plan was for Milo to give a quick overview of how the Yes side was polling: indicate areas of strength, neighbourhoods that could be written off, and neighbourhoods with a large number of undecided voters who might be swayed by a face-to-face visit from a committed volunteer. After that, experienced volunteers would give last-minute instructions to the newbies, and people would hit the streets.

Given people's work schedules and quotidian duties, I had counted on seventy-five of the one hundred and fifty volunteers who'd knocked on doors for us during the election campaign showing up – plenty to help handle the two hundred and fifty new volunteers who'd offered to work for the Yes vote in the referendum. By 9:45, only twenty experienced volunteers were sitting around drinking coffee and casting surreptitious glances at the door, but none of our new volunteers had appeared. At 9:50, Peggy Kreviazuk put a comradely arm around my shoulder and stated the obvious: "Well, Ms. Smarty, it looks like nobody else is coming to our party."

"Time to change the agenda," I said. The volunteers had seated themselves in the first row of chairs. Milo moved to one of the empty rows behind them, and I pulled over a chair so I faced them.

"Thanks for coming. Eight days to the referendum, and we obviously have a huge problem. We were ahead in the polls. We had enthusiastic volunteers, and our people were committed. We're still ahead in the polls, but that doesn't matter if we can't get out our vote. What happened? Why didn't the others show up this morning? Anybody have any ideas?"

I didn't need to be an expert on body language to realize that my questions had spiked the level of discomfort in the room. People looked at their feet, at the window, at the door – anywhere but at me. There was an outbreak of throat-clearing and clothes-adjusting. "We've been through a lot together," I said. "If you know something, tell me."

Finally, a man with whom I'd gone door-knocking during Zack's campaign spoke. "People are suffering from referendum fatigue."

"The referendum is a week tomorrow," I said. "We're almost there. After Lee's death, we were overwhelmed by people committed to making Lee's dream a reality. That was less than three weeks ago. Now we're in free fall. What changed?"

Peggy turned her bright blue eyes towards the other volunteers sitting in the front row. "Is no one going to answer Joanne's question?"

Colleen Hennan had begun volunteering the day after Zack announced the referendum, and I had shepherded her through her first foray into door-to-door canvassing. She was a pretty blonde who worked as an on-air personality at a local radio station. After three minutes, I knew she didn't need shepherding, but she was young, smart, and deeply committed to sustainable development and I'd stayed with her for an hour just for the pleasure of her company. She had a cat named George Michael and later that evening when we'd had a beer and bitch session with the volunteers at a local pub, she'd wowed us with a hula-hoop display.

Colleen had a great smile, but she wasn't smiling now. "Joanne, you know there were a number of volunteers who were drawn to the Yes side because of Lee Crawford. They saw Lee as an idealist – principled and uncompromising."

"She *was* principled and uncompromising," I said.

"I know that," Colleen said gently. "I also know that we're all human and that even the best of us have flaws. But many of the people who didn't show up today haven't been around long enough to have figured that out. They were Lee's groupies. By joining up with her cause they felt they were part of something larger and more significant than they were. When the rumours started surfacing about her private life, they felt betrayed."

"But people got past the rumours," I said. "We picked up dozens of volunteers."

"Then Bridie Doyle was kidnapped and they backed away again," Colleen said. "Slater Doyle's murder and Bridie's seemingly well-timed return have made many of our volunteers feel that instead of being part of a shining quest, they're involved in gutter politics and they don't want any part of it."

I was livid, but my voice was surprisingly calm. "The people who've deserted us were hoodwinked by the oldest political trick in the book. When you can't win on merits, muddy the waters with personal attacks. But the damage has been done."

I stood and moved nearer to the group. "I understand why the viciousness of this referendum has soured some of our volunteers, but it's also distracting us from the real issue, which is exactly what our opponents want. In the eight days we have left, let's go full force on social media and bring the focus back to the issues at the core of the debate. What kind of city do we want? What kind of relationship do we want between urban and rural neighbours? What kind of legacy do we want to leave for our children?

"I have a list of contact information for all the people who volunteered to help us. We'll be sending out mass emailings telling them exactly what I just told you, and tweets telling them what's happening, but if each of you could take a page of names and contact the people on that list personally to ask them to come back to our campaign, we have a shot at winning. Remind the people you talk to that for us, this is still a shining quest and we want them to be part of it. Any questions?"

There were none, but at least people were again looking me in the eye. "Thanks for coming," I said. "As you pass by the kitchen, please take a box of doughnuts with you. I over-ordered."

I caught Colleen on her way out. "Don't forget your doughnuts," I said.

"Oh, I won't. I'm on my way to the station, so the doughnuts will find a good home. I'll take some lists too."

"Thanks," I said. "And thank you for being frank about the problem we're dealing with. It always helps to get things out in the open."

Peggy stayed behind with me to wash the coffee cups, and the ever-surprising Milo stayed to stack the dozens of chairs Brock and I had so optimistically set out the night before.

When we were done, the three of us sat down with a box of doughnuts. I chose maple; Peggy chose Boston cream, but

Milo wasn't a doughnut man, so when I held out the box to him, he passed.

"Well, you nailed it," he said.

"Now comes the hard part," I said. "Making it happen. Time to go to the agency and tweak our ads for the final week. Are you two free?"

"I have a day of phoning ahead," Peggy said. "Joanne, you still have quite a stack of volunteer lists. I'll take some. I'm sure Colleen is correct about the age of many of our no-shows, and the young tend to be very courteous to the elderly."

I handed Peggy three pages of names and numbers, and she took two more. I felt a rush of gratitude. "You really are the best," I said. "I wish I could clone you." I turned to Milo. "What do you think of the shining quest idea?"

He shrugged. "It's lame, but it will probably work. You've already done the one thing you had to do – you convinced the people at the meeting that you were in charge. People need to be led. Napoleon said, 'A leader is a dealer in hope,' and he got a 99.94 per cent vote in support of the constitution he drafted."

"Napoleon cooked those numbers, Milo. You know that."

Milo shrugged. "A win's a win," he said. "Let's go see what the creative types at the agency can conjure up for us."

Three hours later, Milo and I left the agency with revised media and social media strategies. The last lap was underway.

I called Zack, gave him Colleen Hennan's assessment of the problem eroding our volunteer list, and we agreed her analysis was spot on. And then I called Warren Weber. During the past year, I had come to respect his clear vision and his ability to be objective. I needed both now.

For the first time in a long time, Warren sounded buoyant. "Joanne! I was just about to call you. I have some good news, although, given the circumstances, *good* seems an inappropriate word. I just got off the phone with Asia Libke. The police have determined that the gun that killed Slater Doyle was the same gun that killed Lee. Simon was with us the weekend Slater Doyle was killed, and much of that time he was with a police officer going through proofs of the abandoned buildings he'd photographed."

The cloud that had been hanging over Simon since Angus found him washing the blood off himself in the barn had lifted. "I'm so relieved," I said. "I know you've all been going through hell. This is such good news."

"And there've been other positive developments," Warren said. "Simon has moved out of the boathouse. He spends the nights here at the cottage in his old room, and most evenings he has dinner with us."

"So Simon's starting to connect again," I said. "That's wonderful."

"It is, isn't it? And, although you're too diplomatic to point this out, the fact that Simon was either with us or with a police officer when Slater Doyle was killed gives Simon an alibi. He's finally in the clear. I can hardly believe that myself. I try not to get my hopes up with Simon, but it's hard." Warren's voice grew hoarse. "I love him, Joanne."

"That's half the battle," I said.

"It is," Warren agreed, "but it's only half." I could hear the anger in his voice, and the determination. "From the beginning, I've believed Lee was targeted. Simon has been exonerated, but someone made my son a scapegoat, and I'm going to make certain whoever did that is punished. I have a stake in this, Joanne."

"We all do," I said. "Warren, do you think the same person is behind everything that's happened: killing the birds, the murders, and Bridie's abduction?"

He didn't hesitate. "I've believed that all along," he said.

"Where do we begin?"

"With Lee," Warren said. "She's the starting point." He paused. "Joanne, did you pass along the Harries-Crosby report on Lee to her sister?"

"No. I thought about it, but Maisie's been dealing with so much I didn't want to add to the load. She's grieving. She's back at work, and she and Peter have moved out to the farm. They're planning some major renovations on the house, and they have two babies on the way. There never seemed to be a good moment to ask Maisie if her sister had a love affair before she was twenty-two."

Out of nowhere the image of Lee's bedroom flashed through my mind. The graceful oak four-poster bed; the pristine white chenille spread; and on the bedside table a brass lamp and a framed photograph of Colin Brokenshire, the man with whom Lee had chosen to spend every weekend during her undergraduate years.

Colin was thirty years older than Lee. He would have been forty-eight when Lee started university, old enough to be her father. But he wasn't her father. There was no blood connection. Colin had raised the Crawford twins because there was no one else. He had allowed each girl to find her own path. Maisie had chosen the law, and Lee had chosen agriculture. Had she also chosen Colin Brokenshire?

"Are you still there, Joanne?" Warren's question interrupted my reverie.

"I'm sorry," I said. "Something just occurred to me. Warren, could you get the people at Harries-Crosby to look into Colin Brokenshire's romantic life from the time he adopted the girls in 1990 until he died in 2004. He was killed in a farm accident. It might be important for your investigators to find out as much as they can about the circumstances of the accident."

"I'll get Harries-Crosby on it immediately," Warren said. "Anything else?"

"No, just please tell Simon and Annie how relieved and happy I am."

It was Isobel Wainberg's birthday and Taylor was having dinner with Isobel's family. The weather was pretty enough to barbecue, so I made a soy sauce and lemon pepper marinade that Zack and I liked but Taylor did not, poured it over pork chops, then picked up my list of drop-out volunteers, sat down at the kitchen table, and started making calls.

Twelve of the people I called weren't home or weren't answering, so I left my contact information and a message urging whomever to get back to me so I could talk to them personally about rejoining the campaign. I had good luck with the eight people I talked to. Colleen had been right when she identified disillusionment as the reason we had lost volunteers. I laid out the reasons why the new bylaws were the best option for our city's future growth, waved the shining crusade flag, and was able to convince all the people I reached to join us for the final week.

By the time Zack got home, I'd finished my first list. With martinis mixed and salad made, I fired up the barbecue. A solid day's work. We took our drinks to the terrace and settled in to enjoy the sunshine.

I stretched out on the lazy lounge. "I think I could stay here forever," I said. "How was your day?"

"Debbie's news about the same gun being used to kill both Lee and Slater has certainly alleviated some concerns. Have you had a chance to talk to Maisie?"

"No, I called her office, but she was in a meeting, so I thought I'd try again tonight. I did talk to Warren."

"The Weber family must be over the moon," Zack said.

"More like 'cautiously optimistic,'" I said. "I don't think Warren's experience with his late wife is ever far from his mind."

"That's understandable," Zack said.

"He's determined to find the person who framed Simon for Lee's murder."

"Also understandable," Zack said. "Debbie's determined too. It may take time, but the police will track him or her down." He sipped his drink. "Tell me more about the meeting this morning."

"It ended up being productive," I said. "At least I hope so." I didn't minimize the significance of the dismal turnout at our volunteers' meeting, but I did move quickly to more positive news: the steps we were taking to address the drop-out problem and the media and social media campaign we'd be using during the week before the vote.

Zack nodded approvingly. "Sounds like the Yes side is moving in the right direction."

"For the time being," I said. "Zack, something else occurred to me, and I'm not certain how to deal with it or if I should be dealing with it at all." Zack listened without comment as I told him about asking Warren to have Harries-Crosby look into Colin Brokenshire's private life. When I finished, Zack still didn't say a word.

"You don't approve," I said.

Zack leaned closer. "It's not that. I'm just surprised that you feel the need to pursue this."

"Because it's none of my business," I said. "But, Zack, it *is* my business. I can't take away Maisie's pain, but she says that for her the hardest part of Lee's death is that she can't understand why it happened. I get that. For years after Ian died, I believed he died because he was in the wrong place at the wrong time. I agonized over the fact that if Ian had been on that particular stretch of highway two minutes earlier or two minutes later, he'd still be alive. I had a terrible time sleeping. I'd wake up in the night and read whatever book was at hand. One night it was an old poetry anthology. I leafed through and found a poem titled 'Auto Wreck' by Karl Shapiro. I can still recite that entire poem from memory, but the point Shapiro makes is that a death that's seemingly random forces us to realize that no matter how much we know, we will never be able to answer the question 'Who shall die?'"

"You think finding the answer to why Lee was killed will help Maisie?"

"I do."

Zack took my hand. "Then I'm with you all the way."

Wednesday morning Brock and I had a good run. When we got back to the condo, Brock took the dog's leashes while I started my stretches. "Do you have a few minutes?" he said.

"Of course."

"It's something personal," Brock said. "I've been seeing a man I'm very attracted to. Margot's met him and she likes him too."

"So what's the problem?"

Brock met my gaze. "What's always the problem?" he said. "Michael. He called this morning. He's unhappy and he's confused. He's holding it together for Bridie, but he wanted me to come out to Lawyers' Bay so we can talk."

"What do you want to do?"

"I'm willing to help Michael through this, but I'm not going to get involved with him again. I've tried, but too much has happened. Derek, the new man in my life, is such a pleasure to be with – no drama, no miserable shared history, just two people finding out about each other and enjoying each other's company."

"That's the way it should be," I said. "I'm happy for you, Brock. After the referendum is out of the way, bring Derek by for dinner so we can get to know one other."

"Actually, you already do know him, Jo. It's Derek Fleischer. He teaches at the School of Journalism."

"We were on the union's grievance committee together for three years," I said. "He's a terrific guy!"

We stepped into the elevator. When it stopped at Brock's floor, I said, "Could you give me a call if you decide to spend the night at the lake? You know how Pantera and Esme get if they have to hang around waiting."

Brock's gaze was steady. "I'm not going to stay overnight, Joanne. I've already made that decision."

"Good call," I said, and I pushed the button for our floor.

Zack had a breakfast meeting, so he was dressed and waiting to say goodbye.

He held out his arms to me. As always on breakfast meeting days, he was immaculate, and I was sweaty. "I'd better give you a rain check on that hug," I said. "Brock and I ran hard today."

Zack wheeled closer and drew me to him. "I'll take my chances," he said. When we parted, Zack was beaming. "Great way to start the day," he said.

"The best," I said. "And I have some nice news. There's a new man in Brock's life."

Zack cocked his head. "He's finally over Michael?"

"I hope so," I said. "I know the new man. His name is Derek Fleischer, and he's a professor at the School of Journalism. You'll like him. But it's strange, Derek looks enough like Michael to be his brother: same slender build, same blond spiked short hair, same deeply cleft chin, same ironic brown eyes."

Zack shrugged. "Most guys have a type they go for."

"I wasn't the type you'd been going for."

"Nope, for forty-eight years I was barking up the wrong tree. Then you came along and my barking days were over."

After Taylor left for school, I sat down at the kitchen table with my phone and my lists and began trying to woo back more of the disaffected. Out of thirty-five people I talked to, five told me to go to hell and take the horse I rode in on with me and thirty agreed to show up the next day at the Noodle House.

By eleven, it was time for a break. I made myself a cup of tea and took my phone and tea up to the roof garden. I was checking email on my phone when Harries-Crosby's preliminary report on Colin Brokenshire arrived with a note telling me they'd send the full report and their file on the investigation of the accident as soon as both were complete.

Harries-Crosby's report began on July 1, 1990, Lee and Maisie's eighth birthday and the day their parents died. The information in the report was based on interviews with neighbours in the community around the Brokenshire farm.

The report was bare bones but informative. Fiona Brokenshire, Colin's former wife, left her marriage on the day after Christmas 1990. Eleven months later, in November 1991, Colin and Bette Stevens were in a relationship. They were both thirty-eight. When Fiona divorced Colin in February 1993, everyone expected Colin and Bette would marry. They didn't marry, but they continued to be a couple until 2000 when the relationship ended coolly but without drama. There was a general sense in the community that the affair had simply petered out. Until Colin's death four years later, he and Bette remained friendly but distant, and Colin was not known to be involved with anyone else for the remainder of his life. I read the report again.

It didn't offer much, but it was going to have to be enough.
I called Maisie. She was at the office and she had a half-hour
free at one-thirty. I went home, ate a sandwich, and drove
downtown to Falconer Shreve.

CHAPTER

17

Since I'd met Zack, five women and one man had sat behind the silvery granite slab that was the firm's reception desk. All were as slick as their surroundings; all were unfailingly kind to me. Today's person behind the desk had perfectly oval nails that matched her indigo silk blouse, and her smile was winsome. Her name was Rosalie Wu. She stood to greet me. "It's always a pleasure to see you, Ms. Shreve. I'll buzz Maisie – she's expecting you."

Maisie came out immediately; she ushered me into the boardroom, closed the door, and embraced me. In high heels, Maisie was well over six feet tall. She was wearing a smart ivory maternity suit and the peach blouse we'd admired when she unpacked Margot's clothes. She had a new hairstyle: very short and very flattering.

I hugged her. "You look amazing," I said. "I love your hair."

A sliver of sadness undercut Maisie's smile. "I had it cut yesterday. Every time I looked in a mirror, I saw Lee. I thought having a different hairstyle might make it easier."

"Did it?"

"Not yet," she said. "Jo, what do you want to talk to me about? I know it must be important. That's why I brought you in here. There are always interruptions when I'm at my desk."

"I'm glad we can be private," I said. The table in the board-room was large: sixteen silver-grey leather chairs positioned precisely around a rectangular table of the same silvery-grey granite as the desk in the reception area. Maisie sat at the head of the table and I took the chair to her right. "There's no way to approach this subject gently," I said, "so I'm just going to begin. Were Lee and Colin Brokenshire lovers?"

She flinched. "Who told you?"

"Nobody. I figured it out. Maisie, I've had a hunch that there's something in Lee's past that can shed light on every-thing that's happened since the day after the wedding. When it seemed the police were closing in on Simon, Warren Weber had a firm of private investigators look into Lee's romantic life. I was angry, and I told him so. Later, after I'd cooled off, I realized the report might help us discover the truth about Lee's death, and Warren sent me a copy. He suggested it might be helpful if I shared it with you, but I couldn't bring myself to do it."

"But now you can," Maisie said, and her voice was heavy with defeat.

"I don't have a choice," I said. "The Harries-Crosby report is all we have. It's our only option."

Maisie squared her shoulders. "All right," she said. "Go ahead. Tell me what they found."

I turned my chair so I could watch my daughter-in-law's face. "The first sexual relationship Harries-Crosby could identify began when Lee was twenty-two," I said. "I found that unusual. I tried to talk to George about Lee's past, but he evaded my questions. Yesterday, I asked Warren to have Harries-Crosby look into Colin Brokenshire's personal life from the time he assumed responsibility for you and Lee until his death. Like Lee, Colin didn't have any romantic relationships after the time you and she started university."

Maisie raked her long fingers through her curls. "I was hoping that Lee and Colin's love affair could be kept private," she said. "I'm still hoping that. Jo, they're both dead. Why does the fact that they were lovers matter now?"

I leaned across the smooth expanse of granite that separated Maisie and me. "Because I believe that knowing the truth will lead us to whoever is behind this nightmare," I said.

Maisie tented her fingers and studied them. After less than a minute, she'd reached a decision. It was time to talk. "The relationship started when Lee was seventeen," she said.

"And Colin was forty-seven," I said.

"Don't rush to judgment, Jo. Lee and I never had secrets from each other and she made it clear from the beginning that she was the pursuer. Colin resisted. He cited all the reasons why they shouldn't become intimate. There was the age difference, of course, and the fact that Colin had been our legal guardian. Lee didn't care. She was in love with him, and she knew he was in love with her, and for her that was all that mattered. They were discreet about their relationship – even around me. When I was home for the weekend, Lee slept in the room she'd shared with me from the time we were children."

"And this arrangement continued for four years," I said.

"It would have gone on like that forever. Lee told me there was no reason for Colin and her to marry. They were happy as they were. They were both private people and the idea of the neighbours talking about their affair was repugnant to them. Then Lee got pregnant. That changed everything. She and Colin both wanted the baby and that meant acknowledging their relationship. They were planning to get married, and then Colin was killed."

Maisie walked over to the wall of glass that looked out over the city. Her back was to me, but I could hear the strain in her voice. "Even now, I can't bear to remember how Lee was after Colin died. She had always been so strong, but night after night I held her in my arms and stayed with her until she'd cried herself to sleep. She lost the baby, and I think something died in her then. She felt she had to carry on Colin's work, and I know that for a very long time that was the only reason she wanted to go on living." Maisie turned to face me. "Anyway, that's the story – or at least as much as I know of it."

"You think there's more?"

"Over the years, I've wondered if Colin's accident really was an accident."

I felt a chill. "Colin was Mansell's friend."

"And Bette Stevens was his sister." Maisie's eyes were troubled. "I know it doesn't make any sense. The accident happened four years after Colin and Bette broke it off. And the only two people who knew that Colin and Lee were in love were George Sawchuk and me, and George just learned about the relationship when Colin asked him to be a witness at the wedding." Maisie shook her head impatiently. "Ignore everything I just said. These hormones sluicing through my body are making me crazy. But, Jo, I'm sure you're right. I'm certain everything that's happening grows out of something in the past."

"Do you think George Sawchuk might have some answers?"

"He and I are the only ones left who knew about the wedding." Maisie came back to her chair, folded her arms on the boardroom table, and rested her head on them. She looked like an exhausted schoolgirl. When she straightened, her eyes were filled with tears.

I went to her. "I'm sorry. I shouldn't have brought this up."

Maisie looked up at me. "No. We owe it to Lee to see this through."

"Would you like me to talk to George?"

"I would," Maisie said. "But I should call first. He should know that I want him to tell you everything." She took out her phone, called George, and gave him a lawyerly précis of the situation. When the call was done, she said, "George will be home all afternoon. He wants you to come ahead."

I picked up my bag. "It's time for this to be over," I said.

When I arrived, George was in his driveway washing an already spotless green Ford half-tonne. I parked next to his truck and walked over to him. "You can squeeze out your chamois," I said. "That truck looks as if it just rolled off the assembly line."

"I've been hard at it since Maisie called," George said. "I've always found working on a vehicle relaxing."

"Ironing does it for me," I said.

George smiled. "Come in and have some tea."

The kittens were scampering around under the mother cat's watchful eye. I bent and picked one up. It had a very sweet face. "There's been so much going on that I haven't had a chance to bring Taylor out here, but she's definitely interested in a kitten."

"She still has the pick of the litter," George said. "Now come inside, so we can talk." The Peek Freans Digestive Biscuits were already arranged on a plate on the chrome table. George and I both washed our hands, and then he filled the kettle and we sat down. He got right into it.

"Except for Maisie, no one, including me, knew that Colin and Lee were lovers until two days before they were to be married. After supper that night – it was a

Wednesday – Colin came over with a bottle of Glengoyne. He and Mansell and I always had a glass of single malt together on our birthdays, and on Christmas Day and New Year's Eve. This was mid-September and Mansell hadn't been invited so I knew there was something special.

"Colin poured us each two fingers of Scotch and he told me everything. When he was finished, he said that Lee was pregnant, that they already had a marriage licence, and they were asking Maisie and me to be witnesses to their marriage at City Hall. The wedding was to take place on Saturday. It was a lot of information to process, so I was glad Colin had brought the Glengoyne.

"It seemed that everything was settled, but Colin needed my advice on one matter. There had been a woman in his life before Lee, and he felt he should tell her about the upcoming marriage before it became public knowledge."

"The woman was Bette Stevens," I said.

George nodded. "I advised him not to tell her. I'd known Bette since we were in grade school. She's a good person, but she has a temper. I told Colin that in my opinion if the wedding was presented to the entire community as a fait accompli, Bette would handle the news gracefully, but if he told her privately beforehand, Bette might confront Lee and they would both say things they'd regret.

"He thanked me for my advice, told me the wedding was at eleven o'clock Saturday morning, and that he, Lee, and Maisie would pick me up at ten. He said he'd never been happier." George swallowed hard. "That was the last time I saw him."

"How did the accident happen?"

"The same way farm accidents always happen," George said. "People are tired, they rush, and they get careless. It was harvest – it was a good crop but we were late getting it off because of the weather. Everybody was going full tilt – out in the fields before sunup and still out there hours past sundown. Colin had Lee, but she was just starting her post-graduate work in Saskatoon, and she was only back on the weekends. Mansell and Bette had finished, so they were helping Colin. It was after dark. It was hot and everyone was exhausted. They were unloading, so there was a lot of noise. Somehow Mansell just didn't see Colin. He drove right over him."

"There must have been an investigation."

"There was, and all the physical evidence – the tire tracks and the state of Colin's body – was consistent with what Mansell and Bette said had happened. Bette had wit- nessed the accident and she was in a state of shock. As I said, Mansell was never the same after that – at least he was never the same with me."

As I drove back to the city, I couldn't shake George's account of the collateral damage Colin Brokenshire's tragic death had caused. When I pulled into our parking garage, images of that hot September night were still crowding my brain, I was looking forward to a shower and a peaceful hour prepar- ing dinner and planning for the summer ahead.

The vagaries of fate had long since ceased to amaze me, but even by fate's whimsical standards, the scene I walked into when I stepped through our front door was surreal. Mansell Donnelly and Zack were in the living room, dressed in the lightweight, carefully tailored suits successful men wear in summer. Whiskey tumblers in hand, dogs at their feet, Zack and Mansell were the very model of corporate camaraderie. Mondo bizarro. Esme had positioned herself next to Mansell. When she spotted me, she came running. Mansell took in the reunion with a smile. "Zack said the minute you came through that door Esme would leave me high and dry."

"Don't take it personally," I said. "I have dried liver treats in my bag."

"Mansell and I are just having a celebratory bourbon," Zack said. "Can I get you something?"

"Please – a light one on the rocks. So what are you celebrating?"

"Tomorrow morning the Regina and District Chamber of Commerce is going to announce their endorsement of the Yes vote," Zack said.

"You're kidding."

"No," Zack said. "Mansell has been working on them and they've seen the light. Let me get your drink."

Zack wheeled into the kitchen and returned with a tray holding an ice bucket, a bottle of Jim Beam, and a whiskey tumbler. He poured my drink, freshened his and Mansell's, and then raised his glass. "Here's to the endorsement from the Chamber of Commerce."

I turned to Mansell. "How did you pull that off?" Zack caught the edge in my voice and gave me a sharp look, but Mansell cruised on.

"It was the solid material I had to work with," he said. "It's easy to make a case for building on the infrastructure that Regina has in place while making thoughtful decisions about development. I used North Village as a great illustration – a carefully planned, multi-use community with well-designed homes for families of varying sizes, needs, and incomes." Mansell's laugh was self-mocking. "I don't know why I'm telling you this, Joanne. You probably wrote Zack's speeches on the subject."

I was in no mood to be drawn into their bonhomie. "Just the good ones," I said.

"True enough," Zack said. "But seriously, the Chamber of Commerce's support should put us over the top in Wednesday's vote."

"Bite your tongue," I said. "We'll approach this E-Day the way sensible people approach every E-Day, as if we're fifteen points behind in the polls."

Zack was contrite. "I stand corrected," he said. "But I've invited Mansell to a celebratory dinner at the Sahara Club. If I promise not to crow, will you join us?"

"Absolutely," I said. "It will be fun watching you control your urge to crow."

"Excellent because I've already made the reservations. I invited Taylor. She let me down easy, but she made it clear she'd rather be pecked to death by a duck than have dinner with three people talking politics – even if it was at the Sahara Club."

"Zack, have you told Milo about this?"

"Not yet."

"I'm going to call and ask him to join us for dinner."

"You know he won't come."

"He lives right over the club," I said. "He has to eat sometime."

I went upstairs to make my call. Milo answered with his usual greeting. "What's the sitch?"

I filled him in.

"This is big," he said.

"It certainly improves our odds," I said. "Milo, Zack and I are having dinner with Mansell Donnelly at the Sahara Club at six. I wish you'd join us."

"Thanks but no thanks." For a beat there was silence. Milo broke it. "Jo, there are three people in the world I trust. You're one of them. Mansell Donnelly doesn't even make the long list."

"Same here. Mansell seems sincere, and he's offering proof of his commitment, but I'm still uneasy. Anyway, we'll have a chance to see him in action tomorrow. Zack, Mansell, and the president of the Chamber of Commerce are making a media statement at City Hall at nine in the morning. It would be great if you could be there."

"Then I'm there."

"Thanks. Milo, is Zack one of the three people you trust?"

Milo didn't answer immediately. When he did, he sounded faintly amused. "Jo, when I came to work for you I was thirty-three years old and there were two people on my list. Now there are three. One a decade. I don't believe in rushing these things."

When I met Brock downstairs for our run the next morning, the pungent zing of ozone filled the air and the sky was dark. A storm was on its way. Brock held out his hand palm up. "No rain yet," he said. "Shall we chance it?"

Esme and Pantera were straining. "The dogs are making their wishes known," I said. "Let's go."

The Chamber of Commerce's endorsement of the Yes vote was important enough for us to break our pattern of not talking while we ran. Brock seemed pleased, but he never offered his opinion until he'd had a chance to think a situation through, so after I shared the news, we didn't revisit the matter. Brock didn't mention Michael and neither did I.

We'd just turned onto Halifax Street when the wind came up and rain began lashing our faces. A garbage can had blown over and the contents were sailing down the street. Seconds after a thunderclap, a bolt of lightning slashed the sky. Without conferring, Brock and I turned up the heat and raced with the dogs for home.

We were all soaked. Zack had gone to the office early so Brock came up and helped me with the dogs. When Esme and Pantera were dried and fed, Brock went downstairs to shower and change. I invited him to come up and have waffles with Taylor and me when he was ready. So there were three of us for breakfast.

Taylor was in fine fettle. She and Declan had tickets for a rock concert that weekend, and Declan had scored backstage passes. Taylor had her tablet on the table between us, and she was showing Brock and me videos of the band they were going to see when the phone rang.

Warren Weber's rumbling bass filled my ear. "Zack just called to tell me about the Chamber of Commerce. That's welcome news, Joanne."

"It is," I said. "Are you and Annie still at the lake with Simon?"

"Yes. It's pleasant here, and that's the other reason I called. Is somebody staying at your cottage? Simon was canoeing yesterday and he saw a man and a child on the beach in front of your place."

"I'm sorry, Warren, I should have called you, but it's been crazy around here. The man is Michael Goetz, and the little girl is Slater Doyle's daughter, Bridie. She's been through so much. We thought Lawyers' Bay might be a good place for her to recover."

"Are you and Zack coming up this weekend?"

"I wish, but I'll be knocking on doors and Zack will be making discreet phone calls. Next weekend for sure. Meanwhile, I'll call Michael and tell him that he and Bridie can have a quiet weekend at the lake."

While I was on the phone, Brock had cleared the table. After I hung up, he came over and sat down. "About Michael . . . ," he said.

"How did that go?" I said.

Brock raised an eyebrow. "It was painful. Zenaya took Bridie down to the beach so we could be alone. You *did* know that Zenaya has come back to take care of Bridie?"

"I knew," I said. "Michael called and asked if it was all right if Zenaya stayed with them. I was relieved to hear that she was back in Bridie's life. Bridie needs to feel safe."

"It's going to take a while," Brock said. "She still isn't speaking."

"Apart from that, how does she seem?"

"She's fearful, but Michael says that since Zenaya's been with her, Bridie seems better. Bridie likes the beach and she's enjoying Madeleine and Lena's old toys, so Michael is hopeful. And I'm hopeful for him."

"But you're not going back to him."

"No. That's what Michael wanted, but I told him it was over. He didn't seem surprised. There's been too much grief and too many painful memories. When I said we both needed to start with a fresh slate, he understood."

"Did you tell him about Derek?"

"Yes. I know that must seem like rubbing salt in the wound, but there aren't many secrets in the Regina gay scene, and I felt Michael should hear it from me first."

"I agree. Any idea what he's planning to do next?"

"Short-term he's looking for a cottage to rent somewhere not too far from the city. Michael thinks Bridie would benefit from a summer at the lake. It would be good for him too. He's found a publisher interested in his book on strategies to support high-risk and gang-involved youth that he started way back when we were together, so he's going into high gear on that."

"Did he mention Slater?"

"Just to tell me that when Slater left the house the day he died, Michael asked where he was going, and Slater said, 'To do the right thing.'"

"Further confirmation that Slater knew who was behind the abduction."

"Apparently, and whoever it was killed him."

"Michael *has* told the police this," I said.

"Yes, and they're ripping Michael's house apart looking for something that might identify the killer."

"But they didn't come up with anything?"

"No. So far, they have nothing."

———

Brock had a staff meeting at Racette-Hunter, so I drove to City Hall alone. It was a wretched drive. The rain came down so heavily I could barely see the road ahead. A power outage in North Central had knocked out the traffic lights, and as I inched along, the wind whipped leaves off the trees and onto my windshield. I didn't exhale until I pulled up in staff parking.

Just as I got out of my car, Milo steered his Harley into the space beside me. I was dumbfounded. He had on a full-face helmet and when he took it off, his face shone with exhilaration. "Now *that*," he said, "was a ride."

Milo's joie de vivre rankled. "Are you out of your mind – being on a motorcycle in this weather?" I said.

A sharp crack of thunder was followed almost immediately by a bolt of lightning. Milo raised his face to the heavens. "Time to take it inside," he said. "I'm risk-averse."

The look I gave Milo was withering, but he was nonchalant. "Before you give me a lecture, check out what I'm wearing: a quality rain suit, waterproof boots and gloves, and . . . " He waggled the thumb of his glove. "That little squeegee thing on my thumb keeps my visor clean. Jo, I know what I'm doing. I never ride in the first fifteen minutes of a rainstorm because that's when all the crud on the road mixes with the water and turns the road into greased owl shit. And when it's raining, I take it slow." His eyes met mine. "Convinced?"

"No, but I'm backing off."

He grinned. "My lucky day, but we really should get inside. Getting struck by lightning while I was with you would be a sweet exit, but if we got fried, there would be no tweets from the mayor's office about the big man's announcement."

I'd assumed the lobby would be deserted, but it was filled. Zack, Mansell, and a smartly turned-out woman I didn't recognize were standing under a mural chatting while people toting media equipment milled about. I started towards them, but Milo touched my arm. "Something has come up that I'm not cool about sharing with Mansell."

"I'm exercising caution there too," I said. "So what is it?"

"The police have checked the messages on Slater's phone, and my source tells me that on June 4, Slater sent Piper Edwards a text saying, 'We know you did it.'"

"And Slater was murdered that weekend. Do the police think Piper killed him?"

"No, and she didn't kill Lee either. She has iron-clad alibis for the time of both murders. On the day Lee was killed, Piper went straight from the CPG meeting at Lee's to a meeting with her constituents about an old swimming pool in their neighbourhood being closed because it was deemed unsafe. The meeting lasted four hours. The constituents came and went, but Piper was there the whole time. The weekend Slater died, she was in Winnipeg with friends. She left Thursday night and came back Sunday."

"Then what was Slater alluding to?"

"The heritage birds. The police brought Piper in for questioning as soon as they found the deleted text. She denied everything and her alibis for the murders checked out, so she walked away. Last night, Piper's Honda was on the receiving end of a rear-ender. When the cops opened the trunk, they found a container that piqued their curiosity. They asked Piper about it, and she freaked, so they took it in for testing. It turned out to be cyanide."

"Why would she leave cyanide in the trunk of her car?"

Milo gave me a lazy smile. "Piper's a responsible citizen. She was probably just keeping the cyanide out of harm's way till Hazardous Waste Disposal Day."

"That's in May," I said.

"Piper was prepared to wait," Milo said. "Anyway, I just got a text saying she's at police headquarters and she's signed a confession."

"Milo, where are you getting this information from?"

"Just around," he said.

"You're talking to me now," I said. "I'm one of the three people in the world you trust, remember? I'd like to know where this is coming from."

"Okay. I'm friendly with an IT guy at police headquarters. You know how it is with IT guys. Everybody ignores them. All I have so far is what I've told you."

I shivered, and Milo put his arm around my shoulders. "Are you okay?"

"I'm just trying to process this," I said. "I've been assuming that one person was behind everything that's happened. Now we know that's not the case. But it makes sense. Piper was jealous of Lee's relationship with Bobby Stevens, and during our vetting process for slate candidates, several people mentioned that Piper has a mean streak. I just never thought she was capable of killing innocent creatures."

"So you think she just lost it?"

"It happens," I said. "I guess the note she left for Lee in the mailbox said it all. 'Now you know how it feels to lose what you love.' Whatever her motive, Piper's going to pay in hard coin for this."

Milo nodded. "Yeah, there's the legal thing and then there's the political thing. Getting the vote out for a killer of heritage birds will be tricky."

"You could do it," I said.

"Possibly. But I'm not going to. Those birds were stellar. So was Lee. Moving right along – Jo, the big man will hear about Piper Edward's confession from the chief of police within the hour. Until he does, what I've just told you stays between us."

I met his eyes. "Understood."

"I never have to dot the i's and cross the t's for you," he said, and then he cupped my elbow in his hand and pushed me gently forward. "Time to join the party."

———

Usually the announcement of an endorsement was as stylized as a Kabuki dance: the big reveal, a few minutes of grip-and-grin photo ops, and occasionally a question or two. But today, something was clearly amiss.

When she saw us, Norine MacDonald approached. "The power's out. One of the elevators is stuck between floors. Someone trapped in the elevator is having a meltdown. Workmen are trying to fix the elevator and a psychologist is trying to talk down the person inside. Incidentally, if I were in that elevator, I would be that person."

"I can't imagine you losing control, Norine," I said. "So how's Zack?"

"You know Zack. Play it as it lays. He, Mansell, and Lydia Mah from the Chamber of Commerce aren't going to bother waiting for the power to come back on. They're just going to go ahead with the announcement. The quality of the TV video won't be great, but all that really matters is the endorsement." She glanced across the lobby. "Looks like they're ready to go."

I moved so that I'd be in Zack's sight line, and he smiled and introduced Lydia Mah. I liked her statement. It wasn't effusive, but her explanation of why the chamber was urging people to vote Yes in the referendum was cogent, and her voice rang with conviction when she said that careful planning and respect for the environment were key to our city's future growth.

Then Zack asked for questions. Surprisingly, the questions were aimed at Mansell. They came in a barrage, and they were tough. What had Mansell's sudden support of the Yes vote done to his standing with his former colleagues at Lancaster? Did it end his marriage to Quinn Donnelly? Was his decision related to Bridie Doyle's kidnapping? Could he offer the media any insights into who might have killed Slater Doyle?" Mansell handled the questions well, and the press conference ended without incident – smiles and hand-shakes all around.

"Anything I can do here?" Milo said.

"Nope – it's a lovefest."

"In that case, I'm going to take off."

"Stay in touch," I said.

Milo paused. "Always," he said, and then he walked away.

By the time I joined Zack and the others, the power had been restored, the passenger trapped in the elevator had been released, and Mansell was on his phone. I introduced myself to Lydia and told them I thought that, given the cosmic pyrotechnics, the session had gone well. We chatted briefly, then Lydia left for a meeting, Zack went to talk to Norine, and Mansell ended his call. He seemed upset. "Is something wrong?" I said.

"Bette felt the questions were too personal, and that Zack should have stepped in and cut them off."

"If Zack had stepped in and cut off the questions, it would have looked as if he didn't trust your ability to answer them truthfully."

"That's what I told Bette."

"Siblings can overreact," I said. "And Lee told me you and Bette are as tight as ticks."

It was a playful phrase, but Mansell's face darkened. "In what context did Lee say that?"

"Nothing specific. She wasn't being critical, Mansell. It was just an affectionate observation."

"Well then," he said. He started to walk away but changed his mind. "Joanne, it might be wise if you and Zack stayed away from my sister for a while. She can be . . . erratic."

It was a peculiar comment, but Mansell didn't give me time to respond. He simply cleared his throat, excused himself, and walked across the lobby and out into the rain.

———

It was five to ten when Mansell left City Hall. The day was young, and I had work to do. I spent the morning sitting on an exercise ball in the Noodle House pondering the significance of Mansell's warning about Bette and waiting for Zack to call about Piper Edwards's confession. While I pondered and waited, I checked through the lists of voters we knew would support us. I'd just finished the lists when Milo arrived, rolled an exercise ball over to the space next to me, sat down, and ripped open a Crispy Crunch.

"News about Piper Edwards," he said. "Or have you already heard?"

"Zack hasn't called, so all I know is what you told me."

"Maybe I'm not the only one with a trust issue," Milo said. "The chief of police must be playing her cards close to her chest." He moved closer and inhaled deeply. "Rosemary and mint – a heady blend," he said. "You've changed shampoos."

"I used Taylor's this morning," I said. "I'll tell her you approve."

"That scent really does it for me," he said. "But enough moon-bagging – time for reality. It seems Quinn Donnelly and Lee Crawford aren't the only ones who share a history." He bit into his Crispy Crunch. For a man who apparently subsisted wholly on chocolate, Milo had the most beautiful teeth, dazzlingly white and even. When he'd finished his first bite, Milo turned to me. "Piper Edwards is the daughter of the academic adviser with whom Lee had the affair. Piper blamed Lee for breaking up her parents' marriage."

"So Piper sees Lee as the woman who destroyed her family and took the man she loved away from her."

Milo rocked back and forth on the exercise ball. "Yes, and when she and Quinn met at a women's networking dinner, they struck up a friendship. When they discovered they both hated Lee Crawford, they became besties."

"But their differences over the referendum issue put an end to their friendship?"

"Not necessarily. For both Quinn and Piper, Lee Crawford was the enemy. It's conceivable that they teamed up when the need arose."

"That possibility makes my blood run cold," I said.

"Mine too," Milo said. He jumped up, rolled his exercise ball across the room, and headed for the door. "My guess is the boys and girls in blue are digging into that intriguing possibility even as we speak."

CHAPTER

18

Piper Edwards's confession that she had killed the heritage birds eclipsed every other news story the weekend before the referendum, but there was no public mention of a connection between Piper and Quinn Donnelly. Piper did not speak directly to the press. She was in seclusion. At noon on Friday, her lawyer, Paul Bellerive, delivered a brief statement saying that Piper had confessed to poisoning the birds and that she deeply regretted her actions. He refused to answer questions about motive, about the possible effect Piper's confession would have on the referendum vote, or about Piper's political future.

Debbie watched Paul Bellerive's statement with us at the condo. When he finished, Debbie filled us in on the investigation into Piper's background. I was relieved that Zack was finally made aware of the link between Piper and Quinn Donnelly, but Debbie told us that the link had proved to be insignificant. Both women were open about the fact that they hated Lee, but after hours of questioning both Piper and Quinn about their activities since May 17, the RCMP and the Regina police had come up empty. Both women's alibis for the time surrounding Lee's murder were solid. Piper had been meeting with her constituents. When I'd challenged Quinn about her whereabouts the afternoon she had agreed to meet me, Bette had been quick to volunteer that Quinn had been caring for her, and when the police questioned her, she'd stuck to her story.

Piper's confession torpedoed our campaign's plans, calibrations, and calculations once and for all. The message on social media came through loud and clear – a pox on all their houses. People were sick of politics, sick of politicians, sick of lies and betrayals and hypocrisy. Our campaign had been grassroots, based on the premise that if we identified and got out our supporters we could win. The latest news about the referendum had been tabloid-worthy, and I fretted over the possibility that our volunteers, even the seasoned ones, had had enough.

All we could do was put our heads down and carry on. The next four days were a blur. Zack was at City Hall dealing with the business of the city and the fallout from the fact that a heretofore-trusted colleague on council was facing criminal charges. I was at the Noodle House doing everything I could to breathe life into the dying Yes campaign.

At four-thirty on the day before the vote, I picked Taylor up at school, dropped her off at the condo, and drove to the Noodle House. Milo was there waiting. He grinned when he saw me. "I've been waiting for you. I have news."

"What's the news?" I said.

"We're fucked," he said.

I laughed. "Tell me something I don't know."

That night Zack sent out a final tweet urging people to remember what was at stake; consider the options and remember to vote. The outcome of the referendum was out of our hands, and I slept more soundly than I had in weeks.

———

On the day of the referendum, Zack and I voted at Racette-Hunter with Brock and Margot. They brought Lexi and Kai along because they wanted the children to see them vote. My late husband, Ian, and I had done the same thing with our kids when they were little. For us it was always a great photo op.

At three-thirty on Referendum Day I was sitting on my exercise ball in the Noodle House exchanging texts with Milo. The writing on the wall didn't take long to appear. As we'd anticipated, voter turnout was dismal, but our diehard volunteers had been diligent about ensuring that our most faithful supporters made it to the polls. Mansell Donnelly was proving his worth in rubies by getting his friends in the business community to urge their associates to vote Yes. Warren Weber, too, was a powerful weapon, and Milo's readings of Facebook and Twitter indicated that Zack's tweet had nudged some people into making the effort to cast a ballot.

I took heart in the fact that Milo reported the No vote was as weak as ours and it was possible we might squeak out a win. If I squinted hard I could see the silver lining in the cloud, but I had the hollow feeling in the pit of my stomach that I had every E-Day. Until the polls closed and the last vote was counted, I always waited for the surprise – the dragon that would slink out of the ditch and destroy everything we'd worked for.

The dragon who strolled through the door of the Noodle House was a nice-looking young man badly in need of a shave and some sleep. He carried a travel-worn Regina Rams backpack. He looked around the room. "Is Milo here?"

"No. I'm Joanne Shreve. Milo and I've been working together on the referendum vote. Can I help you?"

He shifted his backpack. "I don't know. This is a bit complicated," he said. "Maybe I'd better wait for Milo." His body swayed, and I reached out to keep him from falling.

He laughed. "Or maybe I'd better not wait. As you can see, I'm dead on my feet." He held out his hand to me and gave me a smile that was brief but real. "My name's Dustin Kovac."

I thought his face was familiar, but I'd taught university for two decades and over the years, there'd been many young faces. Dustin Kovac might have been a former student or a volunteer, or both. Racking my brain for context was pointless.

"Pleased to meet you, Dustin," I said. "What can I do for you?"

"I just got back from Belgrade," he said. "My grandfather was dying and my parents hoped I'd get there before he passed." He waited expectantly until I picked up my cue.

"Did you make it?" I said.

"Yes, but it was pretty much a disaster. My grandfather thought I was my father when he was young, and he got mad because when he talked to me in Serbian one of my aunts had to translate so I could answer. He kept yelling 'stmjika stmjika' at me. That means 'stubborn.'" Dustin shrugged. "At least now I know one word of Serbian."

"I'm sorry it didn't work out for you."

"It was okay," he said. "I got to meet my dad's family. They're pretty cool, and the old man gave me a kiss before he died. When I put my arms around him, he said, 'I don't know who you are, but they say you're mine, so here's a kiss.' Then he said, 'Next time we speak Serbian.'" Dustin laughed and shook his head. "Why am I telling you this?"

"Because you're jet-lagged," I said. "Did you come straight from the airport?"

"Yeah, I figured better late than never, and I thought Milo should see this." He slid his backpack off and took out his phone. "It may not mean anything, but I'm studying journalism and they say that if something seems suspicious, we should record it."

The significance of the video didn't hit me at first. A man and a woman were in the parking lot of a strip mall having what was clearly an intense discussion. The pair was too far away for the camera to pick up their words, but their identity was unmistakable. Slater Doyle and Bette Stevens certainly made an odd couple. Slater was upset. Bette was trying to calm him down. Finally, she took out an envelope, put it on the hood of Slater's Lexus, and wrote something. Slater looked at the envelope quickly, nodded, then got into his car and drove off. Bette's red truck wasn't far behind.

As I stared at the video I felt a frisson of excitement. "Dustin, do you remember when you took this?"

"Yeah, Friday, June 5. The day before I left for Serbia."

"And today's June 17," I said.

"Right," he said. "Have you ever been to Serbia?"

"No, I haven't."

"It's like another world. When I was there, I didn't think about Regina once. Then on the plane home, reality hit. I realized today was the referendum – the subject of my major paper for my investigative journalism class – and I didn't have a clue what had been going down for the past two weeks. When I checked on my phone, I saw that Slater Doyle had been murdered. I thought I recognized him as the guy in my video and sure enough . . . " Dustin rubbed his chin stubble. "As part of my research I was at a lot of the CPG meetings. So was Bette Stevens, so identifying her was no problem. Anyway, I decided to talk to Milo about how to handle this."

"Why didn't you go to the police?"

"Because Milo's a cool guy. I trust him and I knew I could count on him to do the right thing until I got some sleep. Lame, eh?"

Dustin's young face was grey with weariness. "Not lame," I said. "Send me the video, but please don't do anything else with it. I'll get it to the police. The authorities will want to talk to you, but I think tomorrow will be fine. Just leave your contact information with me and I'll pass it on."

As soon as the door closed on Dustin, I called Zack and told him about the video. When I finished, Zack was all business. "Send it to Debbie. Let her handle it. You have enough on your plate."

"You don't know the half of it," I said. "Zack, before I do anything, we need to talk."

I could feel the concern in his voice. "Is everybody okay?"

"Everybody's fine."

"Then whatever it is, we'll handle it. I can be home in thirty minutes. Let's order in pizza and watch a movie until the results come in."

It was Taylor's turn to choose a pizza, so we were having the all-dressed vegetarian from the Copper Kettle. Zack was a meat man. The fact that he never once bristled at Taylor's choice always struck me as a mark of his love.

We took our drinks out to the terrace. The sky was rain-washed and blue, and the air was soft. We sipped our martinis and Zack raised an eyebrow. "Ready to talk?"

"I am, but I want you to listen like a lawyer. I need your opinion on whether I've got enough evidence, for lack of a better word, to take to Debbie."

Zack cocked his head. "Okay," he said. "Let's hear it."

"This morning after the press conference, Bette Stevens called Mansell. I could see he was upset and when I asked what the problem was, he said Bette was furious because you hadn't stepped in to stop the personal questions directed at him. Mansell understood why you didn't interfere. He and I talked a little about overprotective siblings, then he said goodbye and started to leave. After he'd taken a few steps, he turned back and told me that you and I should stay away from Bette for a while because she can be 'erratic.'

"When I went to the Noodle House to work, Mansell's words stayed with me, and I stitched together a scenario. There are holes in the storyline, but I think it hangs together."

Zack's smile was encouraging. "Go on," he said.

"I think Bette Stevens is at the centre of everything, starting with Colin Brokenshire's death. I believe that, contrary to George Sawchuk's advice, Colin went to Bette and told her he was marrying Lee, and I think that Bette was driving the truck that killed Colin and that she killed him intentionally."

"But Mansell took responsibility."

"He did, and Mansell's guilt about what he did ruined his life. I think Bette's hatred for Lee grew over the years, but she knew that to protect Mansell and herself, she had to control it. Then Lee agreed to marry Bobby, and Bette lost it.

"She told Slater that when Lee was seventeen years old she'd initiated a sexual relationship with her guardian because she wanted the Brokenshire farm. That was what Slater alluded to when he called Lee 'St. Lee of Assisi' the day he almost ran me over after the CPG meeting. Bette had stayed close to Lee during the years after Colin died, and she would have known about the men in Lee's life, including Simon. Quinn Donnelly would have told her sister-in-law about Lee's affair with her dissertation adviser, and that would have fuelled the fire.

"At Peter and Maisie's wedding, over a hundred people saw Simon sitting in the yellow canoe throughout the wedding and reception. He was clearly disturbed. When Lee's birds were poisoned, Bette assumed Simon was guilty. She had found the perfect scapegoat for her own crime.

"After Lee's death, Bette needed an alibi, and when she overheard me asking Quinn where she went after she left the office on the day she was supposed to meet me, Bette jumped in. Quinn seemed confused when she heard Bette's story about the sciatica attack. At first, I thought Bette was protecting her sister-in-law, but if she was creating an alibi for herself, Bette was also giving Quinn a weapon.

"And when the balance shifted to the Yes side after Lee's death, Quinn Donnelly knew the only way to redress the balance was through an event as dramatic as Lee's murder. Slater was desperate. He proposed the abduction. Quinn approached Bette about helping Slater abduct his daughter. Bette refused, but Mansell had told his wife what had really happened to Colin, and Quinn was beginning to suspect that Bette was guilty of Lee's murder too. When Quinn threatened to go to the police, Bette couldn't refuse.

"After I showed Slater the second picture of his daughter, he contacted Bette, saying that he would go to the police if she didn't return Bridie. To protect herself from repercussions from Quinn, Bette moved Bridie to a new hiding place. The video Dustin took recorded the moment when Bette, seeming to capitulate, gave Slater the keys to the farmhouse where Bridie had initially been held. When Slater arrived at the house, she shot him."

As I'd spun my tale, Zack's dark eyes had been coolly analytical. When I finished, he shook his head. "It's a compelling argument, Jo, and for what it's worth, I think you're probably right, but it's not enough. Everything's based on premises that could be false. A lawyer like me could shoot holes in this so fast the Crown wouldn't have time to duck. That said, the video is valuable. It shows that just before his death, Slater Doyle met with Bette Stevens. It gives the police an angle they didn't have before. They haven't looked into Bette Stevens's activities at all. Her connection with all this seemed tangential. This video proves it wasn't, but, Jo, you have to send it to Debbie immediately. She'll have questions she wants answered right away. I'll try to stave her off. Until the final vote is in, we have to deal with the referendum. I think she'll agree to meet us here tomorrow morning. You can tell her your theory then."

"Holes and all?" I said.

"Holes and all," Zack said. "You've raised a lot of points that are worth pursuing. Bette will have no reason to suspect the authorities are onto her, so that will give the Regina police and the RCMP a head start."

When the polls closed, I exhaled. It was finally over. Milo, Zack, Taylor, and I watched the results at Margot's. Lexi and Kai were asleep, so the sound of the TV was kept low. Our mood, too, was muted. The results seesawed all evening, but in the end the city voted Yes. We shared hugs and handshakes, but we were far from jubilant. The referendum had inflicted a devastating toll. Our victory was Pyrrhic, and we knew it.

We'd planned a rally, but after Piper's confession, I had cancelled the venue we'd rented and we had announced that when the results were in, Zack would make a statement at City Hall. Milo was taking his Harley, so Zack and I drove to City Hall alone and in silence.

All the media outlets had sent their second stringers, and Zack's statement was brief. He praised the people's wisdom, thanking those who'd endorsed him, especially Warren Weber and Lydia Mah and the Chamber of Commerce, and promised that, as it had been since he was sworn in as mayor, everything the executive director of City Planning and Development did would be absolutely transparent. He also announced that David Christopher would continue with his post. Zack praised Christopher for coming out of retirement, for doing exemplary work during the transition period from the Ridgeway to the Shreve administration, and for his office's fair and balanced policy that informed the new bylaws.

After Zack finished, the media had questions. As I listened, the accumulated weight of the past month hit me and I began to cry. Milo and I were standing by the door. He put his arm around my shoulders and led me into the deserted hallway.

"It wasn't worth it," I said.

"It will be," Milo whispered, and then he stroked my hair and murmured reassurances till I was calm enough to go back inside.

The next morning when I got back from my run, Debbie and Zack were sitting in the kitchen having coffee. I poured myself a glass of juice and joined them. Debbie's phone was on the table in front of her. "I've looked at this video a dozen times," she said. "Zack says you got it from one of your volunteers."

"His name's Dustin Kovac," I said. "He brought it to the Noodle House late yesterday afternoon. I should have sent you Dustin's contact information last night, but I honestly didn't think you'd have much luck with him until he got some sleep. He'd just come back from his grandfather's funeral in Belgrade and he was jet-lagged."

Debbie checked her watch. "He's probably still sleeping. I can wait a couple of hours. I already have every frame of this video memorized." She picked up her phone and turned her eyes to the screen. "Bette takes out the envelope, puts it on the hood of Doyle's car, writes something, and then hands the envelope to Doyle," she said. "End of transaction." Debbie shifted her eyes from the screen back to us. "Doyle had the key to the padlock with him," she said. "But no envelope. We're still looking for that.

"There were footprints in the dirt outside the cabin," she continued. "Someone tried to scuff over them, but whoever did the scuffing must have been rushed. You know that Aesop fable about the lion and the fox? The lion invites all the animals into his den to pay their respects. When the lion asks the fox why he's the only one hanging back, the fox says, 'I see many hoof marks going in, I see none coming out.' Anyway, despite our suspect's attempt to obliterate the footprints, the RCMP was able to determine that two people went into the cabin that night but only one came out. The one who came out was wearing western boots. Not unusual around here, but I notice that in this video Bette Stevens is wearing western boots."

"I've seen those boots, and I imagine they were specially made for Bette." I said. "When I asked her where she got them, Bette said they were a gift. My guess is they were from Colin Brokenshire."

Debbie frowned. "We knew they had a relationship, but it was so far in the past, we didn't pursue it." She rose to leave. "Maybe we should."

I motioned her to sit down again. "I agree," I said. "Deb, there's more. This is all conjecture, but Zack and I both think there might be something here."

As I laid out my theories, Deb's pen never stopped moving. When I finished, she looked up at me. "I don't want Bette Stevens to know we're digging around. Anyone I talk to will have to be discreet. Any suggestions?"

I gave Debbie George Sawchuk's contact information and questions he might be able to help with. Debbie took her mug to the sink and rinsed it. "I'll be in touch," she said. "Are you going to be around?"

"We're planning to go to the lake after Taylor gets home from school tomorrow," Zack said. "But until then, we'll be in the city."

"As long as I can get in touch," Debbie said. "Joanne, thanks for this. I've been banging my head against the wall. A fresh perspective will help. It's time to start nailing down evidence."

———

After I'd showered and eaten, I called Michael Goetz and told him we'd be at the lake by dinnertime the next day. No one would be using our family's extra cottage so he and Bridie were welcome to stay there. His relief was obvious. "This means a great deal to us, Joanne. Bridie's not talking yet, but she's starting to engage more, and I don't want to risk the progress she's made. I know it's late to look for a rental, but I'm hoping we can find a place on the lake for the summer. Money's not a problem, so if you hear of anything, please let me know. I'm trying to keep a low profile, but Simon Weber has been asking around for me, and he put up a notice in the Point Store, so I have some feelers out."

"I'm glad you and Simon are getting acquainted."

Michael laughed. "Simon and me and Bridie and Old Yeller."

"I take it Old Yeller is a dog."

"He is. Apparently he showed up at the Webers's cottage last week, and he's appointed himself Simon's sidekick. He's a golden lab crossed with something very large. Simon was a fan of the movie *Old Yeller*, hence the name. Simon's Old Yeller loves the canoe and he loves to chase sticks. The only time Bridie smiles is when she's with that dog."

"Animals are the best therapy," I said. "We'll see you around five tomorrow night."

"We've restocked the groceries, so no need to shop."

"You didn't have to do that, but thanks. Give Old Yeller a head scratch for me."

I spent the morning at the Noodle House cleaning up the detritus of the referendum campaign. It was mindless but necessary work. Around half past ten, Milo came by. "I knew you'd be here," he said, and he began boxing up unused brochures. He turned on the classic rock station and we worked in companionable silence for an hour. Zack called at 11:45. "Are you free for lunch? It's liver and onions day."

"Sounds tempting," I said. "But I'm at the Noodle House clearing out referendum stuff and I'm making good time. I think I'll just stick with it."

"Want me to call somebody to go over there and help you?"

"I'm okay," I said. "Milo's here."

For a moment there was silence. "There's a picture of you two that's getting some serious retweeting,"

"Of Milo and me?"

"Yeah. Somebody took it last night. You might want to check it out."

"I will. Thanks for the lunch invitation. Next week for sure."

"Yeah, next week for sure," Zack said, and our call ended.

"Zack says we should check out Twitter. Apparently there's a picture of us."

The picture was taken after Milo led me out of the room because I was crying. We had our arms around each other and he appeared to be kissing my hair. The caption read "Joanne Shreve and her very young assistant, Milo O'Brien, doing a victory lap."

"Why would anyone put that on Twitter?" I said.

"Why does anyone put anything on Twitter?" Milo said. "To strut or to make trouble. It'll be something else tomorrow. Do you think you should call the big man?"

"I'll talk to him about it later."

"Fair enough. Hey, do you want to get something to eat?"

"Are you actually going to put food in your mouth?"

"Yeah. Once in a while I go crazy. A new deli just opened on Scarth Street. Let's finish off here and grab a sandwich."

Cleaning out the Noodle House was dusty work, and when I got home, I had my second shower of the day, looked at my bed, and gave into temptation. I awoke from my nap refreshed and ready for action. Remembering Debbie's parting words, I reached for my phone. It really was time to start nailing down evidence. I punched in Peter's cell number, and he answered on the first ring.

"Perfect timing," he said. "I was just going to call you, Mum. I could use some help. Sixteen Narragansett turkey poults are going to be delivered within the half-hour. They're two days old and they need to be hand-fed both food and water as soon as we receive them. Apparently, they can't learn to do that by themselves. I've got a water-trough brooder set up, but I'm nervous. Colin's notes are reassuring, but the literature says that turkey poults can die off easily."

"I'll be there in half an hour," I said. When I started for the door, Esme was right behind me. "Okay, you can come," I said. "But you have to stay in the house. I don't think the turkey poults are ready for you yet."

The poults beat me to the farm but not by much. They were already squirming to get out of their box when I arrived. I put Esme in the house, and then washed my hands and joined my son. We each picked up a poult, dipped its beak in water and then in food, placed it in the brooder, and then picked up another poult and repeated the process. By the time we'd fed and watered everybody, the poults were running between the waterer and the feeder themselves.

Peter and I gave each other self-congratulatory smiles. "They're quick learners," I said.

"In his notes, Colin said they would be," Peter said. "I never would have tried heritage turkeys if he hadn't been so reassuring. Mum, I know I've said this before, but Colin's records of what he did and how he did it are so detailed I feel as if he's here with me guiding me every step of the way. Lee's notes are the same. I'm in good hands."

"Actually, Colin's notes are what I wanted to talk to you about," I said. "Maisie told me that the notes are not simply an account of Colin's farming practises, that he also includes comments about the events of his day. I think the last entries Colin made before he died might shed light on everything that's happened." As I ran through my suspicions about Bette Stevens's involvement in the tragedies that had begun with Colin's death, Peter listened intently, his expression shifting from uncertainty to disbelief and, finally, to horror.

"Let's go take a look," Peter said. He gave the poults a final check and we went into the house. After we washed up, I followed my son into the office on the main floor. The day I'd come out to help sort through Lee's things, Maisie had pointed out the leather-bound notebooks, one a year, lined up on the bookshelves. The black ones were Colin's; the dark-green were Lee's. Peter took down the black notebook marked 2004 and flipped through the pages until he found what we needed and passed the notebook to me. Colin's handwriting was small, neat, and cautious, but I could feel the fear in the words he wrote. "Telling B was a mistake. I've never seen such hurt and such rage. L and I will have to take a break from her."

And then nothing but blank pages.

Lee began her own notes in a fresh notebook on January 1, 2005.

I put the 2004 notebook in my bag. "Lee obviously never read this," I said. "I guess she couldn't bring herself to look at Colin's last entry."

Peter put his hands on his knees and dropped his head. "Bette was like a mother to Maisie and Lee. How could she have done this? First Colin and then Lee. Colin died eleven years ago. Why would she kill Lee now?"

"Two days before Lee was killed, she told Bobby she was finally ready to settle down with him. He was planning to tell Bette later that night."

"And Bette found the possibility of her son marrying the woman Colin Brokenshire loved insupportable," Peter said. "Mum, I don't even want to think about what this will do to Maisie. She's already torn apart by the idea that the last face Lee saw was the face of her murderer. Learning that Lee died aware that Bette Stevens hated her enough to kill her . . . " He rubbed his temples. "And Bobby – my God, what will this do to him?"

As Peter walked me to the door of the farmhouse, Bette Stevens's red truck pulled into the driveway. We both panicked. "What do we do?" he said.

"I guess just carry on as usual," I said.

"I don't think I can," Peter said.

Bette got out of her truck and reached back in and pulled out a cooler. "We're going to have to," I said. From the first time I'd seen Esme's reaction to the red truck, I'd been curious. This was the chance to get answers. "Pete, go out and open the gate so Bette can get into the yard with the cooler. Make sure you shut the gate behind you. I'm going to let Esme out."

"Why?"

"Just do what I said."

Peter looked hesitant as he greeted Bette and opened the gate. She entered the yard, and he shut the gate behind her. Esme had found a cool place in the office and she was sleeping. I picked up her leash and called her. After she'd loped up the hall, I clipped her leash to her collar and, holding on tightly, I opened the front door. As soon as she saw Bette, Esme began to growl, pulling at the leash with such power that I could barely hang on as she dragged me towards Bette. Seeing the dog, Bette dropped the cooler and made for the gate, opening it and quickly pushing it shut behind her. Esme was a gentle dog, but the moment Bette started running, she seemed to become possessed. Yanking free of me, snarling and teeth bared, she hurled herself at the gate.

Bette wasted no time getting away. As the red truck peeled down the driveway, Esme ran the length of the fence towards the road. She was still snarling and growling in the direction where Bette's truck had disappeared when Peter and I went to get her.

She was panting heavily and her eyes were wild. Peter and I both knelt to pat her. When, finally, she realized the threat had disappeared, she relaxed. Peter and I were breathing hard. "That was terrifying," he said. "I've been with that dog hundreds of times. I've never seen her like that."

"That's because Esme's never been that close to the person who murdered her owner," I said.

When Peter and I walked into the kitchen with Esme, my phone was ringing. I took it out of my bag and answered. Mansell's speaking voice was usually rich and authoritative, but that afternoon his voice was thin and uncertain. "Bette just called, screaming at me, saying that I have to kill your dog. She was hysterical. She told me you're at the Brokenshire farm, and that I have to go there and kill your dog because the dog saw her in the barn that day." His voice broke, and I wasn't sure if he'd be able to continue. But I knew he had a message to deliver, so for what seemed like an endless moment, I waited. Finally he pulled himself together. "Joanne, she killed Lee," he said. "First she killed Colin and then she killed Lee."

CHAPTER

19

As soon as my call from Mansell ended, I phoned Debbie and gave her a complete report. Bette had given her brother serious cause to believe that she'd killed Lee, and Mansell had told me that Bette had killed Colin Brokenshire. Debbie said she'd talk to Mansell personally and that since the investigation into Bette Stevens's activities would be in Carl Lovitz's jurisdiction, she'd be in touch with him. Before she hung up, she said, "The dominoes are falling, Joanne. I hope to God it's almost over."

When I hung up, Peter's expression was bleak. "I can't get my head around any of this," he said.

"Neither can I, and we still don't know the whole story. Don't say anything to anybody, not even Maisie, until we know exactly what's going on."

Two hours later, Zack and I were sitting on the terrace at the condo. I'd told him everything that transpired that afternoon at the Brokenshire farm. The magnitude of what had happened and of what lay ahead overwhelmed us both. But there was one problem left that had to be discussed.

"After I talked to you, I found the picture of Milo and me on Twitter," I said.

Zack's voice was tender. "You don't have to explain anything to me, Jo."

"I know I don't, and that's why I want to explain. Zack, from the day Maisie and Pete were married, I felt that I was swimming for the surface. I managed to stay afloat but only barely. When the results came in, I fell apart and Milo took me out in the hall to give me a chance to pull myself together."

"I wish I'd been there," Zack said. "But I wasn't, and I'm glad Milo was. It's that simple, Jo. I love you, and if you need something I can't give you, I'm grateful that there's someone else who can."

It's not easy for a man in a wheelchair and an able-bodied woman to manage a satisfying embrace, but Zack and I had plenty of practice. When the entrance buzzer sounded and we finally broke apart, I knew we both felt well and truly loved. Our visitor was Debbie Haczkewicz. We met her at the front door, and she was clearly keyed up.

"Bette Stevens is dead," she said.

Zack leaned forward. "What happened?"

"Carl and his officers went to the Stevens's farm to question Bette. There was no answer when they knocked. The front door was locked, so the officers went around the back. Bette Stevens was lying face down on the grass beside a pond. According to Carl, the scene was surreal. Bette Stevens had shot herself in the base of the head – the never-fail shot. She knew what she was doing. Carl suspects the gun she used will match the one used on Lee and Slater. But what grabbed everyone's attention was the fact that there were six swans gliding around the pond. Carl Lovitz says it was the first case for one of his officers, and the young woman couldn't stop talking about the birds. She couldn't believe there were swans in Saskatchewan."

"I've seen them," I said. "Bette told me that after her husband died she needed a reminder that there was beauty in the world, so she bought the swans."

Debbie shook her head with the impatience of a swimmer getting water out of her ear. "I hate it when we discover that a monster has a heart. And Bette Stevens was loved. Mansell was shattered when he heard she was dead. He didn't want her to be alone so he went straight to the farm. Incidentally, Carl Lovitz said Bette was wearing her western boots when she pulled the trigger."

"So she died with her boots on," Zack said, and he looked as sick as I felt.

Debbie and Inspector Carl Lovitz had agreed to make a statement in time for the late news, so Debbie had to go directly back to her office. When she left, Zack turned his chair towards the door. "We have to tell Peter and Maisie what's happened before the story hits the media."

Normally, it was a thirty-minute drive from the city to the farm. That night Zack made it in twenty. When Peter opened the door, I knew that a bad situation was about to get worse. Bobby Stevens was sitting at the dinner table and he and Maisie were clearly pleased to see us. "Join us," Bobby said. "These cabbage rolls are excellent. Of course, all cabbage rolls are excellent, but we also have beer."

Maisie came over and hugged us both. "Eat now while the freezer's still full of casseroles because when they're gone, I'm the chef, and nobody's looking forward to that."

She looked from my face to Zack's, and her smile vanished. "Something's happened," she said.

"Yes," I said, but I couldn't find the words to go on.

Zack wheeled closer to Bobby and covered Bobby's hand with his own. "There's bad news," he said. "Your mother died this afternoon."

Bobby leapt to his feet. "That can't be true," he said. "I saw Mum at lunch. She was fine."

"Was there an accident?" Peter said.

"It was suicide," Zack said softly. Maisie moved swiftly to Bobby's side.

Bobby brushed his wrist against his mouth. "My mother would never take her own life," he said. "This has to be a mistake."

"There's no mistake," Zack said. "The RCMP had evidence that Bette was involved in Lee's murder. They came to your farm with a search warrant, but your mother had already taken the matter into her own hands."

Bobby always had a high colour. Now the blood drained from his face. "Why would she kill Lee?"

"I don't know," Zack said. "Maybe we should all sit down."

Peter poured a glass of ginger ale for Maisie, then took a bottle of Crown Royal Black from the cupboard and poured the rest of us stiff drinks. Bobby drained his Crown Royal in a single gulp and poured himself another. "Tell me," he said.

Zack started with the death of Colin Brokenshire and from there he left nothing out. As he talked, Maisie, Peter, and Bobby were as motionless as mannequins. The bottle of Crown Royal sat in the centre of the table beside the casserole of cabbage rolls, both now untouched. A political friend of mine used to say, "There's no problem that can't be solved at a kitchen table over a bottle of rye and a plate of cabbage rolls." Until that night, I had believed my friend was right.

When Zack finished, he said, "Do any of you need to know more?"

As he looked at Maisie, Bobby's face was lifeless. "My mother took everything from you. What can I do?"

Maisie put her arms around him. "Be our friend," she said. Once again, the world as she knew it had been shattered, but

Maisie's voice was firm. "Bobby, this has to end somewhere. Pete and I need you, and you need us. Stay close, and we'll get through this."

Bobby nodded, but his eyes were unfocused, fixed on a horror the rest of us couldn't comprehend. His phone rang. He looked at the call display. "It's my Uncle Mansell," he said. He picked up, listened, then said he'd be there soon and hung up.

"Uncle Mansell is at the main house. There are police everywhere. He didn't want my mother to be alone with them. Neither do I." Bobby began clearing the table.

"You don't have to do that," Maisie said.

"My mother brought me up right," he said, and as the irony of his words struck him, he laughed mirthlessly. Bobby waved off our offers of help and continued scraping and rinsing the plates and cutlery. When all the dishes were submerged in a pan of hot, soapy water, Bobby headed for the door, his movements as stiffly mechanical as those of an automaton. "Thanks for supper, Maisie," he said. "I'm going home now."

Maisie, Peter, Zack, and I glanced at one another. "You shouldn't have to drive," Zack said. "Joanne and I will take you."

I went to our son and daughter-in-law. "Are you two okay?"

Peter pulled Maisie close. "We will be," he said.

Bobby was silent during the ten-minute drive to his family farm. We were two days away from the longest day of the year. The sun wouldn't set until after nine, but the sky was overcast, so the police had floodlit the ranch house, yard, and outbuildings. Officers darted from the house and grounds to the vehicles holding the paraphernalia that would allow them to collect and preserve evidence. With luck, they would be able to establish that Bette Stevens had deliberately driven over the man who had spurned her, and then waited eleven years to kill the woman Colin Brokenshire loved.

The driveway was blocked off. We waited until an officer came over to ask us our business. Bobby showed his identification and said he wanted to be with his uncle.

"How long till this is over?" he said.

As she looked at Bobby, the young officer's eyes were wide, and I wondered if she'd been the officer who couldn't believe there were swans in Saskatchewan. "Our part – not long," she said. "A few days at the most. After that, it's anyone's guess."

Bobby's laugh was derisive. "My money's on 'never,'" he said.

He shook hands with Zack and me and walked with the officer up the driveway – a lonely man: his past in tatters; his present unendurable; his future uncertain.

The next day when Taylor and I picked Zack up at City Hall for the drive to Lawyers' Bay, I sent Taylor off to look at some new art the city had purchased to hang in Henry Baker Hall, the room where council met, and then I went straight to get Zack. Trial lawyers are familiar with the dark workings of the human heart, but the horror of what Bette Stevens had done stunned Zack, and the late-afternoon sun pouring into his office showed a man badly in need of a weekend's respite. As soon as we were in the car, Zack turned on Bill Evans. As we had done many time before, we counted on the singing, melodic lines of Bill Evans's piano to quiet our minds and soothe our nerves.

Michael, Bridie, and Zenaya had moved down to the guest cottage. Zack and I had agreed to let Michael choose when he wanted to meet up with us. He came over after lunch on Saturday. He was tanned but still tense and preoccupied.

Zack motioned him to join us in the living room.

"Can we get you anything?" I said.

Michael had perched on the edge of his chair as if he might be called away at any minute. "Thanks," he said. "I'm fine. I just wanted to check in."

"Glad you did," Zack said. "How are you and Bridie doing?"

Michael's brow creased. "I'm hopeful, but it's going to be a long haul. Bridie's made some progress. The night terrors seem to have stopped. She still won't sleep alone, but as long as she can curl up with Zenaya, she sleeps soundly. She's eating well. She's still not talking, but she's trying to communicate through drawing. Kids who've suffered traumas use images much more readily than words; actually, adults who have been badly traumatized do too. Images, symbols, are the way the intuitive right side of the brain moves in to contain unbearable emotion when the cognitive left side shuts down. With Bridie, it's always the same thing: she draws hearts in a kind of pattern that I can't figure out. I encourage her, but it's as if she can't go forward until I understand what the hearts mean."

I leaned forward. "Michael, I have an idea about the hearts," I said. "There's evidence suggesting that Bette Stevens might have acted with Slater to abduct Bridie. Bette was with Slater shortly before he was killed, and she has a farm not far from the first house where Bridie was kept. Most significantly for Bridie, Bette had a pair of western boots with a pattern of hearts tooled into the leather."

I could see the hope in Michael's eyes. "Have the police arrested her?"

"She's dead. When the RCMP went to Bette Stevens's farm to question her about the deaths of Colin Brokenshire and Lee Crawford, they discovered her body by a pond near her house. She'd shot herself in the base of her skull."

"So she's no longer a threat to Bridie."

"No," I said. "But Bridie doesn't know that. How do you want to handle this?"

"We have to take it slow, let Bridie be our guide. But you could help with this, Joanne."

As Michael explained to me how to use drawing to help Bridie talk about the boots, he spoke carefully and with sensitivity. He was as invested as any father could be in his daughter's well-being, and for the first time I understood why Brock had cared about Michael Goetz for all these years. When Michael finished explaining how we might coax Bridie out of her shell, I said, "When do you want to do this?"

"Let's do it now. Zenaya wants to go into town this afternoon and I promised Bridie we'd go down to the beach. When Bridie and I start out, why don't you and Zack just fall in with us?"

At first Bridie held tightly to Michael's hand, but when the dogs rushed for the lake, Bridie ran after them.

"She seems to be doing better," I said.

Michael sighed. "That's why it's so painful to watch her. She appears to be improving, then the memory of what happened overcomes her and she starts drawing the hearts. When she's awake, she never gets through an hour without the ritual."

That afternoon, Bridie lasted twenty-five minutes before the need for the ritual overtook her. As she threw sticks into the lake for Pantera and Esme, and watched the dogs retrieve them, she seemed carefree. Then suddenly she dropped to her knees on the sand, picked up a stick, and, face knotted in memory, began drawing the hearts.

Heeding Michael's instructions, I knelt beside her and watched for a few minutes, and then I took the stick from her. "I wonder if this is where you saw the hearts," I said gently, and I drew a western boot around them. Bridie's intake of breath was sharp. For a time, she simply stared at the boot, her pale complexion mottled with rage. Then she seized the stick from me and began stabbing the boot.

"That's good," I said. "You're making the boots go away. They won't come back. Not ever. And the person wearing them will never hurt you again." When Bridie turned to look into my face, her lips were white with terror. I took her hand and guided it over the wet sand until the image of the boots was obliterated. "You made the boots go away," I said. "They're gone for good. They can't come back again and neither can the person who was wearing them."

Bridie seemed numb, and I wondered if I'd gone too far. She was trembling violently, but finally she spoke. "Promise?" she said.

"Promise," I said. Her small body was racked with sobbing. Michael drew her to him and held her until she had cried herself out. Zack handed Michael a tissue and Michael wiped Bridie's face clean. "Do you want to go back to the cottage now?"

Bridie nodded. "Yes," she said. "But not alone. I don't want to be alone ever again."

Michael carried Bridie up the hill in his arms. Zack and I watched until they were out of sight, and then Zack took out his phone and called Debbie. "Bridie was able to identify Bette's boots," he said. "So I guess this is finally over."

CHAPTER

20

As it always does, life went on. On July 1, Falconer Shreve held its annual Canada Day party. The first Canada Day party that Zack, Blake Falconer, Christopher Altieri, Delia Wainberg, and Kevin Hynd hosted at Lawyers' Bay had been a celebration of their new law partnership. It had been a BYOB-and-burgers beach bash for old law school friends. Guests were asked to provide their own mosquito spray and sleeping bags. Twenty-eight years later, the affair was bigger, slicker, and more corporate. There were still friends on the invitation list, but the party had become a way to say thank you to Falconer Shreve staff and clients. It was always a lot of fun, but the event was now catered, the bar was professionally tended, and the fireworks display was in the hands of experts.

The partners in the firm were still actively involved in the festivities. They usually double-teamed with the firm's associates to drive the boats for waterskiers. That year Zack was able to put his position to good use.

Mansell had moved to the Stevens's farm the day Bette died, and it was clear the move was permanent. Quinn had made it known that she and Mansell were divorcing, and Mansell had resigned from his seat on city council and thrown himself back into farming. The life he had chosen was hard and solitary. Mansell worked fourteen-hour days and saw no one but Bobby. Since Bette's death, Bobby, too, had avoided the company of others. His circle was limited to his uncle and to Maisie and Peter. When Zack told Bobby he could use some help with the boats for the Canada Day waterskiers, the ruse was transparent, but Bobby embraced it, and on July 1 both he and his uncle were on deck.

The sun glinting off the lake, the scent of pines and bonfires, and the need to focus on something other than the tragedy seemed to be tonic for Bobby and Mansell, and as the afternoon passed, they appeared to be enjoying themselves. When there was a break in the waterskiing action, Bobby parked his speedboat parallel to the dock, and I brought him a Coke. He drank half the can in a gulp.

"You look as if you're having fun out there," I said.

"I'm doing my best," Bobby said.

"That's all any of us can do," I said.

Down the beach, Warren and Annie were admiring the sandcastle Madeleine and Lena had painstakingly constructed. Our granddaughters were wearing matching red T-shirts and white shorts. The Webers, too, were decked out in patriotic red and white. They had brought good news to the party. Simon was doing well. Dr. Fidelak's combination of talk and drug therapy was producing promising results. Simon had become serious about photography again, and he and Michael Goetz were talking about adding portraits Simon would take of at-risk youth to Michael's upcoming book.

Beside me, Bobby shifted his position so that he was looking out at the lake. For a long while, he was silent. Finally, he cleared his throat and turned to face me. "My mum always drew faces on the boiled eggs I had for breakfast," he said softly. "Sad faces if she knew I was having a hard time; big smiles if she knew I had something good on the horizon. When I got hit with a puck and ended up with two black eyes, she drew black eyes on my breakfast eggs until the bruising went away. She never missed a school event or a hockey practise. She was always in the front row at my games." He struggled to finish his thought. "She was a good mother."

"You're proof of that." I said. "Bette raised a fine young man."

"Does that make up for what she did?" Bobby's gaze was piercing. "You don't need to answer that," he said, and the hopelessness in his voice brought tears to my eyes.

Virginia Woolf wrote of moments so powerful that, even if the events themselves are inconsequential, the insights they bring are unforgettable. The anguish in Bobby's face as he fought to preserve the image of the mother he had known was heartbreaking. As he pulled away from the dock and turned the speedboat towards a young skier waiting impatiently on the beach, I knew Bobby's wordless affirmation of the power of love would stay with me forever.

Two more such moments, unimportant in themselves, came that evening. Brock and Derek watched the fireworks on the bay with their arms around each other. As the last rocket sputtered into darkness, Brock drew Derek close for a kiss. The men had been so intent on each other that they hadn't noticed Margot and the children approaching. As soon as Lexi spotted Brock and Derek, she called out to them. When they heard Lexi's chiming little girl voice, the couple sprang apart.

Margot was exasperated. "For godsakes," she said. "You're not teenagers. Finish what you started. It's good for Lexi and Kai to see you loving each other." Her laugh was self-mocking. "Not so great for me to see, but definitely good for the kids."

Derek and Brock communicated wordlessly, the way caring couples often do, then reached out to Margot and the children. Their first pass at an impromptu family hug was a train wreck – Derek and Margot bumped heads, and when Margot uttered a choice expletive, Lexi chortled and Kai got caught in the squeeze and hollered. But they tried again. The adults stepped apart. Brock scooped up Lexi; Derek took Kai in his arms; and this time, amid laughter and hissed instructions, they reconfigured and created a passable family hug.

Zack had gone off to talk to Warren and Annie Weber and our granddaughters, so he missed the action, but Milo and I caught it, and he was surprisingly moved by what we'd seen. "That was stellar," he said. "Actually, this entire day has been stellar. Madeleine and Lena both got up on their water skis first try. You taught me how to make s'mores – which incidentally are really gross. Those ski jumps you have are wicked, and Pete's team won the beach volleyball championship."

"Actually, you won the beach volleyball championship," I said. "Angus already has dibs on you for his team next year."

Milo didn't respond. It was too dark to read his expression. "Is something wrong?" I said.

"Jo, I don't know where I'll be next year."

My heart sank. "I was hoping you'd still be with us."

"Part of me hoped that too. Part of me hoped I'd be with you forever, but I'm not a forever guy. This isn't my scene, Jo. I'm a backroom boy, and there's no backroom here any more. Zack won the election. His bylaws passed. He's not running for re-election, and Brock's not interested in being mayor."

"We can't let Lancaster run a candidate who will undo everything we're trying to do," I said.

"Lancaster can run whomever they can convince to slither out from under their rock, but I've got a candidate who can beat them. Now that Mansell's resigned, there's an opening, and I've been talking to a candidate with solid business credentials who has recently discovered her inner progressive."

"Who?"

"Lydia Mah. I've been working on her, and she told me last week she's going to make a run for it. I've already put together a profile and a playbook for her and given it to Zack."

"You told Zack you were leaving before you told me?"

Milo half turned so all I could see was his profile. "Zack was easy to tell," he said. "So was Brock. Taylor, Madeleine, and Lena were harder. And I just kept putting off telling you."

I was hurt and angry, but the sadness in Milo's voice disarmed me. "Well, you've told me now," I said. "Where are you going?"

"Next year is election year in the States, and I've had a lot of calls. Tomorrow morning, I'm going to Tallahassee. The candidate's a thirty-eight-year-old guy who owns a restaurant chain that hires the marginalized, has onsite daycare, offers flex hours for education and self-improvement, and makes a healthy profit. He's running for a congressional seat, but there'll be a senate seat open in the not too distant future, and he has backers for that."

"The perfect candidate," I said. "Why does he need you?"

"Because he's running in a district that is politically to the right of Atilla the Hun, and he's Muslim and gay."

"Your kind of odds," I said. I was close to tears, and Milo knew it.

"Jo. I've been working for you for a year. That's the longest I've ever stayed anywhere." He gestured towards the bonfire and the lake and the sleeping kids being carried to cars by their suntanned parents. "This isn't me," he said. "I'm the guy who comes in when a campaign is tanking. I don't know anybody in the candidate's campaign and I don't owe anybody, so I'm free to do what has to be done. I figure out who's deadwood and who's necessary and I tell the campaign manager to throw the deadwood into the chipper. If the campaign manager is deadwood, I tell the candidate to throw *the campaign manager* into the chipper. After that, you know the drill. I do what I have to until E-Day, and then, win or lose, I move along."

"But you stayed here after Zack won."

"I stayed here because you asked me to."

"I thought it worked out for both of us."

"It did. And it was great. This has been the best year of my life."

"Then why are you leaving?" I reached out and touched his cheek. For a few moments we were as close as two people can be, then Milo spotted something over my shoulder and stepped back. When I turned, I saw Zack wheeling towards us.

"The big man himself," Milo said. "Jo, I want what Zack has, but that just comes along once in a lifetime, and it's already come to you."

Zack was always sensitive to my mood. He waited until the last guest had left and we had closed our bedroom door before he broached the subject.

"You're very quiet."

"It's been a long day."

"Milo told you."

"Finally. After he told you, Brock, and the girls."

"Are you angry?"

"Yes, but not at you. And not at Milo. Just – at life, I guess. I don't like losing people I care about."

"And you care about Milo."

"You know I do. He's made politics fun for me again."

"And without him, it won't be fun?"

"I don't know."

"Do you want a massage?"

"Thanks, but I think I just need to sleep."

"What's that old Russian saying you always quote?"

"'Morning is wiser than evening,'" I said. I leaned over to kiss Zack goodnight, but my heart wasn't in it, and we both knew it.

Milo was taking the early bird five-thirty flight to Toronto and then from Toronto to Tampa and on to Tallahassee. I drove him to the airport. He had protested vehemently, but my argument was persuasive. "I brought you to this dance," I said. "And I'm taking you home."

I picked him up in front of the Sahara Club. He was wearing his uniform of choice – lace-up black Keds, chinos, black T-shirt, and ball cap – and he had a backpack. He looked pale and the shadows under his dark eyes were deep.

I looked at the backpack. "No other luggage," I said.

"My Harley's going business class," he said.

He got into the car and handed me the keys to the flat that had been his home for a year. I dropped them in my bag. "I hate this," I said.

"I'm not crazy about it myself," Milo said.

It was a fifteen-minute drive to the airport, and for the first time in my memory, we didn't speak a word to each other. Milo was absolutely still. When we pulled into the departures dropoff, neither of us moved.

Finally, we faced each other. Milo reached across and took my hand in his. "Did you sleep last night?" he said.

"No," I said. "I kept trying to figure out what was happening."

Milo's smile was shadowed. "Not worth the effort," he said. "I knew what was happening – at least what was happening for me, and it wasn't going to work out." He picked up his backpack. "Maybe in the next life," he said.

"I hate to see you hurting."

He shrugged. "Bob Marley once said, 'Truth is, everybody is going to hurt you. You just gotta find the ones worth suffering for.'" Milo brushed my cheek with a kiss. "You're worth suffering for, Joanne." And with that, Milo slipped out of the car and disappeared behind the departures door.

As I drove out of the airport parking lot, I was overwhelmed by a sense of loss I didn't understand. I wasn't ready to go back to the lake, so I drove to a spot near the levee that the city had built on both sides of Wascana Creek to protect neighbourhoods from floods during spring runoff. I parked not far from the house I'd lived in before I met Zack.

The creek was an oasis of peace and beauty in every season, and over the decades I'd often found solace there. On that hot July morning, the indigenous bushes planted on the creek banks were in full leaf and the wild roses were blooming. Joggers listening to their playlists dotted the bike path. Two Christmases ago, my kids had tucked an MP3 player into my stocking. I had been touched by their thoughtfulness, but I was old school. For me, the sounds of morning were enough, and that morning the creek was alive with the trill of birdsong and the plash of beavers, muskrats, and ducks. Music to smooth the jagged edges.

My emotions were a jumble, but there were some things I was sure of. I was deeply in love with my husband. At our wedding, the dean who married us said that he was certain two people as passionate and thoughtful as we were could make a fine life together, and he had been right. Together Zack and I had more than I could have asked for or imagined. My life was filled with people who loved me and whom I loved. But when Milo walked away from me that morning, I was bereft.

Following an instinct that was wiser than I was, I crossed the bridge to the path on the south levee that would take me by the house where Zack, Taylor, and I had lived before we moved into the condo. Not far from our old yard was a large, flat stone where I had sat whenever our old dog, Willie, and Pantera had decided to check out life on the creek. It was a good place to think, and I needed to think.

Zack and I had fallen in love quickly and intensely. My friends and family had tripped over one another offering reasons why our relationship was a mistake. At first I ignored them, but finally I could no longer turn a blind eye to all the red flags. When the situation came to a head, Zack and I were in an elegant hotel suite in Saskatoon. He was giving a speech at a colleague's retirement dinner, and we'd seized upon the occasion to arrange a romantic getaway. The bed was inviting; the champagne was on ice, and the view of the South Saskatchewan River took my breath away.

Every detail was perfect, but earlier in the week I had watched Zack tear apart my oldest friend in court, and that evening at the reception before the dinner a woman who'd drunk not wisely but well told me Zack would dump me the way he'd dumped the scores of other women he'd taken to his bed. It was too much. Suddenly, in a suite designed for lovers, we became strangers.

Zack knew I was backing away, but he never shied away from facts. "You're finished with me, aren't you?" he said, and his voice was rough with emotion.

When I saw the misery in his eyes, the words formed themselves. "No matter what happens, I will never be finished with you," I said.

"Then it's time we got married," he said simply, and I agreed. We had known each other for five months.

On the flight back from Saskatoon the next morning, Zack pored through real estate listings until he found what he believed was the house for us. By noon, we'd put in an offer. When Charlie McCudden, the contractor who did the retrofitting, asked us to give him our vision of the new house in one sentence, Zack said what we wanted was a solid family house because we were a solid family.

Remembering that moment, I walked down the incline that led from the levee to our old street. I had always said it was kismet that led Zack to choose a house on the creek that I had cherished throughout most of my adult life. When I came closer to the old place, I saw that kismet had struck again. The house was for sale.

I pulled out my cell and dialled the number on the sign. The realtor's name was Amber MacLeod, and her phone rang at least a half-dozen times before she picked up, sounding groggy. I glanced at my watch. It was six o'clock in the morning. I apologized and asked her not to sell the property until we'd talked. She said she'd meet me at the house at six-thirty. Then I called Zack. He was still at the lake, but he was there in half an hour.

Amber MacLeod was a woman of an indeterminate age who had the dimpled prettiness and bubbly exuberance of the actress Betty White. I had told her that Zack and I had owned the house before, and we might be interested in living in it again. From that small kernel of information, she had apparently spun a romantic narrative. When Zack asked if we could go through the house on our own, she clapped her hands in delight. "Of course," she said. "Rekindling old memories. Love truly is lovelier the second time around. My husband always says that the worst days of our marriage are better than the best days of his life as a single man."

When we were on one side of the door and Amber was on the other, Zack grinned. "What the hell was that all about?"

"I told Amber we'd lived here before. I guess she assumed we'd gone our separate ways and were giving it another try."

Zack's face was grave as he took my hand. "Jo, is that what we're doing?"

"I don't know," I said. "All I know is that I love you more today than I did the day we met, and when I saw the For Sale sign on the house, I knew it was time to move back."

Zack held his arms out to me. "In that case, let's have a quick smooch and tell Amber this house is off the market."

Preparing for our move went relatively smoothly. Zack had used his portable access ramp the day we visited the house with Amber MacLeod. We needed to get permanent accessibility ramps installed, but that was hardly a big job. Luckily, the doctor to whom we'd sold the house and from whom we'd bought it back had changed nothing structurally and very little cosmetically. Even the lavender de Provence paint Zack and I had chosen was still on the walls of our bedroom.

Zack, Taylor, and I were not starting at square one, but we weren't far off. Our condo had belonged to Margot's husband, Leland, before he moved in with Margot. Everything in it, right down to the tea towels, had been chosen by Leland's decorator. The entire east half of our house on the creek had been destroyed by an explosion; everything that was left in the intact half was so badly smoke damaged it was unsalvageable. I'd kept the file folder with the notes, contact information, and samples we'd used when we'd had the house retrofitted and again when we had it rebuilt, so I was able to order much of what we needed by phone.

There were enough lazy, hazy days of summer with Zack, the kids, and the dogs to please even me. At Madeleine and Lena's request, Mieka kept Milo up to date about their diving progress. From Tallahassee, he watched Mieka's videos of the girls' dives and sent critiques. The first time they dived off the high board, Milo sent them matching charm bracelets with moonstones, the state gem of Florida. Taylor kept in touch with Milo by text. When Taylor sent Milo a message saying that she'd named her new ginger

kitten "Bob Marley," his answer was one word: "Sweet."
All three girls seemed to view Milo as a cherished older
brother, and that pleased me.

Madeleine, Lena, and I continued to monitor our garden
closely. By August we faced the fact that our carrots had
been a bust, but we had a bumper crop of tomatoes, and Zack
said the tiny tomatoes he loved were the sweetest he'd ever
tasted. Michael found a rental not far from the Webers's cottage and he and Bridie had a quiet summer at the lake. The
Qu'Appelle Valley was a good fit for them, so Michael put
his house in Regina up for sale and bought a place in Fort
Qu'Appelle. Bridie would start kindergarten in September,
and he wanted a fresh start for her and for him.

Change was in the air for us all. I had dreaded telling
Margot that we were moving away from Halifax Street.
She and I had become as close as sisters, but after I broke
the news and we shed a few tears and noted that our families would still be just ten minutes away from each other,
Margot floated an idea that made a lot of sense. She pointed
out that Brock's condo on the third floor was small, and that
if he moved in across the hall from her, he'd be closer to the
children, have extra space, and still retain his privacy.

When Margot told me Brock had been enthusiastic about
the idea, her smile was puckish. "It turns out I may be getting two new neighbours. Brock and Derek are talking about
moving in together. I'm a girl from Wadena, Saskatchewan.
Having the biological father of my son living across the hall
with his boyfriend was never quite in my life plan. But we
can make this work. Besides, Derek can do magic tricks."

Colin Crawford Kilbourn and Charlie Crawford Kilbourn
were born on September 27, my fifty-ninth birthday. They
were healthy little boys with Maisie's springy copper curls
and lankiness, Peter's sculpted features and equanimity,

and my green eyes. In my grandmother's phrase, we were all foolishly fond of Colin and Charlie.

The contractor who had worked on our house was doing the renovations at the farm too, and true to his word he was bringing the project in on time and on budget. The main floor of the Crawford Kilbourn house was now fully accessible; the bathrooms, kitchen, and family room were finished. Most importantly, the nursery and Maisie and Peter's bedroom were ready for the Crawford Kilbourn family the day they came home from the hospital.

They had painted the boys' nursery a warm, lemony yellow; the room contained two of everything, and Taylor's paintings of Lee's heritage birds were hung where Colin and Charlie could see them from their cribs. Maisie loved the idea that the boys would awaken every morning to the vivid beauty of Blue Andalusians, scarlet-combed Langshans, Swedish Flower Hens, Ridley Bronze Turkeys, and pink-billed Aylesbury ducks.

Maisie had asked Taylor to make a painting from the photograph of Lee lying in the field listening to the wind singing through the grass. At first Taylor had been reluctant because she was afraid she would be unable to capture the joy on Lee's young face. But Maisie promised Taylor she would be content with whatever Taylor did. It was not an easy painting, and it took Taylor much of the month of July to get it right.

In my opinion, and Zack's, it was Taylor's best work. Maisie agreed, but she found it difficult to look at the painting without breaking down, and she asked Zack, Taylor, and me to take it until she was ready. When we moved into the house on the creek, Zack and I hung the painting in our bedroom on a wall that caught the morning sun. On warm days, we could leave open the doors to the deck and hear the creek murmur as we looked at Lee's face.

At family dinners, Maisie always made her way to our bedroom to see the painting. Sometimes alone, sometimes with Peter, sometimes with one or both of her sons, she'd disappear into our room, stay until she found what she had gone to Lee for, and then come out and join the rest of us.

When Taylor was working on a painting, she seemed always to gather strange and arcane knowledge about the world that informed her work. The creative process was a mystery to me, and I never quite knew whether Taylor found the information or the information found her.

One day at the lake after she'd spent the morning working on Lee's portrait, Taylor came down to the beach where Zack and I were watching the girls practise their dives. Her eyes shone and her cheeks were pink with excitement. "Did you know that the Sami reindeer herders believe that nature has powerful restorative powers?" she asked. "They say that whenever you're lost in life, you simply have to put your ear to the earth and listen to her heart."

I never really came to know Lee well as an adult, but over the coming months, I would grow very close to the child in the painting. Many times when I felt lost, the girl with the coppery curls going every which way and the gold-flecked eyes filled with wonder led me to the answers I needed.

ACKNOWLEDGEMENTS

Thanks to:

Kendra Ward, my editor, who asked all the hard questions and guided me gently but firmly to answers.

Ellen Seligman for her friendship and for making it possible for Kendra Ward to continue as my editor until *What's Left Behind* was ready for the next step.

Heather Sangster for being an invaluable member of the writer/editor/copy editor troika.

Ashley Dunn for always being the best and the shiniest!

Rick Mitchell, retired Staff Sergeant in Charge of Major Crimes Section, Regina Police Service, for reading the manuscript at a very early stage and supplying much-needed encouragement and information.

Barbara Weller, LICSW, for sharing her experiences in treating children who have suffered psychological traumas.

Najma Kazmi, MD, for being everything a family physician should be.

Wayne Chau, BSP, for his knowledge, his humour, and his friendship.

Ryan B. Eidness, MD and athlete, for knowing the value of the personal best.

Hildy Bowen, Brett Bell, Max Bowen, Carrie Bowen, and Nathaniel Bowen for their endless patience, support, and love.

Kai Langen, Madeleine Bowen-Diaz, Lena Bowen-Diaz, Chesney Langen Bell, Ben Bowen-Bell, Peyton Bowen, and Lexi Bowen, who fill me with joy every second of every day.

Ted, my love of forty-seven years, who makes everything possible.

Our bouvier, Esme, who finally made it into the pages of one of my books. I hope I did you justice, Ezzy.